MARK OF THE ASSASSINS

A COMING OF AGE FANTASY

LANDRI JOHNSON

CRAIG MARTELLE, INC

Contents

Part 1

E verything was fine until Shane and her friend accidentally fell through a portal leading to another world.

Earlier, the evening started just like any Friday night with a high school football game. The home team was losing, there was no doubt about that. The huge, glowing scoreboard behind the goal posts told anyone brave enough to look that the *Steeds* were down by fourteen points, and the game was only in the third quarter.

No one on the home side dared look. Most of them still hoped their school had a chance of winning. The score deficit wasn't insurmountable, to be fair; the *Steeds* had proven that a few games before, when they scored two touchdowns in the last quarter, tying the game, and eventually winning.

Shane, along with her three friends, Reece, Eleanor, and Olivia, were stuffed tightly on the bleachers, their voices lost in the noise of the crowd.

It was cold that night. Cold enough to where Shane's leggings and large sweatshirt weren't enough to keep her comfortable, and people's breaths could be seen in the air. Her hoodie, which covered her dirty blonde hair, did nothing to fight the cold.

"Come on ref," Shane complained, throwing her hands into the air as the middle ref awarded the *Huskies* ten yards for a holding call. "At least call it for both teams!"

"Sounds to me like you're a little too invested in this game," Reece said.

"Really?" Shane couldn't help but laugh. "What gave you that idea?"

She looked over at her sulking friend. The hood of Reece's jacket completely covered her head. She kept her shivering hands between her knees, trying to warm them. The frown on her face told Shane that Reece would much rather be anywhere but there, but Shane didn't care. If she hadn't invited her, Reece would be sitting alone in her room, just like she did every other Friday night since her mom died a couple months before.

"Come on, Reece," Shane said, trying to cheer her up. "I'm sure that this would be way more fun if you actually paid attention to what's happening."

"Yeah, how about 'no thanks.'" Reece shifted in her seat to get into a more comfortable position. "It's bad enough that you forced me to play basketball. I'm not going to join you in your football crusade or whatever it is you're doing."

Shane laughed. "I didn't *make* you play basketball. I just suggested it."

"A lot."

And it helped her get out of the house and be with her friends.

"Hey, Shane," Eleanor interrupted. "Your brother's on the field." Shane recognized the tall boy running toward the huddle. Corbin put his helmet on over his dirty blonde hair. Reece brought her head up to see.

"Oh, great." Shane rolled her eyes. "Have the coaches given up on winning?"

"He's actually pretty good," Reece said defensively, keeping her eyes on Shane's twin brother.

"Oh, so now you're paying attention," Shane asked. Annoyance flickered across her face, but she tried to keep it steady. It wasn't Reece's fault she liked Corbin. She was just like everyone else.

"No."

"Yes, you are." Olivia smiled. "You're too stubborn to admit that you like him."

Reece's face flushed a glowing red, her mouth flattening into a thin line. "No, I don't." She looked away, trying to hide her embarrassment. "By the way Shane, how's Landen?" she asked to take the attention off her.

Shane blushed in embarrassment. "I don't know. I haven't talked to him, and he's out hunting." She cleared her throat and returned her attention to the field. "I honestly don't see what you see in Corbin."

"That's just because you're his sister."

"Don't remind me of that." Just then the *Huskies* hiked the ball and immediately handed it off to the running back. He sprinted toward the sideline in a curved run weaving in and out of players, but Corbin stopped him in his tracks.

"Did you see that? He tackled him, and that's good, isn't it?"

"Sure," Shane said bitterly.

Corbin ran off the field, taking his helmet off and shaking out his sweaty hair. It made Shane cringe. It was hard enough being one of the middle children but having a twin who was everyone's favorite was even worse. Everybody loved Corbin and referred to Shane as "Corbin's Twin." The lesser talented twin. No matter how hard she tried at school and sports, she always fell short in comparison to Corbin. She was average at everything she did, even when she gave it her all.

The seconds ticked away to the end of the third quarter. When the buzzer went off, Shane winced. She didn't want the game to end yet, and it wasn't because she supported the losing team. The game ending meant going home, and that meant facing her father. They'd had a fierce argument just a few hours before over math homework. He specifically told her that she couldn't go to the game. She had, of course, broken that rule. While she tried to ignore it, an overwhelming sense of guilt came over her every time she thought about what awaited her at home.

"Does anyone want something to eat?" she asked, trying to distract herself. "I'm starving."

Reece sighed and slouched in her seat even more. "Sure, but only if you're buying."

"How 'bout you guys?"

Olivia shook her head. "Nah, I'm good."

"Same. I had dinner before I came," Eleanor chimed in.

"So just you, Reece?" Shane asked.

"Guess so."

Shane got up from the cold bleachers as the fourth quarter began. She led the way through the hordes of people with Reece following close behind. They made it to the stairway, and Shane took a deep breath. Being surrounded by so many people was giving her a slight headache and was making her light-headed. Getting out of the crowd gave her a breath of fresh air, though her headache still seemed to intensify.

A huge groan erupted from the crowd as Shane and Reece made their way toward the concession stand. Shane glanced over at the scoreboard to see that the *Huskies* had scored mere moments before, extending their lead by six.

"You know," Shane said kicking a small rock, "I wish that we had a winning team this year." She watched as the extra point kick went up. The ball went straight through the uprights.

"Yeah," Reece agreed glumly. Her hands were stuffed tightly in her small jacket pockets, her head facing the ground. Shane could've said anything, and Reece would have agreed. Shane took notice of this but kept talking anyway. If she could get Reece to talk, maybe it would help.

"I mean, we could've at least made it to the semi-finals." Shane moved forward in the line. "I'm sick and tired of other schools saying we choke during the playoffs."

"But they're sorta right, though."

"That doesn't mean I'm happy about it."

Shane looked back at the field. She let out a long sigh and rubbed her temples. Her forehead pounded, making her wince in pain. Reece furrowed her eyebrows in concern.

"Are you all right?"

"Yeah. I'm fine." Shane winced as a pang of pain washed through her. "Just a headache. Probably a migraine."

"Are you sure?"

"Yes." Her hand went up to her forehead hoping it would help, but it didn't.

"Do you need some Ibuprofen or something? Or do you want to go home?"

"No!" Shane snapped. She took a deep breath, realizing how rude she just sounded. "Look, I'm fine, okay? I'm just gonna take a walk, and I'll come back when my head feels better. It's just all this noise."

Reece looked at the line ahead of them and pursed her lips. "Do you want me to come with you?"

"Nah, I'm all right." Shane reached in her pockets and handed Reece money. "Just buy me something. I'll be back in ten minutes."

Shane left the line and started for the parking lot. Each step she took sent waves of pain into her head. A light, cold sweat formed on her brow. She wiped it away, suddenly feeling very hot at the cheeks and in her core.

All she wanted to do was be alone, but people surrounded her everywhere she turned. There was a small, fenced off wooded area off to her right. With the game still going and everyone otherwise occupied, it was the perfect place to sit in silence and wait for her headache to subside.

Shane started toward it, desperate for some peace. But her headache worsened with each step she took. She couldn't walk straight; couldn't think straight. She collapsed against the first tree she came to, and slid down to the ground with her hands over her ears. Tears welled up in her eyes as the ache in her head grew more intense. The world began to blur around her.

She felt like her body wasn't her own. She watched people pass by, but it felt like she was watching herself in a movie, as if in a dream.

That's when she heard it echoing all around her. Something, someone, whispered her name in a rasping voice, quiet at first, but eventually completely overtaking her.

"Shane! Shane!" A different voice broke through the noise.

"Please make it stop," Shane begged. Through her blurry, tear-filled eyes she could see something moving. She tried to get away from it, but the tree blocked her escape.

"Shane! What is wrong with you?" Reece yelled, coming clearly into Shane's vision. Her heart sped up as she tried to back up but was stopped by the tree once again. It wasn't until Reece grabbed her arms, she fully comprehended who it was.

"It hurts so bad," she whispered to her friend. Her nose started bleeding profusely, dripping into her mouth, rolling off her chin and staining her hand-me-down sweatshirt.

"What the hell, Shane!" Reece took her phone out of her pocket. Her hands shook as she dialed a number. Before she got the chance to make a call, Shane hit the phone out of her hand and pointed above Reece's head.

"What is that?" Shane's voice quivered with pain and disbelief. She didn't know if she was hallucinating or not, but a strange shape, like waves of heat, hovered above Reece's worried face. Shane gripped her friend's arm so tightly she couldn't pull away.

Reece whipped her head around but seemed not to see it. "What is what, Shane? You're really starting to freak me out!" Her voice was on the edge of breaking.

The heatwave moved toward them. Before Shane could even think about warning Reece, it overtook them, and her vision blurred. Her skin began to burn. When it became too hot to bear, a cold sensation like she had never felt before consumed her, a stark contrast from the warmth. It started at her core and spread outward. Darkness soon followed. It filled her vision with utter black. She closed her eyes tightly, wishing that all of it would go away, but it didn't. The weight of the darkness pressed against her chest and made it hard to breathe.

The coldness seemed to last forever, never relinquishing its grip on Shane. It cut through her clothes and straight into her. Still clutching Reece's arm, she refused to let go. It was the only thing anchoring her in reality.

Just as suddenly as the headache started, it stopped, and the pressure prickling against Shane's skin dissipated instantly. She gasped and let go of Reece's arm in a blur of confusion as she opened her eyes, expecting to see the familiar wooded area on the school grounds. Instead, she was greeted by a light blue glow, barely penetrating the darkness. That's when she realized that the tree she'd been leaning on only moments before had disappeared, the twigs and leaves replaced by a damp, stone ground.

What the hell, Shane thought as she looked around, wanting more than anything to find something that could tell her where she was but found nothing.

This can't be happening, she thought. She wiped away the few tears that still clung to her cheeks. And the blood from her lips and chin. It had to be a trick of the mind, that's all. A hallucination. A dream. In a couple hours, she would wake up next to that tree, and everything would be fine. It had to be.

Shane pinched herself to see if it hurt. It did. Shane's breaths came quickly as more tears threatened to come.

"What just happened?" Reece asked, her voice nothing more than a whisper.

"I... I don't know," Shane said, surprised she could even speak.

She stood up, her legs wavering underneath her full body weight. She began to feel her way around, trying to figure out where they were. All she could make out were dark shadows and a few oddly shaped objects jutting out of the floors and ceilings. Stalactites and stalagmites.

"We're in a cave?" Reece asked.

"Yeah. I sorta noticed," Shane said, failing to keep her fear from creeping into her voice.

Everything's fine, she tried to convince herself, even though everything was clearly not. She looked up at the ceiling and more hopelessness than she had ever felt in her life came and sucker punched her straight in the stomach. *What if they couldn't find a way out?*

No, Shane scolded herself. *I can't go thinking like that. Not if I want to get out of here.*

Shane was surprised to discover that the blue light, the reason they were able to see at all, came from down below where they stood, just over a ledge ahead. She walked to the edge, stumbling backward as it began to crumble away. Rocks fell, splashing into what appeared to be water. The blue glow must've been coming from bioluminescent algae.

Shane retrieved her phone from her back pocket, hands shaking. The screen had cracked, but Shane didn't care. All she wanted to do was call for help. Those hopes were dashed when she saw there was no service.

Fear gripped Shane so tightly she couldn't breathe. Everything shook as she wiped away more stray tears that escaped.

"How'd we get here?" Reece's terrified voice broke through the darkness.

"I have no idea."

If it hadn't been for Reece, Shane would've broken down right then and there, but she couldn't do that to her friend. Someone had to take the lead if they wanted to live, and Shane sure as hell didn't want to die. That, and she couldn't show her friend how truly terrified she was. It wasn't part of the persona she tried her best to put out.

"How are we going to get out of here?"

"How am I supposed to know? What do you think I'm looking for?" It came out a little more venomous than it was meant, but she was too freaked out to care.

Reece went silent.

Shane grabbed her phone again and turned on the flashlight. She was disheartened that the battery was only at twenty percent even though only a couple moments before it had been over fifty. She turned on airplane mode to preserve more energy, then focused on what she could control, like finding a way out. She shone her flashlight across the cavernous room. Eventually, it revealed a small tunnel. Would it lead deeper into the cave, or to their freedom? The thought of going into the unknown terrified Shane, but she had to if she wanted to survive their situation.

Shane looked over at Reece, who was standing right beside her. The blue light from the water made her already pale face even paler. Before Shane even got a chance to say anything, Reece cut her off, like she knew what Shane was thinking.

"How do we know it leads out of here?" she asked pessimistically. Those words only played into Shane's worst fears. "For all we know, it could just lead deeper into the cave."

"We don't." Shane's voice was tight as she tried not to sound too angry or scared. "But we have to at least try."

Reece laughed nervously. "Yeah right. Good luck with that." She picked up a rock and threw it at the ground. It slipped and fell off the edge into the water below.

Shane's patience for her friend was at an all-time low. "Aren't you going to try and help, or are you fine dying here?"

Reece looked at her friend with bloodshot eyes. "Is this even real," she said with a shaky voice. "For all I know this is just my imagination, and you're not even here."

"I'm in no one's imagination." Shane took a breath to calm herself, which didn't work. "Look, all I want to do is find a way out of here. That might be the only way. All I'm asking of you is that you try."

"Well, all I want to know is how the hell we got here in the first place!" Reece yelled. Tears began to stream down her face.

"Then why aren't you helping me out?" snapped Shane. "I'm just as scared and confused as you are. But I'm the only one trying to find a way out of here! Unlike you, I want to live through this!"

A thick silence followed. The harsh words echoed around the room. Immediate guilt took over Shane as what she said truly settled upon her.

"Look, Reece, I didn't mean that," she tried to apologize, but was only greeted with Reece's stern face.

"Sure, you didn't."

"Please, I really didn't. I was just—"

"You were just angry. Yeah. I get that a lot." She swiped tears away from her face. "I actually do want to help, believe it or not." Her voice came out gruff, on edge, and Shane felt worse. Reece looked over toward the tunnel and shook her head. "I want to get out of here just as much as you, but I'm not ready to risk my life just for something that *might* be the exit."

Shane pursed her lips and closed her eyes. "If we stay here, we die anyway, so why not try?"

Reece looked over at the opening again, then at Shane, unmistakable fear in her eyes. "Fine."

Shane stuck a clammy hand out for Reece to take.

"I hope we won't regret this," she said, taking Shane's hand.

"So do I." Shane glanced once more at the opening and gulped.

It isn't going to collapse, she had to remind herself as she pointed her flashlight down their only exit. Her phone was at ten percent battery now, and she feared they wouldn't be able to get out of there without it dying. She didn't tell Reece that; she was already going through enough. Shane didn't want to drag her down with even more depressing thoughts.

Smiling uncertainly at Reece, Shane took her first step toward either their freedom or their death.

CHAPTER 2

They walked down the tunnel for what seemed like forever. Shane's phone died after only a few minutes in, and darkness enveloped them. Fear all but paralyzed Shane. It wasn't that she was afraid of the dark. She was afraid of what remained hidden in it. Already they had disturbed dozens of bats; dirt and stone fell from the ceiling with them, making Shane's heart skip. She shivered thinking of what other creatures might be lurking in there.

A breeze brushed past her and her heart sped. If there was a breeze, there must be an exit nearby. She picked up her pace a little more than she should have. A stitch formed in her side as she walked faster toward their possible exit, but the excitement of seeing the outside world helped her to ignore the pain. The fear that the cave would collapse faded as she saw the way out, and they made it outside to the fresh night air. The sense of relief was almost overwhelming.

They were greeted by a small clearing of an overgrown forest that stood before them. The autumn leaves were lit by the full moon's light. Hundreds of stars filled the sky, more than Shane could dare to count. Shane searched the sky for the big dipper and the north star, just like her dad taught her how when they went camping, but she couldn't find them.

The empty feeling of being more alone than she had ever been in her life hit her like a ton of bricks. With that came hopelessness. Even when she was alone before all this, she could always call her mom or her sister, Chloe, for help, but that wasn't an option here. Her phone was dead, they had no service anyway, and they had no idea where "home" was.

Reece yawned beside Shane, bringing her back to reality. She wasn't all alone, she had to remind herself. She still had her friend with her, and if it weren't for Reece, she would've broken down by now.

"All I want to do," Reece said, her voice on the edge of breaking, "is fall asleep in my own bed. But no. Here we are in God-knows-where with no idea how we got here." She slumped down near the entrance to the cave with her eyes closed. Her head leaned back against the mossy stone.

"Why don't you go to sleep then," Shane suggested. She sat against a tall tree and let out a breath. She should have been freaking out, but she was too tired to do so. "Maybe then we'll wake up in the morning and find out it was all a dream." But Shane knew it to be false. She just couldn't help a small part of her from believing it.

Reece didn't buy it. "Yeah, right." She went quiet after that. Within a few minutes, the only noise Shane heard was her friend's light snoring.

Shane smiled. She couldn't even begin to think of what this situation would be if Reece wasn't there with her, but the smile soon faded. She was responsible for Reece being there in the first place. If Shane hadn't invited Reece to come to the game, would she be with her right now? Or would she be at home with her family?

Shane let out a sigh. The adrenaline that had been coursing through her body after their sudden appearance in the strange cave began to fade, instead replaced by an overwhelming fatigue. She couldn't keep her eyes open for more than a couple of seconds at a time, and it wasn't long before unconsciousness overtook her. Uneasy dreams of home were the only things that greeted her.

Shane had been camping before. Every summer she went at least once with her family, and she enjoyed it for the most part. But that was when she had a tent and a sleeping bag to protect her from the elements. What she didn't enjoy was leaning up against a tree that dug into her back, and the only thing keeping her warm was an old sweatshirt.

A mixture of the cold and the uncomfortable ground woke Shane after a fitful night's rest. The sun was already shining through the trees when she finally became aware of her surroundings and the strange noises that came with it, and she sat up straight against the tree. She wasn't in her room. She wasn't at her house. She was on the cold, damp ground of an unknown forest with no idea how she got there to begin with.

Memories from the night before came back to her and she groaned.

This can't be happening, she thought, closing her eyes, rubbing them, then opening them again only to see the exact same thing. The previous night hadn't been a dream. She and Reece were truly stuck in an unknown place with no idea how to get back home.

The thought of Reece broke Shane's heart. She looked up to find Reece sitting with her back against the mossy stone, her eyes open. She had wrapped herself in her dark, fluffy jacket, and was shivering slightly.

"It's about time you woke up," Reece said, a tone of dismay in her voice.

Shane got up from the ground, her whole body groaning in disapproval. Everything was sore. She couldn't bend her neck beyond a certain angle without pain spasming down her spine. "How long have you been awake?"

"When the sun first started coming through the trees." Reece tried to cover herself better with her frost covered jacket. "It's freaking freezing here."

Shane forced a laugh. *That's an understatement,* she thought. The morning dew soaked into her clothes, leaving her sopping wet. Cold like she never felt before creeped its way under her skin. Her fingers tingled with pain, and her entire body was scrunched up to preserve what little warmth she had left.

"Do we even know where 'here' is?" Shane asked hopefully, even though she already knew the answer.

"No," Reece snorted. "I was gonna ask you the same question."

Shane looked and thought she saw what appeared to be an old path, but she wasn't sure. Bushes and small vegetation had overtaken it years ago, and now it blended in with the surrounding woods. She cautiously wandered over, investigating.

"What are you looking at?" Reece asked, getting up from the ground. She threw her jacket around her but still shivered.

"I think this might be a way out of here."

Reece laughed humorlessly. "If you expect me to go down that, then you're sadly mistaken."

"Come on, Reece," Shane pleaded. "If we want to survive this, then we can't sit here and wait for someone to find us."

"Why not?"

"Because," Shane said. "Look at the trail. Nobody's been down it in years, and from what I see, it's the only way to get in or out of here."

"I'm not going down that." She pinched her lips together, her eyes darting from the trail to Shane. "There might be spiders."

"If spiders are what you're worried about..." Shane said. There was no point arguing with someone as stubborn as Reece.

She knew that if she didn't take action and start down the path, they would stay there bickering. "…then I worry for you."

"Wait—" Reece called, but it was too late. Already Shane had ventured several feet into the path.

"I don't know why the hell I'm friends with you."

Reece reluctantly followed her down the path.

Shane had always enjoyed hiking. In fact, she went at least once a week with her dad. It was one of the only things she shared with her father that none of her siblings enjoyed, so she felt she didn't have to compare herself to them. What she didn't enjoy was being the first to use the trail in years and having to force her way through the brush that had overtaken it.

The first few steps were the hardest. Her legs were becoming beaten and torn up, but that didn't stop her. She was used to pain. She had to push through pain when she played basketball and other sports. If someone else got hurt but kept playing, she had to do it too. She couldn't appear weak, especially not to her siblings.

After only a few minutes of walking, the sound of water splashing against rocks could be heard. Before long, the trail came alongside a small creek. Shane suddenly became aware of the dryness creeping its way up her throat, but she didn't go running to the water.

"Don't," she said, holding an arm out to stop Reece from drinking it. "We don't know if it's sanitary."

"So?"

"You don't want to get dysentery or something like that."

Reece grumbled under her breath but continued on anyway. The trail continued alongside the creek, a constant reminder of how thirsty they were.

It wasn't long before hunger started to gnaw at the bottoms of their stomachs. Shane noticed small bushes with red, oblong berries in places, but she wasn't sure if she should try to eat them. Her dad taught her how to differentiate between poisonous and edible plants, but that was a long time ago, and the memories were fuzzy. That, and the berries were like nothing she had ever seen before.

Slowly, the trees began to thin, and the path widened. A familiar salty taste lingered on Shane's lips and in the air. Along with it came a rhythmic roar in her ears. It wasn't until they rounded a corner that they found the source of the noise. Beyond the thick undergrowth of the trees lay a panorama of water nearly as far as the eye could see. The bright sky reflected the sun, nearly blinding Shane.

"Reece," Shane said, eyes fixated on the ocean before her. "Are you seeing this?

Reece stared dumbfounded by the water. Her face drained of color. "But—" She couldn't find the words to finish her sentence.

Shane tentatively took a couple steps forward on the path, trying to get a better view. There was a sudden drop off about twenty feet ahead of her. Waves twice her size collided with the rocky cliff face.

"But Idaho's landlocked," Reece said at last. "How is this possible?"

"I have no idea." Shane continued on the path that led along the cliff.

"Where are you going?" Reece yelled.

"Down to the ocean." That's where the trail seemed to be heading at least.

"But you don't know what's down there."

"Right." Shane wiped sweat from her eyebrows. "But I intend to find out." Then Shane called back over her shoulder, "We need to find a town or someone that can give us some answers."

"You seriously believe there might be someone else here?" Reece puffed, jogging to catch up to Shane.

"Who do you think made this?" Shane pointed toward the path.

"We're probably the first people to walk on it in years," Reece whispered under her breath. "You would think that if people lived here, it would be more worn." Still, she kept walking. Her words played into Shane's fears, but she pushed them to the back of her mind and continued onward. She suddenly had the overwhelming sense of being alone. If anything happened to either of them, no one was there to help.

The path led to a sandy beach. By then they were both drenched in sweat despite the chill in the air. Shane's legs were burning from uneven terrain that she had navigated. She regretted wearing the large, heavy sweatshirt that she had to keep rolling the sleeves up every couple minutes because they kept falling down. If she had known that they were going to be transported to a strange place, she might've prepared differently, but the thought never crossed her mind.

"I don't see signs of anyone," Reece said glumly, dropping down to her knees on the sand.

Shane had been thinking the same thing. All she wanted was to see at least one sign that there were people here, wherever here was. Birds flew from tree to tree, squirrels scampered on the ground, but no people were anywhere to be seen.

Shane slumped down next to Reece, picked up some sand and let it slip between her fingers. Rescue seemed hopeless. She wanted to scream, to yell out. *This isn't fair!* A few tears rolled down her face and fell to the sand below. She didn't bother wiping them from her cheek. The two girls sat there in silence for a long moment, only the sound of the waves lapping the shore broke the stillness.

Something swelled in Shane's throat as her mind drifted to her father. He must think she hated him, that she'd run away because of their argument. All she wanted to do was go back and tell him that it wasn't that way. But she couldn't.

Shane looked up toward the ocean, and her heart skipped a beat. She rubbed her eyes, making sure it wasn't too good to be true, but it was still there, bright as day.

"Reece," she said, wiping tears away from her face trying to compose herself. "Do you see that?"

Reece looked up, squinting, before she let out a gasp. "Is that —" She couldn't find the words to finish her sentence.

A small island could be seen with what appeared to be vegetation like the one they were on. It wasn't the island that excited them, but what was coming from it. Smoke drifted upward from the island, blending in with the clouds. It was faint, but it was most definitely there.

"Do you think people live over there?"

"No, it's just a wildfire," Shane said sarcastically. "Of course, I think it's people." She tried to keep her emotions in check, but she couldn't help a smile from breaking across her chapped lips.

"How are we supposed to get over there?"

"We'll build a raft or something." Shane scrambled to her feet, brushed the sand from her torn, bloodied leggings. Her legs were full of small scrapes from their venture in the woods.

"And you really trust your sailing skills enough for that?"

"Look, Reece," she started, trying to make her voice relaxing. "This may be our only way of surviving this."

"Do we have to rush into this?"

"You've gone swimming with me plenty of times, and I've never seen you like this."

"That's because this is different."

"How so?"

"Because— because I'm terrified of the ocean! The things that live in it, the deep crevices, they're all terrifying." Reece eyed the island, then looked back at Shane, color gone from her face.

Shane stood there, shocked. She was so absorbed in her own issues that she hadn't even comprehended Reece's reaction to the ocean when they first saw it.

"Why didn't you tell me?"

Reece glanced at the lapping waves. "Because it never came up," she said.

Shane pursed her lips and looked back at the island. She understood her friend's fear, but at the same time, they had to do something to get help. "Look," Shane said softly, "it's either we stay here and die of starvation, or we build a raft like I said and sail over there."

Reece remained silent as she kept her eyes locked on the island.

"Please, I want to go home, even if it means we have to cross over to that island. Face it, Reece, no one's gonna help us here."

Shane's response was met with a long silence before Reece finally said, "Fine, but only if the raft has at least a chance of making it. I'm not risking my life for something that won't even make it more than ten feet offshore." She grabbed Shane's outstretched hand and got up from the sandy shore.

"Great, I'm gonna go get some wood—"

"There's no need for that." Reece's attention was fixated over Shane's shoulder. She was just about to ask what Reece was staring at before turning around and seeing it too.

"I guess we aren't the only ones that have been here," Reece commented as she walked over to the small rowboat tucked behind a sharp decline in the ground. It was half covered in sand, blending it into the scenery but for its pointed bow. It hadn't been touched in years, but the oars were still in it. The words on the side had almost all faded away by the beating sun, and the paint was chipped and falling off. The only thing that they were able to make out were the letters A.C.M. carved into the stern of the boat.

"What's A.C.M?" Reece asked, bending down to take a closer look.

"Initials, maybe?" Shane ran her hand along the boat and got a splinter for her effort.

"Do you think that whoever that is, is still here?"

"Yes, Reece," Shane said sarcastically, "Because a boat that has this many cobwebs *definitely* showed up right before we did. Of course, they aren't here. They probably died on this godforsaken island." She knelt next to the boat, inspecting the imperfections in the wood before saying, "I think it will work."

Reece let out a puff of air. "As what? A boat, or firewood?"

Shane rolled her eyes, standing up and carefully brushed off as much sand as she could from the boat, careful not to get any splinters. "Can you help me get it into the water?" She had moved toward the back and grabbed its frail edges, ready to push.

"If even a little bit of water seeps in, I'm not getting in." Reece joined Shane and pushed with all her might. It slid the tiniest bit, leaving a small trail in the coarse sand. They tried again only to see the same result. They continued like this for what felt like forever before the girls were finally ankle deep in the water, ice-cold waves lapping rhythmically against their legs. Shane winced as salt water stung at the small wounds on her legs.

"I don't see any water coming in," Shane said. She grabbed the oars and placed them in their wooden holders.

"It's too early to tell." Reece ran to the shore nearly as soon as the boat entered the water and looked down at her toes, which were bright red from the cold.

"When's long enough to tell?" Shane asked.

"I don't know. Longer than that, though. I don't want to be way out in the water and see that the boat's bringing on water."

Shane rolled her eyes again, but let the boat sit in the water for a couple of minutes. She used that time to shovel out the handfuls of sand that had found its way in after years of neglect. She got as much of it out as she could before turning to the spiderwebs. When she was all done, the only signs of it being neglected were the chipped paint and sunbaked wood.

"Still no water in it," she yelled back to Reece before getting in. It bobbed unevenly in the water, destabilized by the sudden added weight.

"Are you sure?"

"Come see for yourself." Shane grabbed both oars and ignored the splinters that stabbed the skin of her hands.

Reece got up from where she'd dropped back onto the sand. She grumbled to herself as she trudged through the water toward the boat. Shane dug the oars into the sandy bottom of the shore, trying to make sure that the boat didn't move too much in the waves while Reece got in.

"Have I mentioned I get seasick?" Reece grumbled. Shane ignored her friend and pulled the oars toward her with all her might. The boat barely moved. The waves were pushing them back in, toward the sand. She clenched her teeth and tried again, to no avail. Reece joined in, and finally they began moving out, away from land. It was only when they were away from shore that it got easier. By that time Shane's arms were already burning from the effort.

The farther from the beach they went, the more anxious Shane felt, and Reece's fear gripped Shane as well. She had no idea what kind of creatures would greet them if they did somehow manage to crash the boat, or if water overtook it.

"Would you mind rowing for a bit?" Shane asked, trying to shake off that fear.

"You're doing a great job. Why do you want me to do it?"

"Because my arms feel like they're gonna fall off." That much was true.

"I'd do no better at it."

"But it would give my arms a break," Shane said. "We switch off every fifteen minutes?"

Reece looked like she was about to argue, but Shane had already crossed the oars and was working her way to the other end of the boat.

Reece grumbled, but she switched with Shane and held the oars awkwardly in her hands.

A cold breeze picked up when they were three quarters of the way to the island. Reece was rowing as the cold water lapped the sides of the boat, hitting Shane's hands. All the sweat had cooled down, leaving her with a chill that wasn't going away. Storm clouds were gathering off in the distance, slowly making their way toward them.

"You do see that, right?" Reece asked, staring at the brewing storm and looking a little green in the face. She kept rowing but half-heartedly.

"Yes, and right now I'm trying to ignore it."

The clouds blocked the sun, cooling the air noticeably. Shane, already freezing, started to shake involuntarily. A silent scream erupted in her head as the boat went over a wave twice its size. The unsettling thought that they weren't going to make it crept into her mind for the first time.

"Give me the oars, Reece!" Shane yelled, her voice frantic. Reece obliged without argument.

"Shane, I don't want to die." Reece's terrified voice pierced the cold day.

"You won't," Shane lied. She nearly choked on her own words. Never before had she seen a storm move in so quickly.

The waves on the ocean became much greater in the blink of an eye. Water sprayed in their faces, and the salt burned their eyes. Shane's wet hands had trouble keeping purchase on the oars, but she refused to let go. She wouldn't give up that easily.

"Shane! I thought you said that the boat wasn't leaking!" Reece yelled. Her hands were white against the frayed edges of the boat, her face void of any color.

"I did! But something in the boat must've broken." Cold, murky water crept its way around their ankles. Shane dropped the oars and tried to scoop as much as she could out with her hands, but it was no use. They were taking on too much water.

"It's not helping!" Reece cried out, tears streaming down her face. "It's too late. We're gonna die."

No.

No, no, no. This can't be happening, Shane thought. They couldn't have come this far, given this much hope just to end up dying in the ocean.

The water in the boat was up to Shane's shin, and it was only rising higher. Lightning struck in the distance, illuminating the fear in Reece's eyes.

"Listen here, Reece," Shane said, refusing to give up hope. "We have to jump. It might be our only way to live through this."

"But how? How will we survive?"

"I don't know, but it's the only way, unless you want to go down with the boat."

Shane didn't wait for Reece to make up her mind and leaped out the boat. Her head submerged under the dark water, the cold stealing her breath away. It took the last of her energy to push back up once more, but the waves kept pummeling her down. The light of day disappeared as bubbles rose to the surface.

CHAPTER 3

The cold water cut into her like a sharp knife, pressing her deeper into the ocean. Her ears rang from the pressure the farther down she went. Her lungs screamed in desperation for air, and she was so far under she couldn't see the light anymore. She clawed at the water trying desperately to get to the surface, but the undertow kept pulling her back down. All she was doing was wasting energy that she couldn't afford to lose.

She could hold her breath no longer. Bubbles escaped her lips as she looked up, longing for the air above but knowing that it was impossible to get there.

"Shane." A warm, comforting woman's voice came piercing through the dark water. "Breathe."

Shane's whole body went rigid. She straightened out to look for whoever that voice came from, her lungs screaming at her to bring in air. Everywhere she looked there was nothing but darkness to greet her.

"Breathe, Shane." The voice seemed to emanate from all around her, not originating from a certain point.

No really, part of her mind said. *It's not like I'm gonna drown if I do that.* But another, stronger, part was telling her to listen to the voice. She was going to die anyway. Why not make it faster?

She let the water flood into her mouth and nose. It took her a couple seconds to realize that she wasn't suffocating; wasn't drowning. Instead, she began taking in steady breaths, almost like she was breathing through a musty mask in the open air. Except she wasn't. She was underwater.

That's it, she thought, *I must've died, and now I'm a ghost.* She pinched herself to see if it was actually happening, and it hurt as though she were conscious.

"This is real, Shane," the voice said, almost like it could read her mind. A teal glow emitted from Shane's peripheral vision. She whipped her head around and let out a gasp. A stunning, glowing lady wearing a light, flowing dress had materialized next to her. Her long, glowing brown hair shimmered in the ocean's currents, flowing like seaweed.

"What the—" Shane started. She blinked once to make sure her mind wasn't playing tricks on her. "I'm dead, aren't I."

The woman laughed; a warm wave of water came from her direction. "You are anything but dead, but that doesn't mean you aren't in danger."

"What? What do you mean?"

"What lies before you is perilous," the woman said, floating toward her. "You need all the help you can get."

Shane's heart seized. "Reece," she whispered, eyes widening. She had been so focused on herself that she hadn't even given a second thought about her friend. "She—"

"Is fine. When you go to the surface, you'll find her hanging onto the remains of the boat."

"How did you— Who are you?" Shane's mind felt like it was exploding. This couldn't be happening. This couldn't be real.

"I am Mindalin, goddess of the waters and seas."

"What— Where am I?"

"I'm afraid that I can't tell you. I'm already breaking the divine laws seeing you now."

"Then why'd you do it?"

"To warn you of what lies before you and remind you of the promise you made me." Mindalin's glow began to fade, and her voice became distant, like she was yelling through a long tunnel.

"Wait, no!" Shane reached an arm out, trying to grab her translucent hand, but it was too late. She was already gone. "What did I promise you?" she yelled into the dark waters. "You have the wrong person!"

Mindalin didn't answer. She was gone. No matter which way Shane turned, she saw nothing besides dark blue water.

She could've stayed down there all day, trying to decipher the meaning of what Mindalin told her, but the thought of Reece brought her mind back up to the surface. She couldn't leave her friend all alone in the vast ocean. Even if she was currently safe on the debris of the boat, that didn't mean she would be forever. For all Shane knew, she was searching the water for her, probably thinking she was dead.

Shane kicked her way upward. Her head broke the water's surface. Rays of sunlight hit her face, nearly blinding her. The storm that had overtaken them and was now far off in the distance, replaced by bright blue sky. Shane wondered if Mindalin was responsible for the change in weather, but she shook her head. Of course, she was.

"Shane!" Reece's broken voice pierced the air. She tried to yell it out again but succeeded in only a croak.

Shane twirled around, trying to locate her friend. The shallow waves tried to pull her tired body down, but she wasn't going to allow that to happen. Not again. She spotted Reece's body laying against a large set of planks that used to be the boat. Reece had given up calling out for Shane and lay helplessly on the piece of wood. She sobbed silently at the thought that it could be because her friend had given up hope of her ever returning.

"Reece!" Shane tried to yell but was silenced when a wave filled her wide-open mouth with salty water.

Reece's head perked up.

"Reece!" Shane swam forward, feeling the burn in her arms and legs.

"Shane." Reece's sore voice broke. Tears swelled in her eyes. "You're alive!" She kicked over to Shane.

Shane reached out to grab the edge of the makeshift raft, and a wave of relief washed over her whole body. She yearned to be on the sandy beach, but it seemed farther away than she could paddle. The burning in her arms and legs was already bad enough. She couldn't dare to think of how they would feel after swimming over there.

"I thought you were dead!" Reece cried.

Shane cringed, thinking about what her friend must have gone through.

"I thought that you drowned. You can't do that to me." Tears streamed down Reece's face.

"I… I would have. Drowned, I mean" Shane took a deep breath. She was still trying to wrap her mind around what happened below the surface. "I was trapped underwater. I couldn't swim up. The waves kept pushing me down. I honestly thought that I was going to drown, and I couldn't hold my breath any longer. Then I took a breath in. I… I actually breathed in the water." She saw Reece's skeptic look but continued anyway. "Then this… this woman showed up and called herself Mindalin. She said she was the goddess of the sea, and that I was in some kind of danger."

Reece's mouth went agape. "You do realize how crazy that sounds, right?"

"Yeah, I do, but trust me when I—"

"I do."

Shane blinked the salt away. "What?"

"I believe you." Reece paused, trying but failing to hide her tears. One traced its way down her chin. "After all the crap we've been through over the last twenty-four hours, I wouldn't be surprised if you said that aliens kidnapped you," she joked, trying for a smile but failing miserably.

"I can't tell you how much of a relief that is."

Shane felt like crying from mixed emotions, but knew that if she did, Reece and she would never make it to land before nightfall. The sun was already low on the horizon. Shane let out a groan at how much farther they had to swim to reach the beach.

"I don't think I can make it. My legs are shot."

"Together?" Reece asked, a new fire in her eyes.

"Together."

They started kicking against the small waves, but it was hard to move their legs. Shane couldn't feel them anymore, besides the prickling pain of the cold that had taken over them. She didn't complain though. If anything, she was glad for the pain. It showed her that this was real. She was here. She was still alive.

At last, Shane's feet touched the sandy ocean floor. Relief spread all throughout her body. She couldn't help but smile as she let go of the wood and rushed toward dry land arm in arm with Reece. Their legs both gave out the moment they were out of the water. Shane's deep, heavy, condensed breath floated away from her into the cold night air. Goosebumps rose up on her arms and legs, and her hair stood straight out. They were safe from the ocean, but there was still a chance they would die from hypothermia.

The small beach they found themselves on was surrounded by giant cliff faces on every side. Shane gazed up at them, and a small part of her died inside. The smoke was no longer visible from where they stood, and there didn't seem to be a way to get to where they saw it come from.

"You realize that there's a path right there." Reece pointed to a small break in the cliff faces filled with trees and other undergrowth that Shane hadn't noticed before. A small path that looked a little more well used than the one on the island that they came from was right in the middle. Immediate relief coursed through Shane when she realized she didn't have to climb.

"I saw that."

"Sure, you did."

Shane made her way over toward the trail, working her shaking hands to keep the blood flowing. Never had she been so cold. She was glad to be moving, but all she wanted to do was sit down in a warm place with dry clothes on.

Shane led the way up the trail. It started off weaving in and out of the trees at a gentle slope, but soon it took a sharp incline. The rain from the earlier storm turned the path to mud. Every step she took set her backward two more. There were times when she had to go down on all fours just to continue the climb.

It seemed to take forever to climb the path before it plateaued and joined another, more used trail that seemed to follow the coastline. The glow of the moon shone down on their shoulders. The temperature was dropping quickly, and the smoke became visible in the moonlight. It rose high into the sky, clouding the many stars with its dark gray mist, eventually dissipating into nothing. The trail they were now on seemed to be heading in that direction.

"How much farther could it be?" Reece asked through her chattering teeth, her arms tight to her chest, and her lips a light shade of blue.

"It can't be much farther," Shane said, trying to control her own shivering.

By the time they saw the lights of the town where the smoke was coming from shining through the trees, everything on Shane's body had a slight frost over it. Her shirt crinkled slightly with every move she made. Shane's heart raced as the lights grew bigger. Relief began washing over her as she walked faster and faster toward the lights.

"Shane! Wait!" Reece yelled after her, but she didn't listen. They finally weren't alone.

The trail led to the crest of a hill overlooking a town sprawling out below her. Shane stopped, her mouth agape. It wasn't a town, exactly. It was more like a city lit by torches and lanterns illuminating the cobbled streets and stone brick buildings.

On the distant side of the city lay an ocean bay. It was hidden from her view on the other island. Giant sailing ships sat anchored in the bay with their giant sails rolled up against the yardarms.

"Why'd you stop?" Reece's voice came from behind her, followed quickly by a gasp. She stopped right next to Shane. "What the hell?"

Shane still stared down at it, amazed that something so massive had shown up out of nowhere. Then she blinked, drawing her back to reality. "Come on," she said to Reece. "If we don't get moving, the cold will kill us."

They started down the winding trail and before they knew it, they were walking through the twisting cobbled streets. Grass grew from between the uneven stones that threatened to trip Shane and her shuffling feet. Exhaustion crept up on Shane, and she knew that if they didn't warm up soon, hypothermia would take a hold of them.

"Shane. Where are you going?" Reece whispered, her head darting around. Two and three-story buildings surrounded them. Many of the windows had lanterns lighting them.

"I'm trying to find clothes. If we keep wearing these, we're as good as dead." She grabbed her frozen sweatshirt and tugged it slightly. Particles of frost cascaded down it.

She turned down the alleyway. A clothesline drawn from one building to another full of clothes brought a smile to her face. The shirts were way too big for either Shane or Reece, and the pants even worse, but Shane didn't care. As long as they could get out of the damp clothes, she would be happy. She yanked a set of clothes off the line.

"What are you doing?" Reece asked. "Those aren't yours. You can't just steal them."

"Just did." Shane tossed the clothes to Reece.

"But—"

"Look, it's either we do this, or we freeze to death."

Reece went silent, too busy staring down at the clothes in her hands. All the shirts were torn and battered, and a faded beige colors as well. They looked like something peasants would wear in the Middle Ages. Guilt pressed into Shane as she pulled down another set of clothes, but she was quick to dismiss it.

I have to do this, she reminded herself as she removed her hand-me-down sweatshirt and put on the pilfered clothes. The shirt sagged, and the pants kept falling down, but Shane rolled them up until they 'fit'.

"What do we do now?" Reece asked, pulling a misappropriated shirt over her head.

"We need to find a place to crash."

"Right here?" Reece looked around her, fear in her eyes. "What if someone comes and mugs us or something?"

A small chuckle left Shane's mouth. "What would the chance of that be? If a criminal does come down this street looking for money from us, he's going to be very disappointed."

As soon as she said those words though, something humanoid moved on the rooftops. Shane quickly looked up. Someone was there. His masked face peaked out over the side before he used the ledge to start his descent down. The dark cloak that covered his head billowed out around him as he fell the last couple feet to the ground.

Out of the corner of Shane's eye, she noticed Reece opening her mouth to yell. Shane quickly moved to cover Reece's mouth. Her wild eyes screamed to be let go, but Shane couldn't do that. There was still a chance that the man hadn't seen them, and she wasn't going to allow one screech of terror to ruin that. They slowly backed up against the wall, hiding in the shadows.

The man let out a sigh of relief before removing his hood and mask to reveal his surprisingly young face. He leaned his messy brown hair against the wall and breathed in deeply, sending mist floating away with his exhale. A smile spread across his face as he looked up to the sky.

Shane tried to shrink in the darkness, afraid to breathe, fearful that the man could hear her. She clasped her hand over her mouth to stop the moisture from betraying her while skirting her way along the building toward the main street, pulling Reece as she went. She ran her hand along the brick work, feeling her way backward when she accidentally kicked a rock, sending it skittering noisily toward the main street. The man whipped his attention toward them.

"Who in Haytorrow's Realm are you?" he asked in a strange, *British* like accent, surprising Shane. He removed a long knife from the inside of his cloak.

Thump, thump, thump, Shane's heart raced out of her chest as she willed her legs to run away but she was paralyzed with fear. One look at Reece told her that her friend felt the same.

"If you don't answer my question, I'm gonna have to run you through."

Yeah, right, Shane thought, everything in her telling her to run. *The chances of you killing us are probably the exact same if we do tell you who we are.*

The man took a step toward them. They both shrank together. The knife was only inches away from Shane's terrified face.

"I'm waiting."

Shane took a deep gulp as she regained the ability to move her body. Her hand twitched. Without a second thought, she spun around and sprinted toward the exit, not daring to look back. Something moved out of the corner of her eye. She whipped her head around to see the man vaulting across the wall to get in front of her. Before Shane could even think about blinking, he was blocking the only exit to the alley.

"If you think that I'm gonna let you escape, you're sadly mistaken." He flipped the knife expertly in his hand and put it back in his cloak. Now that he was in between them and the exit, he felt no need for it.

"Look, we don't have any money, or anything at all," Shane said. She couldn't stop her voice from shaking uncontrollably.

"You think I want money?" The man laughed, his thick brown eyebrows creasing.

"Then what do you want?" She reached for Reece's sleeve for reassurance that someone else was there with her.

"I want to know who it was who saw me descend the building, and why I didn't see you when I looked down."

A loud bang rang out through the night, and the smell of gunpowder wafted its way toward Shane's nose. Yelling came from the street. For the first time, what looked like fear wavered on the man's face.

"Bloody knives," he mumbled under his breath just loud enough for Shane to hear him. "How do they know I'm here?" His eyes skirted between Shane and Reece, pursing his lips. "If either of you tell them what you saw, I will make sure that your lives will be worse than Haytorrow's Fallen Realm." With that, he sprinted toward the wall, running up it and grabbing a window ledge before gravity could hold him back. Before Shane and Reece knew what was happening, he was gone. Out of sight.

"Where'd he go?" someone from the street yelled. He ran past the alleyway, looking toward the rooftops, an old-fashioned revolver glistened in his hand. Five people chased behind him, all wearing the same, dark green uniforms.

"What just happened?" Reece asked, her voice shaking with fear.

"No idea." Shane made her way toward the street, trying to ignore how shaken up she was by the whole experience. The people who were chasing the boy had stopped where the streets intersected and were busy arguing among themselves. One man, the leader Shane presumed, brought his eyes up to see her and Reece walking down the street. He pointed at them, and he mouthed some words to the others. He started toward them with the five other men in tow.

"Excuse me, ladies," the man said as he took his hat off and held it in both hands, then put the revolver back in its holster. "Did you happen to see a young man wearing a black cloak running on the rooftops?"

Reece looked like she was about to answer, but Shane cut in before she got the chance. "No," Shane said, faking a smile. "I'm sorry, but we just got here, and we were busy trying to find our way around to notice anything like that."

Disappointment flitted through his eyes, but he smiled. "Of course. Would you mind telling me where you're visiting from?"

Shane let out a laugh. "That's a long story, but the short of it is we came from an island that has some kind of cave, but no people on—"

"What?" The smile on the man's face faded away, replaced by a hard look. His hand slowly reached for his gun. Shane's eyes flitted from his hands to his face as fear gripped her. What had she said to get this reaction? "Seize them," he said to his henchmen. They moved too fast for Shane and Reece to escape, knocking them down on their knees and tying their hands with rope.

"What'd we do?" Shane cried. She winced as one of the people pulled tight on the bindings, nearly cutting the circulation to her hands.

"You're under arrest for trespassing on the Island of Eringunner." The leader leaned down. All the sympathy that he had before was gone from his eyes. "If you wanted our help, then you wouldn't have admitted to breaking one of the king's most sacred laws."

Shane's mind reeled with questions as they were hauled to their feet and jostled forward with two men holding each by their arms.

They were led down the winding streets out of the residential area and entered what appeared to be the commercial section. The apartment buildings dissipated, replaced by shops, both small and large. Soon they passed through to the interior of the city. Enormous houses with huge columns and arches that looked like something out of an old, eighteenth-century story book stood in every direction.

Shane could smell the stink of fish from the ocean. In between the houses as they passed, she could catch glimpses of the sea. She wished that Mindalin had told her more about where she was and hadn't shut her down when she asked. Maybe then she would've known enough to keep her mouth shut. She'd know what law they had broken, and they wouldn't be in this predicament.

But no.

Shane looked over at Reece, who hung her head. Shane could tell Reece was crying silently. She couldn't blame her. Her whole life had been turned upside down in less than a day. Shane had always dreamed of something like this happening to her, to bring her out of her mundane, ordinary life, but now that it was, she wished more than anything that she could go back.

"What you lookin' at?" The man beside her demanded, pulling against the rope further tightening it around her wrists. Shane winced but said nothing, her jaw tightening. She returned her gaze to the stone pathway in front of her. The man chuckled menacingly, pushing her forward and making her quicken her pace. She clenched her fists, unable to break her bonds.

Eventually they rounded a curve that was lit by the orange glow of lanterns that crackled loudly in the cold night. Shane brought her eyes up and realized that they had reached where they were heading. The house was the only one at the end of the street, and it was a large, wooden building with huge logs acting like columns. Large windows graced the facia of the magnificent building

"Just wait until you see inside," the man behind her whispered, taking note of the way Shane was staring, jaw agape when she saw it.

They walked up the wooden steps to the front porch. A sudden chill went down Shane's neck. Everything in her wanted to bolt, but she couldn't just run away and leave Reece behind. Even if she could manage to escape the rope and the man behind her, she still remembered the revolver in the holster on his side. She could see it out of the corner of her eye, glinting in the orange glow of the torches that decorated the entry arch.

Shane was pushed forward from behind. She wanted to scream and fight back, but somehow, she managed to hold herself back. The man leaned over her shoulder and pushed the door open. Warmth rushed out of the building. A musty smell overwhelmed her as the man forced her inside. An elegant stairway wound around the walls leading to a landing above. The whole room was lit up by the bright light of lanterns, and a chandelier in the center made from what appeared to be elk antlers.

"Why are we here?" Shane asked through the fear that gripped her. All it got her was a hard slap to the back of the head that brought tears to her eyes.

"You don't get to talk," the man seethed. The person that Shane assumed to be the leader of the guards led them up the stairs.

Shane remained quiet. They went through too many hallways and rooms for Shane to be able to find her way out, even if she could escape the man's grip. At last, they stopped before a giant wooden door.

She looked at Reece as the man knocked on the door. She looked just as scared as her. She nudged Reece with her elbow. "It's going to be fine," she mouthed, but she had trouble believing that herself. For all she knew they were never going to leave that house.

"Who is it?" a deep, croaky voice asked irritably.

The man cleared his throat. "It's Eikaman, sir," he said. Shane took note of the way he straightened out his uniform and stood up straighter.

"Enter!"

Eikaman opened the door and stepped into the room first. Shane was shoved forward, and the doors closed behind her. The two men holding Shane and Reece left as soon as their captives were in the room, leaving them alone with Eikaman and the man sitting behind an ornately decorated desk. His head rested on his hand, which was holding onto a pair of ancient looking glasses.

"Did you bring me the assassin?" he asked, picking up his gaze. When he saw Shane and Reece, the little excitement he had in his eyes dissipated almost immediately. He set his glasses on the table and let out a long sigh. "I told you," he began, his voice harsh, "not to come into my house if you didn't have him with you."

"But Lord Princecon…" Eikaman started, but was cut off.

"Do you know how many lives he's taken, lives—" he pressed his hands against the table so hard that they lost all color, "—like mine. I've already placed guards to protect my house, but that isn't enough for the assassin." His voice rose until he was yelling.

"I'm sorry, sir." Eikaman gulped. "But from what we saw he was on the outskirts of Stoenstill making his way out."

"So?" He spat. "You think that comforts me? Because trust me, knowing that an assassin who murders people like me is still alive is anything but comforting."

"Lord Princecon, I understand, but I found something better."

Something better?

"And what is that?"

Eikaman straightened up. "These two girls." He gestured toward them. Shane could feel Princecon's eyes staring at her, but she refused to meet them. She focused intently on his desk instead. "They were near the area where I last saw your assassin. They claim to have come from the Island of Eringunner."

I never said anything like that, Shane wanted to scream, but she too was overcome by fear to even move.

"Is that right?" Princecon said. His jaw clenched as he tried to keep a reasonable tone. "And do you have any proof of that?"

"No, but—"

"Then why did you bring them to me?

"Because, sir, the king ordered anyone on this island to bring such criminals to you to take to the king."

Criminals?

Was it criminal for them to have no idea where they were and just wanted to go home, Shane thought? Was it criminal for them to have escaped the island they were trapped on, nearly freezing to death the whole way to the city? As far as Shane was concerned, they should at least have a reasonable explanation as to why they were arrested, other than the vague answer that Eikaman had given them before, that they had apparently broken the king's most sacred law.

"Do you see the king anywhere in this room?" The edge in Princecon's voice made Eikaman take a small step back.

"No, but—"

"Then why did you arrest them when you had the simple job of tracking down the assassin who has threatened my life? My life is in danger, yet you have the audacity to stand there like nothing's wrong with two irresponsible children who happened to trespass on the king's sacred island."

"But sir—"

"Quiet!" Princecon said, putting his hand out to silence Eikaman. He clenched his fist, then took a deep breath to calm himself before looking up. "I'm going to give you one more chance. Tomorrow when I leave for the mainland, I'm going to bring the two of them with me, and when I come back, the assassin better be either gone from the city, or dead. No in between. Got it?"

Eikaman nodded.

"Leave me," Princecon demanded as back in his chair. "Take them with you, and lock them in the cellar."

"Yes sir."

Eikaman grabbed both Shane and Reece's wrists and dragged them toward the door. Before they could leave, however, Princecon said, "Don't you dare come into my home again if you don't have news that the assassin's dead."

Eikaman said nothing as he closed the door behind them. He led the girls back down the stairs and through another batch of rooms and hallways until they got to yet another set of stairs leading down, this one not nearly as elaborate as the ones near the entrance of the house. A cold, foreboding chill came up from below with dimly lit torches showing the way to utter blackness. Eikaman shoved them forward, forcing them to go down. Shane obliged begrudgingly, even though everything told her to fight and run away. Nothing good could happen from what lie ahead.

The cells were like something out of a medieval nightmare. Thick, corroded bars stood between them and the edges of the dark, stone room. They ran all the way from the floor to the wet ceiling. The sound of water dripping could be heard echoing all around the room.

Eikaman unlocked the door and threw them both in. Shane waited for his footsteps to recede before meeting Reece's terrified eyes. Together, they both broke down and cried. Tears streamed from both their eyes all night until they could cry no more. The next day, they would leave for the mainland where they would meet the king who hopefully would have mercy on them, but Shane knew better. *We're as good as dead.*

CHAPTER 4

Shane had been rudely awoken from her uneasy sleep by a grating noise against the cell bars. When she opened her eyes, she wasn't surprised to see Eikaman with shackles in his hand meant for them. He put them on so that their arms were in front of their body before taking them out of the cell.

They hadn't gotten breakfast, instead being led out into the cold air toward the docks. Eikaman said there would be food for them on the ship, but Shane highly doubted that. She didn't know much about Princecon, but from what she had seen, he wouldn't care enough about his prisoners to make sure they arrived on the mainland alive.

On the docks, the ocean breeze flung Shane's hair into her face as she waited to board Princecon's ship, the Thalcan. The docks were silent in the early morning mist, the sun not having yet risen over the horizon. The few people on the dock were rushing around silently, all doing whatever job that needed to be done. Shane stood in the middle of this, her hands shackled together, Reece by her side. Eikaman was nearby but said nothing. He seemed to fade into the shadows in the presence of Lord Princecon.

"Is the Thalcan ready?" he asked, staring up at the biggest ship in the whole harbor.

Eikaman cleared his throat. "Yes, sir. Just as you asked."

"Good. Prepare for departure and take them to the brig."

Eikaman gave a curt nod and grabbed Shane's and Reece's shackles. He led them onboard the ship. Shane didn't have much time to look around the deck as they were rushed below. Already she could feel the stagnant stuffiness of the world below deck.

Eikaman led them to a room with bars closing off one side. He unlocked a barred door and shoved them in. The sound of the door creaking shut behind them, slamming into the cell's bars, was the only thing Shane could hear. There was a click of the door locking, then nothing.

She waited for Eikaman to go back to the deck before getting up. "Well, isn't this lovely," Shane whispered under her breath as she walked around the tiny room that they were to be trapped in for the next week or two. At least that's what she overheard Princecon saying. In the corner sat a small bucket for the bathroom. It reeked of urine and poop, and from the looks of it, nobody had cleaned it out for quite some time. So much for privacy.

"That's one way to put it," Reece said glumly, messing with the shackles around her wrists.

"It could be worse." Shane had difficulty believing it herself.

"How?"

"We could be dead right now."

"Ooh," Reece said sarcastically. "That's so much worse than having to live through this."

"Or we could be tortured." Shane sat down on the uncomfortable wooden ground and let out a sigh. There was no comfort to be found where they were kept.

"I'd rather have that happen to me than be on another boat." Reece wiped a tear from her face. "With my luck we'll probably hit a rock or something and we'll all die."

A lump formed in Shane's throat. She wanted to comfort her friend but didn't know how. She was never good at it.

"Look, Reece," Shane finally started. "If you want to talk about it, I'm here."

"Talk about what? How I'm gonna die here?"

"Don't talk like that. We aren't going to die."

A humorless laugh left Reece's mouth. "Face it, Shane." She stopped, trying to keep more tears from falling. "*I'm* going to die here. Not we."

"No, you aren't."

"You're the lovable one, Shane. With any luck you'll be the king's favorite. But me. I'm a nobody."

"That isn't true."

"Yes, it is." Tears were rolling down her face. "The sooner you realize *that* the better."

"And the sooner you realize that you're lying to yourself, you might have a chance of surviving. You aren't a nobody, Reece."

The whole time Shane and Reece were kept below deck with the only light coming from a lantern at the far end of the room. As the days went by, the musty stench only got worse. Reece fell victim to the smells and seasickness, and spent most of the time in the corner, puking her guts out, only worsening the smell. That, and the food didn't help her stomach. They had gotten pitiful amounts, and the stuff they did get was mostly rotten and moldy.

The worst day was when there was a storm. Waves slammed against the side of the ship, sending Shane and Reece stumbling across the celled-off area. Yelling came from above, and Shane prayed that they wouldn't shipwreck again. When the seas finally calmed nearly two days later, Shane hadn't gotten a wink of sleep.

It took a week to reach the mainland. The sound of activity from above deck hinted that the ship finally made it to the docks. Shane picked up her head as footfalls on the ladder suggested someone was coming their way. He wore the same clothes as Eikaman and the rest of the guards had the day of her capture. The only difference was instead of a gun holster hanging by his side, there were a set of keys.

He made sure the shackles that Shane and Reece had been wearing were still well attached before unlocking the door and letting them out. Her wrists were raw from the constant pressure of them. She winced as the man grabbed the chain and yanked her forward, holding back tears of anger and helplessness.

Reece's face had turned a sickly shade of green, and it once again looked like she was about to lose her stomach.

"You ok?" Shane asked out of the corner of her mouth, afraid of what the guard would do if he heard them talking.

"Never better," Reece mumbled.

The guard led them up several decks. The bright sunlight blinded Shane as they stepped out onto the main deck. The fresh air was welcome to her, and the brisk air of an autumn morning rejuvenated her.

The man herded them off the ship onto a rotting dock, continuing until they made it to the shore. The feeling of the ground not swaying underneath Shane came as a welcome surprise.

"What's taking you so long?" Princecon's voice cut through the early morning air.

"Sir," the man's grip tightened on Shane's wrists, making her want to scream, "we just docked."

"King Aarion expects to see me in less than a week, and he doesn't like to be kept waiting."

"I'm sorry, sir."

"Sorry isn't enough." Princecon took a deep breath, rubbing his eyebrows. "Just tie them to the back of my saddle."

The man gave a curt nod and yanked them forward through the crew and dockworkers attending to the boat. They purposely kept their gaze away from Shane and Reece.

The man leading them stopped when they reached a group of horses in the middle of a street. People congregated around the one in the lead, preparing it for a long journey, it seemed. Shane wasn't surprised that Princecon wasn't the one doing the work. That would mean getting his hands dirty, after all.

The uniformed man had a quick conversation with someone getting the horse together before turning to Shane and Reece with a rope in his hands. He looped it through their shackles and tied them to the back of the saddle.

Shane and Reece waited silently as the men who were tending to Princecon's horse talked in hushed voices, stopping only when Princecon showed up.

"Is everything prepared?" Princecon asked from behind Shane. She kept her eyes glued to the ground.

"Yes, sir." One of the men took a step forward. "Everything's just as you asked."

"Good."

The crowd parted as Princecon started for his horse. Shane watched as his pristine boots left the ground, and he got on the saddle. Without hesitation, he spurred his horse forward, yanking Shane and Reece with him. Three guards followed close behind, carrying whatever they couldn't put on the horse. They rounded a corner, and a building blocked the view of the ocean. Shane was fine with that. As far as she was concerned, she would be happy if she never saw a damn sea ever again.

More people showed up in the streets as the sun rose over the horizon. They went on about with their business as usual, but whenever Shane, Reece, and the rest of the group passed, they scurried away, not daring to meet Princecon's gaze. *What kind of power did he have over these people for them to be afraid to look at him,* Shane thought? She peered into a window to see a terrified woman looking out from behind the curtains. Once they passed however, the people continued on like nothing ever happened. When they left the edge of the city, they were bustling around as normal.

The first hour or so of walking wasn't that bad. Eventually though, Shane's wrists weighed heavy from the heft of the shackles. Every now and again she noticed Reece rubbing her weary wrists, cursing silently. They didn't talk one word as they continued onward, afraid of what might happen if they did.

Storm clouds were brewing above the mountains in the distance, and before long rain was falling. Shane was sopping wet and freezing. The shackles felt like they were frozen to her skin, making it more painful than ever to move her arms. She wouldn't have been surprised if she had frostbite on her sopping feet, or trench foot. She shuddered at that thought, painfully continuing onward.

The hairs on the back of Shane's neck stood on end as lightning struck in the distance. The sky lit up like fire. Thunder soon followed.

Not for the last time, Shane longed for home. If the lightning got any closer, she feared that it would strike one of them. Shane and Reece were like walking targets with metal around their wrists. Shane subconsciously counted the seconds in between the lightning and thunder. She remembered what her dad had told her about calculating how far lighting was away. If you count the number of seconds, and divide by five, you get how many miles away the lightning struck. It was fifteen seconds at first, three miles, but soon the rain started pouring down harder, and thunder clapped right after the lightning struck.

The rain didn't seem to slow them down one bit. They kept moving straight through the storm. Lightning reflected off her shackles every few minutes, but finally the rain let up as they stopped for the night in a small clearing. The guards were quick to set up a small camp with two tents. One for Princecon, and one for the rest of the guards. Shane and Reece were left for the elements, not even getting a blanket.

That night they were close to becoming hypothermic. Shane and Reece hadn't been given anything to protect them from the elements, so they huddled together in a desperate attempt to keep from freezing. They also hadn't been given any food to eat. Instead, they had to watch Princecon and the three other guards sit around a nice warm fire and eat their meal. Their stomachs grumbled. Never had Shane been as hungry as she was right then. She swore to herself that if she ever got home, she wouldn't complain about not having any food, or her mom's cooking, because right now anything sounded good, even seafood.

When she awoke from her uneasy sleep in the morning, her neck was stiff.

The rain continued to drench them on and off for three more days before eventually clearing up to an overcast gray sky. If Shane hadn't been marching to her imminent death, her breath would be taken away from her by the views. Everywhere she looked there were mountains jutting into the sky. The autumn-colored trees climbed their way up the mountains like veins, contrasting with the dark, river made valleys. Eventually, she saw a city in the distance.

"There it is," Shane overheard the uniformed guard saying to the people up front. "Rotshall. The place where dreams are either born, or die an insufferable death."

Even though it was far away, Shane could see that Rotshall still had outstanding beauty, located halfway up the mountain on a plateau. Through the clearing in the trees, Shane could see the faint outline of a rushing mountain river running past it. The Castle was a mixture of stone and wood, thrown seamlessly together, making it both look as though it was straight out of the dark ages, yet constructed just a short time ago. The last rays of sunlight hitting the towers created a breathtaking sight. There were no words that she could use to describe it other than a masterpiece.

It took them another day to get to the city; a day of anxiety over what might happen to them when they got there. As the sun was setting the next day, the dirt pathway gave way to stone, and they were led through a huge gate monitored by guards. They eyed Shane and Reece as the group passed but said nothing. Princecon got off his horse and had one of his guards untie Shane and Reece. He gave the horse to the city guard, exchanging a few words that Shane couldn't hear.

The buildings on both sides towered over them, the streets crossing with one another. Even though the sun had almost completely set behind the mountains to the west of the city, there were still plenty of people out and about. Almost all of them wore the raggedy clothes of the poor. The same style of clothes that Shane and Reece had stolen. A lump formed in the back of Shane's throat as she saw the conditions those people were living in.

"Is this the new batch from the colonies?" The voice came from a man who had walked fearlessly toward them.

"Who else would these criminals be for?" One of Princecon's guards stepped forward to get between Princecon and the man.

"I was sent to collect them. The king got the letter from Lord Princecon and sent me down here as soon as he could." The man started to explain. He looked well-dressed with an elegant silk overcoat and fine-looking pants. The guard laughed.

"If you were sent by the king, then I'm Mindalin's Chosen Hero." He shoved him aside. "Get out of my way, peasant."

They continued their march up the streets to the castle. Shane knew they were getting closer when the street turned into a sudden incline. The buildings around them became more elegant, more well organized. Shane thought she saw the remains of what used to be an old wall, almost like the place they were walking through before had been the newer part of the city.

Bringing her eyes up, Shane was surprised to see they were closer to the castle than she had thought. Its enormous presence cast a shadow in the thin crescent moon's light. Shane thought she could hear the rushing waters of the river that she saw earlier, but she wasn't quite sure. Her hands grew clammier with every step she took, and her stomach felt like she was about to wretch.

The group stopped when they reached the castle walls. Shane looked around before her gaze landed on the uniformed city guard walking toward them.

Shane glanced at Reece and forced a smile, cold sweat rolling down her face. Reece's face had a greenish tint, eyes wide with terror of the unknown, exactly how Shane was feeling at the moment. When they passed through the castle gate, she wondered if they would ever see the light of day again?

"Lord Princecon." The city guard bowed. "We've been expecting your presence."

"Did you get my letter?" Princecon asked tiredly.

"Yes, sir. We did." The guard turned his attention toward Shane and Reece. Shane's stomach writhed. "I'm guessing these were the prisoners you were talking about."

"Yes. They are." Princecon motioned for the guard holding them to step forward.

"I'll take them down to their cells as you settle in."

"Thank you." Princecon gave a curt bow of pleasure before turning and walking toward the castle doors.

Princecon's guard handed Shane and Reece over to the city guard. One yank at the rope and they were being led toward the same door as Princecon, but instead of going straight in like he did, they took a sharp left turn down a cold hallway. Light came in through the tiny windows in between the pillars, but it only made it feel more inhospitable.

"Why are we here?" Shane found the courage to ask. She was surprised by how coarse and rough her voice was.

"Because you trespassed on the Island of Eringunner."

"We didn't mean to—" She started but was greeted with a slap to the face. Tears swelled in her eyes from the pain and shock.

"It doesn't matter whether you meant to or not. You still broke one of the king's most sacred rules."

He started forward again, this time jostling the rope around haphazardly. Shane wanted to scream as each swing of the rope caused the shackles to rub against her already raw wrist. Blood dripped down her hand and fell in droplets to the ground.

They headed through numerous hallways and stairwells. They eventually stopped at the end of a corridor. It split off into a tee, but Shane didn't think that they were going either left or right. Instead, a dark, daunting spiral staircase stood ahead of them. Shane already knew it led to someplace bad.

The guard pushed them ahead of him into the stairwell. The darkness consumed them, the only light coming from torches placed at long intervals. Shane's heart began to pound as she looked up. Would she ever see the natural light again, or would she be trapped underground for the rest of her life?

When they reached the bottom of the stairs, the guard took keys from his belt and unlocked a huge iron door to a large cell. It looked similar to the one in Lord Princecon's house, the only difference being that it appeared to be much older. The man pushed Reece and Shane in. The door clanged shut behind them. His footsteps echoed up the spiral stairs, and it wasn't until the footfalls had disappeared that Reece let out a sob.

"We're going to die here, aren't we?" Her puffy red eyes met Shane's.

Shane wanted to lie. Say *no,* but she couldn't bring herself to do it. "I wish I could tell you differently." Her voice was still so hoarse and ragged that it didn't sound like her own.

"Why'd I have to go to that stupid game?" Reece spat, wiping the tears from her face. "Maybe I wouldn't be here if I just stayed home."

"If you blame anyone it should be me." Shane fought back tears. "I was the one who convinced you to go. I was the one who brought you to the game."

"Yeah, but I agreed." Reece met Shane's eyes, only making resisting the tears harder. "I don't want to die here," she sobbed, her voice becoming nothing but a whisper.

"Neither do I." Tears escaped the corners of her eyes, but she was quick to wipe them away. "Look on the bright side," She forced a smile, "At least we won't die alone.

She met Reece's gaze and they both broke down.

CHAPTER 5

S hane awakened to the sound of a food tray clattering to the floor. The sound of footsteps went up the stairs, and Shane opened her eyes. She grabbed the tray and brought it toward her, sighing at the dry bread and chunks of moldy cheese offered on it. It was more food than she had gotten to eat over the last week and a half but not nearly enough.

"Is that breakfast?" Reece's voice came from the corner where she was curled up into a tight ball.

"I'm guessing so." Shane tore the bread in half and tossed it over. She took a bite and gagged at the staleness.

The floor of the cell was uneven. Water dripped from the cold, stone ceiling, hitting the ground with a rhythmic beat and pooling at the lowest point. The night before, Shane had tried to avoid it but had ultimately ended up finding it in her sleep. The back of her shirt was sopping wet with frigid water. Standing next to one of the torches offered the only relief from the cold, however minimal.

"Do you think we'll be seeing the king?" Reece asked. Her small voice cut through the silence.

"I don't know. From what people have said about how bad our crime was, I'd say we'll see him soon enough."

As if on cue, someone's footsteps echoed on the staircase. A guard rounded the corner and stepped into the flickering lantern light of the cell. His hand rested on the hilt of his sword around his waist.

"Good," he mumbled to himself as he adjusted his black uniform, the same as what the man who brought them to their cell wore. "You're already awake."

"That's assuming we even slept at all," Reece whispered.

The guard ignored her. He grabbed the keys jangling on his belt and unlocked the door, making sure it closed behind.

"What are you going to do?" Shane asked, trying to keep her voice from trembling. She pressed her back against the wall as far away from him as possible. She spotted a knife sheath next to his foot, as well as his sword and pistol across his chest. If he wanted to kill them, then he could most certainly do it at any time.

"To separate you two." He grabbed Shane by the shackles and yanked her out of the cell. Shane muffled a scream. Her wrists were already red, swollen, and cut. Every time she moved her wrists, pain flared up her arm, and the guard yanking the shackles didn't help with that.

"What about Reece?" she asked. She looked back and saw the fear in her friend's eyes.

"Someone will come for her later." He twisted his hand against her tortured flesh, pulling her up the staircase. "I'd be more worried about yourself, if I were you."

She wanted to struggle but didn't. He yanked her around, banging her sore body on the rough stone walls. She had to stumble just to stay up and clenched her fist to make sure she didn't try and fight back. She hated being manhandled.

They made it to the top of the stairs, and the guard dragged her down a passage to the right. She made sure to take notice of where they were going. If on the small chance she managed to escape, she was going to make sure that she knew how to find her friend.

At last, the guard stopped her at a small doorway they had to duck through. He opened the door and forced her inside, slamming the door behind her. The terrifying mechanical sounds of a key turning in the lock echoed into the cell. Shane felt fear in the pit of her stomach. There was a table in the middle of the room and two chairs on either side.

"Sit," the guard demanded.

She did, resting her hands on the table. The guard sat at the other end and stared at her, mercifully unlocking her hands.

"Aren't you afraid I'm gonna attack?" she asked, rubbing her sore wrists. She swore that if she ever got out of this, she would never let herself be put into those things again.

The guard laughed. "You? You couldn't hurt a fly."

"Looks can be deceiving."

The man only laughed at her.

"What if I wanted to be captured?" She remembered the first person she and Reece had seen and added, "What if I'm an assassin and I have you all fooled?"

"That's impossible."

"Why?" she asked, surprising herself with her newfound brashness.

He grabbed her hand with speed, pinning it down to the table. Shane gasped as he touched the irritated skin. She tried to retract it, but he kept a solid grip. He rolled up her thin sleeve up to the elbow.

"No mark," he said, letting it drop. "Unless you're a D list assassin, I don't believe you."

She rubbed her elbow. Her mind reeled. What mark was he talking about?

"Why am I here?" she asked, her eyes darting around the room. It was nothing but plain dark stone.

"I think you know the reason."

"No, I don't," Shane said plainly

The man ignored her. He pulled the knife out from down by his feet and expertly twirled it in his hand. "Why were you on the Island of Eringunner?"

"I don't know." Shane took a deep breath in, meeting the guards' gaze. "I just appeared there."

"Sure, you did." Without warning, he twisted her arm just far enough for pain to explode in her shoulder. She cried out as her shoulder felt like it was being ripped out of the socket.

"If you don't answer my questions," the man said through gritted teeth, "then you're going to be in a whole lot more pain than this. Got it?"

She tried to remain tough, but one twist of her arm was too much pain for her to handle. She nodded, wet tears streaming down her face, yet she refused to cry out.

"Good." He let go of her. She retracted her arm and held it close to her body while she rubbed her shoulder. "I'm going to ask you one more time. Why were you on that island?"

"And I'm going to tell you once again that I have no idea." Her voice quavered. She knew that saying that would only cause more pain to her, but she didn't care. She had to at least try and make him believe her. "Me and my friend were at a football game when we somehow ended up on the island."

"I would suggest that you stop making up words and tell me the truth."

"I am. Why do you people find it so hard to believe?" she cried, intently watching the knife slide between his hands.

"Because you can't magically appear on an island."

"But it's the truth."

"If you tell me that lie one more time, you will regret it."

He pointed the knife at her, almost daring her to speak once again.

"I don't know what you expect me to say," she pleaded, knowing that pain would soon follow, but she said it anyway.

"I'm telling you the truth, honestly."

The guard instantly reached forward with his knife and sliced downward over Shane's right eye. Agony like Shane had never known flashed across her face. She screamed and her hands instinctively went to her eye, shrinking back into her seat. When she brought them away, her hands were covered with thick, red blood. The pain was intense; tears began to mix with the blood on her face. The cut had barely missed her eye, but her vision was blurred from blood and tears.

"If you don't give a reasonable explanation as to why you were on the one island that Princess Airel was last seen alive, the next cut will be much deeper." The guard said, wiping off his knife on his shirt.

"Please," Shane whimpered. "I'm telling the truth."

A punch to her face nearly knocked her unconscious.

It continued like that for hours. Every time Shane told the truth, she only got relentlessly beaten until her face grew painfully numb.

Someone had entered the room, but Shane didn't notice. She was barely conscious. Images blurred in her vision. She thought she could hear a voice coming from beside her, and it wasn't long before someone hauled her up from the chair. Her legs buckled beneath her; a nauseating feeling overcame her.

"Where are we going?" she tried to ask, but it came out as gibberish.

"To the throne room."

Through her dim vision, she could see the door open before them. She had to lean on the guard to move even a little bit. She bet that the only reason he allowed it was because otherwise he would have to drag her through the hallways. She was too consumed in her own pain to remember to take note of the hallways.

The large entryway she found herself in was lined with guards with rifles in their hands. They must have been expecting them because as soon as they saw them, they opened the doors for them to continue onward through an elegant hallway that ended with a raised throne. The pillars of the room seemed to dwarf Shane in comparison to the man who sat at the end.

The guard forced her down to her knees. She let out a small whimper as she bowed her head toward the king. He radiated power.

"King Aarion," the guard behind Shane said. "The prisoner, just like you asked."

"Where's the other one?" The voice coming from the throne jarred Shane down to the bones. Something about it was so familiar, yet like nothing she had heard before in her life. She forced her eyes to move up the man's body and let out a shake when she saw his ornate crown sitting atop his blond hair and piercing blue eyes.

"She's coming, milord."

Shane could only assume that they were talking about Reece. She could only hope that her friend wasn't beaten and bruised as badly as she had been, but she feared the worst.

Uneven footsteps came from behind her, and she peered over her shoulder to see Reece. Her heart leapt with relief as she saw that the only thing that had happened to her was a small cut on her forehead. Her face was red in the shape of a handprint, but she looked nothing like Shane felt.

The guard forced Reece down beside her, gasping at the sight of Shane.

"Shane?" she whispered under her breath. "What happened to you?"

That guard heard her and slapped her across the back of the head.

Shane winced but said nothing.

"Were you the only two on the island?" Aarion asked, standing up and stepping down from the throne platform to get a closer look at the girls.

"Yes," Shane said, which resulted in a slap to her neck from the guard behind her.

"Yes, milord." This time a punch didn't come for her.

"You realize that the island is protected land, and you trespassed."

No.

"Yes, milord," Shane lied before Reece got the chance to say anything. She knew that Aarion wouldn't believe them if they told him the truth, so why even try?

"Then why did you go there? Why confess now?"

Shane didn't answer. One look at Reece's pale face told her that she was too terrified to even think about speaking. She got a slap to the back of the head.

"Why were you on the island of Eringunner?" Aarion asked again, his voice taunt. His eyes remained fixed on Shane, but she refused to meet them.

"Because milord. We didn't think."

"That much is obvious." He walked closer to her, his black boots echoing around the room until he knelt in front of her. Power oozed from him, making her want to cower down, but she refused to do so. "You have to pay for what you did."

"How?"

"By watching your friend die."

Shane's heart stopped as she took in a sharp breath. "No!" she screamed. She tried to escape the guards' strong hands but couldn't.

Aarion nodded toward the guard holding Reece. He pulled a revolver out of his holster. Reece's face twisted in horror.

"No! Please no!" She elbowed the man behind her and struggled to pull away. "Don't do this!" Tears flowed from her eyes. "Kill me! Not her!"

"I've already made up my mind. You have to learn your lesson. An example must be made."

"I have!" She looked over at Reece, her eyes screamed for help. "Why can't it be me? She doesn't deserve to die! I made her come with me!"

"Nobody deserves it, but that's just the world we live in."

Shane's heart tore in two as the guard placed the revolver on Reece's chest, finger tightening on the trigger. "Wait! This is about your daughter, Airel, isn't it?" Shane asked, remembering what the guard had said during the questioning.

"So, what if it is?" Aarion's jaw clenched, but he made a motion for the guard holding the revolver to wait.

"She wouldn't want you to do this."

"Don't talk about what Airel would have wanted!" Aarion yelled, spit flying everywhere. "She's gone! Never coming back, so it doesn't matter what she wanted!"

"You were there, weren't you?" Shane asked, hoping she was right.

"Please Shane," Reece pleaded, but Shane ignored her.

"On the island when she died. You want me to feel the way you did that day just because I went to the island of Eringunner, right?"

"So what if I do. You deserve it." He turned to the guard holding the gun. "Do it."

Reece squirmed in his arms. "Please," she begged. "Don't."

Shane elbowed the guard holding her in the stomach and dashed over to Reece. The king stepped in front of her and sliced her face with a knife Shane hadn't seen before. Everything turned red as pain exploded on her face. She let out a muffled cry but kept going. She couldn't allow her friend to die.

The gunshot was deafening.

Shane was too late.

Shane screamed as Reece fell to the floor. She ran forward, no longer aware of the pain in her face.

"No!" she yelled. "No, no, no!" This couldn't be happening. Reece couldn't be dying. This had to be a dream.

Except it wasn't. Reece was laying before Shane in a pool of her own red blood. Her breaths were shallow and faint but still there. Shane reached under her, not even feeling the warm red blood soaking into her shirt sleeves.

"I'm sorry, Reece," Shane sobbed. "This wasn't supposed to happen." Tears streaked down the sides of her face.

Reece's cold hand fumbled to find Shane's and she squeezed it wearily. "I… I don't want to go." Her voice was faint, getting weaker by the second. "Shane, I don't want to die."

"You won't," Shane lied, which tore her heart to pieces. "Just… just keep fighting, okay? You aren't leaving me here alone. You can't do that."

"It hurts, Shane."

Reece's pain filled eyes met Shane's, pleading with her to help. "Just keep fighting, okay." Shane's voice broke.

"I… I don't want…" Reece's limbs became limp, and her breaths stopped coming. Empty eyes stared up at Shane.

"No. No!" she screamed, her voice breaking down. "Come back, Reece. Come back to me." Nothing happened. Reece's body remained unmoving in Shane's arms. "You can't leave me."

"It's dreadful, isn't it." The cruel voice of Aarion came from behind Shane, bringing her back to reality. "To have the person you love the most die in your arms."

Shane remained quiet. She shook slightly as silent bloody tears made their way down her face, falling on her friend's dead body.

"You feel like if things ended differently, you could have saved her." Aarion continued.

"You did this!" Shane was up on her feet before she knew what she was doing and leaped for Aarion. Before she could get her hands around his neck though, a guard grabbed onto her shirt and yanked her backward, choking her. "You're the one responsible for this!"

"Are you sure about that? It never would've happened if you hadn't been on the island of Eringunner."

"Then why don't you kill me too?"

"Because it's worse to live with the knowledge that you're responsible for the death of a person you love more than life itself." He nodded to the guard holding her back. "Take her back to her cell, along with her friend's body."

Shane shook with anger, but she was filled with too much shock to try and escape the guard's grip. She allowed him to escort her down the halls to her cell, refusing to look behind her at Reece's dead body in the hands of another guard.

They reached the bottom of the stairs, and she was thrown into the cell. The noise of Reece's dead body hitting the ground reverberated through the dungeon, and Shane didn't realize that the doors were locked until she heard footsteps disappearing.

Shane took one look down at Reece and wretched what little food was still in her body. She gripped her friend's lifeless body as tears and screams left her. With her fingers shaking, she closed Reece's eyes, asking herself why she couldn't have saved her?

CHAPTER 6

Reece's body remained untouched for what seemed to be a week, the smell of decay and her rotting, fly covered flesh becoming more pungent as each day passed. Shane remained against the bars as far away from the body as she could get, trying hard not to look at what was once her best friend. Whenever she closed her eyes, she could still see the gunshot, the bright flash of light and Reece falling to the ground an instant later.

Guards came down every day with a tray of food, but Shane barely touched it. She sat in the corner, not saying a word, when two uniformed guards came into the cell one morning and hauled Reece out. Guilt took over Shane when she realized that she was relieved that her friend was gone.

A short time later she heard more footsteps coming down the staircase. It was the same guard that had questioned her. Shane raised her head at the sound of him unlocking the doors.

"Are you here to beat me some more?" Shane asked weakly. It had been so long since she last spoken that she was surprised that words could even come out of her mouth.

"The king wants to see you."

Shane didn't struggle as the guard hauled her to her feet, put on shackles, and led her out of the cell. She numbly followed him as he led her back to the throne room.

"Is he gonna kill me?" Shane whispered as they entered the doorway.

The guard chuckled behind her. "You're going to wish for death after what's going to happen to you."

The guard pushed her forward, and Shane gasped.

Two classily dressed people were already there, deep in conversation with the king.

"Ah," Aarion said when he saw the guard escorting Shane. "Here she is." He gestured toward her.

The guard made her bow her head before the king, before forcing her to her knees.

"She looks like she wouldn't last a year," said one of the gayly dressed men. She brought her eyes up and let out an inaudible gasp— it was the assassin! From the look on his face, he apparently recognized her as well, even with the dried blood that coated her face.

"Looks can be deceiving. I'm willing to sell her for one hundred fifty Shulhers."

"You've got to be kidding me," said the person standing next to the assassin. "The most Fritz is going to spend is a hundred."

"One twenty-five and we have a deal, Orrik."

Orrik pursed his lips before saying, "Fine, but we want her now. Not in a couple days."

"The sooner she can get out of my sight the better."

The man reached into his pocket and took out a small money bag packed with coins and handed it to Aarion. The king counted the money within. Shane's gaze was fixed on the assassin, and he was staring right back at her. He tried not to show any interest in her, but narrow eyes showed a different story.

"When do you plan on leaving?" King Aarion asked, motioning a guard to step forward. The king then handed him the bag.

"As soon as possible, your majesty. Fritz wants the new slaves there as quickly as we can get them."

"Then make sure I never see her face again." Aarion's blue eyes stared straight into her, contempt flooding from them. "Give her the worst the camp has to offer. I'm thinking the mines."

"Yes, your majesty."

The man bowed before turning his back, motioning for the assassin to take Shane from the guard. He gripped under her arm and yanked her upright. Shane resisted a scream of pain. "You were a fool," he whispered in her ear, his breath hot against her neck. "Nobody in their right mind allows themselves to be arrested by the king."

And I know that now, Shane thought, but didn't say it. She kept her gaze fixed on the man who had done the deal. Did he know that he was working with the assassin the king was looking for? Was he one himself?

They led her down the passageways toward the door, and Shane noticed the assassin handled her more gently once they got out of the king's view. His grip on her arm loosened. Whenever they passed guards, however, he jostled her around, hitting her in the back of the head and pushing her forward.

Once outside, the brightness of the sun and the clear blue sky nearly blinded Shane. Her vision slowly adjusted as they headed down the slope leading from the castle. About thirty people had congregated at the base of the mountain below the keep. They all wore shackles like Shane's, and well-armed soldiers surrounded them.

"I'm sorry," the assassin whispered in her ear as he connected her to the long chain of people in the back of the line.

Sorry for what? Shane thought. *For buying me like a slave, or treating me like an animal when there were the king's guards around?*

The assassin walked over to the guards, turning around every few seconds to look back at Shane. He stopped and talked to another guard with darker skin, motioning toward Shane discreetly with his head. Shane guessed him to be a friend.

"Why was he staring at you like that?" the girl ahead of Shane in the line of slaves asked. She was taller than Shane, maybe a couple years older, and had light brown undertones.

"No idea," Shane lied.

"Does he know you?"

"No, I don't think so." Shane peered over the girl's shoulder to look at the assassin, who was in a much deeper argument with the dark-skinned man. He kept gesticulating toward Shane, no longer trying to hide it.

"Then why is he talking to Archer like that?"

"Who?"

"Archer. He's one of the guards." The girl's smile wavered, but it quickly returned to the way it used to be. "My names Kyaina, by the way."

"Shane."

"Listen up!" the uniformed man yelled. "If any of you talk, you get whipped. You stumble, you get whipped. If you slow us down even in the slightest, whipped. We are expected to be in Verscar in less than a week, and if any of you mess that up, all of you will pay." His gun glinted in the morning light, a malicious smile on his face. "Got that?"

A heavy silence followed. Everywhere Shane looked she saw haggard faces of all ages, hope gone from their eyes. Something swelled inside her when her gaze landed on a young girl no older than her eleven-year-old brother, Henry. A cut ran along her right cheek, and her disheveled hair covered half her terrified face. Nobody of that age should have to deal with this. Nobody at any age should.

The crack of a whip rang out in the early morning air, startling everyone, including Shane. She hurried forward, not wanting the guards to have an excuse to use the whip against her. Kyaina fell silent, her dark hair rolling behind her shoulders as her head faced down toward the ground.

Archer and the assassin stayed at the head of the pack. Every now and then, Shane saw them look back at her and talk between them. It seemed whenever she looked up the assassin's eyes were on her.

Shane walked in a daze of fatigue and hunger; her eyes glued to the ground. A crack of a whip in the distance broke the silence and brought Shane back to reality. There was a cry of agony ahead, and the whole train of people came to a stop just outside the city gates.

"I'd hate to be whoever that was," Kyaina whispered back to Shane, pointing toward the man who had just been whipped. "Bad enough where we're headed, but to be punished here…" She shuddered.

"Where are we going?" Shane tried to get the shackles to where they didn't rest on the sore spots on her wrists, but to no avail. "All I know is that I was sold by the king and brought to this group. I heard something about mines?"

Kyaina looked back and stared. "You seriously don't know?"

Shane shook her head.

Kyaina chuckled. "We're headed for Verscar, the worst labor camp in all of Lyconnexal. Only the worst offenders are sent there."

Shane stopped walking, her breath catching in her throat. The chain yanked her forward and her feet rushed to catch her up. She should've known that nothing good was ahead, but hearing it come from somebody else's mouth made it more real.

"That's why the king sold you," Kyaina said bluntly. "It's where he sends all the prisoners who he doesn't want anymore. Most don't last over a year."

Shane cringed, tears escaping her eyes. A year? With a record like that she didn't think she would live longer than six months.

She was certain she was heading to her own death. She was going to die just like Reece. It was what she deserved.

"Hey you!" Someone behind her yelled. She could hear the whip resonating in the air but didn't register it in her mind. "Stop slowing us down!"

This is it, Shane thought. The whip ripped into her back and the pain was immediate. A muffled cry escaped her mouth. The lash throbbed. Blood trickled down from the giant gash the whip had made on her back, soaking into her filthy shirt. Shane tensed up, expecting another, but it never came.

"What were you thinking?" Kyaina whispered, keeping her eyes on the guards surrounding them. "You're gonna get yourself killed if you keep doing that."

"If I keep stumbling?" The words came garbled and forced out of Shane's throat.

"Pay attention to where you're going next time."

I'll try, Shane wanted to say, but a stinging pain had taken over her, keeping her silent. Every time she moved in the wrong direction, her back rubbed against the cloth of her shirt, sending spasms of pain down her entire torso.

The rest of the day was mostly uneventful. Shane stayed quiet for most of it, too afraid to be overheard by the guards surrounding her. The whip rang out only a couple more times, but nowhere near Shane. She had learned her lesson the first time. Archer and the assassin kept looking back at her infrequently. Shane couldn't help but wonder once again if Archer knew what his friend was.

The group stopped when the sun set behind the snow peaked mountains to the west. They had found a place in a large clearing with mountains surrounding them. It would have been a breathtaking view if Shane hadn't been so fearful for the days to come. She began to wonder whether it would be better to die on the way there than in the actual labor camp. Maybe death would be better than what she would have to endure?

The prisoners weren't given anything to sleep on, and only a thin blanket to cover themselves with. It had started snowing and before long there were several inches on the ground. Shane's arms shivered from the cold as she sat on the ground next to Kyaina, her shackles weighing down her wrists.

"How's your back feeling?" Kyaina asked, eating the tiny chunk of stale bread that everyone had been given.

"Horrible." Shane winced as her shirt rubbed against it. She looked up and spotted the assassin staring at her again. He had changed out of the nice clothes he had been wearing before and now looked just like one of the guards.

Kyaina saw what she was looking at. "Are you absolutely sure he doesn't know you?"

Shane pursed her lips, looking from the assassin to Kyaina. "Before I was at the King's castle, I was in the colonies," she started. "I saw him there." She lowered her voice. "He's—"

Then she noticed the assassin coming toward her, Archer following close behind him. "You two," he hissed. "What are you doing talking?"

"Elias, what are you doing?" Archer asked.

"Something." Elias shrugged Archer off. He grabbed a key from his pocket before unlocking the chain that attached Kyaina and Shane to the rest of the group.

"What are you doing?" one of the guards asked, looking in their direction.

"They were talking," Elias said, as if it explained everything. It must have been good enough for the guard because he let them pass.

Elias grabbed the chain that connected the two of them and yanked it toward the tents away from the entire group, walking past guards and other sentries without a problem. It wasn't until they were past the trees and everyone else was out of view that Elias let the chain go. Shane wanted desperately to run away, but she was attached to Kyaina, who looked quite contemptible sitting there.

"Elias," Kyaina scolded. "What do you think you're doing?"

He gestured toward Shane. "She knows about me." He didn't meet her eyes.

Shane looked at Kyaina with a new terror in her eyes. Were they all working together?

"How—" Realization passed over Kyaina's eyes. "The colonies."

"Are you gonna kill me?" Shane asked, trying to swallow down the fear that had taken over her body. She couldn't show them that she was afraid, not to a group of people who could kill her without batting an eyelash. "Now that I know what you are?"

Elias looked in her direction. "Not unless we have to."

"What do you plan on doing with her then?" Archer asked, leaning on a walking stick. "It's not like we can just let her go. People would notice."

Elias gazed at Shane. He pulled a knife out from inside his jacket and walked menacingly over toward her. "I don't want to kill you, but I'm warning you," the knife mere inches from her neck, "if you tell anyone what you know, I will make sure that you experience nothing but pain for the rest of your life. Even worse than what awaits you in Verscar".

"Tell people what?" She scanned around her, taking in everyone's serious faces. "That you're assassins?" Everyone leaped toward her. Elias put a hand over her mouth, and he pressed the knife deeper into her neck, drawing tiny droplets of blood.

"If you say those words again," Archer said, pulling out his revolver and pointing it at Shane's face, "You won't live to see another day."

"Archer, put the gun away. You're scaring the princess," Elias said, letting her go and putting the knife back into its sheath. He leaned up against a fallen tree.

Shane would've laughed if she weren't so terrified. "My name is Shane, and I'm nobody's princess."

"Well, will you look at that." Elias laughed. "She gets mad when I say her name wrong. Isn't that right, *Shay?*"

Shane flinched.

When she was younger, people used to bully her for her name, saying that it was traditionally a masculine one. They called her Shay, or Shannon in a jeering way. She used to hate her name, and she hated those nicknames even more.

"Look," she said, trying not to show how much Elias had gotten to her. "I just want to live, so if you'll let me do that, then I'll be fine. I won't tell anyone your secret, which by the way, I still have no idea what it is you're doing."

A dry chuckle left Archer. "If you wanted to live, then why'd you let yourself get arrested? Most people don't even last a year here."

"Then why are you here?" Shane looked over at Kyaina, who pursed her lips.

"It's complicated," she said. "And we're not going to stay long."

"Then why don't you take me with you."

Elias let out a sharp chuckle. "That's out of the question."

"Why?" Shane paused, trying to hold it together. "You can teach me to be an assassin." She would say anything to get away from where they were going.

"That's not going to happen."

"Why not?"

"Because we don't accept princesses like you, Shay." Shane flinched slightly. "And even if we did decide to take you with us, you have to be tested."

"Tested, how?"

"It's too much for you, both mentally and physically," Elias said, looking back at the rest of the camp, not meeting Shane's eyes.

"Everything that I had to live for is gone." She wanted to tell them about Reece, but the words wouldn't come. "Look, I know you don't want to let me come with you, but I just want to live, no matter what that means."

"Not this life," Elias said.

"Then why do you do it?"

Elias' shoulders tensed as he got up from the fallen tree and walked over toward her. She was afraid that he was going to hit her, or worse, but all he did was say, "Why would I tell someone like you that?" He started walking back toward the camp. "Do whatever you want with her, but I don't want her coming with us on the way back."

"Don't mind Elias," Kyaina said, breaking the silence as Archer led them back toward the camp. "He's very private."

"What happened to him?"

"That's his own story to tell." She sighed. "Nearly everyone who works this kind of job has some kind of trauma in their past but, trust me when I say this isn't the life you want to live."

"So, you're saying that being stuck in a labor camp is better?"

"No, but—"

A whip snapped off to their right, cutting Kyaina off mid-sentence. A cry for help erupted, but no one made any attempt to assist. The camp remained silent, afraid that if they talked, the whip would find them as well.

Shane laid herself down on her blanket. She closed her eyes, but sleep evaded her. Even though she was tired, her mind was racing too fast for her to relax. What were the assassins doing here? She shifted her gaze toward a heavy-set man with a whip hanging from one hip, and a revolver on the other. Even though he changed out of his fancy clothes, Shane could still recognize him as Orrik.

Shane glanced at Kyaina. "Are you gonna kill him?" she asked, motioning toward Orrik.

"Maybe." Kyaina's eyes went between him and Shane. "Unless you want to get whipped again, I'd suggest you go to bed."

Shane didn't argue. She laid her head back down and remained still.

If she did become an assassin, would she be able to face the fact that she— someone who was willing to murder to survive— lived instead of Reece? She already felt responsible for her death. She felt like Reece was watching her from the Underworld, judging her every move and scrutinizing it harshly, just like her parents would if they were there. If she did find a way home, she wouldn't be able to look them in the eyes, knowing she was the one responsible for Reece's death. She already saw herself as a disappointment. She didn't need anyone else to point it out.

I'm probably overthinking this, she thought, trying to fall asleep.

In the morning when the sun rose, Shane was more exhausted and sorer than the day before, but she forced herself to get up as ordered. She couldn't help but notice Elias and Archer skulking in the distance. Shane could only imagine what they were up to.

Shane and Kyaina started walking with the rest of the group. They wouldn't stop until the sun set once again. The whip rang out all through the day, but Archer and Elias were nowhere near where it sounded out.

That's one good thing, Shane thought bitterly. *At least they have enough human decency not to torture people, just kill them.*

This continued for the next week and a half. They had been given food at the beginning and end of the day, but it wasn't nearly enough to satisfy their hunger. The snow grew heavy on the ground as they continued walking, and soon it was up to Shane's ankles, chilling her to the bone. When they reached an overlook of the valley below them, Shane felt a crazy mix of relief and fear as she saw the encampment below. She knew that being there would only lead to more pain than she could possibly imagine, but her legs grew numb and weary of walking. If they had to go much further, she was afraid she'd collapse.

They started down the hill, giving Shane plenty of time to take in the horrible sight before her. Large walls surrounded the camp. It was bigger than Shane expected. A lake sat at the western side. The west wall cut it in two, leaving half of the lake inside, the other half out. Buildings mostly filled up the empty space in the camp, but there were piles of dirt everywhere. Four mines were in each of the corners. Shane could only wonder which one she would go into, and if she would ever come out again.

Occasionally she could hear a gunshot. There were giant torches on the walls, as well as lanterns lighting every couple of feet on top. The distant figures of guards could be seen walking along the top of the wall. Fear gripped her when she realized they weren't there to keep people from coming in, but to keep the slaves from getting out.

It was getting dark as they wound their way down the path to the camp, but they didn't stop. The orange flickering lights could be seen ahead, and they trudged on, stopping only when they reached the gate. They were untethered for just a moment before they were split into three groups, then bound together once again within their groups.

Even before Shane could even consider running, someone made a break for it. He had somehow worked his way out of the shackles and started sprinting, screaming in terror. He made it fifty feet before a gunshot rang out in the night. He fell to the ground, dead. Shane gasped as she was led away with the rest of her group.

The guard brought them through the streets with shacks on each just big enough to fit a few people. A large building towered over them, but they were led to what Shane assumed to be the center square. A huge platform with a bloodied axe wedged into a block formed the centerpiece of the square. She wondered what horrible things she would have to do to end up there.

"You should feel lucky," Orrick said as he led them to an open shack. "After this week, you'll sleep down in the mines with the rest of the scum."

He pushed Shane and the others inside before taking a step back, blocking the only exit. "After today, your lives are going to be worse than those in Haytorrow's Fallen Realm." He slammed the door shut. She could hear the sound of a lock being closed as she sat down on the ground with the rest of the prisoners, wondering how her life had gotten so messed up.

CHAPTER 7

In the morning, Shane stood in a line inside a long, hot building. Her shackles dug deep into her wrists. She was connected to the rest of the prisoners by a long, rusty chain, not that anyone really needed it to stay where they were. After what had happened the night before, everyone was too skittish to even think about running. Nevertheless, guards still surrounded them with their guns always at the ready.

Shane moved a step closer to where they were being herded. Fires were ablaze on either side of her, but it was the one ahead of her that had her worried. A metal rod sat in it, making it glow a simmering shade of red. Whenever the prisoners got to the front of the line, they were forced to sit down in a rickety wooden chair, and someone would take the metal out of the fire and place it against their collarbone. Screams of desperation and agony filled the chamber. From there they were led into another room.

Shane hadn't seen Kyaina that morning. She wouldn't be surprised if Elias and Archer somehow got her out of doing this. If she got the mark, it would mean that she was the property of Verscar. Shane doubted that they would want that for their fellow assassin. But for her? They couldn't care less what happened to her once she got to the camp.

But that left her all alone walking toward a life of slavery and misery. With each step she took, her heart pounded faster and faster until it was beating out of her chest. By the time she was yanked by the chain to the front of the line, her hands were clammy and shaking. Every ounce of her being urged her to run, completely ignoring the chain and the guards surrounding her, but her own sense of self-preservation kept her where she was. If she wanted to live, she had to remain still. But she wasn't sure if living was what she wanted anymore.

Shane closed her eyes, trying to hold the tears back, when a guard took her by the arm and yanked her toward the chair and forced her to sit. The rough chair dug into her back. The guard held her shoulders against it. No matter how much she struggled, she wasn't going anywhere.

The guard in front of her, Orrik, returned the metal to the fire to reheat it. He looked into Shane's terror filled eyes. Shane's heart raced faster the longer she waited, imagining all the pain that she would endure in the next couple seconds.

"Scared?" Orrik asked, taking the poker out at last. Shane realized that it wasn't just a spike. At the business end of it was a hollow circle with a V in the middle. V for Verscar. He held it right in front of Shane's face, close enough to feel the heat radiating from it.

Shane didn't say anything, only gulping down the fear that had taken a hold of her body, paralyzing her in place. She tried to back away from the metal as it slowly made its way toward her skin, but the chair was fixed in place, and the guard's grip on her shoulders was too tight to do anything except sit there.

Orrik took his time positioning it over her right collarbone. Sweat raced down Shane's forehead as he forced it down. Nothing happened at first, but then a strangled cry rose out of her mouth as the burning raced down her shoulder and torso. It seared her skin layer by layer in excruciating pain. The sizzling of her skin grew louder, the fire taking over her body as she struggled against the guard's grip. There was no way to escape the pain.

The metal spike tore away from her collarbone trying to pull burned flesh with it, but the agony didn't disappear. Her new brand radiated a burning heat that came in never ceasing waves. Shane heard people's voices, but they were too muddled together in her head to tell them apart or what they were saying. It wasn't until the guard's pulled her from the chair and threw her into a room with the rest of the prisoner's that had been branded before her.

It took several minutes for the pain to cease enough to where Shane was once again aware of what was going on around her. She was placed in another line with the rest of the prisoners. Her legs shook as she took a step forward, surveying the guards surrounding her. They acted much more lackadaisical than the ones in the room that she had just come from, but that was probably because all the other prisoners were in incapacitating pain just as she was at that moment.

There were multiple guards at the front of the room, and all of them had knives and a bag in their hands. The prisoners were forced to sit down in one of the many chairs at the front, this time for tattoos. Shane knew it was going to be painful, and it was going to be further proof of her slavery to Verscar, but she would gladly take getting a number tattooed on her left collarbone than be branded again. She was pretty sure that dying would be preferable to what she had just gone through

Her shackles jangled as one of the guards grabbed her and brought her to a chair at the far end of the room. *Ironic,* Shane thought as she sat down, the guards strapping her arms to the chair, *how I'm now being shackled down rather than when I had a reason to run.*

That thought left her mind when the guard left her to attend to the rest of the prisoners. The guard with the tools stepped forward and a shudder went through Shane's entire body. The knife was much longer than she originally thought, and it appeared that it had just recently been heated in the fire. Her eyes widened in fear with the thought of it slicing her skin. She was wrong when she thought this would be less painful than what had happened before. It was going to be so much worse.

The man's face remained expressionless as he bent down, holding it close to her tender skin.

"B-31082," someone read behind her, but she didn't pay any attention. Her focus was on the scolding red knife right in front of her. The man dipped it in the bag, and it came out with black ink dripping from it. The man's wrists slowly moved toward her other collarbone, and Shane tried to inch away, but there was nowhere to go. She took in a sharp breath as it made contact, a silent cry for help escaping her. It dug deep into her skin to where it would scar. Tears leaked from her eyes as she shut them, trying to escape the agony that had taken over her. She thought she knew pain, but that was before being sold to Verscar.

The ink burned into her skin, the heated knife leaving no blood behind. The room went black for Shane, and the next thing she knew she was being dragged out of the chair. She was in total agony as she was muscled toward the exit.

By the time she got back to her shack, the pain no longer overwhelmed her. The guard tossed her inside. She fell straight to the ground, not bothering to move, as the guard made sure to lock the door behind her, leaving no escape, even though that was the farthest thing from Shane's mind.

There were bodies inside the shack, and Shane couldn't tell if they were dead or alive. Almost everyone remained still, their muffled sobs being heard in the crisp air. The sobs were the only thing assuring her that the bodies around her were still alive. She cried as she writhed on the floor. A wave of lightheadedness succumbed her. A cold sweat washed over her as she curled into a ball, silent tears rolling down her face.

Nobody tried to assist her, and she couldn't blame them. Most of those surrounding her suffered the same as her, worrying only about their own survival. Shane was doing the exact same thing.

She peered down at her left collarbone and shuddered. Her tear-soaked eyes fixed on the blurry image.

B-31082.

That was what she would be called by these monsters. Was she nothing more than a number? Nothing more, nothing less?

She closed her eyes and sobbed, not wishing for sleep to come. But she was going to need as much rest as she could before the next day. She cringed at the thought of the mines she had seen on the way in.

In the morning, still in tremendous pain, Shane opened her eyes to the sound of the door opening. She had barely slept that night, only getting a few minutes here and there between flashes of pain on her collarbones.

Orrik took one step in, silhouetted against the light coming from outside. Another guard could be seen standing just outside and blocking the door.

"Anyone die last night?" Orrik laughed, a cruel smile spreading across his face as he motioned a guard forward with a chain in his hands. He unraveled the chain before connecting it to the people's shackles, tying the people together. There would be no attempts at escape. Orrik took the first person, forced them to their feet and out the door.

Instead of heading for the mines, they went straight for a large, elegant log house. The closer they got, the more intimidating it looked. The guards led them through the doors, its long, dark empty hallways gave off a sense of foreboding that sent a chill to Shane's core.

Orrik took the lead through the house, eventually ending up at a door that looked unremarkable from the rest in the building.

Shane had a strange feeling in the pit of her stomach as Orrik opened the doors, and the guards began herding them through.

Inside there was a desk with a man sitting behind it. Shane guessed he was in his mid to late thirties. He had short cut dark brown hair, and a goatee on his slim, malicious face. Something evil glinted in his eyes.

Orrik bowed to him. "Fritz."

"These are the slaves you brought me?" Fritz asked, placing the paper that he had been reading down on the desk.

"It's the first group, yes." Orrik cleared his throat. "At least the ones who survived the journey."

"How many were there when you first started?"

"About a hundred, but we lost ten on the way."

"And these are the ones headed for the mines?"

"Yes."

"Good." Fritz stroked his goatee, leaning back in his chair. "You can leave us," he said, shooing Orrik off with a wave of the hand.

Shane quivered with fear as Orrik stood next to the door behind her, and Fritz's attention turned to them.

"I don't care," Fritz began, an evil gleam in his eyes, "why you're here. All of you will be punished the same." A smile formed on his face. "All of you will be in the same mine, working in the same conditions. You will be given a pickaxe at the beginning of the day, and it will be taken away at the end. We have a quota here. If you don't get at least a cart full of limestone, you will be punished."

He paused, waiting for anyone to speak up. When nobody did, he continued. "If you couldn't tell on your way into Verscar, guards are posted nearly everywhere. They are down in the mines to make sure that you comply with our rules, and to stop any of you that might get ideas of… uprising. If you do somehow manage to escape the mine, however, you may have noticed the guards stationed all around the perimeter wall. Trust me when I say that they aren't there for your protection. They are armed with both guns and bows, and they can use them. Nobody escapes Verscar alive."

Shane gulped, keeping her eyes focused on the ground in front of the desk. If she hadn't already come to terms with the fact that she was going to die there, she certainly did now. A tear streaked down her face, but she was quick to wipe it up.

"Take them away," Fritz ordered, motioning to Orrik, and he complied, opening the door and leading them down the hallway and out the front door to the harsh, outside world.

They walked for what felt like forever through the shoveled, snowy streets of the camp. Lanterns sat ablaze along the sides of the streets, illuminating the way as the sun rose behind them. Shane wanted so badly to look back and see it one more time before delving into the darkness, but she was afraid that if the guards saw her doing that, she would get whipped or even shot. There were whips at the ready on the guard's belts, and Shane didn't want to ever feel the wrath of one of those again. She could feel the sting from the one lashing she received on the trek from Rotshall.

"You look like a Geistluck," Shane heard someone whisper behind her ear as they passed through the entrance of the caves on the eastern side of the encampment. She looked back and wasn't surprised to see Kyaina standing right behind her, looking much better than Shane did.

"What?" Shane asked, returning her attention to what was happening in front of her, even though the tunnel was barely lit enough to see more than ten feet ahead.

"A Geistluck. You know, a spirit who's being punished in Haytorrow's Realm."

"You would too if you were there yesterday," Shane said bitterly. She pulled at her shirt to reveal the tattoo and brand. Both were still bright red and blistered. Kyaina winced, but before she could answer, Shane continued. "Let me guess, Archer and Elias didn't want you to be branded and tattooed."

"Archer didn't, yes. But Elias left as soon as we got here." Kyaina messed with her shackles. "He just helped us get in."

"And why would you want to do that?" Shane sneered. "If this place is all it's cracked up to be, then I would run as far away from here as possible."

"It's complicated."

They reached the entrance to the cave, and Shane's chest tightened. So many pounds of dirt and stone over her head, she had to fight past her claustrophobia to go any farther. But the chain pulled her forward, and she unwillingly entered the mine. She savored the last rays of sunlight she would see before continuing onward to where the sun could no longer reach.

As they went deeper into the mine, the tunnels splintered off in several directions. Rails for minecarts led the way. Sounds of pickaxes hitting the stone wall's echoed throughout the cavern, and it wasn't until they finally reached the end of a tunnel, that an armed guard distributed a pickaxe to each person.

When he got to Shane, he pressed a pickaxe into her hands, pushing her back slightly. It was heavier than she had expected. She grew tired even thinking about using it.

Someone yelled at them to start, but never specified where to hit. A sickening feeling shuddered through Shane's body as she saw the person ahead of her— a young man— swinging it toward the wall. The sound of pickaxes striking stone ahead of her solidified her reality. She was certain she would die there, and nobody would remember her.

Shane lifted her pickaxe and swung it against the wall. It stung her hands as it hit. Little chunks of rock sprayed out everywhere.

Shane's arms trembled after what she guessed was only an hour, but she wouldn't have been surprised if it were much less. Sweat rolled down her scarred face, but she had to continue for what felt like twelve more. The whip rang out through the cavern every couple of minutes. That, mixed with the sound of metal against rock and the cry of slaves, were the only noises that she heard all day.

She tensed every time a guard walked by. She was worried that they would find something wrong with what she was doing. She wiped the sweat from her face as she tried to keep her focus on the wall. The guards seemed to be watching her. Every time the pickaxe slipped from her hands, she feared the worst would happen.

When it was finally announced that the shift was over, Shane's arms shook with exhaustion. Her hands were bright red with fresh blisters. She tried to touch them but recoiled with pain as soon as she grazed it. The guards came around to collect the pickaxes, and she gladly gave it up. She had just barely met the quota given to her that day, and she didn't want to think about what would happen the next day. Her stomach rumbled with hunger as she collapsed to the ground.

"Why would you want to come here?" Shane looked at Kyaina, exhaustion filling up her eyes. "To this hell?"

"Because I was told to." Kyaina sighed, wiping the sweat away from her face. She pursed her lips. "My father assigned me a mission, and I can't disappoint him."

"Your father sent you here?" Shane got up from the uncomfortable wall and stared. "Is he crazy?"

"Most people think so," Kyaina said. She kept her eyes down as she fidgeted with her shackles.

"Why, though?"

Kyaina sighed. "Because my father's in charge of... us." Shane assumed she meant the assassins. "And if we don't listen to him, let's just say that bad things happen."

A shudder ran through Shane's body. It was hard to think that someone who looked so young and innocent was part of a group whose sole purpose was murdering people for money.

"But why are you *here*?"

"I can't tell you."

"Of course, you can't." Shane sighed, laying her back against the rocks once again and closing her eyes. Getting information from Kyaina, or any of the assassins, was like pulling teeth.

They were expected to sleep right where they were, given no pad or sleeping bag to protect them from the cold. Shane shivered all night, not sleeping at all. The guards switched posts in the middle of the night. Shane could hear them whispering but couldn't make out a word.

In the morning, they were awoken by the loud bang of a pickaxe colliding against the wall. With the pickaxes, they were also given a pitiful amount of food that consisted of moldy bread and cheese, the leftovers from what the guards had eaten a couple weeks before. Shane picked at it with her fingers but left the moldy sections for the mice.

The prisoners were also given small animal hide flasks that got filled halfway with water. Shane wondered if the water came from the lake.

The blisters on her hands had only grown worse from the day before. She cringed when it came time to start mining. She barely managed to pick up her pickaxe, much less swing it. She narrowly scraped by with the quota that day. When the minecarts left behind them, a huge sigh of relief went through Shane.

After that day, the pickaxe became easier to hold. The blisters became callouses. Soon her hands were no longer as soft and delicate as they had been before.

It only took Shane a few months to get used to the rhythm of the mines. Kyaina was the only person she talked to, and that didn't happen often. At the end of each day, she was too exhausted to think about speaking to another person.

Everyday her stomach rumbled with hunger. She guessed that she must've lost at least ten pounds already. She was nothing but flesh and bones.

The lack of food affected her performance tremendously. It got to the point that she struggled to get her quota. Eventually she was only able to fill her minecart halfway by the end of the day.

When the guard took the pickaxe away from her, he took note of her light haul. He breathed in sharply, making Shane look back only to see the man smiling slyly. His right hand went toward the keys on his belt and unlocked her shackles from the chain, keeping one hand gripped on her shoulders. Kyaina said nothing, only pursing her lips.

"Please," Shane begged as he threw her against the other wall. Her face hit the stone. "I'll try harder tomorrow."

"You know the rules." The guard's thick, baritone voice echoed around the tunnel.

She did. "Fifteen lashes for everyone who didn't bring in the quota for the day." Her body tensed as he grabbed for his whip, cracking it mere inches from her face.

"Please," Shane cried again.

The man didn't listen. The whip sounded out through the cavern and immediate pain took over Shane's entire back. She let out a strangled cry as the next lash came, stinging worse than the first one. All the breath left her body. Tears rolled down her face, but she didn't notice it because the man whipped her once again.

Shane lost count of the number of lashes, but after what seemed like forever, the whipping stopped. Shane remained still with her head against the stone, tears falling freely from her eyes. Her entire back exploded with agony. The man grabbed her, her shackles jangling against each other as he returned her to the same spot she left on the chain of people.

"Gods, Shane," Kyaina said, yanking on her chain to get closer to her. "I'm so sorry."

Shane couldn't speak. Blood raced down her back, soaking her already dirty, ripped t-shirt, mixing with the dirt and sweat that already coated it. Her jaw clenched as her sweat entered the cut, a gurgled plea for help leaving her mouth.

"This is gonna hurt like Haytorrow's Fallen Realm." Kyaina searched behind her, grabbing a small animal hide flask. Shane wanted to protest, saying that she didn't need her help, but Kyaina continued anyway, pouring it onto her back to clear away the dust from the mines. Shane let out a gasp as it contacted her broken skin, stinging more than ever, followed by some welcome relief.

Sleep came difficult for her that night. Every time she changed her position even the slightest bit, her back rubbed against the torn shirt. When she finally did get to sleep, it felt like only moments later she was being woken back up by the same clanging against the wall. She winced standing up, but it surprisingly felt much better than the day before. It still hurt like hell, but in a more manageable way.

"Your back," Kyaina whispered to her as the guards handed them their pickaxes. "How does it feel?"

"Still hurts." Shane ignored the blisters on her hand and swung the pickaxe toward the wall.

Kyaina peered behind her and gasped.

"Does it look bad?"

"No," Kyaina said, peering around to make sure that nobody overheard her. "The exact opposite actually. It's already scabbed over and healing."

"Great," Shane said with no emotion in her voice. "Only means I'll have to spend more time in this hellish place." A small part of her had hoped that it would get infected, and she would die. Then she would be able to see Reece and apologize to her for what she was about to do.

"How is that possible?"

"I don't know." Shane pursed her lips, looking around her to make sure no guards were around. "Look, you want my advice? Complete whatever it is you were sent here to do, then leave."

Kyaina's eyes flickered up to the exit of the tunnel, then back to Shane. "I'm trying, but it isn't as easy as that. Most of my missions only take me a week at most, but this one's more difficult."

"Why are you waiting so long to do it?"

"Because right now, I'm just trying to find a way out of here and not be killed." Kyaina sighed. "My father said this would be challenging, but I never thought it would be near impossible."

Shane scanned the area around her, a plan forming in her mind for a way to get Kyaina out. "Does it matter how you escape?"

"No, but—"

"Good," Shane said, swinging her pickaxe, making rocks fly up from where it landed. "Just wait about a week for me to heal, and I'll help you."

"Why?"

"Because," Shane said, her face remaining emotionless, "I want to help with whatever it is you're doing and wreak havoc on this godforsaken place."

"Gods."

"What?"

"Godsforsaken place."

"Whatever."

CHAPTER 8

"Are you aware of how stupid this plan is?" Kyaina asked as she swung her pickaxe halfheartedly.

"Yes. I am fully aware."

Several days had passed since the whipping, and Shane's back felt significantly better. During those few days, after their pickaxes were taken away and they were expected to sleep, they went over the details of the plan they were making with hushed voices. Plan was too generous of a word. It was more like a suicide pact.

Shane looked at the prisoner in front of her and took a deep breath. If she were going to do this, then there was a good chance she would be killed. All she hoped for was a chance to be brought before Fritz once again. Then, Kyaina could finish whatever she was sent there to do. During their late-night planning, she had promised Shane she would come back and get her. Maybe, just maybe, if they survived all that, they would be able to escape the hell hole they were in, and Shane could start her life over again.

"Ready?" Shane whispered to Kyaina, adjusting the pickaxe in her hand.

"As ready as I'll ever be."

"Good." Shane drew in a shaky breath before bringing down her pick, but it wasn't on the stone. Instead, it contacted the rusty chain that connected her to the other prisoners. The loud, metallic echoing noise of metal against metal was camouflaged by Kyaina's own pickaxe striking the stone wall at the same time. Shane winced. If a guard heard it… Shane shuddered just to think about it, but nobody came. All she had to do was break through the chain, and it would be good. She brought the pickaxe up one more time, and when she brought it down, the chain snapped in two.

"What are you doing?" Kyaina yelled to get the guards' attention. "Guards, she's trying to escape!"

"Would you shut up," Shane hissed, trying to get rid of her shackles the same way she broke the chain.

"Guards! She broke her chain!"

"Shut up!" Shane walked toward Kyaina, heart pounding. She slapped Kyaina across the face leaving a giant red welt where her hand made contact.

"You hit me!"

"And I'll do it again if you won't shut up."

Saying that was a mistake. Kyaina's elbow pummeled Shane straight in the stomach, doubling her over in pain.

"What in Haytorrow's Fallen Realm are you thinking?" the prisoner in front of them hissed. "You're going to get us all killed!" The young man stepped between them and grabbed Shane by the shoulders.

"Get off me." Shane tried to shake his grip off her, but to no avail. The other prisoner wasn't supposed to get involved in the fight.

The chain broke behind Shane, and Kyaina lunged toward the prisoner. "Let go of her." She kicked the man's legs behind the knees, taking him down and Shane with him. She let out a cry as her arm was twisted in its socket.

The sound of the whip rang out through the caves. "What's going on here?" A guard flew forward and gripped the prisoner that attacked Shane. Seconds later someone grabbed Shane's arms and pinned her against the wall. She wasn't prepared for the elbow that went straight for her face, breaking her nose instantaneously. She cowered on the ground, too weak to fight back.

"Both of you are crazy!" the other prisoner yelled, flailing around in the guard's grip. "Fritz is going to kill all of us!"

"I should kill you right here!" said the guard holding Shane. Her eyes widened as he reached for his gun.

"Wait." Orrik's cold voice came from the shadows. His footsteps echoed loudly around the cave and stopped a couple feet away from Shane. Shane couldn't help but notice the smile forming on Kyaina's face, then disappearing the moment it had appeared. "Bring them to Fritz."

"But—"

"Was I speaking Yalog?" Orrik bent down to get a better look at Shane's bloodied face. "Let him decide what to do with them." He looked over at the slave that had attacked Shane and smiled before getting back up and wiping the dirt off his hands.

The guard hauled Shane up. He kept both ends of the shackle chains in his hand, keeping her arms together. Shane winced as he put his hand on her back and pushed her toward the exit.

Blood ran freely from her broken nose, but she didn't complain. Her eyes met Kyaina's. She mouthed the words, *thank you* as Orrik led them and the other prisoner away.

When they made it to the surface, Shane was nearly blinded by the bright sunlight reflecting off the crisp, white snow. She closed her eyes, black spots dancing in her vision. She never remembered the world being so bright, but she had never been underground for months at a time.

The guards took them to the house of Fritz, and an uneasy feeling settled on Shane. She glanced over toward Kyaina, who kept her eyes locked on Orrik. She was probably waiting for the right opportunity to kill him when no one else was around. Shane was starting to wonder when that time would be, and if it ever was going to happen.

The guards opened the door and led the slaves through the same hallways that they had walked a few months earlier. Shane felt the urge to vomit as they knocked on the door to Fritz's office before opening it up. What had she been thinking when she decided to help Kyaina? She knew that the chances of dying were high, but hadn't realized how high until right then.

There was a man and a woman with Fritz in his office. Fritz looked up and frowned when he saw who had entered his space.

"Why are they here?" he asked. The two people that he was talking to looked back, and Shane gasped. The man. She knew his face. It was so familiar, yet she was sure that she could never have seen it before.

"They started a fight in the mines," Orrik explained, motioning for the man holding Shane to come forward. "This slave broke through the chains." The man holding her grabbed Shane's dirty hair and twisted it, "Show him your wrists!"

The woman pursed her lips, her dark face looking at Shane with pity. It looked like she wanted to say something, but she remained quiet.

"But why are they here? I thought I told you to deal with any uprisings where it started?" Fritz let out a sigh, turning to the people that he was talking to before. "I'm sorry for this, Lethik, Eska."

"Fritz, your son was part of the fight."

Fritz's jaw clenched. "I have no son."

Shane looked over in shock at the young man who had tried so hard to stop her and Kyaina from fighting. He had the same twisted smile and malicious look in his eyes as the man sitting in front of her. What had he done to deserve being thrown in this slave camp by his own father?

"Hate you too, father." The young man spat on the ground, then looked up at Fritz and smiled.

"You dare speak to me?" Fritz's hand moved for his side. Before Shane even got the chance to realize what was happening, he had a gun in his hand and was pointing it at his son. "One more word out of you, slave, and I will end you."

"Fritz," the woman said, finally finding the courage to speak. "Is this really necessary?"

"Yes."

"He's your son!"

Fritz sneered. "Blood doesn't mean anything. If it weren't for him and his soft heart, I never would've had to put down a slave revolt three months ago."

"You were the exact same as him when you were his age."

"And I hated myself then," Fritz yelled, traces of spit accentuated his words. "If my father hadn't knocked some sense into me, I would have ended up a low life merchant."

Lethik's jaw clenched. "At least give him a chance."

"I already did! And he ended up here." Fritz motioned for Orrik to bring his son forward. He was forced to his knees, and Fritz put the gun against his head. "My father should've done this to me when I acted out."

The gunshot came suddenly. Before Shane could scream, blood splattered from the boy's head. Shane stared in horror as he fell to the ground, lifeless.

"Get rid of them," Fritz said, motioning with his hand for them to be gone. The guards hesitated. The man holding Shane tightened his grip on her shackles and started dragging her away, but Fritz stopped him. "Wait. Keep her here." He pointed at Shane.

The guard obliged. The man who brought in Fritz's son hoisted his limp body over his shoulder and carried him out. Shane couldn't look. It reminded her of Reece too much.

Shane's eyes met Kyaina's, who, though was being hauled back outside, looked like she had everything under control. *Thank you*, her gaze seemed to say before being brought out the doors.

"What's your name?" Fritz asked, no emotion in his voice.

"Sh—" The guard behind her grabbed her hair and twisted again, kneeing her in the back. She gritted her teeth. "B-31082."

"Why'd you start the fight?"

Shane let out a cold, ruthless laugh. "I didn't. That girl did. She saw what I was trying to do and tried to stop me."

"And that was?"

"Escape."

In front of Fritz, Lethik's face twisted in what looked like pity.

Fritz stared at Shane for a couple seconds before searching on the bottom drawer of his desk for something, and when he brought it out, Shane's eyes widened. A curled whip sat in his hand.

"Nobody escapes Verscar alive. You asked how we punish our slaves." Fritz turned his attention to Lethik. "How about an example."

Lethik's face seemed to pale slightly, but he didn't protest. Eska, who was standing next to him, curled her fist into a ball.

Shane struggled to get away, but the man behind her pulled up on the shackles, torturing her already raw skin. A strangled cry left her mouth as Fritz got up from his chair, uncoiling the whip for show. She tried to yank away from the man, wanted to run away, but he kept her still.

Fritz let loose a crack.

"Please," she begged. "Don't do this."

"If you're lucky, death will come for you and quickly at that," Fritz whispered in her ear, just loud enough so that she alone could hear him.

He made a motion for the man holding Shane to leave before cracking the whip again. Shane winced and clenched her eyes closed, waiting for the whip to hit her.

First there was the crack, then came the pain. It was worse than being whipped in the cave. There was a giant, deep slice in her back that stung with every breath she took. The whip hit her back again, and an overwhelming sense of agony spread up her arms and down her legs.

Again.

Again.

Again.

Tears fell from her eyes as her blood dripped down onto the already red carpet.

"Stop!" Shane could hear the words coming from Eska but didn't understand what they meant. "She's just a girl! You can't kill her!"

The whipping stopped as she ran forward, falling to her knees next to Shane. Her worried face looked at her with concern.

"Are you aware of what this *girl* did?" Fritz spat, letting the blood-stained whip lay haphazardly in his hand.

"Does it matter?" Eska tried to wipe the blood from Shane's face, but she winced as she touched the bridge of her nose.

"You of all people should hate her, Lethik. She trespassed on the Island of Eringunner." There was a malicious darkness to his eyes.

Lethik's face paled more than it had before, but he said, "That doesn't matter. She's just a girl, and I think that the rule the king made is stupid."

"Funny to hear that, coming from you." Fritz smiled. "I wonder how Airel would like to see how her husband would treat her death."

Lethik's face tightened. "Shut up."

Fritz rolled up the whip and set it on the desk, motioning for the guard to take Shane once again. She felt paralyzed with pain.

"Take her away with the rest of them," he said, refusing to take his eyes off Eska and Lethik.

Shane didn't even realize she was being escorted out until she heard the doors slam behind her. She had to use the guard for support, her feet dragging along the floor.

He led her down different hallways than when they first entered the building, but Shane didn't find that surprising at all. She assumed that she was being brought to the dungeon. When she was led down dark stairs, it reminded her of the dungeon in the castle.

Where Reece's dead body had lain for over a week.

A sob escaped her as she was tossed into a cell. She stumbled, falling to the hard ground like a rag doll. The door clanked shut behind her and the lock turned, leaving her all alone with her own thoughts. And pain.

The water seeping through the wall soaked into her clothing, making her back sting almost as bad as when the whippings first happened. She winced in pain, and then the pain stopped. It was the same thing that had happened when she was whipped in the cave. Almost like magic.

Shane's heart skipped a beat as she recalled what happened the first day she and Reece had gotten to the world. The boat mishap, Mindalin. It all came flooding back to her. It felt like it had happened a lifetime ago, even though it had been several months.

She felt her back with her hand. There was nothing but deep scabs and dried blood. The cuts were no longer open. They had somehow healed themselves.

"B-31082!" A voice yelled from outside the cell. She brought her eyes up to see a guard walking toward her cell, keys in his hands.

"What do you want from me?"

"It's time for you to leave." He unlocked the door and grabbed her by the broken chains that hung uselessly from her wrists.

The guard dragged Shane out into the hallway and back up the stairs that she had just come down. Everything in her body tensed up, telling her to run far, far away. An uneasy feeling entered her stomach as the guard led her down different hallways, but fortunately not going back to Fritz's office. Had Kyaina succeeded in assassinating Orrik? She hoped so, or else she had endangered her pitiful life for nothing.

When they left the building and entered the cold, snowy outside, they didn't turn toward the mine that she had been taken from. Instead, they continued straight. Shane's hands became sweaty, and she couldn't help her eyes from darting to the mines. They rounded a corner in the road, and she suddenly felt ill. Ahead of her stood the podium that she had seen when they first entered the camp, but two people stood on it, one with shackles on, and the other with an axe. Kyaina smiled down at her.

CHAPTER 9

"Kyaina, what are you doing here?" Shane whispered as she was led up the stairs to the top of the platform. The man tied her hands tightly, cutting off the circulation. She unsuccessfully tried to get out of her restraints.

"It won't do you any good," Kyaina mumbled to Shane. "I've already tried." Shane couldn't help but notice the blood splatters on Kyaina's clothing.

"What happened? Why are you here?"

"There were... complications." Kyaina pursed her lips, growing quiet as the man heaved the freshly polished axe over his shoulder.

"Did you do it?"

"Yes." Kyaina was fiddling with her shackles. "But I was caught before I could get to you."

Shane's heart fell. She was going to come back for her.

"Do you have a plan for this?" she asked.

"Just follow my lead." Kyaina winced as she messed with her hands behind her back. Shane was surprised to see the rope that had tied Kyaina's wrists fell to the floor. Shane stared with amazement as Kyaina popped her dislocated thumb back into place. The guards never saw a thing.

"How did you…?" Shane started but was quieted by Kyaina's glares of warning. Without hesitation, she lunged for the man with the axe. Caught off guard, he fell to the ground as Kyaina's body collided with his own. The guard next to him fumbled for his gun as Kyaina ripped the axe free from the man and brought it around, striking the man with the gun square in the torso. Without hesitation, in a flash of blood and steel, the axe had found its way into the chest of the other guard.

Blood coated Kyaina's front before she turned to Shane, a crazed look in her eyes. "Turn around," she ordered, and Shane did without question. No need to disobey the woman with the blade who wasn't afraid to kill. Kyaina cut Shane's bonds, letting them fall to the ground. Shane massaged her poor, chafed wrists. It was the first time in months they were free from bindings.

"Remind me never to get on your bad side," Shane said, stepping over the dead men to follow Kyaina to the stairs.

"We have to get out of here. It won't be long until more guards come. This was supposed to be a public execution." Kyaina heaved the axe over her shoulder and jumped down from the platform.

"What about the gun?" Shane asked, pointing at it in the dead man's hands.

"Grab it."

Shane tore the gun from the man and leaped down from the platform, running as fast as she ever had in her life just to catch Kyaina. The heft of the axe must have weighed Kyaina down because it wasn't long before Shane caught up. They weaved in and out of the streets until they saw three guards walking toward them.

In an instant, they ducked behind a wall to hide from the guards. Shane's breaths came ragged as she supported her frail body against the nearest building

"Kyaina, do you see them?" Shane asked.

Kyaina brought the axe down from her shoulders. "Yes, I do."

"They have three guns, and we only have one."

"I'm fully aware of that, thanks."

A loud bang rang out through the complex. A split second later, wood snapped an inch away from Shane, sending splinters everywhere as the bullet went straight through.

"How thin are these walls?" Shane breathed, eyes wide as she shrunk down into a ball, trying her best to disappear.

"My guess is pretty thin." Kyaina angled the axe so that its metal blade acted like a mirror, letting her see what was happening in front of them. The three men slowly made their way toward them, guns ready. They heard someone yell to sound the alarm, and a sinking feeling went through Shane. If that happened, then the entire compound would be on high alert for escaping prisoners. "Aren't you going to shoot back at them?"

Shane stared down at the gun in her hand and fought back the fear that was trying to paralyze her. She shot with her dad at the shooting range, but it seemed so long ago. She'd been aiming at targets then, not actual people. "I… I can't."

"Then give me the gun."

Kyaina set the axe down and took the gun from Shane's hand. She peered around the wall and fired at the men. Six deafening gunshots sounded in Shane's ear. Immediately after, all she could hear was a high-pitched ringing in her ears.

"Dammit," Kyaina swore as she tossed the gun to the ground. "I never was good at aiming with these."

"Did you hit them?"

"I hit a couple, but I don't think I killed them."

Kyaina rolled her left sleeve up, revealing a dark, black, circular tattoo with a knife in the middle. She pressed down on it, wincing as a little wave rippled through it.

"What are you doing?" Shane asked, peering around the edge to see the guards running for them, one holding his arm. "People are trying to kill us, but you're busy admiring your tattoo?"

"I'm calling for help."

"A lot of good that does us," Shane spat sarcastically. "What are we going to do about them?" She motioned with her head.

"You're going to run out there and cause some chaos."

Shane stared at her, mouth agape. "Are you crazy?"

"I thought we already decided that." Kyaina took one look around the corner. "The guns that they have only hold six bullets, and they already wasted one." Another gunshot sounded through the street and another hole blasted through the wall. "Make that two." She pursed her lips. "From what I've seen, they don't have good aim with moving objects. They only have sixteen bullets left. If you can get them to use those, then they'll have to use their swords."

"Am I the only one who sees a flaw in your plan?" Shane asked, gulping down fear. Kyaina didn't listen. "Why can't you do this?"

"I can, but why would I?"

"So, you're telling me—"

"Just go." Kyaina tried to push her out from behind the wall. "They'll be on us any second."

"If I die doing this," Shane mumbled, getting up off the ground, "you are dead." Taking in a deep breath, she ran out. Almost immediately a gunshot sounded.

"Fifteen," she thought she heard Kyaina say, but she was too busy running to pay attention to what was going on around her. The guards had stopped sprinting toward her and were positioning themselves across the thin street to cut her off. Their guns were aiming at Shane, hands remaining steady.

Another shot went off and Shane felt a sting in her arm. She looked down in horror to see it coated in blood. There was a slight tingle of pain, and it was getting worse by the second.

She kept running zigzags down the street, refusing to allow one wound in her arm to slow her down. The guns fired fourteen more times, and Shane felt the air bend around her ear, the bullets whizzing past her head. Her heart pounded faster and faster the closer she got to them. One by one their guns clattered to the ground, and they reached for their swords.

She skidded to a stop, placing her bloody hand on the nearest wall. Her arm pounded with pain. Shane guessed that she wouldn't die right away from her wound, but that didn't make it any more pleasant.

The guards moved forward, blocking any escape. She wanted to run back and let Kyaina deal with them, but her friend was nowhere to be seen.

"If you're going to act, I would do it now," Shane yelled.

One look behind her told her Kyaina was busy fending for her life against more guards. Her heart sank as they fired their guns, but not toward her, toward Kyaina. The bullets pinged off metal, and Shane could only hope that her friend was all right.

Shane's nearest assailant raised his sword, about to strike her when an arrow pierced his stomach. He took one look down and fell to the ground in a puddle of his own blood, the sword clattering from his hand. The others hesitated, looking for where the arrow came from. Another arrow flew down from Shane's right impaling itself into a wooden wall, missing the nearest guard by inches.

"I was never good with the bow," a deep, familiar voice said, dropping down from the tall building to Shane's right. Archer took an arrow out of his quiver and shot it at the nearest guard to him, almost point blank. In the blink of an eye, he launched another one at the last remaining guard.

"I was going to do that," Kyaina said, stepping out from behind the wall, covered in blood that hopefully wasn't her own. It dripped off the blade of her axe.

"But you didn't." They switched their weapons. Kyaina looked much more comfortable with the bow in her hands. Archer looked at Shane, having trouble hiding his irritation. "Why did you bring her with you?"

"I'll fill you in later."

Shane followed the two of them down the street, holding onto her bleeding arm. Archer said, "Kyaina, you risked your *own* life just to help her escape too?"

"Yeah, that sounds about right" she said, taking a quick glance at Shane. "I have a good feeling about this one."

"Gods, I hope you're right."

The pealing of a bell rang out through the encampment, making them stop dead in their tracks. Shane's heart raced, seeing guards running on the top of the distant walls, and multiplying in numbers.

"Bloody knives," Archer whispered before clearing his throat. "We have to split up. Make it so they have to search the whole camp to find us."

"But—" Kyaina tried to argue but was cut off when a bang sounded behind them.

"You take Shane and meet me outside by the shore of the lake." Archer sprinted away, disappearing into the streets.

"Damn him."

Shane looked behind her only to see more men running their way, revolvers out. They slowed down only to aim and shoot.

"Kyaina…" Shane didn't finish the sentence before Kyaina gripped her sleeve and yanked her forward as the first bullets ricocheted past them. They veered into a small side street and sprinted for their lives. If they kept zigzagging through the streets, Shane realized as she looked hopelessly at the walls surrounding them, they would never find a way out.

Kyaina let go of Shane's sleeve and sprinted ahead. Shane swore at Aarion and Fritz, who made her body so frail. She was beginning to feel the effects of her time as a prisoner. She passed a small street, trying desperately to catch up to Kyaina when a guard came out directly in front of her. She tried to stop, to run the other direction, but her momentum carried her right into him. He grabbed her and held her firm.

"Got one of them," he said to one of his fellow guards nearby.

Before Shane could scream for Kyaina, the man holding her put his hand over her mouth and pushed the point of a knife into her back. If she made a sound, she was sure he would stab her and that would be the end. Her eyes watered as she watched the assassin round the corner far ahead, unaware that Shane was no longer with her.

"Take her back to Fritz while I deal with the others," the other man said.

No. She couldn't go back to Fritz. She would rather die than see his twisted face again. Shane tried twisting and fighting back, but the man only dug the knife deeper into her back. A cry escaped through his fingers.

The man tightened his hand over her mouth. Her jaw clenched without thinking as she drove her teeth into the man's fingers. The metallic taste of blood soaked through her mouth, nearly gagging her, but she stayed steady. The man's grip around her body loosened as she pushed away from him, slipping from his grasp and knocking the knife out of his hand. Shane pounced on the fallen blade before he even realized what had happened, the hand of her injured arm closing around the hilt.

Blood dripped from the corners of her smile. She pointed the knife toward the man, who was holding his wrist and staring at his hand.

"You little wench!" He seethed. "You bit me!"

"And I'll do it again." She spat the blood and bits of finger at the guard's feet in defiance. Before the man could respond, she was already sprinting away.

The sun was setting behind her, casting the world into a red glow. Shane smiled as the light faded away. It would be easier to hide at night, and she was planning on using that to her advantage.

She twisted and weaved through the streets. She wouldn't be able to climb the outside wall, she thought. And even if she could, there were too many guards manning it, ready to strike down at anyone who tried. The entrance to the camp was out of the question. Everyone was on high alert, leaving only one option for her escape. The lake.

From what she remembered seeing on the way in, the water was both on the outside and inside of the camp, the wall cutting it in two. She theorized that there would be a grate in the wall that allowed the water to flow from one side to the other below the waterline. But if there wasn't… She preferred not to think about that.

She sprinted through the shadows, hoping no one saw her, but her hopes were dashed when she heard feet hitting the cobbled streets with force. Glancing back, her heart sank. Two men were coming for her, one of them the man who she had bitten.

Shane ran faster than she thought was possible. The lake was near, maybe a hundred yards away. The length of a football field. Snow covered its icy surface, and Shane's only hope was that it was thin enough for someone like her to break through. If it wasn't, then she was certainly dead.

She was about fifty feet away when a gunshot sounded. Something warm and wet ran down her right leg and she stumbled, limping. With a mixture of horror and shock, she looked down at her leg to see blood oozing its way down, the burning pain of a gunshot confirmed her worst fears.

"No!" she cried, still limping toward the lake, but the men were gaining ground. She had to make it. Had to escape. For Reece. For her family. For her friends. She couldn't die here.

Another gunshot sounded when she was only feet from the lake. It tore into her shoulder, making the knife fall from her hand. She screamed in pain as she continued to limp forward, refusing to give up. Pain burned through her shoulder, pulsing. Tears blurred her eyes as she fell forward onto the ice and broke through, her whole body submerging into the frigid water, blood turning the water red.

Breathe. Just breathe.

It was difficult when the cold water displaced all the air from her lungs, freezing everything in her body. Her hurt arm tingled with relief, but the gunshot wounds still throbbed like nothing Shane had ever felt before. Taking in a deep breath of water, she swam forward a little ways, trying to ignore the pain. It wasn't until she was a couple feet away from where she broke through the ice and nearly to the bottom of the lake that she stopped and breathed in a sigh.

This was far from over.

There was still the chance of bleeding out if she didn't get those bullets out, not to mention the possibility of dying of hypothermia. Already her fingers were becoming numb from the cold.

Just take it one crisis at a time, she reminded herself, waving her uninjured arm in the water to keep her still. The light down there was poor, and she could hardly see a thing, but she didn't let that stop her from plunging her free hand into the wound on her leg. She cried out, bubbles floating up as a sharp stinging shuddered throughout her entire body. Black spots danced in her vision; the pain nearly made her pass out. Her fingers dug deeper trying to find the bullet. She winced as she grabbed onto it, yanking it out of her leg. Almost immediately she felt relief as the wound began to heal itself. The bullet in her shoulder came out equally as painful.

Blood pooled ahead of her, mushrooming outward, floating to the surface. She could only hope that it told the people on the surface that she was dying or already dead. She must have been underwater for a couple of minutes, and there was no way a normal person, especially one as weak and injured as her, could survive that long with no air.

Shane looked at the surface through the clouded, thick red water. She thought she could hear people yelling, but nobody dared to go near the lake.

She turned her attention to the wall that cast a giant shadow over her. Through the murky water she saw what appeared to be an algae-covered round grate with metal bars and openings no bigger than what a fish could pass through. Shane kicked up from the sandy bottom, swimming in pain toward the grate. The cold bit into her like a knife, and she knew that if she stayed down there much longer, her fate would be sealed.

The wall appeared in front of her through the darkness. It wasn't long before she found the grate. Water had eroded away some of the metal, and the grate was half-covered on the bottom with sand. She spotted a bar that appeared like it had deteriorated enough to be weak and started digging around it. If she could eliminate at least one of the bars, she might be able to squeeze her way through.

She worked fast, the cold creeping its way through her body, making everything numb. She couldn't feel the rusty bars when she tugged. It made a small noise, moving only a little bit. She tugged at it frantically, and finally, it broke free. She let it drop to the bottom and made her way through. For a moment she feared her hips were stuck and her heart raced, but with one final tug and a kick, she slipped through the grate.

She was free! But she didn't have time to get excited. She had to get to the surface before she froze to death.

Shane willed the muscles in her legs to move as she kicked for the surface for all she was worth. Her thighs rubbing together felt strange, almost like they weren't her own, but she kept swimming, refusing to let the ever consuming bite of the cold beat her. Her legs pumped viciously, and her arms flailed about, trying their best to find the surface.

One hand touched the ice unexpectedly and Shane's stomach dropped. She tried pounding on it to break it, but that did nothing. Her arms were too weak and tired to do anything. Her legs stopped pumping as she feared there was no getting out. She was too close to death to have the strength to break the ice.

She sank to the bottom, too weak to cry. It was ironic, really, to waste all her energy on escaping only to die this close to freedom. She wanted to scream about how unfair it was.

But then she heard a noise, a voice. Something hard hit the ice, reverberating through the water. It happened again and the ice cracked open. Shane looked up to see Archer's face peering down at her and a newfound strength coursing through her. She wasn't going to die! Her legs pumped as fast as they could toward the hole, her head coming clear of the frosty water. She made it. She was outside.

CHAPTER 10

"**H**oly gods," Kyaina said, rushing across the ice toward Shane. Now wrapped in Archer's arms, Shane was desperately trying to absorb all the warmth from him she could. "What happened?" she asked, taking off her jacket and draping it over Shane's shoulders

"Now isn't a good time to be asking that question." Archer helped Shane to her feet, allowing her to lean on him.

Kyaina's eyebrows creased. "Right. Can you walk."

Shane tried to talk, but she couldn't find her voice. Instead, she nodded shakily. Everything in her body told her to lie down and give up, but she forced herself to remain upright in Archer's arms. *That's just the hypothermia talking*, she had to remind herself.

"Good." Her lips pursed. "We need to get you to camp and out of those clothes and into some dry ones."

They stumbled across the ice. Shane felt sorry for Archer, who had to practically carry her near lifeless body the whole way, but she knew that if she tried to walk by herself, she would only slow them down.

"Which way?" Kyaina asked. A sickening feeling went through Shane as she realized that Kyaina had no clue which direction to head. Had she never been to Archer's camp?

Archer pointed his chin straight to the tree line. "It's past those."

They were almost to the tree line when the warm glow of the fires lighting up Versar disappeared behind a hill. Shane should have been filled with relief, but she was too close to death to feel anything besides pain. The high alertness she felt while escaping the camp was replaced by slow, sluggish movements and exhaustion. All she wanted to do was fall onto the fluffy snow. It looked so soft, so inviting, but she forced herself to ignore it. Her eyes narrowed as she tried her best to put one foot in front of the other.

Through the branches came an orange glow of a smoldering fire. Memories of sitting by the fire, drinking a warm cup of hot chocolate with her friends, and laughing gave Shane the inspiration to continue on over a well packed path that led down to Archer's camp. The fire, it appeared, had almost completely gone out, but Shane didn't care. She could still feel the warmth emanating from it.

"Set her down next to whatever that is," Kyaina said, gesturing over toward the smoldering logs.

"It's a fire."

"If that's a fire, then I'm Princess Airel." Shane pulled Kyaina's jacket tight around her, sinking into its fuzzy inside, sleeves dangling helplessly on either side.

"Th-thank you," Shane managed to say, teeth chattering so loudly that she was surprised she could hear herself, "for the jacket."

"Rekindle the fire while I get her some clothes." Kyaina said as she retrieved a leather rucksack from a branch of a nearby tree. She pulled a shirt and pants from the bag and tossed them at Shane. "Change into these."

Shane didn't even wait. Archer averted his eyes and focused his whole attention on restarting the fire as she tugged her frozen shirt off her body and replaced it with the warm, dry one. She was suddenly stricken with nausea when she looked at the clothes she had been wearing for months. They were nothing more than shreds of cloth, bloodied and torn so bad she could hardly recognize what they had been.

When Archer stepped away from the fire, it was blazing high into the sky. The heat radiated toward Shane, and she managed a smile as it began to warm her bones.

"Feel better?" Kyaina asked, slinking down on the fallen log next to her.

"Oh yeah," Shane said sarcastically, "The best I've ever been in my life."

"At least you're talking now."

"How'd you find me?" Shane asked, pulling Kyaina's jacket tighter.

"Me and Archer met outside Verscar as planned, and I realized you weren't behind me. Archer was about to give up when we heard the banging on the ice, so we ran to see what it was. When we saw that it was you, well…" She looked over at Shane, her eyes watering. "I thought you were dead, Shane. When I looked back and saw that you weren't there…" She took in a shaky breath. "Then when we found you under water, I was sure that you had drowned."

"What can I say," Shane said, faking a smile. "I'm good at holding my breath." She didn't think it would be a good idea to tell Kyaina about Mindalin and water breathing. Shane was perfectly fine with not telling anyone about it.

Archer cleared his throat. "I don't mean to dampen the mood here, but what do you plan on doing with her, Kyaina?" Archer said, gesturing to Shane.

"We're gonna bring her back with us."

A dry laugh left Archer's mouth. "You're kidding right?"

"No. I'm not." Kyaina turned her attention from Shane to Archer. "I promised her that she could come with us if we managed to escape, and we did."

"Does she even want this?"

"Yes," Shane cut in. "I do. Everything that I have ever loved has been ripped away from me. Reece's dead," her voice cracked. Saying it out loud made it seem more real. "And I have nothing left of my old life."

"And I'm sorry for that, but you should start a new life, away from Lyconnexal. Find one of your cousins or someone and live with them, but don't become a killer like we are."

"What did you not understand about what I just said? I have nobody in this world. No family. No friends. All of them were taken away from me."

Kyaina looked up at Archer. "She's already proved that she has what it takes. She helped me with my assassination, and she escaped the guards. Why not at least give her a chance?"

Shane gazed at Archer's golden flecked eyes begging, pleading with him to allow her to come with them. She didn't know what she would do with herself if he decided to let her go, and she didn't want to think about what it would be like if they did.

Archer turned toward the fire. "If your father kicks her out, don't be surprised when I tell you I told you so."

A smile spread across Kyaina's face. Shane couldn't help but to allow herself a small bit of happiness even after everything that had happened to her. For the first time since she had been in that world, she knew what she was doing, what she was working for.

But the happiness that she felt soon faded away from her face, replaced by a small frown. What would Reece say if she were here right now? If she were alive, could she even look Shane in the face, knowing the decisions that she made to survive?

Shane noticed everyone staring at her, and she blushed red when she realized that she had been caught up in her own mind to even hear the question.

"What?"

Archer sighed. "I asked if you were hungry."

Shane's stomach rumbled when he mentioned food. With shock, she realized that the last time she had eaten was the day before, and her frail body was only growing weaker by the second. "Yeah, I am."

"I would be surprised if she wasn't." Kyaina laughed, trying to wipe the dried blood off her hands. "Given how little we were given to eat in Verscar."

Shane forced a smile. "Why were you in there?" The question had been burning in the back of her mind ever since she found out that she was an assassin, but only now did she articulate what she was thinking. "I mean, couldn't Archer have remained acting as a guard, and you could've performed the assassination that way?"

The smile on Kyaina's face wavered. "He could've, yes." Her tone was much darker than it had been before. "But after I messed up our last mission, my father had to punish me. To test me."

Shane's face went slack. "I still can't believe your dad did that to you."

"I deserved it." Her gaze went up toward Archer, who was tending the flames. Sparks flew into the dark, cloudy night sky as he threw another log on. "I nearly got both Archer and me killed."

"Can we please not talk about this," Archer interjected. He rubbed his chest, massaging it. "It was bad enough that I had to live through it once."

"Fine." Kyaina sighed, blinking her thoughts away. She rolled up the sleeve of her left arm and outlined the tattoo that she had on the inside of her elbow. Only now that Shane wasn't being shot at could she tell the intricate details that went into it, unlike the tattoo that Shane had been given on her shoulder. Shane's hand instinctively went toward it, feeling the scarring tissue. B-

31082. Even if she never saw the scar again, she would never forget that number for as long as she lived.

"When we were being shot at, you did something to your tattoo, saying that you were calling for Archer? How did that work?"

Kyaina sighed, unrolling her sleeve and bringing it down to her wrist. "Every assassin has a partner, someone who you can trust with your life, and Archer's mine. Whenever either of us press down on our tattoos, the other person's arm tingles and burns. It's mostly used for life and death situations."

"But how does it work?"

"The tattoo is the mark of the assassins. Legend has it that we're Haytorrow's Chosen Heroes, and he gave us the gift as his blessing."

Archer laughed. "That's just a load of bullshit."

"Do you not believe in the gods?" Shane asked, thinking about Mindalin visiting her in the ocean. She wished that it never happened. Ever since she'd come to visit, her entire life had gone to hell.

"Oh, I believe in them all right," he said, laying down next to the fire. "But us being Haytorrow's Chosen Hero's is a myth."

"That's just because you don't want to be anyone's Hero," Kyaina said.

He let out a dry laugh. "Look at Princess Airel. She was apparently Mindalin's Chosen Hero and look where she is now. Dead. A whole lot of good Mindalin did her in the end."

"How did she die?" Shane asked, trying to hide her grimace. If Airel was Mindalin's last Chosen Hero, what did that mean for *her*? Would she die the same way that Airel did, or an even worse death?

"No one knows." Kyaina said. "One minute she was in the colonies, the next she was on the Island of Eringunner, dead."

"Probably because of Mindalin." Archer sighed, yawning. "If Airel hadn't died and sent King Aarion into a downward spiral," he spat, "I would still be with my family now." He didn't elaborate, and Shane didn't push it. Archer tossed Shane a cooked chunk of meat, rabbit, Shane guessed. She took a couple bites out of it, relishing the taste. She finished the chunk, before eventually succumbing to exhaustion.

Chapter 11

S hane awoke as the sun broke the horizon. Both Kyaina and Archer were already moving around, packing up camp.

"Good," Kyaina said. "You're awake." She tossed a bag in Shane's direction. "You're carrying this."

"Um, okay." Shane wiped the sleep from her eyes, stood up, and slung the straps over her shoulders. Her left arm was still sore from the gunshot wound the day before, but it didn't hurt nearly as bad as she thought it should have. She guessed she had the water to thank for that.

"I suggested we leave without you if you didn't wake before we were ready," Archer said. He kicked out the last sparks of the small smoldering fire. "Would've been better for you that way."

"I'm sure you would've." Shane said, a little shaky from the day before, but overall, in a much better mood than she'd been in for what seemed like forever. "Where are we going anyway?"

"Assassin's Underground in Conlar. It's north of here. We'd better get moving if we want to make the most of what daylight we have," Kyaina said before turning to Archer. "Is everything packed up?"

"Yes." Archer tied down the last strap on his backpack. From the looks of the area around them, it appeared that no one had been there at all. The only sign was the charred wood, and that was quickly being hidden by snow.

Archer started walking down the path that had led them to the campsite the day before. A gust of wind caused some tree-trapped snow to fall on Archer's head. Kyaina let out a small chuckle before passing him.

The relationship between Kyaina and Archer reminded Shane of her own siblings. She smiled sadly as she thought about Cloe, her older sister. They used to talk to each other like that, one minute jabbing at one another, insulting them, then the next laughing at their brothers. She didn't realize until now how precious those moments had been until it was too late.

When they made it to the main trail, they turned North, away from the horrors of Verscar. Shane would've been perfectly fine if she never saw those damn walls again. Even thinking about the place brought Fritz's grinning face to her mind, making her shudder. Every time she closed her eyes, all she saw was him.

"So, Shane," Archer said after a while. "Where are you from?"

"Why do you want to know?"

"I thought that since we're gonna be together for a while, at least until we get to Rotshall, we might as well get to know a little bit about you, and what makes you so special."

Shane looked back at Kyaina. "Rotshall..." she said, trailing off. "I stole something from a food cart, got myself arrested, then I was sold to that hell that we just escaped from." The lie was easier than the truth.

"So, you have a criminal background."

"Yeah, I guess so." *Even though I have no idea what I did wrong,* she thought, but grinned instead. "I hope that doesn't ruin my chances of joining the assassin's."

Kyaina chuckled. "We don't have a very clean record either."

"You could say that, with all the killing you do."

"Those are just the perks that come with the job."

"Just can't wait." But a sickening feeling tugged on Shane's stomach. Once again, the thought of Reece came into her mind.

They continued walking. The landscape around them changed as the days went by, from a dense forest to a wide, open field with mountains looming over them, their spiky, snowy peaks were enough to take Shane's breath away. Add the setting sun casting a glow on the hillside, and it was beautiful. She could imagine a camera in her hand, taking the perfect picture.

"Conlar's up there." Kyaina pointed up the mountains. "It's one of the biggest cities in all of Lyconnexal, a perfect place for a hiding spot."

"I'm sure it is."

They camped on the foothills of the mountains for the night, then in the morning started the ascent to Conlar. Shane had hiked mountain trails before, but not like that. There were almost no switchbacks in the trail, and when there were it was only because the climb was too steep to climb straight up. It didn't take long before her legs were feeling fatigue, but she refused to stop.

"We're almost there," Kyaina said after several hours, noticing Shane struggling. "Only a couple more hours."

"Great," Shane puffed sarcastically, her hands on her thighs and breathing heavily. "Hiking on a mountain trail is my favorite thing to do."

The clouds had taken over the sky, and small, dry snowflakes drifted to the ground, making the path more slippery. With every step they took, they seemed to slide back two. But eventually the terrain leveled out and the lights of the town appeared in the distance.

Archer sighed, his shoulder's relaxing. "Home at last."

But to Shane it was the exact opposite. Nothing felt like home to her here.

"We would've been here weeks ago if you'd thought to bring horses," Kyaina mumbled under her breath, arms crossed.

"I didn't know how long you were going to be in that camp, and I didn't want to worry about horses that long," Archer said.

People were crowding the streets when they made it to the city. Soon they were among them, and Shane felt uneasy. The last time she had seen so many of them was when she was being branded. Her heart raced as cold air tried to suffocate her. *It isn't real. It isn't real. It isn't real.*

"So," Shane cleared her throat, hoping her words didn't seem as shaky as they seemed, "where's… the Underground?"

"Just up here." Kyaina sprinted forward, dragging Shane and Archer along. They weaved their way through the hordes of people before turning down a small alleyway, surrounded by tall buildings. Shane stopped and raised an eyebrow.

"You're joking, right?" she scoffed, looking at the dilapidated, rundown inn at the end of the alley. Wooden boards full of splinters covered all the windows.

"Does it look like I'm joking?" Kyaina walked up to the door and pulled it open, the hinges squeaking. "Are you coming or not?"

I've gone mad, she thought, rushing to enter the building. The warm air on the inside caressed her cold face. The inside was much more furbished and better looking than it had on the outside, but it was small, and in no way a functioning inn. There was a desk at the back of the room and that was all, nothing like what Shane imagined the Assassin's Underground to look like.

"Am I missing something?" Shane asked. "Is this some kind of elaborate joke you guys are playing on me or something?"

A deep chuckle came from Archer. "Do you think this is it?" he asked, eyes sparkling with entertainment and trained on Shane.

"Look," she started, "I don't see anything that could possibly lead to— I don't know— a secret room or something like that."

"That's exactly what we were going for." His eyes shifted toward Kyaina. "Do you want to do the honors?"

"You're closer to it," she said.

Archer let out a sigh and rolled his eyes as he pushed himself off the wall and headed toward the desk. Leaning down, he grappled for something underneath. With a click, the whole building began to shake ever so slightly. At first Shane thought it might be a small earthquake, but then she noticed the floor in front of the desk beginning to lower, opening up to a slope that was growing steeper by the second.

"When we said Assassin's Underground," Kyaina said, walking down the still moving ramp and jumping the last couple feet, "did you think that we didn't mean that literally."

"No," Shane said, watching as Archer followed Kyaina into the darkness. "I just didn't think that it would be this dramatic." The ground stopped shaking and the ramp stopped at the floor below.

"Are you coming?"

"Yeah, I am." Shane gulped, taking the first steps down.

The darkness seemed to go on forever, and Shane couldn't help but be reminded of the caves she had managed to escape from a week before. She once again could feel the weight of the shackles weighing down her poor, frail wrists, imagining the jangling of chains as she descended into the cave in Verscar.

Stop.

Shane blinked, clearing her head. *I'm not there anymore,* she had to remind herself, taking the first step onto the stone floor. She looked around as Archer pushed a lever to make the ramp return back to its original position.

The only lights that could be seen were torches, and they were few and far between into the depths of the earth. The passage narrowed, ending at a spiral staircase. The steps were carved perfectly out of solid stone. Archer had already disappeared down them, leaving Kyaina just ahead of Shane.

"Aren't you going to catch up to Archer?" Shane asked Kyaina, trying to distract herself from the weight of the earth above her.

"Nah. He can find his way to his room perfectly fine by himself." Kyaina didn't meet Shane's eyes. "Besides, I have to introduce you to my dad and see if he wants to keep you as an assassin."

"And if he doesn't?"

Kyaina remained silent.

The hallway opened to a giant chamber with smooth stone walls and giant lanterns fixed to the stalactites above. A few people were strolling around. Shane spotted Archer heading down a passage and wondered if that was where the living quarters were. In the middle of the giant room was a railing overlooking the rest of the compound below.

"Come on," Kyaina said, nodding her head and yanking Shane along by her jacket sleeve. "My father's room is this way."

Shane took a deep, calming breath and followed close behind. She had so many questions pinging around in her mind, but she was too scared to ask them. What if Kyaina's father dismissed her before even seeing her? Or if he saw her and how weak she truly was and pushed her aside for someone more worthy?

"Gods." Kyaina laughed, sounding too tense to be real. "You look like a Geistluck."

"I'm fine," she said, forcing a smile.

"Sure, you are." Kyaina twisted the doorknob leading into her father's room and walked in without even knocking. Shane followed behind, trying to stay hidden from sight for as long as possible. Her palms grew clammy as she shut the door behind her.

The room was small, with only a cluttered desk near the far wall. A man sat behind it, peering over a file of papers before throwing it on the rest of the papers cluttering the desktop. When he looked up to see who had entered his office, a smile spread across his face. It wasn't reflected in his eyes

"Kyaina," he said, taking notice of Shane behind her. Something flickered in his eyes and his smile faltered, like he'd seen a ghost, but before Shane could even blink, his jubilant expression returned. "Who is this? I don't think I've had the pleasure of meeting her before?" There was something in his voice that told Shane that what he said was not completely honest, but she couldn't remember ever seeing the man before.

"Father, this is Shane." She stepped to the side, motioning Shane forward. Reluctantly, Shane obliged, taking a step closer to the desk. "She helped me with my task."

"And did you complete it?" he said with doubt in his voice, as though he expected the worst.

"Yes. Orrik's dead." Kyaina seemed tenser than Shane had ever seen her before. What used to be a laid-back young girl was now a nervous wreck. "Shane got me out of the mines so I could do it."

"Why'd you bring her back here?" He eyed Shane. She stiffened but managed to fake a smile. If she wanted to survive long enough to leave the room, she had to act the exact opposite of what she felt: Confident.

"It's my fault, sir," Shane said, not looking at Kyaina, but instead staring at the man straight in his bright blue eyes. "I had nowhere to go after I escaped, so I begged her to take me with her."

"Call me Wikter." He stuck out a hand, and Shane shook it, surprised by the coarseness of his skin. He paused, taking a moment to collect himself after bringing his hand back. "You do realize what we do here, don't you? I'm sorry if I'm judging you too quickly, but you don't look like an assassin?"

"Neither does Kyaina. Looks can be deceiving."

Wikter let out a hearty chuckle. "Too true, they can." He turned his attention to Kyaina. "What makes you believe that she'd be a good fit here? The last person who came died within a week. What makes you think she could possibly do any better?"

Died within a week? Shane wiped her hands against her coarse pants, trying to slow her heart rate. She couldn't be like that person. She had to survive.

"She escaped the camp with just a little help." She told him the story. What happened in the mines, how they managed to leave, and their eventual escape. Shane interjected a few details, stuff that Kyaina missed, all the while, keeping her gaze on Wikter. When they got to the part with her being trapped underwater, she noticed his eyes narrow. He noticed that Shane was staring at him, so he cleared his throat, his face relaxed. Did he somehow know about Mindalin's visit?

Shane chided herself. Of course, he didn't. She had only told Reece about that.

"Did you really bite the guard's hand?" Wikter asked, not being able to suppress a laugh.

"He had it coming to him. He was in the way of my escape." She could still taste his warm blood in her mouth. It was enough to make her recoil.

Wikter let out a laugh. "I'm sure he did." Then he turned his attention to his daughter. "I have to say, Kyaina, you were right. She has the potential to be an assassin."

Shane's shoulders sagged. She wasn't sure she heard him correctly, but the words kept echoing around in her mind.

She had the potential to be an assassin.

Relief washed over her, followed by immediate guilt for the feeling. Why was she happy about becoming an assassin?

"Really?" Kyaina asked, beaming. Her whole body had lost its tense look that it had had before, replaced by the same Kyaina that Shane thought she knew for the past month.

Wikter held his hand out once again as he stood from his desk. "Welcome to the assassins," he said. Shane leaned forward to shake it once again. As soon as her hand made contact though she knew she'd been tricked, but it was too late. Wikter clamped his hand around hers, yanking her forward and slamming her into the desk. Papers went flying everywhere. A knife appeared in Wikter's free hand, and in an instant it was thrust downward toward Shane's terrified face.

Without thinking, Shane yanked herself to the side, the knife impaling deeply into the desk exactly where her face used to be. In the moment of his distraction to extract the knife from the desktop, Shane twisted and freed her arm. Without thinking, she dove for the knife, using her momentum to yank it free. She held it steady inches away from Wikter's neck, her mouth straight in a tense line, what just happened still processing in her mind.

"You just tried to kill me," Shane fumed.

"Yes. I certainly did not expect that from you." Wikter wasn't fazed at all by the knife at the bottom of his neck. "But like you said earlier, looks can be misleading." He reached out with his index finger and moved the dagger from his throat.

"Was this some kind of test?" Shane blushed, dropping the blade on the desk.

"Yes, and I must say, you passed with flying colors." Wikter noticed the frown on Shane's face and laughed. "You didn't expect to be accepted without first being tested, did you?"

"No, but I didn't realize that it would include someone trying to kill me." She paused, trying to collect herself. "Seems a little excessive."

"This job is hazardous. If you don't like danger, then I'm afraid you're in the wrong place." He motioned for Kyaina, who had been extremely silent for the last couple minutes, to come forward. "Take her to Elias. It's been a while since he's had a partner."

"Elias?" Shane almost laughed. She had to make sure that she heard the name correctly. "The person who wants me dead?"

"He technically never said anything like that," Kyaina mumbled to herself, giving Shane a warning glare.

"He might as well have." Shane returned her attention to Wikter. "Please, I'm begging you. Pair me up with anyone else.

Just not him."

"I've already made my decision. He's about your age, and he could use someone he can trust."

Shane snorted. Like that was ever going to happen.

"You can leave now." Wikter whisked them off with a wave of a hand, and before Shane could argue further, Kyaina tugged at her shirt and led her toward the door.

"You should be glad my father didn't eviscerate you there," Kyaina said after closing the door quietly behind her. "Nobody argues with him."

"Lucky me." Shane rolled her eyes. "I don't see why he made me partner with Elias."

"I can." They started walking toward the area that housed most of the people in the underground. "You guys have nearly the exact same personality."

"Great. Just another thing to change about myself," Shane mumbled under her breath. She cleared her throat and said a little louder, "Where are you taking me, exactly?"

"To Elias' room, like my father told me to."

"Do I have a room?"

"Yeah. It's conjoined with your partner's."

"Yay. Anything else that I have to share with him?" Shane rolled her eyes. Kyaina saw it and couldn't help but smile. "Why are you laughing at me?"

"I'm not." They stopped next to a door like any other in the hallway, and she knocked. "But I will enjoy watching this."

"You're evil, you know that?"

There was a stirring behind the door and a voice pierced through the wood. "Come in," Elias said, making Shane's stomach do flips. Before she could protest, Kyaina pushed the door open. Elias was sitting at his desk at the far end of the room.

"Oh, it's you," he said, acknowledging Kyaina. "I was expecting—" He saw Shane.

"Elias, meet your new partner."

The quill in his hand fell to the desktop, his mouth agape. "You're kidding, right? This is some kind of sick joke?"

"No. My father told me to bring her here." Kyaina couldn't suppress a smile. "He specifically said that she was going to be your partner, Elias."

"Well, you can take her with you when you leave. I'm not taking her."

"I'm no more excited than you are," Shane grumbled, but Elias completely ignored her.

"Yes, you are, Elias, like it or not," Kyaina said.

"No, I'm not." He got up from his cluttered desk chair and started walking toward them. "When you leave, you can go remind Wikter that I work alone."

"He already knows that. That's why he assigned Shane to you." Kyaina winced, rubbing her left arm. "Archer's being impatient, so I have to go." She looked over at Shane as she walked out the door. "Good luck," she murmured before closing it behind her.

Elias rolled his eyes. "I'm sure that you're nice, and all, but I don't do this whole partner thing, *Shay*, so if you could just leave too, that would be great."

"My name is Shane, and I'm not leaving." She looked around the room, surprised by how comfortable it looked, despite it being a mess. There was a sitting area off to her left, so she decided to go over and plop down on the couch.

"Don't sit there," Elias said, glaring down at her.

"Why not?"

"Because it's my stuff."

Shane laughed. "I didn't know that you were such a child."

"And I didn't know you had to be so rude to sit on my couch without even asking, *Shay.*"

"Well, I'm sorry," Shane started, getting up from the couch, "but I have nowhere else to go *Eli.*"

Something flashed in Elias' eyes, and he took a small, nearly unnoticeable step back. But it quickly passed. "Did you come up with that name all on your own?" He asked dryly, making her cheeks flush with color. "Because if you did, let me tell you how unique that truly was."

"You're insufferable, you know that."

"Yes, actually, I do." A smile stretched across his lips. "People tell me that all the time. It's one of my most prominent features."

Shane raised her eyebrows, blinking. "Look, I know that you wanted to get rid of me when you saw me in the group of prisoners heading toward camp, and I know that your feelings toward me haven't changed the slightest bit. But you heard what Kyaina said. We're partners, whether you like it or not. Trust me when I say that I hate it just as much as you do."

"No, we aren't." He turned around and returned to his desk, taking a seat and leaning back in his chair so he could still keep an eye on Shane. "Both people have to agree if you want a partnership, and I don't agree. I'll talk to Wikter tomorrow and see if he can fix this."

"And if he can't? Or won't?"

"That's not going to happen."

Shane's jaw clenched. "You owe me."

"For what, exactly?"

"For not telling Eikaman in the colonies where you went."

Elias laughed. "You actually listened to me when I told you not to tell him what you saw?"

Shane didn't answer. "I never would've been at that damn camp if it hadn't been for you."

"I'm confused?" Elias said, smiling. "How did not telling Eikaman what you saw result in you getting arrested?"

"It's complicated."

"Well, if you hadn't gotten yourself arrested, you never would've been thrown in that camp. I don't see why you're blaming it on me."

Shane flinched, tears threatening to leak from her eyes. With what he was saying came another guilt, once again reminded that Reece's death was her fault. She never would've died if Shane hadn't gotten them arrested.

"Where am I supposed to sleep for the night?" Shane asked suddenly, fighting past the sorrow she was feeling. She had to get out of the room. She wasn't going to allow Elias to see her in such a vulnerable state. "You've already made it quite clear that you don't want me contaminating all your stuff."

Elias let out a forced sigh. "Come with me," he said, walking over to a door on the left-hand wall.

He opened it, revealing a short hallway with another door on the other end. Elias motioned forward for her to go first. She opened the second door, which brought her to a room that was a duplicate of Elias', except the layout was reversed. Instead of the sitting area being on the left, it was on the right, and the four-post bed lay against the right wall with a grandfather clock sitting next to it. The desk sat at the far end of the room. It was just as trashed as Elias'.

"Is this my room?"

"It would be." Elias laughed. "If you were my partner."

"Explains why there's this mess." Shane picked up a shirt and threw it toward Elias. "Let me guess, since you haven't had a partner in gods knows how long, you think of this room as your own?"

"Yes, actually. You're correct." He tossed the shirt into his room. "And I've never had a partner. And I never will. I prefer to do things alone."

"Sure, you do."

Elias rolled his eyes, rubbing his hands against his temples. "Just try not to touch anything, okay? I'll have it fixed by tomorrow and hopefully we will never see each other again."

Shane didn't say anything as Elias left, closing the door gently behind him. As soon as it was shut, she fell apart.

PART 2

CHAPTER 12

" **Y**ou're holding your sword all wrong."
Clang.

The two swords met midair. Shane lost the grip on the hilt, and it fell from her hands. Eli kicked her to the ground with the ball of his foot and pressed his blade into her neck, drawing the slightest bit of blood.

"If this were a real fight," he said as he wiped the tiniest bit of sweat from his forehead, "You would be dead by now."

"Then it's a good thing it's not." Shane crawled on all fours to her sword, gripping the hilt in her hand before getting up with tremendous effort. Everything hurt. They had been in the practice room for what seemed like hours, and Eli hadn't gone easy on her. Repeatedly she would be forced down to the ground with Eli standing over her, sword pointed at her heart or neck. He hadn't given her any instructions on the basics, like how to hold a sword, instead choosing to make a fool out of her. And he seemed to be enjoying it.

Eli had woken Shane up early that morning by knocking on her door. He didn't mention what he was up to, so Shane guessed that his talk with Wikter hadn't gone well. Instead, he thrusted a sword into Shane's hands and led her down to the practice room without another word.

"Let's do it again," Eli said, flipping the sword expertly around in his hand. "Except this time, don't suck."

"That's pretty hard to do when you have no idea what you're doing," Shane mumbled under her breath. Her eyes widened when Eli swung his sword down on her, giving her barely enough time to raise her own to defend herself.

"Hey, that isn't fair." Her feet remained steady on the ground as Eli circled around her. "Usually, you give me at least a warning before you attack like that."

"A real fight isn't fair, now is it, Shay?" Eli got down low and hooked Shane's feet with his own. Her body hit the ground with a giant thud, knocking the breath out of her. "You're being flat on your feet," he said, offering a hand to help her up, but she hit it away. She wasn't going to be embarrassed even more by not being able to get up on her own.

"If you hadn't noticed, I have absolutely no idea what I'm doing and am too focused on trying to survive at this point, so you telling me that I'm flat on my feet but not giving me *any* pointers on how to actually hold my own in a fight really isn't helping."

Eli rolled his eyes, putting his sword back in his sheath. "I honestly have no idea how you passed Wikter's test," he said, walking toward her and yanking her own sword out of her hands.

"Neither do I, but here I am." Shane managed to smile.

"For the last hour," Eli started, bringing his hands together on the hilt, "you've been holding the sword like this, which is wrong on multiple levels." He extended the distance between his hands so that one was on right next to the pommel, and the other against the cross-guard. "This is how you're supposed to hold it." He swung the sword horizontally to prove his point. "Here you have much better control of it, and you won't drop it when I hit it with some force."

"So, you're telling me that I'm not holding it correctly?" Shane said sarcastically as she grabbed the hilt from him. "Why didn't you say so before?"

"Haha. You're so funny." Eli removed his blade from its sheath with a *shink*. "Again."

He attacked at once. Shane brought her sword up to defend. The two blades met with a *clang*, sending vibrations down to the handle. Unlike before, it didn't fall from her hands. She pushed Eli off her, surprised by how easy it was in comparison to what she was doing before.

"Congratulations," Eli said, a smirk rising on his face. "You've successfully blocked one of the simplest blows. You must be so proud of yourself."

Shane stuck her tongue out at him. Once again, their swords met. Shane bounced on the balls of her feet, keeping them a shoulder's width apart. She was glad for perhaps the first time in her life that she had participated in so many sports. One thing that went interchangeably between them was the athletic stance. Nearly every coach drilled it into her mind.

They exchanged a few parries and blows back and forth before Eli was able to disarm her, sending her sword flying across the room and *clanging* off a wall. Sweat dripped down Shane's forehead. Her breaths came ragged and unsteady, but she couldn't keep a smile from spreading across her face. She was never so proud to be beaten.

"Don't be so happy with yourself," Eli said, putting his sword in the sheath once again. "I was going easy on you."

"Sure, you were," she said, retrieving her own sword.

Shane believed him, but that still didn't mean she wasn't proud of what she had done. She remembered when she was younger, and she and her brother Corbin would pretend that sticks were swords. He would always beat her, hitting her in the hands to bruise them. If only he could see her now.

See her becoming an assassin.

The smile faded away from her face as she followed Eli over toward the wall to where the water was. She took a sip from her flask and sat down on the bench that ran along the wall. Eli had only allowed two water breaks before, and they never lasted long. As soon as she sat down, Eli scowled at her.

"Get up," he said.

Shane groaned but followed his directions. Her gaze landed on something gleaming in Eli's bag.

"What's in there?" She asked, pointing toward it.

"Huh?" Eli whirled around, his eyes landing on what Shane was looking at. "Oh, those are knives." He walked over and took them out of the bag. "Much more difficult than swords, but just as lethal."

"Can I try them?"

Eli laughed. "If you want to, but let me warn you that it takes years of practice to master using them."

Shane set her sword down on the bench and grabbed the knives, surprised by how perfectly they fit in her hand. They resembled nothing fancy, just a sharp double-edged blade with an ordinary leather hilt at the bottom, yet Shane couldn't shake the feeling that she should try them.

"Come on," Eli said. "The break's over."

"Yeah, I know." She palmed the knives and started toward the fighting ring.

Once in the middle of the room, Eli started circling around her, sword at the ready, but she was prepared. She kept her eyes fixed on his sword, watching the way it remained steady in front of him. She saw his fingers clench tightly around the hilt and Shane knew that he was about to strike. Her eyes narrowed as she stepped out of the way of his stab, knocking down the blade with the two knives in her hand. She allowed his momentum to carry him forward, turning with him as it happened.

"Where'd you learn to do that?" He laughed after he regained his balance. "It's almost as if you knew what you were doing."

"Who's to say I don't?" Shane lied.

"You said it. If I recall correctly, it went something like, 'I have absolutely no idea what I'm doing.' Or was that someone else?"

Shane smirked. "That was with the sword."

"Oh, I'm sorry." Eli smiled. "Here I was thinking you meant with any weapon."

They started sparring, the area around them filled with swinging and colliding blades. Shane didn't know how, but she knew exactly what to do with every swing Eli threw at her. That was until she got tired. Her movements became sluggish, and it wasn't long until she was down on the ground, disarmed, with Eli pointing his blade toward her face.

"You tire easily," he said, not bothering to offer a hand to help her up.

"I'm sorry. How 'bout you try being in a labor camp for over four months, barely being fed and nearly starving to death."

"All I'm hearing are excuses."

Shane rolled her eyes. She got up off the ground and brushed sweat from her forehead.

"Ready?" Eli asked, hands tensing on the hilt of his sword. "Or are you too sick and tired of having your ass handed to you."

Shane's jaw clenched as she loosened her shoulders. "Bring it on."

But the next round lasted less than a minute. Nearly every instinct in Shane had worn out, being replaced by an empty hole of once again having no idea what to do. Next thing she knew Eli slammed her wrists with the flat of his sword. Her daggers flew from her hands.

"You would've lost your hands right there."

"Yeah, I know. Thanks." She snatched the blades from the ground, ignoring the stinging in her hands as she grasped the hilt.

When Shane got ready to fight once again, Eli only shrugged her off. "We're done for today, unless you want to be bruised up even more than you already are." He sheathed his sword and started for the back wall.

Shane loosened her shoulders, letting out a sigh. By the time she picked up the sword and her water flask, Eli had already grabbed his bag and left, not bothering to escort Shane up to their rooms. Not that she cared. She was fine walking up to her room alone. Nobody to bother her. Nobody to distract her from her own thoughts.

Except those thoughts would only bring back painful memories. Of the mines. Of her family. Of Reece.

The night before Shane had the worst nightmare. All the details left her the moment she opened her eyes besides one. Fritz had been there, in her dreams. His cruel smile filled Shane's mind whenever she closed her eyes, along with his wicked face. She might not physically be at the camps but mentally she still was.

Shane forced those thoughts to the back of her mind as she started up the spiral staircase to her room, her sore and tired legs protesting every step. Soon, she found herself in front of Eli's conjoining room.

Her room.

She twisted the doorknob and entered. The fire had gone out, and a chill had taken over the room. Restarting the fire was a welcome distraction for her. She carefully took her time splitting the logs with a small hatchet into kindling before lighting it, feeding it new pieces of wood until at last there was a blazing fire before her. Anything to keep her mind occupied.

She sighed, sitting on the couch. Her couch. Even though Eli didn't talk about having a conversation with Wikter, Shane knew he had. When he had knocked on her door— the main door, not the one connecting their rooms— that morning, he was distracted and irritated. He didn't mention anything about her leaving, so Shane had assumed that Wikter hadn't made a mistake pairing them together, no matter how much she wished he had.

Shane closed her eyes for just a second, and images of the camp came rushing back to her. She had barely slept the night before. It had been the first time dreams came to her.

She looked at her shoulder where Eli's sword had cut a giant hole into her black sleeve, splattered with blood. She hadn't even realized she had been cut. It wasn't deep enough to bother dealing with it, but she got up to put some water on it, cleaning out the wound in case of infection. With that also came relief. The cut stitched itself together right in front of Shane's eyes, making it appear to be at least a day old, not a couple minutes.

A low, humorless laugh escaped her lips as she returned to her couch. She leaned back and relaxed. If only her from a year ago could see her now. Back then, the worst pain she had ever felt was that of a broken nose playing basketball. Her hand went up to it. It had only somewhat healed from when it was broken in the mine. Her finger caught on a lump, and she sighed, the smile fading from her face.

Shane was about to get up when her eyes landed on one of Eli's shirts strewn across the couch. Her face contorted in disgust. The very least Eli could do was make sure that her room was clean of any of his stuff, but no. He had to throw all his dirty clothes and other crap into it.

She threw the shirt toward the connecting door. If she wanted the room to feel like a home, she had to make it her own.

"You didn't really hit me as the cleaning type person," someone said. Shane looked up, not surprised to see Kyaina leaning against the door frame.

"I'm not, but all this stuff is annoying me." Shane motioned around her to all of Eli's junk that he kept stored in her room. "He thinks that he can just throw his stuff everywhere and someone else will deal with the mess."

"That he does." Kyaina pushed herself off the doorframe and started helping Shane. "I'm gonna be honest," she said, throwing one of his shirts toward the pile. "You look a little rough."

"That's because Eli has been beating my ass all morning with the sword." Shane clenched her jaw just thinking about it. "I mean, he could've at least told me how to hold it before absolutely destroying me."

"Is that how you got that giant gash?" Kyaina pointed to her shoulder. "It's healed up nicely."

"It looks worse than it actually is."

"I'm sure Eli thought that." Kyaina laughed, putting a rolled up piece of paper into the trash can next to Shane's desk. "Let me guess, he just pushed you harder."

Shane snorted. "You could say that. He's honestly insufferable."

Kyaina only smiled, and Shane took notice. "What?"

"Nothing," she said, trying to hide it. "It's just funny to see Eli have a partner. For nearly as long as I've known him, he's acted alone."

"I wish it was still that way." Shane threw the last pair of pants on the pile before shoving it into the hallway connecting their two rooms. "I mean, what was your father thinking, pairing the two of us together?"

"I have no idea why he makes most of his decisions." Kyaina sighed, slumping down in the chair. "Every time I think I understand something, he just does the exact opposite of what I expected him to. It's honestly so annoying, not knowing your parent."

"Don't you have a mother? Why don't you go live with her?"

"Because she died during childbirth," Kyaina said, fiddling with her thumbs. "I didn't really get a chance to know her, if you know what I mean." She tried for a smile, but Shane could see right through it.

"Both my parents have no idea where I am." Talking about them brought tears to her eyes, but she pushed them back. She had to tell someone, even if it brought up some memories that she would prefer to remain hidden. "They probably think I'm dead, which is probably for the best."

"Have you ever thought about going back home?" Kyaina asked.

"All the freaking time." A numbness came over her body as she held back her tears. "But it isn't that easy. I highly doubt that they could even look at me, knowing what I did. Or what I'm going to do."

"I don't have that problem." Kyaina laughed dryly.

"Count yourself as lucky." Shane watched as a burning log broke, sending sparks flying up into the air. She wiped the tears from her eyes, clearing her throat. "Why'd you come here? Cause I doubt that it was to hear my sob story."

Kyaina smiled. "Gods, do I need an excuse to see my friend?"

"You consider me your friend? How touching."

"That, and I came to see how you were adjusting."

Shane let out a chuckle. "Honestly, life here's much better than in that godsforsaken camp. And the king's dungeon." Shane's smile wavered as her memories of what happened in that cell came back to her, but she suppressed them.

"Do you need help finding stuff or anything? Because believe it or not, I know this place pretty well."

"Actually," Shane said, a thought popping into her mind, "you can. Does this place have a library?"

CHAPTER 13

S hane walked down the passageways in her hand-me-down cloak that Kyaina had given her shortly after arriving in the Underground. She looked at the directions that Kyaina had written for her on a scrap piece of paper to lead her to the library. It had been a week since they had last talked. Training had taken up most of Shane's days, and when she wasn't in the practice room with Eli, she was trying to soothe her sore muscles. She couldn't even think about taking some time to herself.

Following the map to a small hallway, she was directed to a door bigger and more elegant than all the others she had seen in the Assassin's Underground. She stuffed the paper into her pocket and pushed open the door and walked into the room. As the massive door closed behind her, she gasped at the enormity of the library.

Even though she had never been into books, something about being surrounded by hundreds of thousands of books was awe inspiring. Shelves upon shelves lined the walls all the way to the ceiling. Lanterns hung every few aisles giving the room a nice, calming aesthetic. It was like something she had only seen in movies.

She took a deep breath and headed toward one of the many aisles making up the library. She passed a group of people sitting at a table with stacks of books in front of them. She had some idea of what she was looking for, but that went completely out the window when she saw the massive amount of books. It was overwhelming. Shane wished there was a librarian to help her sort through everything.

History books. That's what she needed. She was sick and tired of being ignorant of the world she was stuck in.

She traipsed through one of the non-fiction aisles, hand brushing past the different sized volumes before her finger got caught on one with a larger spine. She stopped and took it out of the shelf without even looking at the title.

She made it to the title page and read, *The History of Lyconnexal's Rulers.* It wasn't exactly what she wanted, but she took it with her anyway and continued down the aisle. She continued scanning for anything that would catch her attention. After only a few minutes, her arms were full of books she hoped would tell her the history of the land.

She started toward the tables when her eyes caught on someone sitting on the floor of an aisle with an open book in his lap. She was about to walk past when he looked up, his brown eyes piercing into her.

"Eli?" she asked, trying but failing to hide a laugh.

"What?" he asked. His face flushed with bright red colors. Before Shane could read the title of the book he was reading, he hid it behind his back.

"I didn't expect to see you here."

Eli cleared his throat. "I was just reading up on my next target."

"Sure, you were." Shane raised her eyebrows as she peered at the plaque at the end of the shelves. "In the fiction section?"

"I decided to sit down here." Before Shane could say anything, he added, "My room's too drafty, and the people sitting down at the tables up front are annoying."

"Of course, they are." Shane couldn't suppress a sly smile. "Why'd you choose the fantasy section? Isn't it easier to stay where you got the book?"

"There's more light here." He got up from the floor. "I'm honestly surprised to see you in the library. I didn't know a peasant like you could read."

Shane bit her tongue. "I guess that looks can be deceiving," she suggested. "For all you know I could have come from a wealthy merchant family."

"Oh, you're right." He bowed low, a mischievous grin on his face. "I'm sorry, princess. That I made assumptions, I mean."

Shane rolled her eyes. Her brother was exactly like Eli, making snide remarks to get her to react. She knew, in theory, that it was best to just ignore him, take the high road, but where was the fun in that.

"If I were the princess, I would be thirty-six years old, and dead. Last time I checked, I'm none of those," Shane said. "If I'm not mistaken, I would've died fifteen years ago today exactly."

"I never said that you were Princess Airel. Just a princess, probably to Ginacallo, given your brutish appearance." He went around her, her mouth agape. "If you'll excuse me, now that you've disturbed my reading place I'll be heading back to my room."

Brutish appearance?

Shane had been called many things, but never anything like that. It was enough to make her laugh. Sure, the scar she had on her face might make her less attractive, but definitely not brutish.

Shane started toward the exit, completely ignoring an open table and left the library. She continued to her room distracted by what Eli said, surprised when she found herself at her door. She let herself in and plopped down cross-legged on her bed with the books piled high on her desk.

She looked down at her hands, calloused and blistered from her time at the camp. Was this what Eli meant by brutish appearance? A sigh escaped her as she glared over at the door connecting her room to Eli's. Why did he get to her so much? What gave him the right?

But she already knew the answer to that stupid question. She gave him the right when she confronted him in the same snarky way he did. The only real difference between the two of them was that Eli didn't allow Shane's comments to get to him, or at least he didn't show that he did.

Shane got up from the bed, refusing to allow his remarks to ruin her day. She sat wearily at the desk. She couldn't help but swear at Eli for training her so hard. From the other pairs she had seen sparring over the last couple of weeks, none of them had been at it as hard as she and Eli were. She hadn't complained, of course. She couldn't show him how weak she was. She couldn't break in front of him. But she felt like she was breaking. Inside.

She picked up the nearest book and placed it gently on the nook above her desk, afraid that if she acted too carelessly with it, the spine would split. It was already well used, well read. She continued doing that until there was only one book left on the desk, and when she picked it up a crumpled paper came fluttering down from underneath. She picked it up and read the handwritten words on it.

Meet me at my room when you can

-Kyaina

Shane threw the crumpled paper into the trash. Of course, Kyaina had been in her room.

So much for my relaxing day, she thought as she got up. She didn't want to see what would happen if she ignored Kyaina's request.

Shane had never been to Kyaina's room before, but she had a hunch as to where it was. As soon as she stepped into the passage, she gazed in the direction that Kyaina walked every time she had seen her. But, she didn't have to guess which door was Kyaina's though. When she started down the hallway, she caught sight of Kyaina's wavy brown hair farther up the passage.

"Kyaina!" she yelled as she chased after her with a grimace on her face. "Wait up."

Kyaina turned and slowed down a bit for Shane to catch up. "You got my note, I presume?" she asked when Shane was beside her.

"Did you really have to hide it on my desk? Wouldn't it have been easier to just knock on my door or something?"

"It would've, but I didn't know when you were getting back." They stopped at a door and Kyaina opened it. "Besides," she said as she plopped herself down on the couch. "It wasn't hidden in your desk. It was right on top."

"I set my books down before I saw it."

Kyaina sighed. "I don't see the point in reading."

"Neither do I, but I have to try new things," Shane lied. "Even though I don't have much free time."

"How are you enjoying having a day off of training with Elias?" Kyaina joked. She smiled, and Shane wanted to wipe it off her smug little face.

"He's the absolute worst."

"You'd better get used to him because he's coming over later."

Shane's knees almost gave out. "He's what?" she asked after she was able to regain her breath. "Why?"

"Because he's friends with Archer, and believe it or not, Archer's my partner and we get along, unlike *some people I know.*"

"Hey, that's not fair. I didn't want to be partners with *him.* Your father just paired us together with no rhyme or reason."

"Oh, trust me. He had a reason, even if it doesn't seem sane." Kyaina let out a sigh, a faraway look in her eyes. "He's always scheming. Always one step ahead of his enemies, which is pretty much everyone. By Haytorrow's Realm, he probably sees me as a threat to the assassin's kingdom." Kyaina cleared her throat and returned her gaze to Shane. "You should at least give Eli a chance. He's been through things just as bad as you have."

Just then the door flung open, and Archer stepped through, his arms full of glasses, as well as a bottle of what appeared to be wine. "Where do you want me to put this? Hey Shane."

Shane waved a hand in acknowledgment. *Unlike someone she knew*, Archer had acted much more friendly to her when she started training as an assassin and passed Wikter's test.

"The table's fine." Kyaina motioned for Shane to help clear off the top, which was crowded with different kinds of deadly weapons.

"Didn't know we were having a party," she whispered as she laid a sharp knife next to Kyaina's bed.

"It isn't a party. It's just four people hanging out." Kyaina helped Archer with the glasses. "Besides, how can we not when fifteen years ago princess Airel died."

"Doesn't it seem a bit morbid to have a holiday and celebrate this? I mean, shouldn't we pay our respects or something?"

"That would make sense, but the people of Lyconnexal deal with death with a celebration for their life."

"Then why do we do it fifteen years later?"

"Do you not know any history?" Kyaina laughed.

No, Shane thought. *Not the history here. Not yet at least.*

"I came to Lyconnexal a couple months ago from a faraway continent." A lie with a bit of truth tied in.

Kyaina rolled her eyes. "Could tell that by the accent. The short answer to your question is that the people of Lyconnexal were, for lack of a better term, obsessed with her. She was Mindalin's Chosen Hero, and the people thought that she was going to save them from the war that had been going on for nearly ten years before her death, but then she died, and we had to deal with the war by ourselves." Even though she did well to hide it, Shane could still notice the bitterness in her voice.

"Do you not like her or something?"

"I like her, but not as much as *some people*." She motioned toward Archer with her eyebrows.

"I heard that."

"You were supposed to." Kyaina sighed. "She isn't the only person in the Manderly bloodline. In my opinion my cousin's a bit overrated."

Shane nearly choked on her own saliva. "She's your cousin?" she asked in awe. "Then that means—"

"I'm related to the king." Kyaina looked like something rotten had crawled up her nose. "My father's his brother, but don't tell him I told you. He hates King Aarion as much as anyone else."

Archer snorted. "I hardly doubt that."

"You know what I mean," Kyaina said. "It also doesn't help that Airel used to be friends with Fritz."

Shane nearly choked. "What?" Hearing his name spoken by another human being brought terror coursing through her veins. Her heart beat faster than it ever had, and her hands suddenly became very clammy.

"It was before he got control of the Verscar from his father. Apparently Airel tried to convince him not to inherit it, to shut it down, and it worked for a while. Fritz started his own business, but he went bankrupt after Airel died and he was forced to go back to his father."

"Here I was thinking he was always evil." Shane tried to laugh, but she was shaken. Even thinking about him made her want to curl into a ball and hide.

"Oh, he was, but Airel somehow managed to rein in that part of him."

Something moved outside the door and Kyaina got up to go to the door. "Elias," she said, making Shane cringe, but it brought her attention away from Fritz. "Come inside."

Shane kept her eyes toward the floor, refusing to even acknowledge that Eli walked in. He walked right past her without any kind of greeting.

"Archer." he grabbed his forearm and brought him in for a friendly slap on the back. "How've you been?"

"Are they always like this?" Shane whispered as she walked over toward her friend.

"Every single time they meet up."

"And how often is that?"

"Multiple times a week. It gets rather annoying."

Shane laughed. Kyaina approached the boys, and Shane begrudgingly followed, wondering why Kyaina invited her if Eli was coming too. But that question was stupid, just like every other thought she had. Of course, she would want to push them together. They were partners after all, even if neither of them liked that idea.

"I see you managed not to get lost on your way here," Eli said to Shane.

"I've only been lost once, and that was before I knew the layout of this place." Shane's cheeks flushed with color. Of course, he would try and embarrass her here. Why wouldn't he, being the complete jerk that he was?

"I still don't see how you managed to do it. There are only two main hallways on this level, and even less below us." Eli laughed. "Talk about having no sense of direction."

"Don't you usually wait a month before making fun of the newbies?" Archer asked. "Give them time to adjust?"

"Usually, but that was before Wikter paired me with Shay." Shane's jaw clenched. "I work alone. Always have, always will."

"Must get lonely."

"I like the silence that disappeared the moment that Wikter made you my 'partner.' Ever since then it's like a small, annoying animal has been chattering right in my ear."

"Are you sure that isn't the voice inside your head, 'cause I can only imagine how annoying that would be to listen to it twenty-four-seven."

"No. Your voice overrides it, which I didn't think was possible."

It took every bit of will inside Shane to remain calm and keep from slapping Eli.

"Are you guys done bickering, or can I interest you in a drink," Kyaina cut in.

"Sure," Shane said, feeling her rage diminish just a bit, bringing her attention away from Eli. She grabbed the glass from Kyaina, sniffing it before taking the slightest sip. Her parents had allowed her to try some wine from their glasses from time to time, so she wasn't surprised when it had the same sweet taste she was familiar with, followed closely by a bitterness.

"I think that this day requires a toast," Kyaina said, holding her wine glass high in the air. "To my cousin, and her morbid death."

CHAPTER 14

S hane leaned back against the hardback of her chair and let out a huge sigh. Rubbing her eyes, she closed the book in front of her before placing it back on the nook and grabbing another. So many names and dates swirled together in her head that it was hard to keep them straight. As she turned the cover of the next book, she was sure it would only add to the confusion.

It wasn't that she didn't enjoy learning about the history of Lyconnexal, she did. She had never enjoyed reading in her own world but here she found it to be quite enjoyable. Maybe it was for the lack of TV or internet?

Her mom had been a history teacher. She would always bore Shane and her siblings with "fun facts." She was part of the reason that Shane didn't take a liking to the subject. Here it was all different. History read like something straight out of fiction, with the magic and the gods' Chosen Heroes.

According to a book of gods she'd read, there were a total of six supreme beings, three gods and three goddesses. There was Haytorrow, the god of death, Erasol, the god of the earth, and Feuerbrand, god of fire. Then there was Mindalin, goddess of the sea, Vagen, goddess of nature, and Shiesel, goddess of the air.

Each god and goddess were the 'Patron" of the five different countries, excluding Haytorrow. Mindalin had Lyconnexal,

Vagen had Bulipocs, Shiesel had Celiap, Feurbrand had Iapciz, and Erasol had Ginnacallo. Occasionally, they each picked a Chosen Hero from their Patron country.

Haytorrow was different though. He'd gotten the short end of the stick, being left with the dead in his own realm. The upper Realm was where the good, noble people went, and the Fallen Realm was where the horrible people were sent to suffer for eternity. The worst people, though, had a place reserved for them at the bottom of his Fallen Realm. They became what was known as Geistlucks.

The first, and last, person to be Haytorrow's Chosen Hero was a king named Zaltak. He led the dirtiest life and became the first Geistluck.

Then Shane read the title of the book in her hands.

The History of Lyconnexal's Rulers.

The first book she picked up from the library, and the last one she was going to finish. In the two weeks since she first visited the library, she had already finished most of the giant stack of books she brought with her.

She turned the pages, absorbing every word on them. She was many pages into the book when she came to the heading that read *Aarion* across the top in fancy letters.

King Aarion was one of the most beloved members of the royal family, overshadowed only by his daughter, Airel.

Shane let out a wicked laugh. Aarion? Being people's favorite ruler? It seemed like it was something out of fiction, but she kept reading.

However, after Princess Airel died, that all changed. She was only twenty-one when death took her, ending the never-ending war with Ginacallo while doing so. The whole country went into mourning, but Aarion took it the worst. He, along with Princess Airel's husband, Lethick, had been on the island where her death had occurred, and afterward his whole life

seemed to go downhill. After King Aarion lost his wife to a flu and his son left him, he become sadistic, enjoying other's pain.

With no one to receive the throne after his death, he had to choose someone outside the royal family for the first time in centuries to rule after him. A well-known thief named Vito Bourne, infamous for his heists and his bloodthirsty violence, became the new heir to the throne, much to the people's dismay.

A knock came from the hallway door, making her slam the book closed right before she could turn the page.

"I've been waiting forever," Eli said, his voice being garbled by the door. "I told you to be ready at seven."

Shane blinked and rubbed the sleep away from her eyes. Had she really been up all night, forcing herself to read through dozens of books? She must have because when she looked at the clock. it showed that it was already seven ten.

Shane groaned. Why had she not slept?

She knew exactly why, but she didn't want to face it. The dreams that haunted her during the night were still with her in her waking hours. Every time she closed her eyes images of Verscar, or Reece's dead body lying in her arms filled her mind. Usually, she'd be able to visit Kyaina and Archer when they got bad, but they were gone on another assassination.

"I'll be out in a minute," she yelled, trying to distract herself. She went to her dresser full of Kyaina's hand-me-down training clothes. She hadn't yet gotten a chance, nor did she have the money, to go above ground and buy her own things.

"I'm waiting."

"Shut up." She grabbed a shirt and pants out of a drawer and quickly changed. She put on her shoes as she hopped over toward the door and grabbed her knives from a small hanging rack next to the door.

"Gods." Eli laughed, looking Shane up and down as she stepped out into the passage. "You look like you just woke up."

Shane sneered at him as she pulled her dirty blonde hair back.

"Or don't talk to me," he added. "I'm fine with that too. It gives me a break from your voice."

"Haha," Shane said. "You're so funny."

"I know. I'm told that every day." They arrived at the main area and started down the stairs. Shane fidgeted with her knives, palming them in her hands. Eli let out a humorless chuckle.

"What?"

"You don't need those today. I told you that yesterday, so I have no idea why you brought them."

Shane blushed. "Maybe so I could stab you if you start annoying me."

"I would honestly like to see you try." Eli rolled up his right sleeve, revealing small, throwing knives concealed against his arm. "It's been years since there's been a death here, but if you try to attack me, I'm afraid that that will change."

Instead of going to the normal training room, they passed it and continued down the passage for quite a distance before stopping at a door on the side of the corridor.

"Why do I feel like you only brought me here to kill me?" Shane asked, looking around and seeing no one.

"That's a possibility." He opened the door and allowed Shane to go first. "I'm still trying to make up my mind."

The room was nearly identical to the one they usually trained in, except instead of benches on the far wall, there were dark targets, torn and broken. Shane gulped when she saw a replica of a human with jagged cuts across its stomach.

"Lovely." Shane set everything in her hands down on a bench near the door and turned to Eli. "What are we doing here?"

"What does it look like we're doing?"

"I don't have throwing knives, or a gun or bow." Shane eyed the targets at the other end of the room and wondered whether Eli was going to make her stand there as he threw the knives at her.

"I have some." He grabbed another set of sheathed throwing knives out of his bag and tossed them over to Shane. There were four in total. "We'll move on to guns later."

The knives were heavier than Shane expected. Taking one out and messing with it, she found it fit almost perfectly in her hand. The curve of the handle made it easy to hold, and presumably easy to throw.

"What are you waiting for?" Eli asked. He leaned against the wall and unsuccessfully hid a smirk.

"Oh, I don't know, maybe some instructions." Shane looked down at the targets, eyes narrowing. "But let me guess, you're not going to give me any until I try, and I make a complete fool out of myself."

"You're already catching on."

Shane rolled her eyes. "You're insufferable, you know that?"

"You told me that already."

Shane turned her attention to the array of targets at the other end of the room. She shifted uneasily on her feet before awkwardly chucking the knife toward the target. It left her hand strangely, and it was no surprise when the knife didn't connect anywhere near the target she was aiming for. It bounced off the wall and clattered to the floor.

"If you were aiming for the person behind the target, then congratulations. You successfully managed to give him a big old bruise in the stomach."

"I was actually trying for that."

Shane tried again, except this time, it hit the outer rim of the target, but again, just bounced off. Again she tried, same result. With her final blade, she tried something different. This time, she held it by the tip of the blade, and let it fly at the target. It twirled in the air, finding the outer edge of the target, sticking.

"Did you see that?" She asked. She turned excitedly to Eli.

"You barely nicked his arm, but congratulations." He waited, but Shane did nothing. "What are you waiting for, go get'em and try again."

She imagined Eli chucking at her while she retrieved her knives, but she obliged, keeping an eye on Eli the entire time. He was still leaning against the wall when she returned to the throwing position.

"Are you gonna give me some advice now that I tried, or am I supposed to keep going and learn on my own?"

"I don't see what's wrong with that. Gives me more free time."

"Are you sure you don't just want to watch me mess everything up?" Shane asked, getting into position before chucking the knife once again down the range.

"While that would be fun," Eli admitted, "I have more important things to do instead of being your babysitter."

Babysitter?

"Like what? Read stories?"

Eli remained silent, and Shane grinned. He took aim at the target right next to her and started throwing as well. All the knives hit near the center of the target.

Show off, Shane thought, throwing the knife once again, hitting closer to the center, but bouncing off. She swore as she went down to collect them once again.

"Can you at least tell me what I'm doing wrong?" she asked Eli. He was walking over toward his own target and getting his own set of knives out.

"Watch me and see if you can figure it out." He flipped a knife in the air and caught it before chucking it at the target. Before Shane could even blink, the knife hit the center ring and quivered. He used nearly the exact same form as Shane, the only difference being where his feet were positioned.

"Have a wider stance?"

"Exactly." He threw another knife. It hit in nearly the exact same spot. "And don't face the target straight on."

Shane looked down at her feet, positioning them the way Eli did. It felt awkward at first, but she threw her knife at the target face with surprising ease. It rotated in the air, hitting the outer ring of the bullseye, sticking in perpendicular to the target. Right next to the heart.

Eli raised an eyebrow. "Nice," he said.

Was that a compliment?

"Bet you twenty Schulhers that you can't do that again."

"Is that a challenge?"

"If you can't figure that out on your own, I worry for you." He chucked his last knife, landing in a cluster with the rest of them, right in the middle dot.

They both went down the field to collect their knives. Butterflies appeared in Shane's stomach, but she managed to suppress them. If she missed, she didn't have the money to pay, but she didn't think about that. Eli challenged her, and there was no way in hell she was going to say no. She couldn't back down now.

"You're on," Shane said as she tore the knife out of the dummy's chest.

"You gonna do it anytime soon?" Eli laughed once they made it back.

"I'm going."

Shane took a deep breath to calm her nerves. She made sure that her feet were in the right position before chucking the knife at the target. It left her hand strangely and wasn't going anywhere near where she aimed. It was no surprise when it missed the target completely and clattered to the floor.

"Beginner's luck," Eli said. "I'll expect the money when we make it back to our rooms."

Shane winced for show. "Look, I'm probably the brokest one here. I don't even have a single Schulher, whatever that is."

"Then why'd you accept the challenge?"

"Because I couldn't just decline it. It's not in my nature."

Eli sighed. "Then get down there." He pointed toward the far wall.

"What?" Shane asked, eyes widening. "No way in hell am I going to do that. You'll kill me."

"That's a possibility, true, but since you can't pay me, then the least you can do is be my entertainment." Eli smiled at her, shooing her away.

"You're evil."

"I can name multiple people that are worse than me."

So could Shane, but she preferred not to think about them.

Shane started toward the target, her stomach doing somersaults the entire time. She wiped her sweaty hands on her pants, but that didn't help with the nerves that came with being someone's target. She kept eyeing the target that Eli had thrown his knives at earlier. The gashes in it showed themselves clearly to her, all clustered together. Part of her knew that the chances of him accidentally hitting her were small, but if he intended to…

She shook her head. He wasn't that evil. No matter how much he hated her, he couldn't have gotten that low. But he was an assassin after all. She wondered if her life meant anything to him.

"Ready?" His malicious smile sent shiver's spiraling down Shane's back, but she wasn't going to allow him to see how scared she truly was.

Her jaw clenched, but she managed to fake a smile. "Do your worst."

Eli tossed a knife into the air and caught it by the twirling blade, eyes narrowing. Before Shane could blink, the knife left his hand, flying straight for her. Every instinct in her told her to duck, cover her head and curl into a ball, but she forced herself to remain still as it collided with the target right behind her, catching her sleeve, and a throbbing pain appeared on the outer edge of her arm.

"You just hit me," she exclaimed, tearing her shirt away from the wall. Her hand went over toward her arm, coming away stained in blood. He had truly hit her.

Eli grimaced. "Sorry 'bout that."

Anger like she had never felt before exploded from her. Eli could have killed her, yet he acted like it was just an accident. Her life really did mean nothing to him.

"If you were truly sorry—" Shane yanked the knife out of the wall, allowing all the emotions she had let boil up inside her explode out "—you wouldn't have put me down here to throw your stupid knives at me. If you were sorry, then you wouldn't be so damn rude to me all the time." She could feel tears start to come, but she wouldn't let them fall. She couldn't. "I have gone through what seems like the bottom of Haytorrow's Fallen Realms during these past months, so it would be nice if someone, anyone, had enough decency not to be an absolute bitch to me." She threw the knife down to the ground and for a moment; the clattering of the blade was the only noise to be heard.

"Gods, Shay—"

"My name is Shane." Her voice shook with so many emotions. She couldn't pinpoint the exact one she was feeling.

Blood dripped down her fingers as she brushed past Eli, making sure to hit him with her shoulder. It probably hurt her more than him because of the cut, but she didn't care. She just wanted to get out of there.

"Where are you going?"

"Anywhere but here." She pushed open the door and left Eli behind her.

She ended up back in her room, even though she wanted to be as far away from Eli as possible, and that wasn't possible when his room was right next to her own. She couldn't go up to the surface. She didn't know her way around, and she was too afraid of getting lost. She also couldn't go to Kyaina's, leaving her with only one place to go.

After tending to her wound, she threw herself on her bed, tears leaking out of her eyes and landing on her silky pillowcase. She had had enough. Enough of Eli making fun of her. Enough of him beating her up at everything they did. Enough of him.

She rolled over to look up at the ceiling, eyes burning. She wanted more than anything for things to go back to the way they were a couple months ago. They were so simple then, back when she didn't have to stress about surviving. Back when Reece was still alive, and they were still with their families.

"I'm so sorry, Reece," she whispered. Sorry for what had happened to her, and what Shane was doing with her life that should've been taken from her months before. "It should've been me."

There was a light knock on her door, and Eli's voice came through. "Shane, can you let me in?"

"Yes, but I don't want to." She quickly wiped away her eyes, trying to dry them out as much as she could.

"Please, I just want to talk."

"About what?" she asked opening the door. "My lack of any skill with a weapon? Or maybe, what did you say before? Oh yeah, my brutish appearance?" She let him in and closed the door behind him. "Because I already know all that. No need to add salt to the wound."

"I'm not going to insult you."

Shane let out a low, humorless laugh. "Why the sudden change of heart?"

"Because of what you said."

"Look, if this is pity, I don't want it. Especially if it's from you." Shane flung herself down in her chair near the fire. She sniffled quietly.

"No, this isn't pity." He stopped himself, taking a deep breath in. He fiddled with his fingers, popping them. "I'm sorry about cutting you," he said. The mischievous glow in his eyes was gone, and Shane began to wonder if he was truly being sincere, if she was too quick to judge him before. "I thought I was a better thrower than that."

"Is that why you came?" Shane asked. "To apologize?"

"No, it isn't why I'm here." He took a deep, shaky breath. "Believe it or not, I know what it's like, feeling like you've lost your will to live."

"Why are you telling me this?"

"Can you just let me finish?" Eli laughed uneasily. He was acting vulnerable. For the first time, Shane wondered if he had a heart beating in his chest like real humans?

"I used to have a partner, but that was a long time ago. He betrayed me, and I was forced to kill him."

"Sounds a little morbid."

"It was. Ever since then, I've been alone. So, I know what it's like, what you're going through right now, but trust me when I say that it will get better, eventually. It's okay to feel broken. Everyone does at some point in their life, some people worse than others."

"Are you sure about that?" Shane's voice cracked. She couldn't help her thoughts from returning to Reece.

"It did for me."

"*Why* are you telling me this?" Shane asked again.

Eli's eyes darted around the room as he quickened his finger popping. "Because I wanted you to know that you aren't the only one who's going through something. Everyone here has seen some evil in their lives. You need to move on and focus on the present if you want to make it here. The important thing though is to get up after life knocks you down." Eli paused and pursed his lips nervously. "I also wanted to tell you that I'm sorry for being such a jerk to you."

Shane raised an eyebrow. "Does that mean you're gonna stop?"

"No." Eli managed to crack a smile. "I'm never gonna stop, but I'll back off. A little."

"Thanks for that," Shane said sarcastically.

"You are so welcome." He got up from the couch and started walking toward the door. "Your room's a mess, by the way."

"Yeah, I know."

He opened the door and was about to go to his room but stopped in the doorway. "Get up early tomorrow. We're going on a run."

"Why are we starting now?"

"Because before you were far too frail to even think about it. You'd be blown away by the wind, not that you're any better now."

Shane rolled her eyes. "Fine, Elias. What time?"

CHAPTER 15

S hane thought she knew what it was like to go through hell, but boy was she wrong. The last six months had been nothing compared to what she was doing at that moment. She gulped in air, trying her best to catch up to Eli with her sore muscles and throbbing arm, but the blinding snow that was falling from the sky clouded her sight with nothing but white flakes.

They had been running for a week, not having a single rest day. Everything hurt. Whenever her foot contacted the ground, immediate pain spasmed through her leg, starting with the balls of her feet and ending in her kneecaps. Yet every single day she would get up and do it over again. She couldn't allow a little bit of running to be her downfall. Not after everything she had been through. That would be a disgrace to herself.

A hill loomed ahead, and she cursed through her ragged breaths. A stitch had appeared in her left side, but Eli refused to stop. If anything, he only continued faster, making her push through the pain. Once climbing the hill, her whole body screamed in protest. It begged her to stop, but she knew she couldn't, unless she wanted to hear it from Eli. All she could do was push through the pain. The brain would compel her to stop before she truly reached the point where she could run no more.

"I've been waiting up here for five minutes," Eli said when his silhouette finally appeared through the blizzard conditions.

"You can shut up." Shane came to a stop and drew in ragged breaths. She rested with her hands on her knees. "You're in better shape than me, and you've been doing this a lot longer. Give me a break."

"I'd rather not." He brushed the light, small flakes off his cloak and started forward, moving slow at first but picking up speed.

"Wait!" Shane yelled after him but didn't get an answer back. Groaning, she followed him, hating every single second.

They ran for what seemed to be forever, every step was agony to Shane's already sore muscles. When they saw the lights of the city far below them on the mountainside, a huge sigh of relief left Shane. Her legs seemed more willing to allow her to keep going as she sprinted down the hill. The distance between her and Eli grew, but she didn't care.

Eli slowed to a stop when they passed the first lantern that lit up the streetway. Shane gasped for air; her full body weight rested against a light post.

The biting cold had taken hold of her as soon as she left the Underground. There was a deluge of snow greeting them. It was strange weather for springtime. That didn't stop Eli from taking her on his run.

"I don't know why you do this to yourself. This is torture," said Shane

"And I don't see why you come with me?"

Shane only stared at him. "You're kidding, right?" She started walking with him toward the Assassin's Underground. "That *was* a joke."

"Of course, it was a joke." Eli laughed. "Bloody knives, you have an awful sense of humor."

When they finally made it to the alleyway with the entrance to the Underground, all the sweat that Shane had exuded had frozen. It gave her a chill that she thought would never go away. The warm breeze coming from the stairwell that led down helped, but not nearly enough to make her comfortable. If anything, it only made her hands tingle with pain.

Shane said goodbye to Eli before entering her room and immediately started a fire. Warmth radiated from it, but it wasn't enough to get rid of her chill.

Shane grabbed some fresh clothes out of her messy dresser and headed for the bathroom. She started water in the bathtub, stripped of her sweaty, cold clothes and slipped into the steaming water. She sank lower until her head went underwater, but she kept breathing.

Shane washed her hair, making sure to dig deep into her scalp to get rid of all the dirt that had somehow found its way there. She only took a bath once every few days, and each time she did, a wave of relief washed over her. The warm water reminded her of home, of her friends before she left them. She was afraid that if she did it too often, the memory would become cloudy, nearly non-existent. She didn't want that to happen. At least not yet.

Once she felt completely cleansed, she got out of the bathtub. She dried off, got dressed, all the while careful to avoid looking in the mirror. Ever since she escaped the camp, she refused to do so. She was too afraid of what she might see, what she had become. It became a habit after the first week of being there.

As soon as Shane settled in her chair near the fire, there was a knock on the door connecting the rooms. Shane raised her head, eyebrows furrowing. Eli never knocked there. He always preferred to go to the door in the hallway, yet the knock came again. Cautiously, Shane got up and made her way toward the door. Her whole body tensed as she opened it only to find nobody there. She was about to shrug it off, but it came again from Eli's door.

"What do you want?" She asked, flinging the door open, impacting Eli with a *thud*.

"Hey! That hurt!" He rubbed his shoulder where the door hit him.

Shane rolled her eyes. "You'll get over it." She looked around his room, which was just as dirty as she remembered it. "Why did you knock?"

"Because Wikter wanted me to give this to you." He reached inside his pocket and brought out what looked like a ticket. It had a dark red outline that was intricately woven around the words. Shane had a difficult enough time reading cursive, much less when what she was trying to read was upside down.

"What is it?" she asked as she took it from Eli. The silkiness of the touch of the paper surprised her.

"An invitation to the dance tonight on the surface. Apparently, the governor's having some big celebration. His daughter's getting married or something."

Shane nearly fell over from laughter. "What?" She laughed, having difficulty breathing. "You can't be serious. I can't dance."

"I would've just thrown these away, but Wikter came to my room and told me I had to go with you to, how did he say it, 'teach you how to be a well-behaved lady so you're ready… when the time arises.'"

"Look, it's not that I won't dance, but I can't dance." She handed the invitation back to Eli. "Do you know how much my brothers made fun of me the last time I tried? Because I can tell you, the tormenting lasted for months." As soon as the words left her mouth, a wave of sadness went through her. She would gladly take their bullying now if it meant seeing them one more time.

"And I would say that we could just let this go, pretend like we never got these. I would be happy to do that actually. But Archer and Kyaina are going, and they know that we're supposed to be there too. They'll tell Wikter if we don't show up." He sighed, pursing his lips. "Be ready by dusk, so six?"

"Are you serious?"

"I don't want to go with you as much as you don't want to go with me, but Wikter will be on us if we don't." Before Shane could start an argument, he said, "I'm sure your dancing can't be that bad. I mean, it can't be worse than your running form."

Shane's cheeks flush with color. "Hey, my running form is better than most people's." That much was true. From all the sports she had participated in, she had perfected her running form. "If you wanted to make fun of me for anything, then at least put some thought into it. Like maybe choose to chastise my fighting form."

Eli tried to suppress a laugh. "My mom told me not to make fun of things that people can't change."

Shane was blushing now. "But did you listen?"

"Does it look like I did?" There was a knock on Eli's main door. "Be ready by six," Eli said making his way over to the door.

Shane took that as an invitation to leave and gladly took it. She shut the adjoining door quietly behind her and exhaled heavily.

When she got back into her room, she threw herself on her soft bed, expecting to use the extra time in her day to get some much-needed rest, but as soon as she closed her eyes, there came another knock from her door. She let out a long sigh of annoyance and hauled herself up from the warmth to open the door, only to see Kyaina with her arms full of an assortment of small stuff, as well as a dress. She didn't even wait to be let in before pushing past Shane.

"A hello would've been nice before you barged into my room unannounced," Shane said as she closed the door behind her.

"I knocked, so that counts for something."

"What are you doing here?" Kyaina delicately set the dress down on Shane's messy bed and put the rest of the stuff on the table next to the fire.

"Getting you ready for the dance tonight."

Shane let out an involuntary laugh. "Eli said I didn't need to be ready until dusk"

"Do you realize how early that happens?" Kyaina raised an eyebrow, still continuing to set up. "The sun will be far past the horizon in just a couple hours."

"Yeah? And your point is…?"

"Have you ever gotten ready for any special occasion before?" Kyaina laughed. "It takes time."

"I usually just put on my nicest clothes and go," Shane mumbled under her breath, but Kyaina heard her.

"And what is that? Some handed down training clothes? Most of yours are cut or torn from Eli's training."

Shane pursed her lips, trying to hide her embarrassment. Even though it was true, that didn't mean she was proud of it. "I used to have nicer stuff than that," she lied.

"Yeah. Sure, you did." Kyaina motioned toward Shane's desk chair. "Sit down."

"Why?"

"Because I have to do your face."

Shane scoffed, but she made her way to the chair. "What are you going to do?"

"Just the basics."

"If you can't tell," Shane said, her hands gripped against the armrest, "I have no idea what that means."

"Just stay still and relax, all right?"

Shane only tensed more. This whole situation reminded her of the time the year before when she and her friends were getting ready for the school dance. Reece had forced her to put on makeup. She acted like it was the worst thing in the world, but she couldn't let her friends know she honestly didn't mind. It went against the persona that she put out.

Kyaina looked at her face from all angles, a crease appearing on her forehead before she went to her bag and brought out a large brush. "Gods, calm down." Kyaina laughed. "I'm not going to kill you or anything."

Shane's white hands remained tight against the armrests.

Kyaina started on Shane's face. She flinched when Kyaina touched it with the brush. The bristles of the brush conjured memories of how she got her scars— memories she didn't care to relive.

Kyaina ignored it and kept going. Shane was fine with that. She didn't want to talk about it. She didn't think she could talk about it. Some things were best left unsaid.

She forced herself to remain still no matter how much she wanted to shrink away. It took only a couple minutes before Kyaina was done, and she moved on to the area around her eyes. Shane pitied her. It was going to take a while to finish because of the dark bags she imagined were under her eyes.

Kyaina pulled something out of her bag and brought it close to Shane's eye, and she flinched away. "Can you not?" she asked, laughing uncomfortably.

"What? Put this on?" She looked down at what she had in her hand. "Are you afraid of things coming close to your eyes or something?" Kyaina chuckled.

"As a matter of fact, I am. Your hand could twitch, and you could poke it out."

And it looks like a knife.

Kyaina rolled her eyes, a smile stretched across her face. "I promise that won't happen."

"That's what they always say, and then their hands just twitch out of the blue."

"If that happens, then you can do the same to me."

"If I can even see you." Shane's hands relaxed. "For all you know, you could completely blind me for the rest of my life."

"Then I'm pretty sure I would have more problems than worrying about you poking me in the eye. My father would kill me for ruining one of his assassins. Now stay still."

Shane's laugh was weak.

Kyaina continued applying makeup to Shane's face and was done in no time. When she took a step back Shane felt no different, but she must have looked different because Kyaina put her brush down.

"If you did this more often, you would be beautiful."

"Are you saying that I was ugly before." Shane laughed. "How rude."

"No. That's not what— Just go look in the mirror and tell me what you think."

Shane's stomach dropped. She knew that eventually the day would come where she would have to face herself, but she never realized that it would be this soon. She didn't think she had enough strength to do it. She was a coward.

"What are you waiting for? Go look at yourself."

Shane managed to fake a smile as she got up from the safety of her chair and made her way to the bathroom. She tried to keep her hands from shaking, unsuccessfully. The mirror stood in front of her. What was so difficult about lifting her eyes up just long enough to see herself? What could be the harm in something so simple?

But she couldn't do it. Her fingers gripped the edge of the ceramic wash basin, her arms shaking uncontrollably. Slowly, she brought her gaze up so she could just barely see the bottom of the mirror. She forced herself to bring her gaze up to where the bottom of her chin was visible, and then she stopped. What kind of monster would she see if she looked up farther? Would it be someone her family would be ashamed of? Someone she was ashamed of?

She couldn't wait any longer. She had to face herself eventually, so why not now? Her eyes met her own in the mirror, and she let out a small gasp at her appearance. Kyaina was right. She did look beautiful. Her cheeks had thinned, and the chubby baby face she'd always had was now gone. Even the mole above her left eyebrow that she had always considered ugly looked good.

It was her eyes that told her a different story though. Makeup could only cover up so much of the pain. The eyes staring back at Shane were broken, shattered by the cruelness of the world. The one scar that stretched from the right side of her chin up to her eyebrow was worse than she imagined. Makeup can only cover so much damage.

She was almost unrecognizable from the girl who had left home so many months before. That girl had died when Reece died, replaced by the woman she saw in front of her now.

"How does it look?" Kyaina's voice came piercing through the door, shattering the moment of shock Shane had.

"Good." Shane cleared her throat. "It looks good."

"Is that all you're going to tell me?"

"I don't know what else to say." Shane opened the door, allowing Kyaina to see her. "It was the first thing that came to my mind."

Kyaina rolled her eyes. "You still have to try on your dress." She went over to her bed and tossed Shane the purple, simple dress that she had set out.

"Do I have a choice in this?"

"When have you ever had a choice?"

Shane closed the door to the bathroom once more. She stripped her clothes off, wishing that she could just wear those, but if she came out of the bathroom with them on, Kyaina would kill her quite literally. She slipped on the dress, thankful that Kyaina hadn't chosen a big, fluffy one that Shane had seen Kyaina wear before when she and Archer had been hurrying out the doors, probably headed to a dance to get another assassination done.

"How does it look?" Kyaina asked after a few minutes.

"I'm having trouble tying it." Shane fumbled around with the strings in the back, but every time she thought she nearly had it, one of them dropped out of her hands.

"I'm coming in," Kyaina warned before opening the door wide.

"I can't seem to get it." Shane dropped the strings, turning around so Kyaina could have a go at it, but Kyaina remained where she was. Shane looked back to see what the matter was but was greeted by a face of pure shock and mortification. "Does it really look that bad?" She laughed unsteadily.

"Your shoulders, Shane."

The smile on Shane's face faded, replaced by a frown. "Yeah, I know." She turned back around instinctively putting a hand on her neck where she could still feel the rough scarring. "You should see the rest of my back." She tried to smile, but it just turned into a grimace.

"If I had known that it was that bad I would've… would've…"

"What? Tried to finish the assassination sooner?" Shane let out a sigh relaxing the muscles in her back and shoulders. "It wouldn't have helped. Most of these didn't even happen in the mine. When Fritz heard that I was the one who started the fight, well let's just say that he didn't take to it very well. He would've killed me, if the people he was with didn't take pity on me."

"Gods, Shane. I'm so sorry…"

"Sorry for what? You couldn't have done anything to stop them." She cleared her throat, trying to clear the memory as she turned around once again. "Now, are you going to help me or not?"

CHAPTER 16

It took another hour for Kyaina to get ready as well. Shane was no help to her, besides being there to chat with her. She sat on her bed while Kyaina put on makeup in front of the bathroom mirror. Then she did Shane's hair

"I don't see the point in all this," Shane said pointing at her tortured hair. Kyaina had brushed it and braided it intricately. "I mean, why take hours just for something that will most likely fall apart in no time."

Kyaina laughed, pointing her brush in Shane's direction as she went on to do her own hair. "Because. It won't fall out in thirty minutes, and it makes you look pretty."

Shane raised both eyebrows. "I could still do without it."

"Some people like doing their hair, Shane."

"And more power to them. I prefer simplicity."

Kyaina rolled her eyes and went back to her own hair.

Shane looked over at the door and wondered how Eli and Archer were doing. It was nearly time to go, and she hadn't heard a thing coming from Eli's room.

"Would you mind handing me another bobby pin?"

"Huh?" Shane returned her attention to her friend. "Oh, yeah." She riffled through Kyaina's bag until she came across a fancy looking box with pins in it. "Here you go."

She placed it in her hair. "How do I look?" she asked, turning toward Shane and doing a twirl.

"I'm not sure I'm the right person to ask. I have terrible taste in fashion."

Kyaina snorted. "Yeah. You do." She winced, her hand going straight for the tattoo on her left elbow. "Gods, Archer. Can't you use this like you're supposed to?"

"Is he calling you?"

"Yeah. He and Eli got ready together, but after that he said he'd go back to his room." She sighed. "He could've knocked on your door before leaving, but *no.* He had to be all dramatic and do the assassin's call."

Shane helped Kyaina gather all her belongings strewn across the room and handed them to her.

"Well, see you later, I guess."

"See you at the dance."

They bid farewell at the door.

As soon as she was gone, Shane let out a deep breath and sank against the wall. She didn't know if she was ready to see Eli. She could only imagine how he was going to make fun of the scarring on her exposed shoulders, but she was thankful that the dress covered her brand and tattoo. She didn't think she could dare to be seen by Elias like that.

Also, there was the whole dancing issue. She had never been good at it. She refused to do it ever since her brothers made fun of her at her cousin's wedding long ago.

Groaning, she picked herself up from the floor and headed for the door that conjoined both their rooms. When she was about to open the door to his room though, she hesitated. It would be the first time she had ever been in there without being invited, but she shrugged it off. They were partners after all. Eli had to get used to her being around.

She opened the door and barged into the room, but the moment she saw Eli, her breath stopped. He stood shirtless near his bed, his bare, scarred back exposed to her. Shane guessed that the scars came along with being an assassin. She couldn't move fast enough to leave before Eli turned around.

"What are you doing here?" he snapped. He quickly put on his white undershirt, but Shane had already seen the scar that adorned the front of his body. It was enormous, located just underneath his rib cage on his left side, all mangled and grotesque looking. Just like her back, except so much worse.

"What happened to you?" She managed to breathe after her heart started beating once again.

"It was an accident." His voice was hard. "What are you doing here?" he repeated.

She cleared her throat, trying to dismiss the image of the scar against his near perfectly fit body. "Shouldn't you be able to hear me because you're an assassin?"

His eyes lost the bite that they had had when she first walked in. "Just because I'm an assassin doesn't mean that we pay attention to every single detail all hours of the day." He grabbed his overcoat from his bed. "You should take note, if this is truly the profession that you want."

"Does it look like I'm going anywhere?" Shane asked, now conscientious about pointing her back toward him. How would he react if he saw her shoulders?

"Yeah. Looks like you're headed to a dance." He looked her up and down. "Did Kyaina give you that dress?"

Shane nodded.

He bent down to pick up his freshly polished shoes from the bottom of his bed. "Looks better on you."

"Was that a compliment, Elias?"

"No. It was a statement." He sat down in his chair to put on his shoes.

"Gods, can't you hurry up?" Shane asked. "You're taking forever."

"You want me to slow down?" Eli smiled wickedly up at her. "I can do that if you'd like." His hands, which were already tying his laces at a slow rate, seemed to slow down even more until it was painful to watch.

Shane rolled her eyes. "I'll be outside," she said, walking toward the door and starting down the passage. Only moments later did she hear Eli's quiet, almost inaudible footsteps clatter against the stone floor. She commended herself for knowing his steps by sound alone.

"Shane, wait." The footsteps stopped and she heard Eli gasp.

"What?" Shane turned around, smiling, but the smile soon faded when she saw Eli staring. "The scars? Yeah. I know. Kyaina saw them earlier."

"What… What happened?"

"You didn't tell me how you got yours, so I won't tell you how I got mine." Shane twirled swiftly on her heel and strutted toward the exit, face burning. She could feel Eli's eyes burrowing into her.

"I told you already. Mine came from an accident."

"And if you expect me to believe you then you must be dumber than I thought you were, and the bar wasn't very high." Shane refused to meet his eyes. This was somehow worse than the tormenting that she thought she would receive. At least she was prepared for that, not him actually showing concern. It wasn't the Eli she knew.

"All right. I'll give you that. But these look new. They look like—"

Shane looked over her shoulder to see Eli's face pale in the soft lantern light.

"Bloody knives, Shane. Did they… did they whip you?" His voice was nothing more than soft breath. Shane said nothing. She was too busy trying to keep the tears from falling but was failing miserably as one fell from her eyes and ran down her cheek.

They made it to the staircase and a wave of relief flooded through Shane. All she needed was some fresh, crisp air. That would be able to take her mind off the camps. And if it didn't…. She preferred not to think that way.

"Shane, why didn't you tell me?"

"Why should I have?" Shane's voice shook, but she didn't care. "You have been nothing except the absolute worst to me, so why should I have told you what happened to me in those camps and bring up memories that were best forgotten. Besides," she sniffed, "you have your own secrets that you're not willing to share."

Eli pursed his lips. "Were you ever going to tell me?"

"You never gave me any reason to want to open up to you." Shane took a shaky breath. "Everything from the past six months I want to forget. Pretend like they never happened, but it's scars like those, and on my back, that remind me every damned day of what I had to go through."

Eli remained silent, which Shane preferred. She needed time to be quiet. She never planned on telling Eli what she just told him, but it slipped out. Only the sounds of their hard shoes against the stone staircase echoed through the cold stairwell. Shane's arms shivered, goosebumps appearing as her chilled breaths floated away from her.

She wiped up her tears, careful not to ruin her makeup. She was afraid that they were going to freeze on her eyelashes.

"Did you forget a coat?" Eli asked. Shane sighed, relieved that he wasn't asking anymore questions about her scars.

"Does it look like I have a coat?" She knew she had forgotten something, but it was too late to turn back now. Not with Eli behind her.

"Must be cold right now for you." Shane could tell from the tension in his voice that he was trying to act normal but was still deeply disturbed by the scars.

Shane looked behind her to see him making a show out of putting on his own coat. She rolled her eyes, glad that their scars were behind them.

"It's so nice, having something to cover myself in when I get cold. Too bad you don't have anything."

"I'll be fine."

When they finally made it to the top of the stairs, Shane was shaking from the cold. She tried to keep her arms together and not show it, but Eli took notice.

"You're going to get hypothermia if you go out like that." He motioned with his head. "Go back and grab a jacket."

"I can't."

"Why not."

"Because the best thing I have is that ratty old cloak. And before you say anything, I can't buy a new one because I don't have any money, so I'm stuck with Kyaina's old stuff and what Wikter provided for me."

"Why— Oh." He looked at her like he had never seen her before.

"What?" she asked, unnerved.

"Nothing."

"Sure, it's nothing." Shane pulled open the door and the cold cut into her like a sharp knife. It had stopped snowing and the sky was clear of any clouds. It was a completely different world than it was in the morning. The ground was coated in six inches of freshly fallen snow, and in the alleyway there were only two pairs of footsteps disturbing it.

"Looks like Kyaina and Archer already left," Shane said, trying to distract herself from how cold she truly was.

They rounded the turn together to a more lit up section of the main road. Shane let Eli lead the way and followed close behind, keenly aware of the snow that was now melting in her shoes, making her feet sopping wet and uncomfortable, not to mention cold enough to cool down her entire body.

Other people were milling around in the street. Some were gazing up at the sky while others were hurrying along like they needed to be somewhere. Either that or they didn't want the biting cold to nip at their noses and cheeks any longer. One thing was for certain though: Every one of them, even the poorer folks, were dressed better for the conditions than Shane.

"You look frozen."

"That may be because I am." Shane let out a shiver. "Gods, why did Wikter make us come?"

"That's a question I've been asking myself for hours." Eli took a long look over at Shane's shivering body and let out a sigh. "I'm probably going to regret this," he said as he took off his jacket, "but right now you need this more than I do.

Shane tried to protest, saying that she didn't need his pity, but then they rounded the corner and saw the line of people waiting to be let into one of the nicer houses of the city, the one with the party. She looked at the coat around her shoulders and a new warmth came from it. She no longer protested.

"What about you? Won't you get cold?" Shane eyed Eli skeptically. His white shirt rippled in the slight breeze, blowing his hair back. Shane hated to admit it, but he looked nice that night.

"Nah. I'll be fine." He shivered to show otherwise. "I have… warm blood."

Shane raised an eyebrow. Did he have something to hide? The expression on his face, as well as the pause in his words told her so, but she had no clue as to what it was.

"I see," she said, taking a step forward in line while also keeping an eye on Eli.

It took them far too long to get to the front of the line. Two people ahead of them handed their invitations over to the guard and Shane's heart sank. She had handed hers back to Eli when he first gave it to her.

"Eli, where are the invitations?"

Eli's mouth opened as if to speak, but his eyes widened. His hands immediately went toward his pockets. They came out empty. A crease appeared on his forehead as he searched everywhere else.

"Did you seriously forget them?" Shane scolded. They were getting to the front of the line, and they were left empty handed.

A sly smile rippled across Eli's face. "Of course, I didn't forget them." He made a show of reaching for the pockets of the jacket on Shane's body, making her squirm. "They're right here." He handed one to Shane who tried desperately to look away. "I got you, didn't I?"

"The only thing you did was piss me off. If we had to go back and get in this long line again, you wouldn't be living."

"I see you making lots of threats but never following through with them."

They handed the man at the door their invitations and proceeded inside to the warmth of the building. The interior was exactly what she imagined it would be, even before she had seen the building itself. Long, elegant staircases wrapped around the walls, leading to a second floor full of people. The decorations were fancy and pristine, subtly showing off the governor's wealth without him standing there saying it.

When Shane looked back at Eli, he only stared at her like he just asked her a question and expected an answer.

"What?"

"My jacket. I need my jacket." He looked around the room. "It's warmer in here, so you should be fine, but I'm rather cold, and you look like an idiot with it on."

Eli snatched away the jacket from her shoulders and threw it on.

Shane's cheeks glowed red. "Right," she said. There were so many people there, and at that moment, she imagined everyone's eyes fixated on her shoulders.

Shane instinctively shriveled up, her hand rubbing the back of her neck. The only thing that brought her peace was the fact that her brands were being covered by the dress. Just barely, but still covered. The people dancing around her looked like they would sell her back to Fritz for a handsome amount of money if they knew she used to be his slave.

"Bloody knives, Shane," Eli said over the soft music coming from the room ahead of them, past the stairs. "You look like you've seen a Geistluck."

Shane cleared her throat. "I feel like people are watching me." Shane's eyes darted around the room. So many people were standing around and laughing. Was it aimed at her?

"No one's watching you. You're blending in, or at least you would blend in just fine if you didn't stand like a shriveled animal. It's really terrible for your posture."

Shane stuck her tongue out at Eli but straightened up all the same. Eli was right. Everywhere Shane looked, she saw people talking with their friends and having a good time, not staring at her. She was just being an idiot.

"Shall we?" Eli made a motion with his head toward the music, holding out his right hand. Shane stared at it, nostrils flaring. "Gods, Shane. You could at least pretend to like me."

"I could say the same to you."

Eli rolled his eyes, a slight smile etching across the corners of his lips. "I wouldn't do this unless I had to," he explained. "Those invitations that I had," he lowered his voice so only Shane could hear him, "I may have stolen them from a couple."

Shane's eyes widened. "You didn't."

Eli winced but nodded. "So, unless you want to get kicked out of this damned place, I would suggest at least pretending like you can stand being in my company."

"You were the one who didn't want anything to do with me. Now you ask me if I can behave? Ridiculous."

Eli winked; his hand still outstretched. "What can I say? I'm a good actor. You have to be if you want to follow this career path."

Shane begrudgingly took his hand and allowed him to lead her down the hallway underneath the great chandelier. "I don't necessarily want to become like you. It's more like a need for survival for me."

"You could run away," Eli suggested. "In fact, I encourage you to do so if it would mean getting you off my back and no longer having a partner, like it used to be."

"Except I can't." Shane didn't know why she had said that. Even though he never shared anything about himself with her, she felt the need to vent to him. "I have no idea where my parents are, and I have no family here in Lyconnexal."

"So?"

They arrived at the dance floor and Eli let Shane's fingers slide from his grip.

"So?" Shane laughed. "I don't necessarily want to run away from a job that might pay well only to find nothing and live on the streets of Rotshall like a street rat."

"Are you insulting the street rats? As someone who used to be one, I say shame on you."

"You used to live on the streets?" Shane stared at him.

Before Eli could answer, Kyaina and Archer appeared from the crowd of dancers. "You guys look like idiots, just standing there," Kyaina said. "Come on out here and dance like you're supposed to."

"Shall we, I guess?" Eli didn't sound very amused.

"If we must." Shane took his outstretched hand once more, allowing him to weave their way through the crowd before they were in the middle of the dance floor where everybody could see them.

"I must warn you," Shane said as Eli grabbed her waist and shoulder, "I'm a terrible dancer. I'll probably step on your feet countless times."

"I brought hard toe shoes just for that," he said as they started dancing. "I can't allow someone like you to obliterate my delicate toes."

"Are you saying that you thought I was a bad dancer before I even told you. Way to judge me."

"Well, from what I could tell, you've never been to anything like this before, so excuse me for believing— ouch that was my foot." Shane lifted her foot off Eli's.

"Sorry."

The song was slow and very dramatic. The musicians were masterful from the accents to the dynamics of the piece. Shane stepped awkwardly to the beat, her body as tense as a pulled bowstring. She had no idea where to place her feet, or if she was doing it correctly. All around her she imagined eyes staring at her scarred back, judging her, even though she knew she was being ridiculous.

"I think I counted twenty-three times you stepped on my feet," Eli said as the musicians finished their song and stepped away for a short break. "An all-time record, I think."

"Shut up."

"I'm just saying."

"I told you I have no idea what I'm doing, and while you were laughing your ass off, I was struggling just to keep stepping to the rhythm."

"Is that what you're aiming for?" Eli couldn't stop a chuckle from escaping him. "Well then your timing is all off. It's like you don't even know how to count a beat."

"I know how to count a beat." Three years of band taught her that much. "It's just a little bit of help wouldn't be a bad thing."

When the next song started, Eli grabbed her by the hand and dragged her into another dance. It was slower, more melodic than the previous song, and the dancers reflected that.

"Just follow my lead," Eli said.

"If you can't tell, that's what I've been doing this whole time."

"Then you weren't paying attention."

He pulled her tight and they started dancing. Shane's eyes immediately went down to watch his feet, but then she felt his calloused, yet gentle hand lift her chin so she was looking at his face. "You're thinking way too much," he explained. "Watch my eyes, and let your feet do the rest. You want to move with the music, not with what your brain thinks."

Against her instincts, Shane followed his instructions. Her eyes met his. She had never realized just how brown they truly were, like melted chocolate on a cold winter's day. He kept his gaze locked with Shane's, not wavering one bit. It was a bit intimidating.

Shane tried not to think. Just let the rhythm of the music move her body. She stopped fumbling around. Her body loosened to allow the music to flow through her.

"See how much easier this is?" Eli smiled.

"Shut up. I'm trying not to concentrate." Except that wasn't true. Her eyes were fixed to Eli's face. The rest of the world seemed to blur around them until they were the only two people left in the world. They twirled and swirled all along the dance floor. The mistakes that Shane made were masked by the music. Whenever it sped up, they sped up. Even when she accidentally stepped on Eli's feet, it seemed that he didn't mind.

The song ended and Shane could feel Eli's warm breath against her face. He let his hands fall from Shane's side, and he started back across the dance floor.

"Eli, wait." Shane raced after him. She grabbed his shoulder, but he brushed it off with his fingers like it was nothing. "Where are you going?"

"To get a drink." When Shane kept following him, he sighed, and turned around. "Since you won't stop following me like a lost dog, I guess that you can come too."

"I'm not— you know, never mind."

They stepped out into a hallway and passed a group of people all huddled together. They all wore intricate masks made with expensive looking metals and jewels. Shane opened her mouth to ask why, but Eli answered before she got the chance. "The people in the wedding ceremonies all wear masks like that. A bit stupid, really, but it's tradition."

"But why were they all huddled together like a group of penguins?"

"Because the bride's in the middle. It's custom for the husband not to see the bride, and the group surrounding her are making sure that it doesn't happen."

"How do you know this much?" A server came around with a tray of wine glasses and Eli took two, handing one to Shane.

"How do you not?"

"It's complicated." She took a drink just so she wouldn't have to continue talking.

"As complicated as how you got in the labor camp?"

Shane glared at him but didn't stop him, so he continued. "When I saw you before, you were perfectly fine, on the streets of Stoenstill, and then the next thing I know you were in the king's prison being bought by the slavers."

"Being bought by *you*, actually," Shane reminded him, keeping the glare.

"How did you get there?"

A cruel laugh escaped Shane. "Like I'm going to tell you."

"When are you gonna tell me?"

"When you tell me more about yourself." Eli opened his mouth to argue, but Shane continued anyway. "And I mean no mysterious talk. I mean hard facts about your past."

"Then it looks like we're in a dilemma because that's not gonna happen."

"I guess we are." She took another sip. If Eli wasn't going to open up to her, why should she for him?

Shane was about to set her glass down on the table when she heard a voice. The same cruel, cold voice that haunted her nightmares. Everything in her body clenched up and froze. She was suddenly back in the mines of Verscar.

"Konner," Fritz said. "Good to see you."

The hair on the back of Shane's neck rose. She tried to move, to get away, but everything was paralyzed. All she could do was stare as Fritz and the man Shane assumed to be the governor of Conlar shook hands.

"Bloody knives, Shay." Eli laughed. "It looks like you've seen a Geistluck." He followed her gaze and the smile on his face faded.

"It's been too long, Fritz. How have you been?"

Fritz shrugged. "Good, I guess. I had to tighten up security in Verscar. Two prisoners tried to escape."

"I heard about that," the governor said. "Did they manage to do it?"

Fritz only laughed. "Security's way too tight for that."

"How many guards do you have there now," Konner asked, laughing. "Got to be at least a couple hundred."

"I had a couple hundred before." Fritz smiled. "Now? It's more like a thousand."

Governor Konner let out a low whistle. "How do you pay for all of them?

"The slaves," Fritz explained as he took a drink. "I get a couple hundred Schulhers for each of them, and a couple thousand more for the limestone that they mine. Let me tell you, if it didn't bring in so much money, I would've quit a long time ago."

Eli tugged on Shane's arm. "We need to go before he sees you."

But Shane didn't move. He tugged her again and she tore her attention away from Fritz.

"Come on."

Eli pulled her through the hordes of people congregating at the dance. Before long they were back outside in the open air, but the cold didn't bother Shane anymore. Nothing could bother her more than seeing her torturer brag about how he used people, people like her, for profit.

The trip back to the Underground was a blur, but somehow, they found themselves back in there and entering Shane's room.

"Are you okay?" Eli asked as Shane settled in on the coach.

Shane cleared her throat and tried to slow her racing heart. "As fine as I'll ever be," she whispered. She brought her tear-stained eyes up to Eli. "He was talking and laughing like he did nothing wrong. Like he wasn't responsible for thousands of people dying under his hand."

"I know, Shay. Trust me, I know." Eli sat down next to her. "I hate him just as much as you. What he does is despicable."

"No. No you don't." Shane's voice was barely a whisper. "Unless you were there, in Verscar and subject to his punishments, you have no idea how much I hate him."

"If you want to talk—"

"I don't want to," Shane cut in. "I just want to be left alone."

But that was far from the truth. She wanted to be with someone who cared about her, someone she could cry on. Being alone was the farthest thing from her mind.

"Are you sure?"

"Yes." *No.*

Eli got up and it took everything Shane had not to pull him back. He headed for the door but stopped before he could open it. Maybe she didn't have to beg for him to stay. "You asked about my scar earlier?"

"What?" Shane asked, completely taken by surprise. "Yes, but why are you asking?"

"Because, Shay, like it or not I need to work on my trust."

"Really?" she sarcastically said. "Could've fooled me."

"I'm saying I'm trying to trust you," he said, popping his fingers.

"Why?"

"We are partners, after all." Eli closed his eyes and sighed before continuing on. "I had an older brother named Alek."

"Had?"

"Yes. Had. He was my partner three years ago. On our first mission, he betrayed me. Stabbed me in the back quite literally. I would've been dead if the target's neighbor hadn't found me."

Realization struck Shane and she gasped. "You... you killed him?" Eli didn't say anything. He only nodded.

"After my parents' death, he was the closest person I had. He was like a father to me, which only made it more difficult. I guess that's what made it easy for him to do this." He pointed to where his scar was, right underneath his ribcage. "Apparently I was holding him back from what he wanted in life.

"Nobody knows this, besides Archer and Kyaina. Everybody else thought that Alek ran away. That it was too much for him. Now you know the truth."

"But why? Why tell me?"

"Because we're partners, and partners are supposed to trust each other with their lives. And that's kind of hard to do when you keep secrets from them. That's what happened in my last partnership, and I'll be damned if I get stabbed in the back again." Eli laughed weakly.

"Why do I feel like you only told me that so I would tell you how I got in the labor camp?"

Eli shrugged. "That may have been part of the reason." Something about his eyes seemed off, but Shane ignored it. He had just told her something that he had kept secret for years. Of course, he was shaken up.

She debated for a moment whether she should tell him the full truth but decided against it. If she did, the chances of him believing her were low. She had a hard time wrapping her own mind around what happened.

"About six months ago," she started, voice shaking, "I found my way onto the island of Eringunner. And before you ask questions, I don't feel like explaining how, or why. The point is I was there." Shane took a shaky breath in and wiped her dry eyes. "I took a small boat back to Stoenstill and the waves picked up and I crashed."

She left Reece out of the story. She couldn't bear to tell anyone about how she got her killed. That would make it more real, and right now she was perfectly fine keeping it suppressed.

"I was so cold when I made it to shore that I thought I was going to die of hypothermia. I didn't have any dry clothes to change into, so I found my way into that alley and got some dry clothes off the clothesline. Then you showed up, and after you left, the guards found me," she continued. "They somehow figured out where I had been and put me in Princecon's dungeons."

When Shane finished telling her story, all the way until she and Kyaina managed to escape the camp, her voice was raw. She showed him the brands as she spoke about them, and told him exactly what she told Kyaina and Archer, that she was good at holding her breath. Either Eli didn't care that it might be a blatant lie, or he believed her.

"Bloody knives, Shane. Why didn't you tell me?"

Shane. Not Shay.

"Because you gave me no reason to." She wiped a tear that had escaped her eye. It was bad enough that Eli heard the shake in her voice. She couldn't let him see the tears that fell. Shane couldn't deal with that kind of humiliation. "If you had, then maybe I would've told you earlier."

CHAPTER 17

S weat beaded on Shane's forehead as she swung her knife at Eli's torso. She made sure to keep one eye on his sword and another on his body. He jumped backward and rained down on her with blow after blow. She was barely able to defend herself.

When his sword made a downward strike, Shane crossed both knives stopping the blow, and Shane immediately twisted the daggers, ripping the sword from Eli's hand. It landed a couple feet away from him, but before he could lunge for it, Shane blocked his path and put her knives at his throat. A smile spread across her face.

"Well done," Eli said sarcastically.

"For beating you?"

"No. For not paying full attention." As soon as the words left his mouth, he kneed her straight in the stomach. The contact sent her back several steps, allowing him to slam his arm into the top part of her body. She hit the ground hard, her knives tumbling from her hands. She tried to take in a breath, but the wind had been knocked from her lungs.

"I think," Eli said as he picked up his sword, "I won." He kicked her two blades away and pointed the sharp edge of his sword toward Shane, drawing the slightest bit of blood from her neck.

"But you have to admit that I was close." Shane pushed the blade away and painstakingly got up from the ground.

"I was pulling my punches."

Even though everything in her body was in pain, and she now had a slight cut on her neck, she had never been happier in her life. That was the first time in months she had ever been so close to beating Eli. She wasn't going to allow his comment to dissuade her from her happiness. True, there had been times where it looked like Eli had her overpowered in that fight, but she persisted.

Three months had passed since she first arrived at the Underground, and she had improved greatly from the moment she first set foot in the training room. She was no longer that weak girl who came back to her room with cuts and bruises everywhere. She forced herself to get into better shape, and it showed. What used to be arms of pure sinew and bones were now full of toned muscle.

Eli forced her to practice with a larger array of weapons every week, but she found that knives were what she liked the most. Something about them brought comfort to her. Eli made fun of her for it, of course.

"Why go for the weapon where you have to get closer to your enemy," he had said one day, "when you might just as well have a sword where you're less likely to get cut up and injured, because trust me when I say that will happen."

"I don't know. I just like them."

Now Eli stood there with his sword gripped loosely in one hand, the other holding his water flask. He gulped it down. Sweat dripped from his hair, which only made Shane smile. He had broken a sweat trying to beat her. Something that hadn't happened before.

They returned to practicing and kept going for another hour. They only stopped when both were too weak to lift their weapons anymore, not that Shane was complaining about that.

Training with Eli gave her time to distract herself from the dark thoughts that she fell into when she was alone. She would much rather face an actual life or death situation than the demons in her mind.

Shane collected her knives and went over to the benches to grab her stuff, as Eli followed. *Strange,* Shane thought. He was usually the first to leave without even so much as a goodbye. Yet there he was, standing right next to her.

"Yes?" She asked.

"I just wanted to tell you to meet me above ground tonight," he said. "Wear black, if you can, and make sure you bring something to keep you warm. I'm not going to give you my jacket again."

Of course, he would bring that up, even though it was mid-June and nowhere near as cold as it had been the night of the dance. "I'll try not to forget." She paused in the exit. "What time?"

"When the sun sets, so seven thirty?"

"Was that an answer or a question?"

"Meet me up there in a couple hours, okay?"

"Fine." Shane continued down the hallway and made her way toward her room. She would've gone to Kyaina's room, but she and Archer were once again on an assassination. Kyaina left a note in Shane's room saying that they would be back in a couple of weeks, leaving Shane alone with nothing except the company of her own thoughts. And Eli.

She set her stuff down in a pile by the door and looked over toward the clock in her room. Three fifteen, meaning she still had plenty of time before heading up.

Shane bathed quickly before sitting down in her chair next to the fireplace. A book sat on a small table next to the chair. She picked it up and turned to the page she had left off. She had moved on from history books to fiction. Too many names and dates floated around in her head that she thought she might explode. She knew the basic history of the land, and that was enough for her.

Shane had discovered a new love for reading. With no television or computers, it was the only pass time that would keep her entertained. She had tried drawing but quit when she realized that it was much more difficult than she perceived it to be, and it required paper, something she didn't own and couldn't buy.

So, she had turned to books, and she rather enjoyed them. Even though the stories she was reading now were fiction, it allowed her to be caught up in people that have a worse life than her own, and Shane found comfort in that.

She was too busy reading, being sucked into her own world, to even realize how quickly the time had passed. When she looked up, she was surprised to see that it was already seven.

Her eyes widened as she threw the book down and hurried for her dresser. Eli said wear black, but was he talking about everything being black? He also said to bring something warm, but since he didn't specify that it had to be fancy, Shane grabbed her cloak from the top of her dresser and changed quickly. She wasn't going to be late. Not again. She could only imagine how much Eli was going to torment her if she were.

The two of them had gotten along better since that night at the dance. Eli still teased and poked at her, but she did the same to him. The jokes were now just that. Jokes.

Shane left her room in a hurry. She passed a couple assassins, but none of them said hello. If she had learned one thing in the last few months it was that assassins weren't the most trustworthy of people.

When she made it up the stairs into the open air, the sun was just setting behind the mountains surrounding Conlar. The clouds were alight like fire with the sun's final rays. It would make a perfect picture if she'd only had a camera with her.

"What are you staring at?" Eli's voice startled her as he appeared from behind.

"Gods, you can't do that," Shane said once her heart had slowed to a reasonable rate.

"Do what?"

"Sneak up on me like that?"

A smile cracked over Eli's chap lips. "Scare you, did I? Shay, a little scaredy cat?"

"No, I'm not," she said. Shane sighed, trying to calm herself down. "Look, whatever you wanted to do, can we just get it done with?"

Eli nodded toward the setting sun. "We have to wait for the sun to fully set."

"Why?"

Eli brought his cloak hood over his head as a strong, spring breeze blew past them. "Because" he said quietly "we're about to do something illegal, and I don't want people to see us?"

Shane nearly choked. "Are we going to… kill someone?" Getting those words out of her mouth was more difficult than she thought it would be. She had been training to be an assassin. Those words shouldn't sound as foreign to her as they did.

"No. Of course not." Eli chuckled. "But that doesn't mean it won't get us thrown in prison if we're caught. Trust me when I say that someone as weak as you wouldn't survive a day in there."

"Then what are we doing out here?"

"I'm teaching you how to move around properly on rooftops."

Shane's eyes widened as she stared at him, so he continued. "All assassins have to be fairly good at this, and you should feel lucky to have me teach you. I don't mean to brag, but I'm one of the best at it."

"Pretty sure that you're full of yourself." She should've known that this was coming. It wasn't like an assassin would walk on the street to their next target. Yet why was she so paralyzed when Eli suggested it?

They stood in silence as the sun set behind the mountains. The last minutes of light were quickly being replaced by the cold darkness of the night. Eli grabbed her by the sleeve and started toward the main road. He weaved his way through the torchlit streets before finally turning down an alleyway full of abandoned looking buildings.

Shane stared up at the rooftop, her stomach doing somersaults. When she looked back at Eli, he only stared at her, as if waiting for an answer. "What?"

"Are you gonna start climbing first, or should I?" There was a bit of annoyance in his voice, but he did a good job hiding it. The dim crescent moon was rising above the mountains, barely giving enough light to see.

Shane looked up once again. She never realized just how tall the building was. "You can go first." Her voice was nothing more than a whisper.

Eli audibly sighed with annoyance. "Don't tell me you're afraid of heights?"

Shane remained silent and let her pale white face tell him the truth.

He let out a low, humorless chuckle that soon gave way to roaring laughter. "Of course, you are," he said, glaring at her. "'Cause why not? Wikter paired me with the one person in the world who can annoy me on so many levels. Just great."

"I don't see what's funny here."

"Of course, you don't." Eli pushed his hair away from his face. "That might be because there is nothing funny about this situation. The only reason I'm laughing is because there's nothing *to* laugh about."

Shane pursed her lips, glaring at Eli. "Look, can we just get this done with?"

"Yeah." Eli suppressed a laugh poorly. "Try and make sure you don't fall."

With that, he ran up the wall and leaped upward, grabbing the nearest windowsill, and hauled himself up. He continued scaling expertly up the wall like a spider before reaching the top.

"Come on." He yelled. "It's easy."

"Maybe for you." *But unlike you, I'm not nearly six feet tall.*

She walked up to the wall, brushing her hand on its rough, stone surface. She gripped the bricks so tightly her fingers turned white. She took a deep breath before hauling herself up, bringing her feet off the ground. She didn't bother looking up to see where the windowsill was. *Too far. It's too far.*

Slowly, inch by inch, Shane climbed her way up the wall. Her arms shook when her hand landed on the sill. Relief washed over her body as she used every muscle in her body to pull herself onto it. She sat there for a moment, taking in deep, laborious breaths. It shouldn't have been that difficult to climb up maybe ten feet.

Shane let out a sigh of annoyance as she looked out at the building across from her. She couldn't even see the top of it from her vantage point. She still had a long, long way to go.

Just don't look down.

Those words rang through her mind as she once again found more hand holds in the wall. She shifted her entire weight onto them, and her arms were shaking uncontrollably from exhaustion. How far was it to the ground? How much would it hurt when, not if, her arms gave out?

Shane cleared her mind and kept climbing. The winds seemed to increase the higher she got, as did her heart rate. Her clammy hands made her fearful every time grabbed onto another exposed rock face. What if the rock she was grabbing onto fell away from the wall? Didn't most climbers have chalk or something? Where was hers?

She had nearly made it to the top when a strong breeze came up, nearly knocking her straight off the wall. She gripped tighter, breaths coming in uneven gasps. Then she looked down. If she messed up here, she would most definitely die, probably painfully.

Don't think. Just do.

She continued upward, and finally the top ledge loomed above, an arm's reach away. She shakily reached up, her hand grasping it firmly. She followed it with her other hand and within seconds she was lying on top of the building with the warm breeze blowing over her. Her breaths caught in her throat, and she was too numb with shock to even register Eli standing over her.

"If I'm not mistaken," he said, not bothering to offer a hand to help her up, "It took you nearly three times as long as it took me to get up here."

"Shut up." Shane had already been through enough that his words bounced right off her. "If you wouldn't mind being a gentleman, would you help me up?" She was about to stop there, but something about his windswept hair, and mischievous smile made her add, "And also not chuck me off the building."

"Now why would I do that?" He stuck out a hand and Shane wearily took it.

"Because you have that look in your eye that you have every time you're about to make fun or make a fool out of me."

The breeze blew harder, making Shane stumble, but Eli caught her before she fell off the roof. "And what look is that?"

"I don't know. An evil one."

Eli shook his head and started across the roof of the building. It had rained earlier that day, the roof was still wet and puddles had formed in the dipped areas.

"Where are you going?" Shane asked.

"You know, for someone who's afraid of heights," Eli turned around, but continued to stroll backward, "you're rather talkative in the face of your fear."

"You didn't answer my question."

Eli stopped near the edge and looked out across the entire city. "I want you to jump from this building to the next." He pointed down at a smaller building that still looked dangerously high. It was only about seven feet away, but the thought of jumping terrified her.

"You're joking, right?" Shane kept her distance from the edge. She was too afraid that the wind was going to pick up once again and blow her off. "You do realize that I am absolutely terrified of heights?"

"Then why did you climb up?" Eli stared her straight in the eyes. A challenge. "If you were so afraid, why'd you do it? No rope. No net to catch you. There was absolutely nothing to save you if you fell, so why? Why in the world did you do it?"

Shane remained silent, paralyzed. Him saying those things didn't make her want to jump even more.

"You aren't really scared of heights. Your brain has been conditioned to believe you are when in truth you were perfectly fine climbing up here."

"I'm pretty sure that *all* fears are just in our heads."

Eli ignored her. "Come here," he said, holding out a hand.

Millions of thoughts flooded Shane's mind before she made the dumbest decision of her life and took his hand. He brought her closer to the edge than she was comfortable with. Looking down from this height made the roof beneath her feet sway underneath her.

"See? Nothing to be afraid of."

"Except the extreme height and sheer drop off right in front of me," Shane grumbled. "You're right, nothing to be afraid of."

"Now jump."

"I don't think you understand how this whole fear thing works. You saying that it's all in my mind isn't really helping me."

"Would you prefer I say that you're being too much of a wimp and you just have to jump, even though you're absolutely terrified that you might fall?"

"Believe it or not, but that's only making it worse." Shane tried to back away from the edge, but Eli's arm was there to stop her. It gripped her body tightly making sure that she didn't go anywhere.

"Jump." Eli's eyes remained fixed on her, boring into her soul.

"You know—"

"Just. Jump." He let her go. "I'll let you get a running start."

Looking back, Shane gulped. "It looks rather slippery. Are you sure this is a good time for this?"

"Jump."

Shane let out an exasperated breath. There was no way to back out of this. She looked out to the building she was supposed to be landing on, and something hard fell into her stomach.

Before she could make up her mind of when she was going to do it, something hard slammed into her back. She lost balance on the edge and was only standing on one foot about to fall off the edge when something inside her took over. She pushed with all her might, leaping off the building and falling faster than she ever had in her life. Her mind filled with inaudible screams; no coherent thought could be heard. The cries got caught in her throat. Even when she tried, the wind against her face only whisked the scream away.

As suddenly as the falling started, it stopped. Shane's entire body slammed into the ledge of the building she'd been aiming for. The little breath she had in her lungs got knocked out. Sheer reflex allowed her to grab hold of the ledge before her body slid down the side. The only thing supporting her was her arms, and though they were shaky, she managed to pull herself up.

Lying on her back looking toward the sky, she heard the sound of Eli gracefully rolling on the ground next to her. "You... are an evil, evil man.”

“Don’t know what you’re talking about.”

Shane picked herself up from the ground with tremendous effort. “What happened to not pushing me off? Huh? Or did your sadistic mind forget.”

“You had trouble finding the courage to jump, and I fixed that.”

“Yeah. By punching me in the back and giving me no choice.”

“I actually kicked you.”

“Same difference.” Eli stuck out his hand to help her, but she pushed it away. “Don’t you dare touch me.”

“All you needed was a little nudge in the right direction.” He paused. “I didn’t realize how close it would be. I’m sorry, okay?”

Shane let out a humorless laugh. She was about to say something, but just then they heard a voice come from across the roof. A man dressed in shabby clothes with a full, dirty beard came out of the darkness. He appeared intoxicated.

“What are you doing here?” he asked, his words slurring together.

“Run.” Eli’s quiet voice was right in Shane’s ear, breathing down her neck. He took her hand and sprinted away, nearly yanking Shane’s arm off.

“Why are we running?”

A gunshot sounded behind them and a blinding pain appeared on the outer edge of Shane’s arm.

“Because of that.”

“Elias.” Shane breathed. She looked down at her arm to see drops of red blood coating it. “He shot me.”

“It’s only a graze.” He started sprinting faster. “Now come on.”

He ran in zigzags making it more difficult for the man to shoot them again. They kept getting closer and closer to the edge.

Before Shane could complain, it was already too late. Eli hurled himself off the building, bringing Shane with him.

They let go of each other's hand's midair, the wind blowing them apart. When Shane's feet touched the ground, she instinctively went in for a roll, like she had seen in so many parkour videos. Little did she know that one day her life would depend on it.

Eli kept sprinting, and Shane followed. Wherever he ran, she ran. When he jumped from one building to another, so did she. She watched as Eli would do something and she did all she could to recreate his every move, no matter how sloppy she might have been. He was trying for efficiency, and she was too.

Shane lost count of how many perilous leaps she made. Her heartbeat was faster than it ever had ever been in her life as she vaulted over obstacles. Her bleeding arm pulsed in pain with every passing moment, but she couldn't focus on that unless she wanted their pursuer with the gun to shoot her again. The only thing she could do was keep moving forward.

She followed close behind Eli as he ran along a slanted rooftop. With every step Shane prayed to whatever god would listen that her feet wouldn't slip out from under her on the slippery surface. They must have answered because the next thing she knew she was hanging from the ledge right next to Eli. He dropped, so she did the same. The adrenaline coursing through her veins helped her not to worry about the height.

She hit the ground and scrambled to get into the alleyway away from the flickering lantern light in the street and any prying eyes. Eli grabbed her by the arm once again and dragged her into a tight space behind a trash can, hidden from view. Eli held her so tightly that Shane could feel his pounding heartbeat on her chest. Someone was making noise on the roof, but a few moments later the noise disappeared.

"I think that we lost him," Eli said after a few minutes. He looked Shane in the eyes and both of them started laughing. "I think we both can agree that this night was a disaster."

"You think?" Eli released her from his warm embrace. "I don't know about you but getting shot in the arm while on the run was most definitely on my bucket list."

She made her way into the street where there was more light to see by to assess the damage the man did to her arm. Eli was right, saying that it was nothing more than a graze, but it still hurt like Haytorrow's Realm. She winced when she tried to wipe away debris from the wound.

"Can I see?"

Shane offered her arm to Eli and grimaced as his rough hand grazed against it. "We need to clean this out with some blukreg to stop it from getting infected?"

"Really? I was just gonna leave it as is and hope for the best." Shane shrugged Eli off her bloody arm and started making her way toward the main street.

"Wait." Eli ran up to catch her, his cloak hood falling off his head. His messy brown hair glinted in the lantern light. "I think we both can agree that your fear of heights is fake."

"So what? I've just been running around thinking that I'm afraid when truly I'm not?" Shane laughed. "Yeah right."

"It's all in your head." Eli tapped his temple. "If it weren't then you wouldn't be able to jump buildings without hesitation."

"Or it could've been the adrenaline rushing through me." Shane looked over at Eli and knew she was wrong, but she wasn't about to admit it. He was right. She didn't hesitate when it came time to jump. If anything, there was a sense of exhilaration that came with it.

"Come on," she finally said. "I don't want to lose an arm because some old drunkard shot at me."

CHAPTER 18

S hane and Eli had been on the road for six days, and Rotshall was still half a day away. They were both exhausted from the long days on horseback. Half a day out, Shane started to get uncomfortable in the saddle, and it only got worse after that. Eventually it was chafing so bad against her thighs that when she got off it took her several minutes to walk correctly.

Not that she was complaining.

Wikter had come to her and Eli a week before and had stopped them on their way back to their rooms after the first training session of the day.

"Elias," he had said. "I have a mission for you, and I would like you to take Shane along."

Eli laughed uncomfortably, popping his fingers. "Do you really think she's ready? I mean, have you seen her practicing? No offence."

"None taken. Yes, actually, I have. That's why I want her to go with you. She knows the fundamentals, but she needs to know what it's really like out there." He paused, looking at Shane strangely. "You never know if you're ready until you jump in completely."

This was the first time since she had come to the Assassin's Underground that she was allowed to go outside the city. The smell of warm, fresh air and the sun shining down on her made it all worth it. The clouds over the mountains were disheartening, but the mountains dispersed them before they could hit the valley of Rotshall.

The castle was ahead, and she noticed its tall, white stone with windows covering its exterior. It stuck out from the landscape like a sore thumb.

"Gods, I hate that building," Shane muttered.

"I hate this city."

Eli whipped his horse with his reins and galloped along the winding trail, leaving Shane no choice but to do the same to catch up.

The horses carried them into the valley leading to the outskirts of the city; Shane could smell the freshly planted farmland that spread out around them.

"Why do you hate it here so much?" Shane asked. She was surprised by the number of people bustling around them as they entered the city. They dismounted, and she noticed that Eli held the reins in a death grip.

"Despite the fact that this was where I got stabbed and left for dead by my dearly beloved brother, this was where we lived before leaving for Conlar."

"Shouldn't you have good memories then? Of your childhood?"

"Oh yeah. Just great ones of being homeless, wondering each day where our next meal was coming from."

It seemed to Shane that everyone in the city was out and about, and she couldn't blame them. It was a beautiful day to be outside. Navigating through the crowd to the inn they were staying was a bit difficult.

"I hate people," Eli mumbled under his breath.

"You aren't the only one."

They led their horses down the twisting street along to the city walls before arriving at a rundown stable. Dirty hay covered the ground, along with horse manure. The stench in the air made her gag.

"I can only wonder how the inn is," Shane quipped as she tied her horse's reins to one of the posts.

Eli stared at the building across the street. "My guess is not good."

The building's shingles were falling off the roof, and it was stained with water damage. She tried not to judge it too harshly, but that was hard not to do when everything she had seen so far pointed to the direction of it being one of the worst establishments she could sleep in.

"You first," Eli said, holding open the door while taking in a deep breath. Shane went through.

It was a new smell that Shane noticed inside the inn, but no less unpleasant. The stale dust in the air attacked Shane's sinuses, and a sneezing fit took over. The musty smell mixed with damp mold wasn't helping.

An old lady with white hair sat behind the desk, which by the looks of it was the newest thing in the entire inn. A hallway off to the right of her led back to the rooms, Shane suspected.

Shane allowed Eli to go talk to her while she stayed back. She heard coins clanging together, and Eli motioned for her to come with him down the hallway.

"She overpriced me by a lot," he whispered into Shane's ear, looking back to make sure that the old lady didn't hear him. "Cost me an extra twenty Schulhers just to use the stables."

"How much does it normally cost?"

"For a place that doesn't smell like shit? About fifteen for both horses."

Shane let out a low whistle. "Why are we here then?"

Eli stopped at his door and handed Shane the key to her own. "Because we don't want to draw attention to ourselves. We go somewhere small like this, and nobody notices us." He opened his room and immediately gagged. "Bloody knives."

"Good thing we're only sleeping in here," Shane said half-heartedly. She went into her room and shut the door behind her. She tried not to breathe too much, afraid that if she did it would only lead to a sooner death. There were mold spots in the corners of the room and next to the dirty window. A giant beetle-like thing crawled over her pillow, and she almost screamed.

It's just a bug, she had to remind herself. *It can't hurt you.*

She had to steel up her nerves as she brushed it off the bed and stepped on the scurrying creature with a satisfying crunch before setting her bag high on a dresser. She didn't have much. Just a change of clothes and some stuff for hygiene, but she didn't want them to get infected, or infested.

"We have to get out of here," Eli said, bursting into her room. "I can't stand the smell anymore."

"We have to stay the night here," Shane reminded him, even though that was far from what she wanted.

"No, actually we don't." He looked over his shoulder. "Just grab your stuff and leave through the window. I don't want to see that lady again. She reeks of death."

"Uh, okay." Eli left Shane alone in her room. She gladly picked back up her pack and opened the window with a great amount of effort. The ground was at a slope along the edge of the building, so when she let go of the sill she still had quite a ways to fall, but it was worth it in the end. She welcomed fresh air into her nostrils, and then let out a sigh of relief.

Eli was already on the ground pressed against the side of the building. When Shane joined him, he motioned for her to follow.

"What about the horses?" Shane asked when they made it back to the main street and disappeared into the hordes of people.

"We'll get them back before tomorrow."

"And the money you spent getting those rooms?"

Eli laughed. "You owe me some for that once you get your own money, but right now it doesn't matter." Shane stared at him to continue, so he did. "I'm rich, Shay."

Shane raised an eyebrow. "Off of blood money, I presume?"

"That," he shrugged, "and something else."

"Are you going to elaborate, or am I supposed to figure it out on context clues?"

"That'd be great. Thanks."

Shane rolled her eyes.

She didn't know where they were going, but Eli must've because they continued walking with a purpose. She had known Eli long enough to figure out that if she asked any more questions, he would get snippy. So, through the crowds of people they went, sticking close together. Shane made sure nobody got in between her and Eli. She wasn't about to lose him. Not in Rotshall.

Eli turned down a side street and continued to weave through the streets and back alleys as though he knew the place like the back of his hand, as Shane assumed he did. He had grown up here.

When they finally stopped, they were in a sketchy neighborhood near the outskirts of the city. Boarded up, dilapidated buildings surrounded them. Eli was staring at an old, burnt down apartment building. Shane was about to speak, but then she saw the expression on Eli's face. Hurt, mixed with sadness and grief.

"Was this where you lived?" she asked after allowing a few moments of silence.

Eli cleared his throat. "Yeah. It was." He shouldered his pack and headed for the burnt building.

"Wait. Are you sure that it's safe?"

"Yes. I'm sure." He ducked under a partially fallen beam and disappeared. "Me and Alek made sure of it before we moved in."

"So, it was always burnt down?"

"I mean, it wasn't always burnt, but that was over ten years ago." Eli's head popped up over the rubble. "Come on. You aren't too much of a wimp to come in, are you?"

"No," Shane lied. As she started in, she scanned for any weak spots both beneath her feet and over her head. She couldn't help but imagine the whole building collapsing on them, burying them under thousands of pounds of black charred wood.

"It's a little tighter than I remember, but we'll fit." Eli bent over a tiny hole in a wall just above the floor, no bigger than the width of one person.

"You're joking, right?" Shane asked.

"I mean, if you want to go back to the Cockroach Inn, be my guest. It's already paid for."

Shane stared daggers at him before taking her bag off her shoulders. "I hate you. You know that?"

"You remind me every day."

Shane handed him the bag and tried to relax her shoulders, but they were tense with fear. All she had to do was get through that tiny, tiny hole in the wall, hope it doesn't collapse on her, all without hyperventilating. Sounded simple enough, but it was the execution of it that worried her.

She laid on her back and started sliding through the small hole feet first. The smile on Eli's face told her that she most likely made a mistake by choosing to go in that way, but she didn't care. She wasn't going to allow her back to be her only escape path.

When Shane was halfway through, she started having doubts, but pushed them down into the deepest parts of her mind. She wasn't going to allow Eli to see her back out of something so simple and trivial as crawling through a tight space.

She tugged herself through until at last she was able to breathe again. Her whole body relaxed as she leaned against the interior wall wiping a cold sweat off her forehead. Moments later, Eli crawled head first through the hole, and rested next to her.

"That was among the worst things I have ever done in my life."

"It was fun watching you struggle your way through it." Eli laughed.

"Haha." Shane's voice dripped with sarcasm. "Very amusing."

She brought her eyes up to see that she was in a small room maybe seven feet tall. Two beds with moth bitten blankets sat along the far wall. It was strange thinking of a young Elias and his brother sleeping in them, but Shane didn't have trouble picturing it. Eli went over to a bed and placed his pack down. Shane could picture him, maybe five years younger, doing the exact same thing. The only difference was that it was Alek with him, not her.

"Why'd you decide to live here of all places?" Shane asked.

"We didn't decide. We *had* to."

"But why?" Shane knew she'd already asked enough questions for the day, but this one was burning at the tip of her tongue.

"Because." Shane wasn't going to accept that answer, and Eli must've known that. He sighed. "My brother tried to find a job, but he couldn't so we had to live off the streets."

"Sounds rather unpleasant."

"It was." Eli tossed his bag to the side of his bed. He didn't elaborate.

Shane cleared her throat and decided to change the conversation. "So, are we going to sit here until night falls, or do you have something else planned."

"I had something else in mind."

"What is it?" Something about Eli's tone of voice, and the glint in his eyes, made Shane uneasy.

"You'll see. Come with me."

He led Shane back out through the tiny entrance, and this time it was easier for her.

Eli took her back out to the street and led her to the main square. People were gathered everywhere. They all formed into little clusters, their full money bags jingling by their sides.

"Watch it!" Eli barked at a young boy who accidentally bumped into him in his haste. He shoved him away.

The boy recoiled in fear. "Sorry," he mumbled. "It won't happen again."

"I would sure hope it doesn't."

The boy ran along before Shane could get to Eli. "What in Haytorrow's Realm is wrong with you?" she asked. "That was just a boy."

"A boy with money." Eli held up an old, black coin sack filled to the brim.

Shane gasped. "Did you just…?"

"Pickpocket him?" A smile reached Eli's face. "Yes, I did."

Shane punched him in the shoulder

"He was just a boy."

"A rich, entitled, snobby boy." Eli sighed and pocketed the coins. "Trust me when I say that I know what they're like. I used to be one of them."

Shane laughed. "You? Rich and snobby?" She looked him up and down. "I can see it. As far as I'm concerned, that's what you are right now."

Eli laughed.

"Is that your plan? To teach me how to pickpocket?" She wasn't sure how she felt about that. She knew that eventually she would have to do much worse, but it never really felt real. It was just a fantasy that would never come true.

"Yes." Eli escorted her over to the fountain of Mindalin in the middle of the square. "You see that girl right over there?" He pointed to a girl standing at a vending cart. Shane nodded, and he continued. "I want you to go over there and try and steal something from her."

Shane eyed a guard walking around the square. There were multiple others hidden within the crowd. "What if I get caught?"

"Don't."

"That simple?" Shane sarcastically said. "Who would've known?"

"Just wait until you see no guard near her and go." Eli pushed Shane's shoulder, and she started toward the girl. She looked back only to see Eli give her an encouraging nod. Not helpful. "Make sure you don't freeze up."

Shane wiped her clammy hands on her pants as she approached the vendor. What was she going to do? Why did Eli always put her in situations and make her figure out how to get out on her own?

The girl put her money bag away on her left hip and grabbed what looked to be food of some sort from the vendor. She turned around and started walking toward Shane. Their eyes met momentarily, and Shane couldn't help the fear from showing in her own, but the girl averted her attention and continued onward toward the fountain like she had seen nothing.

Shane's eyes narrowed as she stared down at the girl's waist. It should've been simple. Bump into her, untie it, and let her walk away without noticing it was gone. It was getting up the courage to do it. That was the hardest part.

The girl was about to sit down at the fountain when Shane ran up to her.

"Thank the gods," Shane said, placing her hand on the girl's shoulder. "I've been looking for you everywhere."

"I'm sorry?" The girl shifted on her feet, her eyes darting from Shane to the guard. *Please don't call them over here.* "Do I know you?"

"Do you not recognize me?" Shane sounded taken aback when in truth she was freaking out. "It's me, Kathrine."

"I don't know a Kathrine." She removed Shane's hand from her shoulder and walked away in a hurry.

Shane tossed the bag of money into the air before putting it in a pocket. She had snagged it from the girl's belt when she had turned to go away.

"Nicely done." Eli appeared behind her. "What'd you say to her? Or did she just give it to you out of pity?"

"I just acted like I knew her." Shane dug into her bag and grabbed twenty Schulhers and presented it to Eli. "Now I don't owe you."

That's how they spent the rest of the evening. When the sun was about to set, they were many Schulher's richer than they had been when they started the day.

"If it's that easy," Shane said as they made their way back to the place they were staying, "I'm envious of your old life."

Eli cracked a smile. "It's a lot more difficult when there aren't that many people. Today's the celebration of New Life, and it was a good day. Of course, people were out on the streets making it easy."

"I think you're just jealous."

"Of what? Of you being a good petty thief?" Eli paused in the street. "If you haven't figured it out, we have a lot more to worry about than that. Tonight, you get to witness your first assassination."

Chapter 19

I t was dark by the time they got ready to leave. Clouds had moved in, blocking the moonlight from illuminating the streets and rooftops they would be running across. With their black under layer, cloaks, masks, and fingerless gloves, they would be nearly impossible to see unless they were standing in the middle of a lighted street.

Eli guided the way down the now deserted street. They kept off the well-lit main roads to keep out of sight and it wasn't long before they stopped in a dead end alleyway lined with low buildings.

"What are you waiting for? Get up there," Eli said, pointing to the building on the right.

"You sure you want me to go first?"

"Yes, I'm sure." He motioned with his head to hurry up. "That way if you fall, I'll be able to catch you before you hit the ground and cause a ruckus that will most definitely get us caught."

Shane pursed her lips. "Thanks for the faith in me."

Every night for the last two weeks before they left for Rotshall, they had gone to the surface and practiced moving around on the rooftops. Shane had gotten better at it, but nowhere near as good as she wanted to be. Her fear kept getting in the way, stopping her from what she knew she could do.

"Don't freeze at the top," Eli said when she hauled herself up.

Shane's face burned bright red. "Have I ever done that?"

"No, but you came close."

She started climbing and continued until her hands caught onto the ledge to the rooftops, and she scrambled her way up. Shortly after, Eli appeared at the rooftop with her.

They moved like wraiths in the night silently across the rooftops. Eli had taught Shane over the past few months the ways of stealth. It was hard to sneak up on someone when your footsteps betrayed you.

Eli leaped from a building, and Shane was close behind. She jumped without thinking, because she knew that if she did, she might freeze. She hit the roof rolling and continued to chase after Eli.

They continued for quite some time before Elias stopped at the edge of a rooftop, motioning for Shane to do the same.

"That's the target's house," he said, pointing to the building across the street.

He took a quick inventory of his weapons. He hadn't brought a sword because it was too big and heavy to carry around with him, but he wore knife sheaths hidden on his thigh and arm. Shane also carried a knife, but for her it was only for self-defense. She wasn't ready to go for a kill. Not yet.

The target's name was Nordin Wayne. He was thirty-seven years old and the captain of the Royal Army. His name had been whispered in fear everywhere they traveled, and Shane couldn't blame people for being afraid of him. He was the one who executed the king's orders, no matter how horrible they were. King Aarion had banished all the people of Ginacallo descent, and Nordin ordered them to be killed.

And that was just the beginning of his atrocities.

It was no wonder someone wanted him dead. They were willing to pay handsomely if it was done on the night of New Life, which was what Eli and Shane intended to do.

"Why doesn't he live in the castle?" Shane whispered, crouching on the ledge that looked down at the small balcony that was attached to Nordin's bedroom. They were in the wealthier part of the city.

On the mountains above loomed the castle in which the King lived. Shane couldn't help but shudder every time she looked up. Images of Reece's bloody, dying body flooded her mind every time she did. No matter how much she tried to force them away, she couldn't.

"Because only the King, his heir, and his Thirteen Advisors live there."

The thirteen advisors. Just as powerful as the king, but without the public face.

"And besides," Eli continued as he joined her at the edge, "if I were him, I would want a little personal space."

Shane cracked a fake smile.

Eli got up and started leaping from building to building around the square, Shane close behind, until he stood on Nordin's roof. He leaned against the chimney billowing woodsy smoke. Shane snuck over to him and sat down. Her eyes stared at the flickering lights from Nordin's room reflecting on the buildings across the square. As soon as they went out, she knew Nordin would be in bed, meaning they would only have a short wait before they could make their move.

Shane's eyes glazed over as the coldness of the night crept over her. She pulled her cloak tight around her, but still shivered in the cold breeze. Time seemed to stand still.

"Aren't you cold?" she whispered to Eli who didn't show any signs of being so.

"Not really."

"But h—"

"Lights have been out for a while now. He's probably asleep."

Eli pushed himself from his perch on the chimney and silently crept his way toward the drop off to the street. Shane followed close behind. She stood near the gutter as Eli dropped down and hung onto the ledge, then dropped silently on the small balcony. Shane was right behind him.

Eli slid behind her and started on the lock. He pulled some tools out of one of his pockets and went to work. Every minute that Shane had to wait for the patio door to come open was agony. She was sure that someone would come out to the street and see them any minute.

Before they left for the assassination, Shane tried to convince Eli to choose to enter a window on a side street because fewer eyes could see them there, but he refused. Apparently, all those windows led to the servants' chambers, and Eli didn't want to waste any unnecessary lives that night.

So, he chose the direct path into Nordin's room.

Eli put his lock picking tools away and slowly opened the door. Every creak made Shane's heart leap into her throat. Once open, Shane was the first to enter the room. Though she couldn't hear Eli's footsteps, she knew he was there. She could feel his presence.

There was a glint of a knife as Eli pulled out one of his many blades and made his way quietly over to the tall four-poster bed. He gestured for Shane to follow, and she complied even though every instinct in her told her to run away. She made sure to place her feet exactly where Eli had for fear that if she didn't, she would step on a squeaky floorboard. Her heart was beating so hard she was afraid that it would wake Nordin.

"Ready?" Eli mouthed from across the bed.

Shane felt like if she talked, she would puke, so instead she nodded.

Eli raised the knife in the air. Its silver blade reflected what little light that was in the room. Nordin seemed so peaceful just lying there, yet Shane knew this was far from the truth. He'd murdered hundreds, if not thousands, of people. If anyone deserved to die, it was him.

Time slowed as Eli brought his knife down on Nordin's throat. Shane wanted to look away, but her eyes were glued to his face. Something felt wrong about killing him while he slept, but before Shane could say anything, the knife sliced through Nordin's neck, and blood sprouted out of the deep wound. His eyes sprung open, and they met Shane's own, confused, pleading with her to help him. Blood ran down his neck, soaking into his hands now holding his throat as he convulsed in the bed.

Then he was still.

Bile rose in Shane's throat as the room began to spin around her, like her head was caught in a tornado.

His eyes. Oh, gods his eyes. They still stared up at her as if to say, *how could you do this to me?*

Shane stumbled toward the patio door. She didn't care how much noise she made. She just wanted to get out of the room.

Fresh air. That was what Shane needed. Anything to get the sickening smell of blood out of her nose.

It was hard to climb the slanted roof with her head spinning, but she managed. When she finally made it to the chimney her stomach tightened and the bile that had risen in her throat finally found its way out. She wretched her guts out, the vile taste of stomach acid being the only thing that seemed real at the moment. Everything else was numb. Numb to the cold. Numb to the touch of stone and numb to the world around her.

A hand touched her shoulder. "Are you all right?" Eli asked, worry in his voice.

She nodded wearily, wiping the vomit from her chin with her sleeve. "Let's just get out of here, all right?" Her voice was nothing but a whisper in the night.

Eli peered at her warily like he was going to argue, but after making sure his cloak was covering his head, he ran toward the edge of the building. Shane was no longer afraid to jump. She wanted to be as far away from the scene as possible. Every time she closed her eyes, she saw the room. All its details jumped out at her. The smell. The feel of the bed sheets grazing against her fingers. The sound of silence filled her head until it consumed her.

Shane shook her head, tears springing from her eyes. Nordin had deserved to die, she had to tell herself when in truth she was having difficulty believing it.

Eli was the first back on the street where they started. When the balls of Shane's feet touched the ground, pain flared up in her knees, but she ignored it. Anything that could distract her from what had just happened was welcome.

They were quiet as they made their way back to the burned down building. Neither said a word until they were both safe inside Eli's hidden room.

"Are you all right?" Eli asked again.

"I'm fine."

Shane tried to take off her cloak, but her hands were shaking too much to untie the simple knot. She frowned as she yanked at it, trying to break the strings off and get the thing off. Eli saw her struggle and held her arms down.

"You're going to hurt yourself if you keep doing this."

"Why won't it come off?" Tears clouded her vision as she tried to elbow Eli in the stomach to get him away from her, but Eli clamped his arms around her, stopping her. Her breaths came unevenly as she sobbed in his arms.

"What is it?" he asked gently. His worried eyes searched Shane's face for any sign of what it was that was bothering her.

"His eyes." *His. Not Nordin's.* She couldn't say his name without feeling sick again. "Oh gods, his eyes," Shane sobbed. "They looked exactly like my friend's before she died."

"Your… friend?" Eli's face seemed to pale.

Shane nodded. "Her name was Reece."

"Bloody knives." Eli breathed. "That day in Stoenstill, there were two people I saw, weren't there? You and your friend."

Shane allowed her silence to answer his question. "We both got caught by the soldiers looking for you." She took in a shaky breath. "The king killed her like it was nothing. He… he held me down and made me watch as it happened. She died in my arms, Elias." She looked up and met his eyes. "I couldn't save her. It's my fault that she's dead."

"No, it isn't."

"Yes. It is." Shane allowed the tears to fall freely from her eyes. "I was the one to convince her to go to the football game. I was the one who forced her."

"The what?"

Shane took a deep breath in. "I haven't been completely honest with you, Eli." She had to tell someone the truth. It had been eating away at her for long enough, and she let it all spill out— the portal, the boat, Mindalin, the water breathing, all of it — to the one person who she should trust.

When she finished, there was silence.

"My gods." Eli rubbed his hand on his mouth, eyes wide.

"I know that it's difficult to believe, but…"

"I believe you."

Those three words shocked Shane more than anything that had happened to her the whole time she had been in that world. "You do?" she asked quietly.

"Yes." Eli cleared his throat. "I mean, if you weren't a complete emotional mess right now, I might not have, but since you are, I can see your sincerity."

A huge sigh left Shane. "I can't tell you how much of a relief that is to hear right now." She wiped the excess tears from her cheeks. "It should've been me. Not Reece who died." Her voice got choked up at the end.

"Don't say that."

"But it's true."

"If that's true then I should've died when I was six." Eli averted his eyes away from Shane. "But here I am, alive and well in Lyconnexal."

"What? Why?"

"Because…" he stopped as if trying to find the right words, "that's when both my parents died. I blamed myself for their deaths for the longest time, but…" He paused. "Trust me when I say that I know what it's like, feeling like you can never be whole again with their memory haunting you every time you shut your eyes. With every move you make you feel like if they were still alive, they would be disappointed in you."

"How do you deal with it?"

"It gets better, but it never disappears." Shane looked up at him with disbelief in her eyes. "You have to just keep moving forward with your life. Don't let the past cripple you."

"You're not really helping me."

"Am I supposed to?" Eli forced a smile.

"It would be helpful if you did." Shane sighed. "What did you mean when you said that you're thousands of miles away from home?"

"Not anything like you." Eli pursed his lips. "My father was the prime minister of Iapciz."

Shane raised an eyebrow. "I didn't realize that we had someone of importance here with us."

"I wouldn't call myself important. Far from it actually."

Shane racked her brain, trying to remember what she had read about Iapciz. "You're Elias Shallowgal?" Shane asked, eyes wide. "Aren't you and your brother supposed to be dead?"

"That's what the world believes, but it was just my parents that died that night. Alek and I were boarded on a boat headed for Lyconnexal by our captors."

"When you said you weren't cold tonight—"

"Yes. That's because I have some of Fuerbrand's Chosen Hero's blood flowing through my veins. Even though it's very diluted."

"That's so cool," Shane said wistfully.

Eli laughed. "Are you kidding? You're Mindalin's Chosen Hero. You do realize that the last person to have that honor was —"

"Princess Airel? Yeah, I do." She must not have sounded very enthusiastic because Eli stared at her, so she continued. "Look how well it turned out for her. I don't know about you, but I don't necessarily want to die."

"Come on. Everyone dies eventually."

"But not when they're twenty-one in a mysterious manner that most likely was violent and brutal like Airel did." Shane let out a sigh. "Why would Mindalin choose someone like me to be her Chosen Hero?" she mumbled.

The question had been burning in the back of Shane's mind since the moment she was chosen. Why her when there were so many other more qualified candidates? Mindalin could have, and should have, at least chosen Reece. At least she wasn't paralyzed by her mistakes. She never would've made the poor choices Shane did to survive.

"Sounds irresponsible." Eli laughed a dry chuckle. "I mean, she at least could've chosen someone with some experience who was born in this world."

"Exactly what I thought."

"Maybe Mindalin wanted someone with a certain set of skills," Eli suggested.

Shane laughed. "Oh yeah. Definitely. With my only skills being too weak and vulnerable to save my best friend, it makes sense."

"You aren't giving yourself enough credit. Would a weak person be able to survive months in one of the worst labor camps on this whole continent? Would they be able to weasel their way into one of the best groups of assassins in all of Lyconnexal?"

"I was just lucky," Shane said.

But was she really? Maybe Eli was right. Maybe she did deserve a little more recognition from herself for what she had managed to endure and survive over the last half a year.

"Why are you being nice to me?"

There was a long silence before Eli said, "Because we're partners."

For the first time since she met Eli, Shane felt like he was telling the full truth.

CHAPTER 20

They were packed and ready to leave before sunrise. Shane was the first to exit through the hole. She made her way through the burnt debris until she was standing on the street with her rucksack, her face covered in soot.

"You have a little something here," Eli said once he joined her. "Makes you look homeless.

"I know that." She wiped a little dirt from her face.

Eli led the way back to the stables and was quick to untie his horse. Shane gagged as she released her own horse. She gripped its reins and led it down the street behind her partner. The sooner they were out of Rotshall and left the castle behind, the better.

It took them a week to get back to Conlar. All the tension and stress that Shane carried on her shoulders seemed to disintegrate the moment they entered the alleyway leading to the Assassin's Underground. She was home. It seemed strange at first to call this place home, but it was true. She had lived here for nearly three and a half months, and it no longer felt foreign to her.

They said nothing to each other as they entered their separate rooms. Shane closed the door and let out a sigh as threw herself on her bed. It had been a long two weeks and what she needed more than anything was sleep.

But it wouldn't come.

The moment she shut her eyes, images of Nordin's dead body lying in a pool of his own blood, and his dead eyes staring at her came flashing through her mind, which quickly turned into Reece's. She didn't know what freaked her out about it so much. She had seen dead bodies before. Verscar was full of them. Yet this one felt different. Was it because she somehow had taken a part in killing him? Or was it because he had been sleeping when it happened, unable to defend himself?

Shane shook her head. She was going to have to get used to that if she was ever going to be an assassin.

She must have drifted off to sleep at some point from sheer exhaustion because next thing she knew she was awakened by a knock on the door. Shane blinked once before begrudgingly getting out of her warm, comfortable bed and going to the door. When she opened her door, she wasn't surprised to see Kyaina standing in the hallway.

"You do realize that you rudely woke me up?" Shane asked, irritated.

"What were you asleep for? It's mid-day."

"Is it really?" Shane sarcastically said. "Why are you here?"

"Because I heard you were back from your first assassination." There was a glow in Kyaina's eyes that should have freaked Shane out, but she was used to it. "How'd it go?"

"I was only an observer."

"That doesn't matter," Kyaina said. "It's your first real step to becoming one of us. So, how'd it go?" she repeated.

Shane sighed. "Well, the assassination went well, but afterward I, um, I puked on the roof of his house." She rubbed the back of her neck as her face grew bright red. She could almost taste the vile, acidic vomit, even now. Every single detail of that night was locked inside her brain.

"So, it went better than mine. A lot better, actually."

Shane stared at her eyebrows raised. "What happened?" If Kyaina had trouble with her first assassination, maybe there was still hope for her after all?

Color rushed to Kyaina's cheeks. "I sort of passed out the minute I saw blood." She laughed awkwardly. "I woke up on a roof a couple houses away with my father leaning over me. He was furious."

"Why?"

"Because I alerted everyone in that house when I hit the floor." Kyaina rolled back her sleeve to reveal a long, white scar running up and down her forearm. Shane gasped, but Kyaina only grimaced. "I got this afterward. I was warned if I ever did anything like that again, I would receive much worse of a punishment."

"That looks awful." Shane couldn't believe that a father would do that to his own daughter, but then she remembered Fritz's son. At least Kyaina's father hadn't thrown her into that labor camp to die. Just to complete an assassination.

"It's not as bad as it looks." Kyaina rolled her sleeve down. "I deserved it anyways. If my father hadn't been there to get me out…" She shuttered. "Let's just say that I never let that happen again."

Shane realized she was still staring at Kyaina's arm, and quickly averted her eyes.

"Does it get easier?" Shane asked. "To kill?"

Kyaina nodded gravely. "It might take a couple more times after your first, but eventually you won't feel a thing as you watch them die."

Was that really what she wanted, Shane asked herself? To grow so used to death that she grew numb to the sight of it?

Kyaina forced a smile. "You should come to my room tonight. For a celebration."

"Let me guess. For witnessing my first assassination?"

"Exactly," Kyaina said. "It'll only be me, you, Archer, and Elias."

"What time?"

Kyaina thought for a moment. "Around five." She looked Shane up and down before saying, "And try to wear something nice. No offense but you look hideous."

"Thanks." Shane laughed, realizing she still hadn't changed from her days on the road.

"And wash up. You smell bad too." Kyaina said with a wink. It had been weeks since Shane had properly bathed.

"See you at five."

Shane let out a sigh as Kyaina showed herself out. She was too awake to fall back asleep, so the first thing she did was take a bath to cleanse herself of all the dirt and sweat. The water was a murky shade of brown when she was finished, but she felt much better.

Shane rummaged through her drawers until she came across a simple light blue dress that Kyaina had given her. She held it up to her body and decided it was good enough before putting it on. She looked in the mirror to see how she looked, but she was pleasantly surprised by what she saw. The dress made her eyes pop.

There came a knock from the connecting door.

"Coming!" she yelled as she hurried to answer it. When she opened it, Eli came right in.

"Notice how I knocked; unlike someone I know." He looked up and blinked. "You cleaned your room up I see. No longer that pigsty that it was."

Shane laughed at the irony. "Funny you should be talking about pigsties. If I recall correctly, this room, before I came here, was filled to the brim with your crap that I assume you had no inclination to clean up one bit."

"That may be true." His eyes sparkled mischievously as he laughed.

"Why are you here?" He had never come barging into her room. That was usually Shane's area of expertise.

"Way to get straight to the point."

"Why are you here?" Shane repeated, making Eli let out a sigh.

"Because we're both heading over to Kyaina's, so why not go together." He looked her up and down. "Nice dress."

"See you look the same as normal." It was true. His light brown pants and rolled up and button up white shirt were the same as when she had first seen him in the Underground, and nearly every day since.

"That's because I don't look like crap, unlike you."

"What happened to no longer making fun of me?"

"I never said that." Eli motioned for Shane to go toward the door to leave. "I might've been nice to you once or twice, but that was only because I'm a good person, and you were quite literally an emotional wreck."

Shane stared at him, and Eli rolled his eyes. "Fine. I'm *sometimes* a nice person."

They left the room and started down the hallway stopping only when they reached Kyaina's door. Shane was about to knock, but before she could, Kyaina flung open the door.

"Well, that was sudden," Shane mumbled under her breath. "Were you watching us?"

"Does it matter if I was?" Kyaina stepped aside and allowed them to enter. "I heard your footsteps stop outside the door."

Shane raised both eyebrows. "Keen ears."

Archer was sitting down on the couch with a glass of something in his hand when he looked up and saw Shane. "Congratulations." He got up and strolled toward Shane, patting her on the back.

"For witnessing my first assassination?" she asked, her voice dull. "Whoop de do!"

"It's a big deal around here."

"Yeah. Kyaina already explained that."

Archer cracked a smile. "I didn't think you could stomach it."

"She didn't," Eli cut in, humor showing in his eyes. "The minute she left the room she was puking her stomach out."

"Thanks for the reminder."

"You are so welcome." Eli went with Archer to sit, and Shane caught Kyaina's eyes. *Don't be surprised if they make fun of you for it,* they seemed to say. Shane already knew that though, and she was prepared.

Shane sat down, and Archer handed her a drink. She accepted it gracefully, took a swig, and then recoiled at the taste. Maybe tonight would go better if she managed to get herself drunk. Less embarrassment for her.

"It couldn't have been as bad as the first one you went to, Elias." Archer said.

"It was worse." Shane expected him to say how she was a sobbing mess afterward, but he didn't. "I wouldn't be surprised if she lost half her body weight with all that puking."

"It wasn't that bad." Shane blushed. "At least it didn't happen in his room."

"And thank the gods for that." Eli laughed and Archer joined him.

"Did Shane slow you down?"

"Not as much as I expected," Eli looked over at Shane, "But a little, yes. That's to be expected though from someone who's afraid of heights."

"Hey," Shane said. As far as she was concerned that was a secret between her and Eli. "I'm getting better."

"You're afraid of heights?" Kyaina asked.

"Yes." Shane sighed, downing the rest of her glass then refilled it. "But at least I don't freeze up as bad as I used to." She remembered when she was riding a ferris wheel with her family. She had hugged the pole the entire time, refusing to let go until they stopped at the bottom.

"That's debatable."

"Before I met you, I used to be way worse." She smiled sadly as she recalled how her siblings would always make fun of her. "I used to not be able to come even close to an edge without freaking out."

"I'd like to see that."

Shane nearly choked from laughing. "So, you could push me toward it again." Shane's sad eyes turned toward the ground. "Trust me when I say that my brothers already tried that."

Kyaina's face contorted in shock. "You have brothers?"

"And a sister." Shane was determined to keep her face free of any emotions. Eli caught her eyes with warning, but she brushed it off. She knew what she was going to tell them and what she wasn't. "Not that it matters. They most likely have forgotten about me."

"What are your brother's names?" Kyaina asked.

"The youngest is Henry, and my twin's name is Corbin."

Kyaina took a sharp intake of breath. "You have a twin?" Shane allowed the silence to answer. "I've always wanted a twin."

"Trust me when I say that there's nothing special about it." Shane let out a long, exasperated sigh. "He's just as rude, arrogant, and selfish as anyone I know."

"I feel like that comment was pointed at me." Eli laughed.

"So, what if it was?" Shane took a drink. "It's the truth."

"How rude."

Kyaina sighed. "It would still be cool. My father's a twin."

"To Aarion."

Kyaina nodded. "He doesn't like to talk about it." The faraway gaze in her eye disappeared in an instant. "Is it true that there's a connection between you and your brother? If you feel pain, does he feel it too?"

Shane laughed. "That's complete fiction, and I pity him if that's true." Shane's hand instinctively went up to her neck and she rubbed it. Kyaina winced.

Archer gave out a snort.

"What do you find so funny?"

"Nothing," Archer said. "It's just that you and I aren't so different."

Eli raised an eyebrow but nobody besides Shane noticed. She eyed him before turning to Archer. "And how is that?"

"My whole family either thinks I'm dead, or like you said, have forgotten about me." His eyes remained dark and hidden, but he continued. "Personally, I hope it's the second. That way I wouldn't have to face them."

"Are you sure about that?" A hole of numbness formed in Shane's chest. She wished more than anything that she could see her friends and family one more time, if only to tell them that she was alive, even if they would hate her for what she had become.

"Yes."

"Why though? Don't you want your family to at least keep you in their memory?"

"I was taken away from them when I was six and brought to a gang where I was forced to steal and kill, then the assassins found me and I joined without even a second thought. I don't know about you, but I wouldn't want to have a son who's a disappointment like that."

"I know about being a disappointment," Shane said sadly, almost to herself. "And I'm reminded of just how bad of one I am when I look around this place full of thieves and murderers." A tear fell from her eyes, but she was quick to wipe it up. "I know what it's like to feel like everyone in your life is looking down on you like you're worthless, and to know it's true."

Tears started to form in the corners of Shane's eyes, threatening to open the flood gates, but she refused to let one fall. Sadness took over her body as her mind drifted to Corbin. So much had changed since she had seen him last. She doubted he would recognize her anymore, even if she stood right in front of him. But maybe that was for the best.

"I almost forgot," Kyaina said, changing the conversation. "I have something for you." She set her glass down on the glass coffee table and headed over to her desk and pulled out a book and tossed it over to Shane. She opened it up to find nothing but blank pages. The blank pages she needed for drawing.

"Wow," Eli said, looking over Shane's shoulder. "It's a blank book. One you could actually read." Shane elbowed him in the ribs.

"I hope you like it. I remember you saying how you wanted something like this a few weeks ago."

"I love it." Shane put the book on the coffee table away from all the drinks.

"I don't understand you people." Archer took one look at the journal and rolled his eyes. "Why would you want *that* when you could get something useful, like knives."

Kyaina hit him. "Because. Most people need a distraction from what we have to do every day."

Shane let out a chuckle. "Tell me about it."

"I wasn't lying when I told you that assassins are some of the most broken people out there trying their best to be fixed."

"Hey," Eli said, "I take offence to that."

"It's the truth." Archer sat back in his chair and let out a sigh. "If anything, you're the most broken of all of us, Elias. I was only taken away from my family and sold around, but at least I wasn't betrayed by my partner."

Who also happened to be his brother.

Eli looked over at Shane eyes wide, but she gave him a comforting look.

"I'm feeling attacked here." Eli laughed.

Shane cracked a smile. "You should."

"You'd better watch what you say." Eli looked at his glass like he did a weapon. "I have a habit of killing my partners," he whispered in her ear just loud enough so only she could hear him.

"I'd like to see you try."

Their eyes met, but before Eli could say anything, Kyaina cut in. "I say we raise a toast for our rotten, crappy lives." They raised their glasses and took a sip.

"You have it the easiest," Archer complained. "Your dad is the king of assassins."

"So? If you think that that means I get special treatment, then you're mistaken. If anything, I have to work twice as hard as you guys to even get noticed by my own father."

Shane felt a twinge of sadness form in her stomach, because she, at least, had two supportive parents who didn't make their kids fight for their lives and mutilate them when they messed up.

"How 'bout we all can agree that our lives have taken turns for the worse," Shane suggested. She raised a cup and took a drink with her friends.

CHAPTER 21

A ll Shane could see was absolute darkness. Silence roared in her ears as she got up from the ground, the world materializing as she did so. Elegant pillars with flickering torches stood at either side of her, and a dark blue carpet lay under her feet leading to a man sitting on a throne.

King Aarion.

Rage boiled inside Shane as she sprinted toward him. She was going to kill him, rip out his throat. But her legs didn't seem to work properly. With every step she took, she moved back two. Shackles appeared on her wrists; she could feel their weight. More appeared around her ankles, and she fell face first into the plush carpet. A guard materialized behind her and held her shoulders tightly.

Shane tried to shake the man off her but couldn't move. Fear gripped her as she looked up at the king hoping that her eyes didn't betray how truly terrified she was.

"What am I doing here?" she asked. She managed to keep her voice steady, but it took everything in her to keep her composure.

The king didn't seem to hear her. All he did was stare down at her while stroking his beard in the exact same fashion as the day he killed Reece. Guilt boiled inside her as she came to a sudden realization. She forced herself to look to her right. A stifled cry left her mouth when she saw her friend still alive and breathing.

Reece's gaze locked with Shane's almost as if she knew what was about to happen.

"Why'd you let this happen?" Reece asked, her voice rough and cracked. "Why couldn't you save me?"

"Reece, I tried." Tears streamed down Shane's face as she struggled harder to move and step in front of the bullet that was inevitably going to hit Reece in the chest, but she still couldn't move. A loud bang echoed around the room. Reece fell to the ground. She no longer felt the soldier holding her down and she could move freely, but she was too late once again.

Shane held Reece's dying body in her arms once again. Her blood soaked into Shane's sleeves, making her hands sticky with a warm red liquid. "Why weren't you fast enough?" Reece whispered as blood leaked from her mouth. "You should've saved me."

"I'm sorry Reece." Shane tried unsuccessfully to control her breaths. "I'm so sorry."

"You aren't sorry enough." Reece took in her last ragged breath and remained still.

Blood.

Blood.

Blood.

There was so much of it seeping out of Reece's body it seemed it would never stop. The room began filling with blood. Reece's body disintegrated in Shane's arms, but the room continued to fill. The guards and the king disappeared in a cloud of dust leaving Shane alone in a room filling with the blood of her friend. She tried to swim, but no matter how hard she kicked she couldn't stay afloat. Her head went under and she took in breath, expecting it to behave just like water, but it only flooded into her mouth, choking her. Red filled her vision as the metallic taste of blood gagged her, and she shuddered as she drowned. She thrashed and kicked, yet the surface never seemed to come.

Suddenly, the blood disappeared, and she was back in the mines with a pickaxe in her hands. Looking around she found people she couldn't remember being enslaved with. Instead of Kyaina standing right beside her, the person was a stranger. They looked down at Shane.

"Dig you idiot." Their voice seemed to come from all around Shane, echoing. "Dig unless you want to get whipped."

Shane looked down at her shackles covering both her ankles and wrists. They were thicker than the last time she was there, meant to stop her from breaking them with the pickaxe. There was no escaping this time.

Shane brought the pickaxe up, surprised by its weight. She managed to cleave it down on the stone, but it never hit the wall. She tried again. The same result happened. Again. Again. Again. Nothing seemed to change. If anything, she was only wearing herself out.

"Dig, if you don't want to get whipped." The voice echoed around in her head, never ending and never relenting.

If she didn't bring in the quota for the day, then someone would come and punish her. She tried to force that idea out of her mind, but the voice kept reminding her. It kept getting louder and louder until she couldn't take it anymore.

"Stop!" she yelled, dropping the pickaxe. "Please stop!"

She felt a guard's hands on her shoulders. He dragged her away from the rest of the chain. The sound of metal hitting stone stopped.

"Where's your quota for the day?" he asked.

Shane physically couldn't bring her eyes up to meet him. "I don't have it," she wanted to say, but instead she choked on the words.

"I said where is it?" He shoved her down toward the ground as the sound of whips behind her grew.

The first whip came as a surprise. It reopened all the lacerations on her back and her blood coated everything.

The whips were worse than when she first got them. Shane didn't realize that they had stopped until she opened one of her eyes to daylight. She was in the main square, her arms shackled to a post.

"How could you?" A familiar voice asked from behind her. "How could a young, bright girl such as yourself become something so despicable that I can't even look at you?"

"Mom?" Shane asked, gasping for air. One look over her shoulder told her that she was right. Everything about her mother seemed the same except her cold, hard face that was once soft. The thing that scared Shane the most was the bloodlust in her eyes.

"You are no daughter of mine," her mom sneered down at her while she unraveled the whip in her hands. "You stopped being my daughter the minute you joined those criminals."

"Mom, I'm sorry," Shane sobbed.

"Sorry isn't good enough."

There was a crack that pierced the open air and once again, pain returned to Shane's back. One whip. Two whips. Three whips. Four whips.

Shane lost count after that. Pain consumed her mind. She couldn't feel the piece of wood that she was gripping onto. All she knew was pain. Never stopping and never ending. Exactly what she deserved.

The whipping stopped, and silence greeted Shane's ears. She dared to open one eye and saw people fill the once empty street. People that she knew, or once knew. People that once loved her, but one look at their faces told Shane that they were far past that and wanted to see her punished.

"You had so much potential, Shane." The tone of the voice was different. Shane looked back only to see that her mom had shifted into her dad. He was holding the whip. "But you wasted it all when you helped that girl." He didn't even say Kyaina's name.

"Dad," Shane managed to say through the pain, gritting her teeth. "I know what you must be thinking."

"No, you don't." The whip lashed out and hit Shane square in the back once again. "I can't tell you how much of a disappointment and disgrace you are to this family." He whipped her again, but she didn't cry out. Instead, tears rolled down her face as she endured what she knew she deserved.

Her dad then morphed into Corbin. "You'll never be anyone in life," he said. "Never would've been even if you hadn't fallen through that portal. I was always better than you at everything, no matter how hard you tried." He flicked his wrist, and Shane winced.

He transformed into Henry. "How is it, knowing that even your younger brother is better than you at everything?" Blood poured down Shane's back. "You were always going to be a disappointment."

"You couldn't do anything by yourself." The voice came from Cloe. "You wouldn't survive a day without anyone's help."

"How does it feel, knowing that you wasted my sacrifice?" Shane looked back and let out a sob as Reece brandished the whip. "It should've been you who died. I did nothing to deserve it, yet here you are. Still. Living." With each word she lashed out.

"How do you live with yourself? Knowing that I still would've been alive if it weren't for you. If you hadn't convinced me to come with you to that game, I would still be living with my family. Happy. Unlike you." Reece smiled maliciously, something Shane never thought she would see.

"Reece, I'm sorry."

"You're sorry for a lot of things in your past, yet you never seem to learn." One whip. Two whips. "When will you realize that you hurt everyone you love? Your parents? Your family? *Our* friends? They think you ran away."

"Reece"

"Would you return even if you could? Could you look your mother and father in the face and tell them what you have done, or what you plan to do? Could you look at my family and tell them why I died? That you were too selfish, and you valued your own life more than mine?"

"Reece—"

The whip came once again, and the pain was too much for Shane to bear. Darkness consumed her once again.

Shane woke in a cold sweat to the sound of her own screams, tears streaming down her face. Blankets surrounded her, choking her like the blood. No matter how hard she tried to kick them off, they just kept getting more tangled, more stuck

She heard a door open and could see someone running toward her, but she didn't fully realize it wasn't still part of the dream until Eli grabbed her shoulders and started shaking her.

"It's okay," he said, trying to calm her. "It was just a dream."

The words went unnoticed as she curled up in a ball with her arms tightly across her torso, sobbing into her pillow.

It took Shane several minutes and many more deep breaths to calm down enough to become aware of her surroundings. Aware of Eli's hands gripping her shoulders. Aware of the dying fire. Aware of the open door between their rooms. Aware enough to speak.

"It's fine," Eli assured her.

"They were so real," Shane said, her voice nothing but a whisper. "They were torturing me."

"They aren't here now."

"But they were." Shane sniffled while getting up from the fetal position. "My family. They were with me in the camp, except they were the ones whipping me." More tears leaked from her eyes. "Then Reece came. Oh Reece."

"It was just a dream."

"It felt so real." Shane's voice quavered as she touched her back, wincing at the memory of the pain that wasn't even there. All the scars were still just that. Scars. She'd had dreams like that before, but they were never as intense.

"What happened in it?" Eli asked. He must have seen the panic in Shane's eyes because he quickly added, "You don't have to tell me if you don't want to."

"No, it's fine." Shane took a shaky breath in. She knew that if she didn't tell someone about the nightmares, they would only grow worse until they would take over her life. She told him everything about the dream, the blood, the whippings, her mom and dad. "I woke up when the pain was more than I could bear," she said when she was finally done.

Shane looked into Eli's eyes. They glowed in the faint ember glow of the last dying embers of the fire in the hearth. "I know that it was just a dream, but what if they were right?"

"Shane—"

"You don't understand."

"Shane, I understand what you had to go through. But you did what you had to do, that was survive."

"Are you sure about that?" Shane let out a sniffle. "I could've run away the moment I left that camp, but I stayed with Kyaina and Archer even though I knew what they were." A question had been bothering Shane since she first set foot in the Assassin's Underground, and now was the first time she found the words. "Am I a bad person?"

"What? Of course, you aren't."

"I decided on my own to train to become an assassin." Shane got up from the bed and went over to the fire, refusing to meet Eli's eyes. "If I'm not a bad person, then something must be wrong with my head."

"I could've told you that." Eli laughed halfheartedly forcing Shane to smile, even though it was a sad smile. "The world isn't split into good and evil, Shay. You did what you had to do to survive, and that's the best any of us can do. We all do what we must to survive, and sometimes we aren't proud of it, but that doesn't make us bad people."

"You really think that?"

"Of course. You and I aren't that different. We're both survivors even when the world is against us."

Shane wiped her now dry, puffy eyes and turned toward Eli. Without thought or warning, she gave him a hug. He was as stiff as a board at first, but quickly relaxed and returned the hug she needed so desperately. "Thank you," she said, her face nuzzled into his shoulder. "I can't tell you how much I needed to hear that from a friend."

"So, we're friends now?"

"How else would you describe our relationship?"

"Partners." Eli smiled down at her. "Go back to bed. It looks like you need it."

"What about training?"

"I'll cancel it for today."

"Why?"

"Because you're an emotional wreck and you might end up hurting yourself."

Shane forced a smile, rolling her eyes. "Thanks for the confidence, but I'm fine." Her shaking hands told a different story.

"I'm not changing my mind." Eli walked over to the door. "Go back to bed and get some sleep."

"I can't." Shane pursed her lips. "What if I dream again?"

"You can't try to run away from dreams. They'll catch up to you eventually, good or bad." Eli stared at Shane's face and became too aware of the dark bags underneath her eyes from lack of sleep. "Trust me. I've tried."

"I know that," Shane lied, "I just don't want them to come rushing in on me right now."

Eli sighed, his hand still resting on the doorknob. "Then do whatever you want with the rest of the day. I'm going back to sleep because someone rudely woke me up." He let out a yawn and closed the door behind him.

Shane sighed as she sank into her bed. She couldn't sit here for the rest of the day, and she didn't want to read. What she really needed to do was get out of there. Go to the surface for just a day by herself. No one to bother her. No one to order her around. Left alone to her own thoughts.

Grabbing some clean clothes out of her messy dresser, she got dressed and snagged a pair of boots from under her bed. She then put on a cloak, not only to keep her warm, but to hide her face from watchful eyes. The one thing she had learned from her time with the assassins was how to blend in nearly everywhere she went.

Before she left her room, she grabbed a coin sack from her bedside table, filled with the money she'd stolen. She hadn't been paid for the assassination. According to Eli, she wouldn't receive payment until she became a full-fledged assassin.

Shane continued for the door, grabbing her two knives on the way and sheathing them to her waist, hidden by her billowing cloak. She went up toward the surface, stopping for nobody. When the fresh air hit her face, she breathed it in deeply. That was what she needed to clear her mind of the dream. A nice day with fresh air.

She joined the rest of the people on the busy street headed for the main square. It was a nice day out, and nearly everywhere Shane looked she saw happy faces filled with life and joy. She had a hard time believing that those emotions still existed in a world so dark and cruel.

She had gotten to know the layout of the city well from Eli's late night training excursions. The town clock tower was ahead of her. It was in the middle of the town near the center square.

"Never climb that building, unless you're desperate for escape," Eli had explained one night. "The closest building is nearly twenty feet away, and even if you are able to jump that far, you'll end up shattering your bones just from the sheer height that you dropped."

That had been all the warning she needed to not find a reason to climb up there.

Shane visited various shops buying different things, mostly food, with the little money she had. The one material thing that she bought was a simple, grey dress so that she no longer had to borrow Kyaina's whenever she needed one.

Most of the day she spent out by the fountain eavesdropping and people watching, but as the sun started to set and the streets began to thin, she decided that it was time to start thinking about heading back to the Assassin's Underground. She hopped down from the fountain and started walking back down the streets the way she came, wondering what might greet her when she got back to her room. What kind of nightmare would she have tonight?

When she turned to go down the alley that led to the Underground, she stopped abruptly. A group of four people, two men and two women, stood near the dead end, exactly where Shane needed to go.

"Well," one of them said, spotting Shane walking down the alley. "What do we have here? Are you lost?" He hopped down from the half wall that he had been sitting on and walked toward Shane.

"Far from it, actually," Shane mumbled under her breath. She became all too aware of the bag in her arms that weighed her down.

The man whistled and the others came up to join them. Their ragged appearance made them look docile, tame even, but Shane knew not to believe appearances.

"Looks like we have a young damsel in distress."

A cruel laugh left Shane's mouth as she set the bag down beside her and reached instinctively for the knives hidden under the fabric of her cloak. If these people were going to stand between her and where she wanted to be, they were going to pay.

"Leave me alone and no one gets hurt."

The man looked behind him to the rest of his group, a twinkle of amusement in his eyes. "You hear that? What does she think she can do to us?"

"A lot." Her hands still rested on the hilts of her daggers, but she waited patiently to draw them, her muscles itching to lash out. But she wouldn't unless they refused to let her pass.

"Would you mind enlightening us?" A girl no older than Shane with red hair asked, smiling.

"I will if you don't move out of my way."

The group had taken up the whole alleyway making sure that she couldn't pass.

"I'll make you a deal," the lead man said, eyeing her money pouch on her side. "You give us whatever you have in there, and we'll let you pass."

"And why in Haytorrow's Realm would I do that?"

Annoyance flickered over the man's face, but he continued to smile. "Because if you don't," he took a step forward, "we will make you."

"I'd like to see you try."

The man leaped forward and tried to grab Shane's arms, but she was prepared for that. Almost as soon as he moved the first muscle in his legs, she had already drawn the daggers. The familiarity of the deadly weapon in Shane's hand calmed her. She easily sidestepped the man and hit him in the back of the head with the pommel of her blade. He fell to the ground and stayed there.

"Who's next?" Shane smiled wickedly.

The other man in the group laughed. "If you expect us to be afraid of you just because my idiot brother wasn't expecting a blow to the head, then you're mistaken."

"So, I take it you want a go too?"

The man looked back at the two girls.

Shane's smile continued to grow when all three of them took a step forward. Maybe this was what she needed. A way to release all the pent-up rage and aggression that had built inside her, festering for a way out during the last couple of months.

The remaining man drew a hidden knife from his belt, much like Shane's. He swiped for her head, taking the few strands of hair as she fell to the ground. She was quick to recover and was back on her feet before the man could even blink.

She blocked and parried the jabs and slices that came her way all while paying close attention to the two girls circling around her. One of the girls lunged forward and punched her in the arm. Shane responded with an elbow to her ribs, and the girl went down. Shane ignored the pain pulsing down to her arm and jabbed at the man once, nicking the flesh on his stomach.

"You cut me." The man's eyes were wide as he touched the wound with his hands, drawing away the blood. Shane rushed him and tackled him while he was distracted. They hit the ground hard, and she quickly scrambled to her feet.

A blow came from behind her right shoulder, catching her off guard. She stumbled forward, dropping both knives. She turned around to see the two girls.

"Are you guys sure about this?" she asked the girls.

They said nothing, instead choosing to attack. Shane managed to keep their blows from connecting too hard. She dodged and ducked under as many as she could, returning their blows. She kicked fiercely at a girl with red hair who made the mistake of lunging at her. Shane's foot made contact with her stomach, and she doubled over.

One remaining.

The girl, realizing she was the last one standing, clenched her fists even tighter, and bounced on the balls of her feet.

Shane wasn't about to let her make the first move. She attacked with a swift kick to the arm, but it seemed to have no effect on the girl. The next thing Shane knew fists were flying in her direction. She managed to dodge most of them by being quick on her feet. If she could get the girl to wear herself out without causing any real damage, the better it would be for the both of them.

Shane could read the girl's body language and used this to her advantage. She moved in close to the girl and gripped her arm. The girl tried to move away only to find Shane's leg behind her.

"I said," she breathed heavily as she slowly let go of the girl's arm, "to get out of my way. Now *go away*.

"You *bitch*." The girl spat before turning to run away.

She knew she technically could have done worse to each of them but had pulled her punches. Looking down at the two men lying on the street, she eyed her knives. She could end it right now for them. Teach them a lesson. But why would she? The more she thought about it, the more that she realized that she physically couldn't bring herself to do it.

Shane grabbed the bag with the dress and her knives and hurried for the Assassin's Underground as the sun was setting over the horizon.

CHAPTER 22

S hane twiddled her thumbs as she paced nervously around in Eli's room. Eli had been nice enough to let Shane stay with him after training to calm her nerves, and there were a whole lot of them.

"What if I mess up?" she asked, looking up toward Eli's bed where he sat with both elbows on his knees.

"You won't mess up." He had assured her of that at least a hundred times in the last week, but today he had to keep reminding her of it constantly. "And if you do, chances are you'll be too dead to face the consequences, which will be placed on me for not training you well enough, so you'd better not fail."

"You're not very good at calming someone down." Shane threw dagger eyes at him.

A week before, Wikter had come knocking on Shane's door looking to talk to both her and her partner. Wikter explained to Shane how he thought she was ready to take on the responsibilities of a full assassin.

"There will be a test," he explained. "Within the next week to determine whether or not you're fully prepared."

When Shane asked what the test would be about, Wikter chuckled. "You'll know when you see it."

With that, he left, leaving Shane at a loss for words.

She was far from ready to become a killer. She never thought she was going to be ready. That day on the surface a month back proved that. Something in her kept her from committing that final blow. The killing blow. Shane didn't know whether to be happy or unnerved that she was still uneasy about striking a fatal blow, even after months of intense training. She'd gone on more assassinations with Eli, and each time she grew more and more used to the idea of taking someone's life, but she still wasn't comfortable enough to do it herself. What would Eli do if he knew the truth about her? That she was too weak to kill?

But the test wasn't about killing. It was about whether or not she was ready for the challenge.

"The assassination comes after the tests," Eli had explained to her one day while training when she wouldn't stop pestering him about it.

"Tests?"

"There will be more than one if that's what you mean." He stopped her before she could say anything. "And before you ask, the tests depend on the person."

"What were yours?" If she knew that, then maybe she would be a little more prepared for her own.

"Me and Alek were sent to steal a flag from Wikter's room while he was sleeping."

Shane's face paled. She had enough trouble with staying quiet when she witnessed Eli's assassination, and she didn't think she had enough stealth skill to enter the King of the Assassin's room without being noticed.

"And your other one?" Shane's voice was nothing more than a whisper.

A grimace passed over Eli's face. "It doesn't matter," he said, trying to sway the subject away to something else. "Wikter never gives partners the same challenge."

"You and your brother had the same challenges." Shane peered hopefully into Eli's face, trying not to look like she was about to vomit her guts out. "Why won't you tell me?"

"Me and Alek were… different."

"Tell me."

Eli sighed. "You won't stop until you know, will you?"

"Nope, but as soon as you tell me I'll stop asking questions."

"Fine. You win." Eli took a sharp breath in before starting. "Me and Alek were the only partners that I knew about that had been trained together. Usually, it's the same dynamic that you and I have where one person's the teacher and the other ones the mentor, but Alek and I were inseparable back then, or at least I thought we were."

"When is this going to get to more useful information?" Shane asked.

"I'm getting there. I just thought that you needed a little backstory." Shane remained quiet, willing him to continue. "Wikter put us against each other for a fight. Not to the death like the Assassins *Harassad*, but we had to last at least half an hour before we were allowed to go."

The Assassins *Harassad* was a battle for rulership of the assassins. According to Kyaina, it was very rare to see. The last one occurred when Wikter became the king of assassins over thirty years before.

Shane's face contorted. "Couldn't you guys pull your punches so you would make it no matter what?"

"No." Eli's eyes tore away from Shane toward the ground. "I mean, yes, but my brother wasn't having any of that." He rolled back the neckline of his shirt and showed Shane a long, jagged scar on his left shoulder. Shane reached out a hand instinctively to touch it but forced it back. "I should've known then that he wanted to kill me. Wikter did. That's why he made us do it. To make sure that nobody held back." He let go of his shirt and it covered the scar once again.

"My gods, Eli. I'm sorry."

"I'm pretty sure that that was the first and only challenge like that, so you have no need to worry."

Yet here Shane was, six days later, stuck pacing around Eli's room. At least now she knew Wikter was going to test her that night or the next day. The days before had been utter agony as her anxiety crept in, affecting nearly everything she did. She couldn't give it her all while training that week because she was too preoccupied thinking about when it would be. Eli took note of this, she was sure, but didn't say anything about it, which Shane was grateful for.

"You're going to do fine at whatever it is," Eli said as he got up from his bed.

"I know that."

"Then will you stop pacing around my room?" He grabbed her shoulders to still her, yet her foot still tapped anxiously on the floor. "Bloody knives, Shay." Eli looked down at her toes. "You really need to learn how to relax."

"You aren't really helping." Shane grabbed both his wrists gently and took them off her shoulders. She didn't know how he could stay so calm and loose while she was such a mess.

"You know what my test is, don't you?" Shane asked as she studied the way he stood so relaxed.

"Maybe." Years of training couldn't keep a mischievous smile from spreading across his face.

"You sick bastard." Shane shoved into his muscled chest enough to knock him back, but nothing more. "Why don't you tell me."

"Because Wikter will flay me alive if I do."

"Well, Wikter can go rot in Haytorrows Fallen Realm for all I care."

"I'm not sure he would like it if he heard you say that."

"Well then tell him to piss off." Shane threw her arms into the air. The anxiety that had taken over her body only got stronger with each passing second. "You're my partner, so you should tell me what it is."

"I'll give you a hint if you want it that badly."

"What is it?"

Eli motioned with his head toward Shane's room. "You should go to bed. You'll need as much rest as you can get."

"I'm not sure you're getting this whole hint thing," Shane complained.

"Go." He pointed toward the door, smiling that evil smile he always had whenever he was planning something. He was no better than her own brother at hiding it.

"Fine."

If he had something planned for her, then she wasn't about to get in the way, no matter how much she wanted to know what the test was going to be,

Alone in her room, she threw herself on her bed and closed her eyes but sleep never came. Instead, she was greeted with visions of what might happen the next day. Even as her eyelids felt heavy, her mind would not shut off.

When she finally drifted off, she was greeted by nothing but darkness. No dreams could bother her any worse than what she might face the next day. She was about to become an assassin.

Shane woke suddenly to the cold, pressing feeling of being watched. Her eyes snapped open as she sat bolt upright in her bed, sheets soaked with her cold sweat, her heart hammering in her ears. Every way she looked, all she saw was the dark, almost imperceivable outline of the furniture in the room. Nothing seemed out of place or touched in any way, yet she couldn't shake the uneasy feeling. The hairs rose on the back of her neck.

A cold shiver ran down her spine. She fumbled blindly at her desk for a candle holder. Her fingertips brushed against the fallen wax from the day before and soon found the cold metal of the holder. She quickly snatched it up, grabbing the matches in the process and lit the candle. She then found her two knives on her bedside table. Just having them in her hand calmed her racing heart.

The candle illuminated only a small section of the room. The rest was still cloaked in the shadows of darkness. What little Shane could see gave no signs of being tampered with, but something told her to keep looking. She got out of her bed and placed a log on the smoldering embers, still hot from the fire the day before. With a little bit of kindling, it didn't take long until the fire was once again blazing.

The flickering light around the room increased, but Shane still didn't see anything suspicious. Her hands gripped the knives tightly, and she was aware of every callus that touched the leather grip. From all her training to be an assassin, her ability to see past the mundane stuff that she saw every day improved greatly. She had the ability to tell if someone had been in her room by the way that dust sat on objects, or the lack of dust that had been there the night before.

A noise came from her bathroom. Shane whipped her head around to face it, noticing the way the door was ajar. She had closed it the night before.

"I know you're in here," she said, successfully keeping her voice steady. If she acted confident, hopefully she would feel confident.

Silence. Everything had a strange stillness to it. Shane stepped forward to the door. Her arms tensed as it opened the slightest bit, only confirming her suspicions.

Without thinking, she picked up a throw pillow from the couch and chucked it at the door. It opened, revealing a tall figure cloaked in darkness.

Shane's heart skipped a beat as the masked figure took a step out. She wanted to cower down in fear, but months of training stopped her from doing it. She had to act calm, even when beneath the surface she was a mess.

"Who are you?" Shane's voice boomed through the thick layer of silence.

"My name doesn't matter." The man spoke in a gravelly, deep tone. He took a step forward.

"Who," Shane repeated, "are you." Her knives in front of her as she squared her shoulders, getting ready for the fight that was inevitably coming.

"I am shadows and darkness." He took another step, but Shane's solid gaze stopped him. "I am both death and rebirth."

"Cut the monologue." Shane licked her lips nervously bouncing on the balls of her feet. "Who sent you?"

"The god of death himself."

"So, you're an assassin?" Shane asked. Who had she angered so badly they wanted her dead? She hadn't talked to anyone in the Underground besides Eli, Kyaina, and Archer.

Her eyes flicked toward Eli's door calculating how long it would take to get over there and warn Eli, but the man only let out a small chuckle.

"You can try, but all the doors that lead out of this room are locked."

"That's impossible." He had to be bluffing. The only way they locked was from the inside out, not vice versa.

"Is it?" He presented something from the interior pocket of his cloak. From the metal that glinted in the light, Shane guessed that it was a key.

Shane pushed past the feeling of dread that had built up inside her. If he was speaking facts, she was trapped in here. Trapped like she was in the mines. Trapped like she was in the dungeon.

"Even if it wasn't locked," the man continued as if reading Shane's mind, "I don't think your partner would even help you."

"That's not true." Shane's hands trembled.

"Are you sure about that?" Even though his face was hidden by a mask, Shane was certain he was smiling underneath. "You are a disgrace to anyone who knows you or used to know you."

"You're lying."

Shane tried to calm herself, but she instead was seeing red. Who was he to throw insults like that at her? Her fingers shook as she tightened them around the handles of her knives, the only things that kept her anchored to a world that was spinning faster with each passing second.

"You are a liar." He took a step forward. "A thief." Step. "A murderer." Step. "If you think that anyone likes you then I worry for your sanity."

Before Shane could even think about what she was doing, she reached for the throwing knives that lay on her table. Blind anger and rage fueled her throwing arm, so it was no surprise when it hit the back wall a mere second later.

The man remained silent before reaching his hand across his body and brushing it along a small flap of cloth that had once been tight against the arm. "You missed." He flicked the tiniest bit of blood from his fingertips and reached behind his back where he drew two slightly curved katanas.

Shane ignored the fear that built up inside. Her knives ready in her hands as she took a step forward.

I will not be afraid.

I will not be afraid.

I will not be afraid.

Shane took a step forward, projecting a false sense of confidence in herself.

The man lunged forward, blades flying in every direction. She blocked the first blow that nearly made her drop her knives. The man's other sword came flying toward her neck and she barely had enough sense to duck. If Shane had reacted a moment later, her head would have been rolling on the floor.

The man's attacks pushed her back toward the bed. All Shane could do to keep herself from getting killed was defend. The man was too good, too well trained, to allow Shane to go on the offensive. His blades were a whirlwind of death, and Shane was nothing more than an ignorant girl trying her best to survive, just like she was when she first came into this world.

He used both blades in a downward blow that Shane barely had time to defend. Acting on pure instinct, she crossed both of her knives as it hit. Before Shane could even think about regaining herself, a foot came flying toward her stomach. It knocked all the breath from her. She stumbled back and fell on her bed. Her knives clattered from her hands.

"A pity, really," the man in darkness said. "I was expecting more of a fight from you."

Shane reached desperately above her, looking for anything to give the man a distraction so she could get up when her hands rested upon her pillow. Without thinking, she gripped it with all her might and chucked it at him. He caught it easily and tore it in two, feathers flying everywhere.

"Did you seriously think that this would stop me?" he asked.

"No." Shane managed to get up as the man made his way through the feathers. She dove for her knives on the ground.

Before she knew what was happening, the man was upon her, and the fighting commenced once again. Shane's thighs burned as she danced on her toes, barely managing to keep out of the blade's path. She knew she couldn't keep doing this forever. Already her blows were getting sloppy, and her feet weren't moving as quickly as she would have wished. The man was wearing her down.

They circled around the coffee table. It didn't look like there was any way to turn the tide of the fight in her favor. The man pushed Shane backward, her foot catching on the rug and she stumbled, barely able to remain upright. The man's blade flashed toward her. Shane's deflection was less than perfect, and it sliced into her shoulder.

The intense pain clouded her thinking. Everything turned a shade of red. The color of blood. The thick liquid dripped down her arm at a steady rate and she wanted to scream from the pain. Wanted to sit down and cry, but she couldn't. The man kept bombarding her with blows and slices. It was a miracle that one of his blades didn't find a way into her stomach. With only one arm to defend herself, she knew that it would happen soon.

"You are weak." He thrust with his katana; Shane barely managed to deflect it. "Arrogant," again, "fool."

He pushed her into the table. The knives flew from her hands, landing too far away to grab them. She tried to crawl, but the man shoved one of his feet onto her stomach. Her eyes widened. His blade was right above her neck, glimmering in the light of the fire.

Fire.

The sword came down.

Shane contorted her body and the blade only grazed her neck as she scrambled frantically for the candle holder. Her hands closed around it, the cool metal welcome to her fingers. She thrust it into the man's face. The mask was the first thing that caught fire. It quickly spread to his whole face, cloak and hood were nothing but a giant flame.

The man stumbled back trying to swat out the flames that were spreading to the rest of his body. Shane didn't hesitate to lunge for her blades.

The fire was out quickly, but the man was still distracted by the burns to his face. Shane used this as an advantage as she tackled him toward the fireplace. She stabbed both knives in his shirt sleeves so he couldn't move and stared into his evil, dark black eyes that showed no emotion. She kept one arm pressed against his neck.

"You scar faced bitch," he hissed, his voice nothing more than a gravely whisper from smoke inhalation.

"I've been called worse before."

"Why don't you kill me?"

Shane remained silent as the fire drew her attention to it. Without thinking, she bent over and grabbed one of the half-burnt logs and thrust it into the man's side.

"I will," Shane lied. "Just not yet."

The man let out a strangled cry as his clothes tore at the knives, trying to get free from the torture.

"Why did you try and kill me?" Shane asked.

"It was a test," the man gasped. "And you passed."

The log fell from Shane's hand, only having enough sense to kick it back into the fire when the floor began to smolder. How could she have been so stupid and have forgotten that today was the day the test was supposed to happen? After spending all night worrying over it, she shouldn't have forgotten that easily.

"My gods," Shane gasped, removing the knives from the tunic. "I'm sorry."

The man removed his already burnt mask and took off his hood to reveal a fair-haired young man no older than his mid-twenties. His face looked familiar, and Shane remembered seeing him around the Assassin's Underground before. She believed his name was Jaylen.

She heard the door to Eli's room open behind her as the man got up and brushed himself off.

"You." Shane turned on her heel to face Eli, pointing an accusing finger at his chest with her unhurt arm. "You knew what I had to do, and you didn't warn me?"

"Where would be the fun in that?" He ran a hand through his disheveled brown hair, yawning. "I'm sure that there are salves to help with those burns you got there," he said over Shane's shoulder.

"Yeah, I know," Jaylen spat. He put his blades back on his back and went for the door, not saying a word to anyone.

"He's a little bit of a crank," Eli explained once he left. "If it hadn't been Wikter to ask, he would've most definitely said no."

Only now did Shane realize truly how much of a mess her room was. The feathers were the worst part. Everywhere she looked she could see little, tiny white dots scattering across the floor. Not to mention the blood splatter on nearly everything.

Her shoulder throbbed in pain. When Eli looked over to see what was bothering her, he reached out, but Shane shrank away.

"You don't touch me. I'm still mad at you."

"For what?"

"Not helping me."

Eli rolled his eyes. "I couldn't help you. Wikter made that explicitly clear. And even if I did want to, that would mean leaving the comforts of my bed and grabbing my swords and—"

"Yeah, I get it." Shane grabbed a clean towel that was thrown across the floor and applied pressure to the wound.

"I was sleeping perfectly fine until you started clanging your knives around like your life depended on it."

"That's because I thought that it did." Shane winced as more pain came from the wound. "Why don't you go back to bed, where you so wanted to be instead of helping me."

"If you don't want my help, I will."

"Good."

Eli turned before leaving. "Congratulations. On beating the test, I mean."

Shane looked up. "Thanks."

"If you keep it up, I might actually have a partner before the end of the week." Eli laughed. Before he could close the door, he said, "Get some blukreg on the cut."

"I was going to do that."

"Sure, you were."

It was only when Shane threw the torn-up pillow at Eli's door that he finally left her alone.

CHAPTER 23

A cold breeze rushed past Shane's head, whipping her hair everywhere with the night sky looming above.

Earlier in the day, Wikter had come to Shane's room and informed her that her last test was to be that night.

"Tonight, there will be a race. If you win, you become one of us," Wikter had said.

"And if I lose?"

He pretended he didn't hear the question. "The rules are simple. You and your opponent start on the same building. When you hear a gunshot, you both have to find where it came from. I don't care what path you take, as long as you beat them."

Of course, he hadn't told her who she was going up against.

Now, she walked the streets in silence with Kyaina escorting her to the start line. She wished Eli was with her as well, but he had left them to go with Wikter to the end of the race. It felt strange, wishing for the company of someone who she swore she would never like.

It had almost been a year since she and Reece first washed up on the Island of Eringunner, but it felt like a whole other lifetime since she had last seen Reece's face. Since she had last felt the comforts of her home. Since she had last been truly happy. Every smile since then, every laugh, felt forced.

If she beat her opponent in the race that night, she would get the tattoo that marked her as one of the Underground. It felt surreal. It was something that she had worked so hard for over the last six months, yet it seemed unobtainable until it was staring Shane in the face.

If she beat her opponent, everything was going to be different.

"You nervous?" Kyaina asked, peering down at Shane.

"What? No?" she said sarcastically. She wiped her clammy hands on her pants. "Nothing *to* be nervous about. Only the threat of death looming over me if I don't win."

Kyaina laughed, but the tension between the two of them remained the same, if not more tense. "I'm sure I can talk my father into letting you go if you don't beat your opponent."

"With me knowing all your secrets? I don't think so."

They continued down the street in silence.

Just this one challenge, Shane reminded herself, *and I'm free to go.*

Free was a relative term. If she did win, she would still have to work as an assassin until the day she died. Even though Wikter never implied it, she doubted that he would allow people to walk freely away from the Underground knowing everything about the assassins.

"How much farther do we need to go?" Shane asked after ten minutes.

"Not much farther," Kyaina said as she took a sharp turn down a small, rundown street.

"Have you ever done this before? Race people as a test I mean."

Kyaina pursed her lips but answered. "Once before," she explained. "When it was Archer's tests, I had to, but it was a different route than this."

Finally, they turned down an alleyway that ended at a tall, stone building. Kyaina motioned for Shane to start climbing as she watched their backs. Shane used every part of the rough walls to find foot and hand holds. The pipes. The windowsills. Anything would work. It wasn't long until she stood on top, a cold autumn breeze threatening to blow her off, but she remained near the edge. No longer was she going to hide from her fears.

Kyaina's hand appeared on the ledge only a couple seconds later.

"Where's my opponent?" Shane asked as she helped Kyaina up.

"He'll come."

As if on cue, there came a small noise from below them, and moments later someone scrambled their way onto the roof. His mask covered his face, but when he looked over at Shane, she could tell who it was.

"Jaylen?" Shane asked in surprise. She turned to Kyaina. "I'm racing Jaylen?"

"He asked for it specifically," Kyaina explained.

"That way when you lose, I'll be the one to kill you." He took off his mask and Shane gasped. Burns mangled his face. Jaylen saw her squirm and smiled cruelly. "You're going to pay for this, you know."

Shane could only imagine what he meant by that. She felt nauseous.

"You know the rules?" Kyaina asked, trying to bring Shane's attention back to her.

"Yes." All she had to do was make it to the finish line first. Simple yet daunting.

Kyaina gave Shane a hug. "You'd better beat his ass," she whispered in her ear. Shane smiled.

"I'll try," Shane said as they broke apart the hug.

"See you at the end." Kyaina turned away and headed back toward the street.

Shane returned her attention to Jaylen as she bounced on the balls of her feet. She shook her arms and hands to shake out the nerves that were building inside her. Her cloak waved wildly in the frigid wind.

"Your friend wish you good luck?" he asked cruelly.

"I won't need it."

"Are you sure about that?" He smiled. "Where was your luck when you got that scar that butchered your face?"

Shane's face hardened. "You're not one to talk, or did you forget about your burns."

"You're going to pay," he repeated.

"Ooh, I'm trembling," she sarcastically said as she lined up next to Jaylen, preparing for the gunshot.

"Scared?"

"You wish."

The gunshot sounded. It had begun. Shane started to sprint, but Jaylen pulled her back with his full force, propelling himself forward. Shane's eyes filled with surprise as she fell back. She regained her balance just in time to see him launch himself off the building onto the next.

She scolded herself for thinking Jaylen would play fair as she scrambled to catch up. Of course, he would play dirty— he had a score to settle.

Shane followed his footsteps without thought. Her feet hit the roof of the next building, and though pain shot up her shins, she kept running. Much worse would await her if she didn't beat Jaylen.

Shane had always been a fast sprinter. She used it to her advantage on the flat terrain. It wasn't long before she was neck and neck with Jaylen. Buildings flew past as they grappled for the lead. He used everything in his power to slow her down, whether that be fist or foot. Shane managed to dodge most of the blows. Nothing was getting in her way of victory.

Shane elbowed her way to the lead and jumped off a building when she felt a tug on her cloak suddenly clotheslined and yanked back. She let out a strangled cry as she fell. Only by instinct was she able to grab the ledge as Jayden leaped across the gap above her.

Shane fell to the small patio underneath her, collapsing on the railing as she tried to bring in rapid breaths. Everything in her wanted her to stop, to let him win, but she couldn't give up. Not yet. Not when doing that meant death.

Shane stood up, leaning heavily on the patio railing as she brought in heavy breaths to regain her bearings before she forced herself to stand on the railings and launched herself toward a sewage pipe on the building across the alley. She grabbed hold of it and scrambled her way to the roof, hauling herself up just in time to see Jaylen's head drop from the edge of the other side of the building.

Shane was sucking in air. Everything in her body groaned in protest as she continued onward, leaping off the edge and landing on the next building.

He was a hundred yards away, and Shane was already slowing down tremendously. Her legs shook with every step. No matter how hard she tried, she couldn't bring in enough oxygen to satisfy her needs. She needed a short cut, a way to catch up without digging so deep within herself that she would burn out and fail.

Shane leaped off the side of the building. Her entire body weight smashed into the other building's wall, but she was ready and didn't let go of the lip on the roof. She hauled herself up, realizing that the distance continued to grow between her and Jaylen. It was too immense to cover before reaching the finish line.

But she couldn't give up like that. She sprinted faster than she ever thought she could as she let out a cry of pain. She was so close, yet so far from reaching her goal.

Grappling her way up another obstacle, Shane's arms turned to lead. She barely managed to make it up the wall, and the distance had only grown larger between her and Jaylen.

She imagined Jaylen standing at the end of the race, smiling down at her with triumph in his eyes. She could only imagine the ways he would kill her.

No. She couldn't allow that to happen. She couldn't accept defeat so easily. She couldn't let Jaylen win.

A new fire burned in Shane as she scanned for a shortcut, something that could help her win the race. The gunshot fired again, and Shane was able to pinpoint where it was. Her eyes narrowed as she saw outlines of people standing on a roof. Her heart sank when she also noticed that Jaylen was already nearly there.

It was now or never.

Now, or death.

The area around her was familiar. Shane and Eli had run up here countless times, and she saw a building rising high up in the sky ahead of her. Jaylen avoided it, but Shane expected that. It was the clock tower in the center square. The one Eli had warned her never to climb up.

But Shane was desperate, and it was her only option. Either way she would end up dying, regardless of what she chose, so why not do it on her own terms? If she could make the jump, it would cut her time nearly in half, and she could use that. She veered toward it, scrambling up.

Her heart hammered when she reached the top of the tower. The cool breeze had picked up its pace, but Shane didn't mind. It helped cool her and distract her from what she was about to do.

Closing her eyes, she took the first step toward the edge, picking up speed with every step that followed. She didn't bother looking down as she leaped off it, arms flailing wildly. She seemed to float for a couple seconds before gravity and the sheer terror of what she had just done became reality. Fear like she had never known flitted through her mind with each passing second as ground came rushing up to meet her.

Tuck your elbows in, feet together in front of you. Keep your muscles loose. Bend your knees.

All those steps went through Shane's mind in an instant. Her feet hit first, and she immediately went into a roll. Pain exploded across her body, especially at her knees, but she rolled onto her feet and kept going, completely in awe of what she just managed to survive.

But she had, and the race was very much still alive.

Pure adrenaline coursed through her body, and it was the only thing that kept her going. Her legs were in shock with the pain and stress that she had put them under, but Shane forced them to obey her and limped her way toward the nearest wall. She climbed it and forced herself to focus when she saw Jaylen right in front of her. Shane was too late, even with the jump. All the excitement that she had felt mere moments before disappeared in an instant.

She let out a cry as she continued onward despite her body's protest. She wasn't going to lose. She couldn't allow herself to.

But the building where Eli and Wikter were waiting loomed ahead of them. Eli's silhouette could be seen hunched over on the edge, probably wishing Shane on, even though it was clear that she was going to lose if she played fairly.

So, she wasn't going to.

Rules were meant to be broken, and those who break them are the ones who truly live.

Shane fumbled around with the ropes that tied her cloak to her neck all while trying to remain balanced. The chilled breeze pierced her bare shoulders, but she had more to worry about than that. If she could just get close enough to Jaylen… She forced her legs to move faster. Against all the odds, she began to gain ground. When she was an arm's length away, she chucked her cloak toward Jaylen's legs with all her might, holding onto the hood with one hand. The thick fabric of the cloak caught

Jaylen's legs like a lasso. Though he stumbled, he remained on his feet, but by then, Shane had caught up.

Shane pushed Jaylen to the ground with all the remaining force in her body before launching herself off the edge. Her hands caught on the ledge of the next building, and she hauled herself up, not bothering to get up off the roof. She was in too much pain to realize what happened.

Her heavy breath floated away from her as Eli ran toward her and gazed down at her exhausted body.

"You bleeding idiot," was all he said as he held a hand out to help her up.

"Did I win?"

"Yes, you won, but that doesn't excuse the fact that you are an idiot."

Shane brushed herself off.

"You could've died."

Shane winced. "You saw that?"

"Of course, I saw it." He pushed his hair back, pursing his lips.

"Is that concern I hear in your voice, Shallowgal," Shane joked.

Eli rolled his eyes. "I just don't want to see my partner dead because she couldn't gauge how high a jump was."

Partner. Pride bloomed out of Shane as she realized what that meant. She had finished the tasks. She had successfully become an assassin. The feeling was surreal.

Just then Shane saw Jaylen's hand appear over the edge and his body soon followed.

"I think you deserve congratulations," Wikter said. "For beating the challenges I've given you."

Shane couldn't help herself from beaming. Any fear that she had before that moment disappeared in the breeze that was blowing past her. What she had been working for the last six months had finally come to fruition. Every concern she might have had before suddenly didn't matter.

Wikter turned to Eli. "I assume you have everything you need to give her the tattoo?"

Eli nodded. "Yes. It's in my room."

"Good."

With that, he turned away and made his way to the ground, not acknowledging Jaylen's presence.

"You scar faced bitch!" he sneered as he made his way toward her and gave her a shove.

"Jaylen," Eli said, placing himself between them. "Calm down."

"No, *Eli*." Elistiffened. "Your so-called partner first burned my face, then made me an embarrassment in front of Wikter!"

"What? Are you afraid she ruined your chance to be his heir?"

"You—" Jaylen started forward, but Eli brought out a concealed knife. Jaylen stopped in his tracks.

"One more step toward her, and I'll give you a real scar," Eli warned.

"I'm going to kill you," he said to Shane over Eli's shoulder.

"Oh, really?" Shane couldn't help but laugh. "Join the long list of people who have already tried."

Jaylen stiffened, nostrils flaring.

"Leave," Eli demanded, holding the knife closer to Jaylen's face.

Jaylen pursed his lips, eyes darting between Shane and the knife. "Fine," was all he said as he straightened out his cloak and made his way toward the ground. Shane hadn't realized her hands balled into tightly wound fists until he was gone. What he said should've scared her, but it amused her instead.

"Don't mind him," Eli said when he disappeared. "From the first time I met him, he had it out for me."

Only moments after Jaylen left, Kyaina crawled her way to the roof. "Why'd Jaylen leave so angry?" she asked.

Shane shrugged. "I beat him."

A huge smile spread across Kyaina's face. "You did? Congratulations!" she said, gripping Shane's calloused hands. "You're finally one of us." She could barely keep her excitement contained.

"I'm surprised that Shane did it, with that stunt she pulled," Eli cut in.

Shane rolled her eyes. "You're still mad about that, aren't you?"

"Yes. If you had died, then Wikter would've given me another partner that I most likely wouldn't get along with."

"We get along? That's surprising."

Eli somehow managed to keep his face straight, even though Shane could tell that a smile was about to crack on his lips. "Better than most people I meet."

"What stunt did she pull?" Kyaina asked. Shane remembered that she was walking toward the end when it happened.

"I launched myself off the clock tower to catch up to him."

Kyaina stared at her. "And you didn't break anything?"

Shane shrugged, her shoulders hurting more than she would like to admit. "I have thick bones."

"That was suicide," Kyaina said, looking shocked.

"That's what I tried to tell her."

Shane rolled her eyes. "I survived, didn't I? And if I didn't risk that jump, I never would've caught up to Jaylen, and I would've died anyway because I didn't complete the challenge."

"Still…" Kyaina looked Shane up and down. "Don't ever pull something like that again. I don't know what I would do if you died."

Shane shivered as the cold wind picked up. She threw on her cloak, but it didn't seem to help.

"You must be freezing," Kyaina said. "We should get you near a fire."

They started down the building taking their leisurely time. Everything in Shane's body groaned in protest as she scaled the walls. All she wanted to do was get to her room and sleep, but she felt like even when she was lying in bed, she wouldn't be able to lose consciousness. Not with everything that had happened that day rushing through her mind.

She had done it. She had become an assassin.

Even saying the words in her head felt wrong, but it was true. She had done it. Six months of hard work had finally paid off and she was about to get a tattoo to show for it.

If only her family could see her now. A wave of sadness went over Shane as she pictured her father standing next to her, a frown of disapproval on his face when he saw what had become of his youngest daughter.

She blocked those thoughts out of her mind. She would most likely never see her father again.

They spent the rest of the walk back to the Assassin's Underground in silence. As they went down the spiral staircase, Shane truly felt as if she was headed to her home. A home that she could truly enjoy now that she no longer had to stress about taking the tests. Those had come and gone, and now she felt like she truly belonged here.

As Shane bid farewell to Kyaina, she turned to Eli.

"How does it feel?" he asked. "Officially being one of us?" Eli asked.

"No different than before."

He opened his door and allowed Shane to go first. "I have the stuff for the tattoo in my bathroom," he explained.

While Eli went into his bathroom, Shane situated herself on his couch. When he came out with a needle and ink, Shane's heart raced with excitement, along with a tiny bit of guilt for what she had done with Reece's sacrifice. If there was an after world, Shane shuddered to think what her friend would think of what she did.

"You ready?"

Shane took a deep breath, forcing a smile. "As ready as I'll ever be."

So, Eli began. He started with a light, charcoal outline of what was soon to become the mark of an assassin.

Shane winced as the needle repeatedly pressed down into her skin but didn't allow herself to complain or move once Eli started.

When he took the needle away, he let out a long breath.

"That shouldn't have been that stressful," he said, returning the needle to the box in which it came from. "How does it look?"

Shane looked down at her irritated left elbow. The skin was red around the black ink that now lay permanently in her skin. It looked identical to Eli's. There were mountains in the background of the circle, and an intricately drawn knife with blood dripping from it in the foreground. A huge smile spread across Shane's face as she looked up at Eli, eyes burning.

"I love it."

CHAPTER 24

S hane's muscles ached more than ever before as she sprinted through Conlar, trying to catch up to Eli who had run up ahead. According to him, she was going too slow to even call it running, and she couldn't disagree. It had been a week since she had taken the final task, yet her sore muscles were still recovering.

The night after the task she had difficulty sleeping. Her elbow still burned slightly from her new tattoo, but that was only part of what kept her awake. She still couldn't wrap her head around what had happened. She was an assassin. The words just felt wrong to her.

It also didn't help that months previous, Kyaina had promised a party for Shane once she finally became one of them. Shane shuddered just thinking of what she might have in mind, but when the day came, she was pleasantly surprised to find that Kyaina hadn't gone completely overboard. Instead, Shane hung out with Archer, Eli, and Kyaina in her own room. Eli brought over drinks as everyone reminisced over getting their tattoos.

Eli remained silent for most of that night, only chiming in with a couple snide comments, but that was to be expected, considering he had such a rocky history with his brother and the assassins. Every time Shane looked in his direction, he pretended to be normal, laughing at all the jokes, but his eyes showed the real story. They appeared to grow older, more pained as the night went on.

Eli had allowed the first couple of days after the race to pass with no training, and Shane was much relieved. Now, as Shane sprinted through the empty, early morning streets of Conlar, she wished more than ever that he could've extended it another day. Her legs groaned as they bore her weight with each step she took.

But deep down she loved it. Loved the pain. Loved the scenery. Loved the city. Now that she no longer had the test to be anxious about, everything appeared more vibrant, fuller of life. This was the first fall she spent in Conlar, and she loved every second of it. The colors of the shrubbery surrounding the city popped out against the dull mountain in the distance.

The smell of fresh rainfall greeted Shane's nostrils as she left the outskirts of the city. She followed the same path leading out of the city that she and Eli had run for the last couple months in hopes to catch up with him. She knew the trail like the back of her hand, and she could probably run it with her eyes closed.

"Took you long enough," Eli called down from the top of a small incline. "I'm pretty sure a sloth could beat you at the rate that you're going."

"I'm sore." Shane sprinted up the hill, meeting Eli at the top.

"That's no excuse."

"Well, I'm using it." Shane said, breathing heavy. "Can't you slow down a little?"

"Can't you speed up a little?" Eli cracked a smile and started going again. It took everything in Shane to chase after him, not for the last time wishing she could still be in bed.

They followed the usual route up the mountains until at last Conlar came into view. Eli, who was already a hundred feet ahead of Shane, picked up the pace, yelling at Shane to hurry up. She forced her legs to move faster. The only reprieve was that the rest of the trail went downhill. Less work for her lungs, and her overused legs.

The sun had risen fully above the mountains by the time they made it back into the city. More people were out on the streets, all of them huddled in warm clothes. Shane didn't mind that it forced Eli to slow to a walk, allowing her to finally catch up. Her legs shook beneath her with every step she took, and her breaths came unevenly.

"Looks like the couple days off didn't really help you," Eli said as they weaved their way through the crowded streets.

"Or it could be that I'm still sore from last week."

"You've had a week to recover. You should be fine."

Shane rolled her eyes. "You try jumping from the clock tower and walk away unscathed. It hurts."

"Well, that sounds like your problem." Eli laughed. "Most sane people know not to do that, unless they want to die."

"Then it's a good thing I'm not sane."

Eli raised his eyebrows. "That's for sure."

"Hey!" Shane said.

"What? You said it first."

"Yeah, but you weren't supposed to agree with it." They turned around a familiar corner and entered the small side street leading to the entrance of the Underground.

"How was I not supposed to agree with it when you were telling the truth?"

Shane forced a laugh. "Like you're any better. Most people don't go around killing their partners."

Eli stared at her with a stern face as he held open the door. "And if you say that again, I'll go back to not having a partner." The door closed behind him and he pulled the lever for the floor to descend. "Besides, he had it coming." Eli held open the door, allowing Shane to go in first before joining her and pulling the lever for the floor to descend. "If he hadn't tried to kill me first, then it never would have happened."

"And we never would have been partners?"

"Well." Eli shrugged. "He was always going to run away from the assassin, so technically I was never going to be his partner, so I guess we would have been."

"What do you mean?"

"He wanted to take my father's place as Prime Minister."

Shane let out a low whistle. "How well did that work out for him?"

"Pretty well, actually." They stopped at the top of the stairs. "He had a way with words and knew how to sway people to join his cause."

"So, the exact opposite of you?"

Eli ignored her comment. "He was working his way through the ranks of Iapciz when I found him and killed him."

"How lovely." Shane cracked a smile.

"If he hadn't tried to kill me, he might still be here today."

"Have you ever heard of forgiveness?" Even as Shane said the words, she knew that if either of her brothers had stabbed her with the intent to kill, there was no way in hell she was going to let them go easily.

"I've heard that I'm a very vengeful person."

Shane nearly choked on laughter. "No kidding."

"Hopefully you'll get your first assignment soon. Then we'll see if you're any better than Alek." Eli said as they walked down the stairs.

Everything in her itched to get out of Conlar, but the very thought of having to slit someone's throat sickened her. Kyaina had explained that nearly every assassin's first assignment was like that.

"It's to see whether or not we're truly ready for our jobs," Kyaina had said. "Slitting someone's throat makes it more personal, a better test for new assassins."

Thinking back on the conversation now made her feel nauseated.

"Do you think I'm ready?" Shane asked Eli in a small voice as they continued down the stairs.

"For what?"

"For this job." Shane rolled back her sleeve to reveal the healing tattoo. Every time she looked at it mixed emotions coursed through her veins. "I mean, I know I passed the tests, and I am technically an assassin, but do you think I'm ready to… to kill?"

Eli stopped dead in his tracks. It was the first time Shane had voiced her concerns out loud, and she was sure that it made her sound weak, but she didn't care. She had to tell someone, even if it meant being scoffed in the face.

But Eli did none of that.

He looked Shane in the eyes, the flickering light of the lanterns illuminated his worried face. "Honestly I still ask myself that question to this day." He took in a shaky breath, looking down the stairs to make sure nobody was coming. "When I confronted my brother, a part of me still wanted him to live, even after everything he did to me. It still lives in me to this day."

"How do you deal with it?"

"You don't," Eli said. "It's those feelings that make you human, no matter how much they suck."

"Does it ever get better, less intense?"

"Yes." Eli's grave face shocked Shane.

"When?"

"When you've killed enough people that you're numb to their deaths."

"Has that happened to you?"

Eli nodded, tearing his eyes away from Shane's face. "It happened a long time ago." He started down the stairs again.

They reached their doors and Shane stopped. "How long do you think it will take for that to happen to me?"

Silence followed. "It depends on the person," was all Eli said before opening his door and entering.

Shane entered her room and let out a deep sigh. She closed the door, leaned her back against the wall, and slid down to the floor. Would she ever be ready for this? To kill without feeling any emotion? Lose part of her humanity?

If she ran away, would Wikter send someone after her to end her life? Would it be Kyaina that would hunt her down? She didn't think she could stand looking her friend in the face, knowing that she was just another disappointment to someone else. All because she couldn't kill.

Shane looked up at the ceiling, eyes watering as she got up to go to the bathroom. When she started walking away, her eyes caught on a piece of paper on the floor next to the door that she had somehow missed when she first came in.

Shane's hand shook as she bent down to pick it up. Nausea returned when she realized what this was. Her first assignment.

She unfolded the paper. Her eyesight was too blurry, and the handwriting too small and twirly to read it in the dim light. Shane didn't mind though. She didn't think she could stand to look at who her first kill would be. At least not alone.

Shane folded the paper and headed toward Eli's door. She knocked but didn't wait for an answer before barging in.

"What are you doing?" Eli asked. He was seated at his desk with a book.

"I got this." Shane's voice shook as she held the folded paper in her hand.

Eli's face lost all the color it had had moments before.

"I didn't think I could read it alone in my room."

Shane had known it was coming, but some small part of her refused to believe it.

Eli got up and went to Shane. "Do you want me to read it for you?"

"No, I just," Shane took in a shaky breath' "I just needed someone's company." She stared at the letter, unsure if she would have the guts to open it.

Taking a deep breath, she unfolded the paper once again and held it next to the lantern to see it. She read one word, and her face paled. Her hands went slack, and the paper fell free from her hands.

"What?" Eli asked, his voice full of worry. "What is it? What does it say?"

Shane looked Eli straight in the eyes, trying her hardest not to throw up all over his room. "Fritz," she whispered. "I'm being sent to assassinate Fritz."

Images of the camp flashed before Shane's eyes. The whippings. The mining. The branding. All of it came rushing back, and she wasn't sure she could even go within sight of the compound, much less in it.

But none of that mattered.

The one man who she had envisioned killing, the one man who deserved to die more than anyone in the world, was who she was sent to assassinate.

Eli sucked in a sharp breath. "That means you have to go back to the camp, doesn't it?"

Shane nodded.

"Do you think you can do it?"

Another nod. "I want to do it." Shane's voice had no emotion in it. No fear. No anger. Nothing.

It should have frightened Shane, but it did the exact opposite. For the first time since she had become an assassin, she no longer doubted she could go through with the kill. After everything Fritz did to her, death would be the best thing she did for him. He deserved to suffer the way she did.

Shane picked up the letter and continued reading. It gave her information about the target. She gazed over it. She didn't need to know anything else about Fritz. What she knew already was enough to make her crave his death more than anything. The only information she needed was that she was to steal a ring from his finger to prove she had done it. She tossed the paper in the fire, watching as it burned brightly then turned to smoldering bits. Ten thousand Schulhers to kill the one man who deserved death more than anyone.

"You really hate him, don't you?" Eli cautiously asked.

"Yes." Shane took a quick look over to Eli. "Every night since I escaped, I've dreamed of his blood coating my hands." Her eyes met his. "He's the one person I've been wanting to kill for the last six months."

Eli pursed his lips, and Shane was afraid he was going to say something to stop her. Instead, all he said was, "I know the feeling."

"Your brother?"

Eli shook his head. "No. The people who kidnapped me and killed my parents."

"Did you kill them?"

"Yes. After I killed Alek, I tracked them down and ended their lives."

"After it happened, did you feel better?"

A nod. "I didn't feel anything when I stabbed them. Even afterward I didn't, but I guess a small part of me was glad that they couldn't hurt anyone else."

Shane remained stone faced, fighting to hold back her tears. "Do you think that I won't feel anything?"

Eli let out a sigh and gripped Shane's shoulders. "I can't tell you that," he said, staring into her eyes. "You decide whether or not he deserves to control your emotions."

Shane nodded, wiping away the tears that had escaped the restraint. "Thank you."

Eli tentatively let go of her shoulders. "Yeah, well I wouldn't want a balling mess in my room. I just cleaned it."

Half a smile found its way on Shane's face. "You call this clean?" She looked around her to find stacks of clothes and other miscellaneous things thrown all over the floor.

"It's my version of clean."

"I'd hate to see what your version of dirty is."

Eli laughed, turning toward the smoldering fire where the paper's remnants quickly disappeared. "When do you want to get ready to go?" he asked.

Shane too looked at the fire, the warmth burning at her face. "As soon as possible."

CHAPTER 25

E li and Shane had been on the trail for several days, and the long, relentless hours were starting to wear on them. Shane, at one point, had dozed off on her horse, nearly falling off. It was Eli's sharp words that brought her back to the moment.

They had packed their things in a rush. Shane didn't have much to add to her bag. Just a couple sets of clothes and food. Her weapons remained on her body, giving her reassurance. The feeling of her daggers strapped to her body and legs was almost enough to give her confidence. Almost.

They left the day after Shane had gotten the letter. That night Shane couldn't sleep; not with thoughts of Fritz and what he had done to her running through her head. When she finally lost consciousness, whips dominated her dreams. Whips, biting against the fragile skin of her back. She awoke in a pool of cold sweat, but she could still feel them thrashing against her back. Still hear Fritz's laugh when she begged him to stop.

Now, as Shane's horse trudged on through the mud-covered trail, she kept her hands tight against the reins. Lightning crackled ahead of them, followed closely by thunder. She was soaked and miserable. All she wanted was to get to the camp, even though she knew what nightmares lurked there. Lightning flashed once again ahead of her.

"We should stop for the night," Eli said, forcing her to lift her cloaked head. "Unless you want to get struck."

Shane pursed her lips. No matter how quickly she wanted to get to Verscar, she knew it would do her no good to hurry through the oncoming storm. She had to be at her best when she got there, and that meant she couldn't get any sicker than she already was.

"Fine."

She pulled the reins back, stopping the horse in its place at the edge of the trail in a nice clearing. Everywhere she looked, mud and puddles covered the ground. No good place to sleep for the night. It would be ironic, really, if Mindalin's Chosen Hero fell to a deluge of water.

Sighing, she went to her soaking wet bag on her horse's side. All her clothes and her blankets were sopping wet, but she ignored them and rummaged through the bag until she found a water-resistant cloth that she could use to keep the rain from pounding down on her. She strung it between two trees over the driest spot she could find to make a makeshift tent. She pinned the corners down using rocks.

"Here," Eli said, taking a dry blanket from his bag and tossing it over to Shane. "Use this."

"I don't need it." But even as the words left her lips goosebumps rose on her arms and a cold shiver went sprawling down her spine.

Eli raised an eyebrow. "Are you sure about that?"

"What about you? Don't you need this?"

He got to work setting up his own dry spot. "I mean, it would be nice, but you forget that I have Fuerbrand's Chosen Hero's blood flowing through my veins." He looked over at Shane. "And it looks like you're half dead. I don't know what I would say to Wikter if you just dropped dead right here."

Shane stuck out her tongue at him, but gratefully took the warm, woolen blanket. She already felt much better than before.

They didn't talk much before settling down for bed, but Shane struggled to get to sleep. She was too afraid of what, or who might visit her in her nightmares. Her eyes remained open throughout the night. The occasional lightning strike lit up everything around her. The booming sound of thunder and the pitter patter of rain helped soothe her nerves. The closer she got to the camp, the worse her anxiety became.

Eventually, the world began to grow lighter with the rising sun, and the rain began to taper off. The thunder and lightning had moved off into the distance somewhere in the night, headed north for the Lynese mountains.

"How long have you been up?" Eli's voice came from the spot where he had hidden himself the night before

"All night." Shane let out a yawn that had been building for the last couple minutes.

"Are you serious?"

Shane shrugged. "Couldn't sleep."

Eli took note of the dark bags under Shane's eyes. "How many nights do you think you can stay awake before you eventually cave in?"

Another shrug. "A couple more." Shane saw Eli open his mouth to argue, but she interrupted, "Once Fritz is dead, hopefully the nightmares won't be so bad."

Eli remained quiet for a few seconds. He looked like he could say something to contradict what Shane just said. "Hopefully," was all he said as he got up and brushed the water from the folds of his clothes.

"Here." Shane held out Eli's blanket that he had so kindly given her the night before. "Looks like you need it more than I do."

Eli said nothing as he grabbed it from Shane's hands.

"How'd you manage to keep it dry?" Shane asked.

"Kept it in a waterproof part of my bag." Eli showed her. "Only the rich can afford stuff like this."

"Are you calling me poor?"

Eli blinked. "I thought that was obvious."

Shane rolled her eyes, getting up from the ground with a groan. All her muscles had stiffened the night before. "After tonight, that'll all change."

"We'll see about that."

It took them a couple of hours before they reached a vaguely familiar part of the forest. Dread rose in Shane's stomach as her horse trotted along the muddy trail taking her closer and closer to her destination. When she reached an overlook of the valley, she held her breath, afraid that if she exhaled, tears would soon follow.

"There it is," Shane spat, gazing through the thick foliage. Images of the cruel whippings, and starved people flooded Shane's mind, but she forced them back. That wasn't going to happen again. This time, she came here on her own terms, not Fritz's.

Verscar's tall walls rose in the distance. Even though it was too far away to see clearly, she thought she could see people walking on the battlements.

"I think I'm gonna be sick."

"I won't judge you," was all Eli said as he stared down as well, his face a shade whiter than it usually was. "Are you sure you're up for this?"

Shane nodded. "I wanna make sure he can't hurt anyone ever again the way he hurt me." The scars on Shane's back prickled as though she had just been lashed. She could picture Fritz behind her, laughing as she screamed out in pain for someone to intervene.

Eli started down the trail, forcing Shane to take her thoughts away from Verscar. No longer being able to see it helped remind her that she wasn't going there as a slave, but as an assassin on a mission to kill. She couldn't help herself from grabbing the leather handle of one of her knives, just as reassurance that she wasn't going in there unprepared. When she looked at Eli ahead of her, she smiled. She had a friend that would help her if things went badly.

When they made it into the small valley, they slowed to a stop. The trees ended just ahead, and through the branches stood Verscar, so close they could smell it. They were near the place where she, Archer, and Kyaina had stopped after escaping.

"We stay here until nightfall," Shane said with a frown, swinging her legs off her horse.

The sun had peaked through the clouds, lighting up the world once again. Shane used it to her advantage and laid all the clothes in her bag on a branch, hoping the black clothes and mask she would wear that night might dry before then.

"It's not going to work," Eli said, realizing what she was doing.

"Yes, it will." Shane was already having a horrid day, and she refused to accept having to put on damp assassin's clothes that night.

"No, it won't." Eli walked over to her. "At least not in the short time we'll be here."

"Then do you have a better idea?" Shane whipped her head around, anger rising in her. "'Cause a fire will bring smoke, and I don't want that kind of attention."

"Bloody knives, Shay." Eli forced a laugh. "You get angry when you're tired."

"Believe it or not, I've been told that before." Shane returned to setting her stuff about to dry out.

"You should really get some sleep."

"I don't need your help. This is my mission, so I don't have to listen to you."

Shane could feel Eli's worried stare, but she didn't look back. "It's not like it's an order. It's a suggestion."

"Well, I'm not going to listen to it." Shane reached into her bag to grab a pair of pants, but Eli grabbed her arm before she could. His warm hand kept a tight grip on her so she couldn't escape.

"You need rest."

"No, I don't."

"Yes, you do." He let Shane's arm fall from his grip, and she didn't go for the rest of her wet clothes.

"I can't sleep." Tears swelled in her eyes. Shane didn't bother trying to hold them back. "Every time I close my eyes, I see the whips. I can feel them hitting my back, Elias."

Shane started shaking and crying. He grabbed her, hugging her tightly against his chest. Shane allowed her tears to soak into his cloak. He held her close, reminding her that she wasn't there on her own. Someone else could help her carry the pain away.

"I keep seeing his face," Shane cried. "Every time I fall asleep, he's there."

"I won't even pretend to know what it was like for you in there." Eli pulled back but still holding her shoulders at an arm's length. His eyes met her own broken ones. "But I can tell you that I know how it feels to have nightmares. I was afraid to go to sleep like you, but you can't keep living in fear."

"Do they get any better?"

"They do once you're no longer afraid."

Eli let his hands fall free from Shane's shoulders. She wiped the tears from her eyes and cheeks.

"You lay down over there and close your eyes, and I'll deal with drying your clothes, ok?"

Shane nodded. She was too tired to argue. She wasn't going to be afraid. She refused to be. She fell asleep almost as soon as she hit the ground.

Shane was awakened by Eli standing over her, nudging her gently with his boot. She sprang up, breathing heavily. It took her a couple moments to realize where she was, and why she was there.

"Bloody knives." Eli laughed. "Are you that weak hearted that a little tap made you jump ten feet."

"You just surprised me."

Shane looked up at the sky through the trees to find utter blackness. The clouds had once again moved in, hiding the moon and the stars. A perfect night to infiltrate Verscar, to finally accomplish what Shane had been dreaming of for months.

"Everything that you brought is dry," Eli said, tossing her the assassin's outfit. The cloak and mask were warm.

"How?" Shane looked from the clothes to Eli, surprised.

Eli wiggled his fingers. "I'm Fuerbrand's Chosen Heroes descendant, remember?"

"Yeah, but that doesn't explain how you managed to do it." Shane threw her cloak around herself to stop the cold breeze from brushing harshly against her skin. The warmth of the cloak felt good on Shane's back.

"Are you sure about that?" He picked up his knife sheath from a fallen log and put it around his arm. "I can heat up my hands at will. Not as good as being able to start a fire, but at least it's something."

Shane thought back to every time Eli's warm hands brushed her arm. Even when they should've been freezing, they hadn't been. "Thank you." She made Eli turn around as she changed out of her cold, damp clothes and put on her dark, stealth clothes.

"How long has the sun been down?" she asked, putting on a soft sole boot.

"About thirty minutes."

Shane let out a sigh. The weight of what they were about to do was finally hitting her. Soon, they would be scaling the wall to make their way toward Fritz's estate. Shane was worried she wouldn't have enough guts to do it, to enter Verscar once again, but she wasn't going to say it out loud. If she said it, it might become a reality. A wall she could never get over.

"Do you know the layout?" Eli asked.

"Like the back of my hand."

"Good."

Even though Shane spent most of her time in the underground, the streets of Verscar were etched into her brain. She could remember the path she took to get out like it just happened yesterday.

Shane looked out across the trees to the lights of Verscar a couple hundred feet away. The exact same way it was when she first arrived, so ignorant and naive of what was to come. She wondered if any of the prisoners she came with were still alive, or if they had died just like she would've if she hadn't had the help of Kyaina and Archer.

"We can't leave the prisoners in there," Shane said out of nowhere. "Before you say anything, I know that I'm being irrational, but we can't leave them there to die."

Eli pursed his lips. "You do realize how crazy that sounds, right?" His gaze remained on the walls in the distance. "We're going to have a hard enough time getting in there and getting out without being seen, but you want us to take everyone in there with us?"

"They'll be the distraction," Shane said. "That'll send the guards away from Fritz, making it easier for us to sneak in there and kill him."

"Shay, I don't think that's possible—"

"Look, I know you don't care about them, but I do."

There was silence.

"I care about them. Gods, I care about them." Eli pushed his hair back with his hands. "What they're going through in there is despicable, but we have a mission. If we fail, Wikter will kill us."

Shane didn't know if that was a true or empty threat. "Please, Elias. That's all I ask of you."

Eli let out a long, slow breath. "All right, but if this doesn't work, *I'm* going to kill you."

A slight smile played at the edges of Shane's lips, but it stopped there. A smile didn't belong where they were about to go.

"Thank you."

"Don't thank me until we get out of that gods be damned place." Eli tightened the holsters around his thighs and arms. "Do you have a plan?"

"Yes, actually. I do."

Scattered parts of a plan, but Shane was going to deal with that later.

"What is it?"

"We get in there, sneak into the mines, break the chains, and set the prisoners free."

Eli blinked. "Sounds well thought out," he said sarcastically. "I don't know why I didn't think of *that* before."

"If that doesn't work, I'll improvise."

"Because we both know how great you are at that," Eli said. "Isn't that my job?"

"Shut up, Eli." Shane let out a sigh. "All I want to do is give them a chance to escape. They can take it if they want, but like you said before, we have a mission to accomplish."

Shane looked over at Verscar, a feeling of dread forming in her stomach. She wasn't the same scared girl who went in there a year ago, she reminded herself.

"You ready?" she asked, refusing to look away from the wall they would have to climb shortly.

"As ready as I'll ever be."

"Well, I'm not," Shane mumbled under her breath. But she forced her shoulders to remain high as she began her confident walk out of the woods and into the barren fields between them and the walls of Verscar. She nervously palmed her knives as the wall drew closer.

Eli was behind her. This was her mission. She had to lead the way. She kept reminding herself that she could do this.

The tall grass that surrounded them made them nearly invisible to any guards on the tall walls, and could be the only thing that might betray them if it moved.

It wasn't until they reached the spot where torchlight lit the area ahead of them that they slowed their pace. Shane placed a hand on Eli's arm, waiting for the guard on top of the wall to pass before sprinting up to the wall, pressing herself as close as she could to the stone fortification. The guards weren't watching the outside, she reminded herself. They were more concerned about keeping people in, than to care what happened outside Verscar. Getting out of the camp once inside was going to be the hard part.

Shane didn't wait long before grabbing hold of the wall and beginning her climb.

Relying on her training, she made her way to the top, stopping when she heard a guard's footsteps directly above her. She waited until they disappeared in the distance before hauling herself up and over the top, onto the battlements. Shane slunk down against the edge, making herself as small as possible. Moments later Eli joined her. His eyes met hers and she was surprised to see that he was waiting on her to make the next move. For a moment she forgot that she was supposed to be the leader.

Shane looked over the ledge, blinded by the torchlight that covered the entire area. She had forgotten just how harsh the conditions were here, and even the light was a reminder of that. It made Shane sick to her stomach.

It also meant that the mission would be harder than she expected.

The soldier's barracks were exactly where she remembered them, as well as the shacks the prisoners were forced to sleep in the first night. The main building stood at the far end of the camp on the eastern side of the lake. Just looking at it made Shane sick.

She scanned the surrounding area before deciding to make her way down the inside of the wall. She did it quickly and sloppily, but she didn't care. Not when so many torches were shining down on her like spotlights.

Her knees buckled as she dropped down the last few feet, a little too far for a painless landing, but she survived unscathed.

Shane didn't wait for Eli's permission before sprinting to the shadow of the nearest shack. Eli wasn't far behind, sinking into the shadows just as the sound of guards' feet could be heard against the hard cobblestone road. Shane let out a sigh of relief as they walked past without seeing them.

Motioning for Eli to follow, she continued down the street, hiding in nooks and shadows as guards walked by. There were more people here than Shane remembered, but Shane remembered Fritz saying they had gone from a few hundred guards, to over one thousand. She just didn't realize how many that really was. Her and Eli were stopped every few minutes.

Finally, Shane saw one of the mines up ahead of her. They had stopped in the small shed that held the pickaxes when they weren't in use. Two men stood guard outside the mine, illuminated by faint torchlight.

"You distract them while I go in," Shane whispered as she grabbed a pickaxe from the wall. It didn't seem as heavy as it had before.

"Do you want them dead?"

Shane thought for a moment. "That would be best, yes." She got up to leave.

"Wait." Eli grabbed her arm, stopping her before she got the chance to go. "Just try and come out alive. It would be embarrassing to say that you died trying to help the prisoners escape."

"I don't plan on dying." A slight smile traced its way across Shane's lips. "But if I do, then make sure the rest of Fritz's life feels like he's in Haytorrow's Fallen Realm."

She shrugged Eli's hand from her arm and started toward the mine. The very same mine that she had come from only six months before.

Out of the corner of her eye, she saw something move in the shadows. She knew it was Eli making his way to his victims.

"I don't see why we need to stand here," Shane heard one of the guards say when she was near enough. "It isn't like the prisoners aren't tied down." Shane crawled forward out of the shadows just enough so she could see them once again.

"We're here because Fritz would have a fit if we weren't."

Just then there came a noise from their left.

"What was that?" The guard went instinctively for his sword pommel.

"Relax, Lonolan." The other man laughed. "It's probably a rat."

Lonolan took a step in the direction the noise had come from. "I'm gonna go check, just in case."

"Whatever makes you happy."

Lonolan disappeared into the darkness. A few moments passed and he didn't return. Her muscles tensed as she prepared to run.

When the guard near the mine wasn't looking, Shane took her first couple steps.

She saw someone walk out of the shadows wearing all black. Eli.

"Hey you," the man said, hand resting on the hilt of his sword. "What are you doing here?"

Before Shane could even blink, Eli was at his throat with a bloody knife in his hand. The man instantly dropped to the ground dead.

"Well, wasn't that lovely," Shane said quietly, stepping out of the shadows.

"It was the quickest way to get rid of them." Eli wiped his blade off on the man's clothes. "I'll deal with their bodies while you rescue your people."

"Thank you," she said over her shoulder as she started into the mine. "Thank you for helping me with this."

Eli smiled. "I'm still waiting for this to fail miserably."

Shane couldn't help but smile. She turned around and made her way into the mine.

The guards in the mines weren't much of a problem. There were more in the mine than she remembered, but they were too focused on the prisoners to notice her, so it was easy to surprise them and knock them out with the butt of her knife. The shadows of the mine helped hide her.

"Who are you?" a small boy, no older than ten asked, his voice full of fear as Shane made her way farther into the tunnel.

Shane couldn't blame him for being afraid. With her mask on, all that could be seen was her eyes, and they looked deadly.

"I am nobody," she said. She took off her mask and the boy gasped at her appearance.

"Ha-have you come to punish me?"

The fear in the boy's voice broke her heart, but all she could do was pin back her emotions and remain confident. "I've come to rescue you, and the rest of the prisoners down here."

Shane brought the pickaxe down and broke the boy's chains that kept him locked down. The boy only remained frozen in fear.

"Why?"

Shane swallowed. "Because I know what it's like to be down here, and I know what it's like wanting your freedom." Shane tugged on her shirt to reveal her own brands. The boy gasped.

"You truly are here to save us."

Shane handed him the pickaxe. "Free the other prisoners," she ordered. "And run like hell once you do."

"Where are you going?"

Shane paused to put her mask back on, and then said, "To murder the man who tortured and enslaved us."

CHAPTER 26

"Did you do it?" Eli asked as Shane's silhouette appeared from the darkness of the mine.

"Yes." Shane felt her thighs for her knives, relieved when her fingers brushed against the cold handle. "Told someone to free the rest of the prisoners."

"And do you think they will?"

Shane nodded. "He wasn't following me, and this is the only way out."

"Are you sure?"

"Yes," Shane said bluntly. "In case you've forgotten, I've been here before."

Eli didn't meet her eyes as they continued onward toward Fritz's estate. They had a mission, and they weren't going to leave until it was finished, Shane would make sure of that, even if it meant killing everyone in the entirety of Verscar.

"How bad was it down there?" Eli asked when he was sure no one was surrounding them.

"Horrible." Shane's eyes suddenly had difficulty holding back tears. "Everything was the same. I… I—" Shane took a deep breath. "It was hard to breathe down there. It was like everything I had done in the last six months didn't happen, and I was waking up from a bad dream."

"You aren't here alone," Eli reminded her. "I'm here for you."

Shane's bloodshot eyes met his. "Thank you," she mouthed, not even able to make the sound.

"We still have to get in there." He jerked his head toward a building that stood taller than the rest, watching over the whole compound. "After you complete your mission, you can thank me."

Shane forced a smile.

They continued onward, ducking and hiding whenever they heard someone coming. Fritz's house was only a short distance away. The moon was already high up in the sky, peeking through the clouds to illuminate the entire compound.

"We'd better hurry," Eli said. "It won't be long until the wind pushes all the clouds away."

Shane looked up and swore. Stars that had been hidden moments before were glowing brightly in the sky. The clouds that surrounded them moved fast, and were quickly dissipating.

Shane waited in the shadows, trying to blend in with the darkness as two guards walked past. Their voices could be heard loudly over the otherwise silent compound, complaining rather loudly.

"It's too damn cold out here," one of them said. "Why Fritz makes us circle around the compound when there are plenty of other people already doing it doesn't make any sense."

"Don't let Fritz hear you complaining like that, or your head will be separated from your body."

"I don't think he has the guts to do it."

"Are you sure about that?" the other guard asked. "Have you ever met the man?"

"Once when I first got the job a couple months ago," he said as they walked closer and closer. Shane's heart pounded out of her chest. If they took one more step forward, they would be seen for sure. Shane pressed herself to the building wall, sucking in as much air as she could, trying to appear smaller than she really was.

"Then you don't know him as well as I do." The guard shuddered. "Before you got hired, two prisoners tried to escape," he explained. "One made it out. The other died in the lake from a gunshot wound. Fritz went ballistic afterward, killing almost all the guards who allowed them escape, at least those that hadn't already been killed."

"Is that why there are so many of us now?"

The other guard nodded. "He more than doubled the surveillance after that. He didn't want any more prisoners ruining his record."

Shane wanted to scream. She wanted to do anything but sit and wait for them to find her and Eli.

But just then, they turned around and walked in the other direction.

Shane let out a sigh, sinking to the ground. Being that close to the guards, knowing they could do nothing but wait to be discovered… It brought back memories that Shane would prefer to forget. She shouldn't be afraid of them, yet she couldn't stop her heart from pounding out of her chest. Couldn't stop her eyes from widening with each step they took, or her breath from quickening.

"Shane." Eli grabbed her trembling shoulders, his warm touch a soothing presence in the cold night, "It's all right. I'm here with you."

"I… I know." Shane let out a shaky breath. "It's just being so close to them… This isn't as easy as I thought it would be, all right?"

"I never expected it to be." Eli's eyes scanned Shane's face. "If you want to back out now—"

"No. I want to do this." Shane forced her shoulders to stop shaking and stood up a little taller. "I want to kill Fritz."

Eli let go of her shoulders and looked up into the sky as the moon poked out of the clouds. "Then we'd better hurry, unless you want to get caught and put back in the mines again. Or worse."

Shane shuddered just thinking about it. She made sure her hood was well over her head, and her mask snug to her face, she peered around the corner of the building and saw no one. She motioned for Eli to follow as she sprinted through the wide opening. She could only pray that nobody on the wall was looking down. She realized she'd been holding her breath all the way across the street, exhaling only when her fingers touched the wooden wall of the estate Fritz resided in.

"Do you know where his room is?"

Shane nodded, gazing up at the building. She knew it was on the second floor— the paper told her that much— and on the far north side, but other than that it would all be guesswork.

With Eli watching her back, she started climbing. It was a harder climb than the fortress wall had been because the surface was smoother, less room for hand and footholds, but a conveniently placed rain gutter made it a little easier. She reached her cold hands up the last couple feet and grabbed a window ledge with flowers growing on each side. Ironic, that something so beautiful could survive in a place full of death and despair.

She peered through the window to make sure no one was in the dark room before she hauled herself onto the sill. She prayed to whatever god would listen that no one would come in as she started on the window. It wasn't locked. Why should it be when it was surrounded by thousands of guards and a giant wall?

It was a slow, tedious process, trying to open the window silently, but it paid off. When the window was open enough for a body to pass, Shane squeezed her way through, rolling silently on the floor.

Shane waited for Eli to join her before sneaking for the door. She opened the door and made sure the coast was clear before slinking out in the hallway, Eli right behind her. There were lanterns everywhere, lighting the hallways.

Her hand instinctively went to her collar bone where her brand and tattoo were, and she winced. It seemed like just yesterday that she was forced down this exact same hallway toward Fritz's office.

"You okay?" Eli asked, in a whisper.

"Yeah." Shane whispered her reply, hoping her emotions didn't betray her. "Fine."

She nodded and they started down the hallway. They slinked their way to where the hallway turned, backs pressed against the wall.

Shane's ears detected footsteps coming down the hallway somewhere behind them. Her eyes widened as she stared at Eli, his expression the same.

"Hide," he mouthed as he flung himself into a doorway.

Shane was about to follow him when three guards rounded the corner. They took a couple steps down the hallway and stopped. Shane tried to push herself further against the wall, trusting in her black clothes and mask to hide her in the ill-lit hallway, but it was too late.

Shane was forced to open her eyes when the sound of the men taking their blades out of the scabbards echoed down the hallway.

Before anyone could blink, Shane's hands immediately went to the handles of her knives. She lunged forward, meeting the men midway down the hallway. Metal clanged as she sliced downward. The guard was barely able to raise a sword to defend himself. Shane had caught them off guard, but that didn't last for long.

"So much for staying discreet." She heard Eli's voice behind her along with the *shink* of his own daggers leaving the sheath.

Shane didn't have time to answer him. The guard that she was fighting took a step forward, trying his best to fend off her knives. The two others joined in, and it took all her concentration to just stay alive.

But not for long.

A throwing knife thudded into one man's chest. He fell to the ground almost instantaneously, gasping for breath. A lung hit.

Without hesitation, Eli was fighting by her side.

The man in front of Shane was a whirlwind of blades and steel. Her eyes narrowed as he took a swipe over her head. She ducked and rolled toward him. She jumped back to her feet and kneed the man square in the stomach. He stumbled backward, gasping for breath. Right in the diaphragm.

The man tried to push himself up and go after her, but he was sloppy. He took one wide swing with his sword arm. Shane crossed her knives in front of her stopping his sword in its path. She twisted her arms to the right, and the sword was thrown from his hand.

Shane took her leisurely time stepping forward, not that she had any. But she took pride in knowing that she was beating one of the men who may have tortured, whipped, and beat her not so long ago. He deserved to feel it. Deserved to suffer the way she did. Deserved it nearly as much as Fritz did.

She twirled her knife in her hand. The fighting behind her stopped and all she heard was a deafening silence.

"What are you waiting for?" he breathed, crawling backward trying to get to his sword, but Shane kicked it away.

The knives in Shane's hands felt heavier than they had before. She raised it high, but the point shook too much. Looking down at the man and how helpless he appeared made her hesitate. She should kill him right here, right now. That's what he would've done if the roles were reversed. Yet...

"I'm saving it," Shane said.

Just then Eli walked up behind her with his blades in his hands. They dripped with blood that was not his own.

"Want me to do it?"

Shane nodded. Eli took a step forward and the man didn't bother trying to fight. He took in a sharp breath as Eli slit his throat. Dark red blood covered his blade when he retrieved it.

"Thank you."

"You keep saying that." Eli wiped off the blood on the guard's pant leg and returned his knife to the sheath on his shoulder.

"And I mean it." Shane took in a deep breath, staring down at the now dead man. "He deserved to suffer more," she said.

"I'm sure he did, but we don't have time to play around." Eli looked over his shoulder warily. "It won't be long before someone finds them, and the rest of the prisoners escape."

They started down the hall. Shane's cloak billowed behind her as she turned the corner at a fast but quiet pace. Eli was right. If the prisoners escaped before they got to Fritz, there was no way to make sure that he was still going to be in his room and not out in the courtyard dealing with the revolt. That, and they needed the distraction to help escape.

As the walls surrounding them blurred past, Shane's eye caught on a door. There was nothing special about it, just stained wood like the rest of them, but something about it made her skin crawl. It took everything in her not to reach out her hand to touch the cool metal handle.

"Eli," she quietly called. "Wait."

She looked the door up and down and knew that it was the one they were looking for. "This is Fritz's room." The name tasted like acid in her mouth.

"You sure?"

"Positive." Even though she had never been in it before, her intuition told her they were at the right place. Something about the door oozed pure evil. Hatred boiled up inside Shane as she reached out and grabbed the handle. Eli watched her back as she slowly creaked open the door, wincing every time it made the slightest noise. Once open wide enough to squeeze through, Shane made her way into the room, Eli close behind.

Shane silently shut the door and looked around the moonlit room. It appeared to be so average. Nothing about the room made it special. There was a desk at the far wall, and a full four poster bed with a man sleeping on it, yet it still reeked of evil. Being in the same room as Fritz made her skin crawl.

"Gods, I hate it here," Shane whispered as she pulled her daggers from their sheaths with a sharp *shink*. She froze, but Fritz kept snoring so peacefully that it seemed a waste to kill him like that. He deserved to suffer more than anyone in the gods be damned camp, not die a quick easy death with a slit to the throat.

"I know that you want to make him suffer," Eli whispered as if he could read her thoughts. "But you can't. Just slit his throat like I taught you, and everything will be fine."

Shane nodded. Her eyes fixed on Fritz, afraid that he would awaken at any moment and come at her with the whip that caused her so much pain.

She took a step forward, careful to distribute her weight evenly as not to make any noise with the squeaky floorboards. With each step she took, her heart beat a little faster. Shane was sure Fritz could hear it. He would wake up any minute now and she would be paralyzed with fear.

Still sleeping. Still snoring.

Shane got to the side of the bed and froze. Here was the man who tortured, whipped, and beat her to the point where she longed for Haytorrow to take her away to his realm, and he was sleeping in his bed like none of it bothered him at all. He had killed so many people but hadn't felt a thing.

He deserved to die more than anyone in the world.

Shane raised her knives slowly, afraid if she moved too quickly, she would start to shake. Her eyes gleamed with murder. She was going to do it. She was going to bring her knife down and end the life of the man who had come so close to ending hers.

Yet as her muscles tensed for the final blow, she hesitated. If she did this, it would only be the beginning of a road of death and destruction. Would she be any better than the man she hated for nearly a year?

Before she could decide, bells rang and yelling erupted from outside. The prisoners had escaped.

Fritz's eyes flung open, and he shot out of bed. His eyes widened when he saw Shane and Eli.

"Who are you?" Fritz asked as he fumbled around his bedside table for something to defend himself with.

Shane shook off her paralyzing fear. "You mean you don't recognize me?" Shane threw off her hood and mask. She hoped that the little light in the room would illuminate the scar that ran down her face. Maybe if he saw that, he would recognize her.

But he obviously didn't.

Eli's eyes met Shane's, and he gave a slight nod. He was there with her, even when it felt like he wasn't. If she faltered, he would help her out.

"I don't know you," Fritz said, still rummaging in his drawers. "And I don't plan to."

He reached into his drawer and brought out a gun. His hands remained steady as he fired it at Eli. Shock filled Shane as Eli took a step back, gasping. The shock was replaced with pure anger and hatred. She couldn't worry if Eli was alive. Not now.

"Get out!" Fritz yelled at Shane. But Shane wasn't going to be afraid of him any longer. Now that he stood in front of her, she realized that he was nothing more than a man, and this one deserved to die.

"I don't think I will." Shane managed to say through gritted teeth. She twirled her knives in her hand and started forward. Shane didn't care about her life anymore. All she cared about was killing Fritz, even if she had to die in the process.

Fritz brought back the hammer of the revolver and Shane's muscles tensed. When he pulled the trigger, she expected pain to flare up in her chest, but nothing happened.

"Looks like you're out of bullets."

I will not be afraid.

"That's impossible." Fritz said, studying the gun in his unsteady hands.

Shane stabbed with both knives aimed straight at Fritz's heart. He dropped his revolver and rolled to the side faster than Shane expected. The knives grazed his arm drawing blood, but nothing more.

Shane forced Fritz back to his desk, stabbing and slashing at him, but he was a better fighter than she gave him credit for, dodging and blocking her blows. Shane sliced with both knives, but Fritz hit her arms away, just like she had expected. She kicked him hard in his stomach, and he hit hard against the desk, falling to the floor.

As Shane was about to bring her knife down for the final blow, Fritz grabbed the chair and swung it at her full force. It shattered, forcing her to stumble back as pain erupted down her side. All the air left her lungs, and she lost her grip on her right blade. The knife clattered to the floor as she backed up against the wall trying to get her wind back.

"I said get out." Fritz got up and picked the knife from the floor. He flipped it expertly in his hand.

"And I said there's no way in Haytorrow's Realm that I'm doing that."

Fritz swung the knife toward Shane's head. She easily ducked and rolled out of the way behind him. With his back to her, she stabbed just below the ribs. Fritz turned to defend himself and quickly went on the offensive, slicing upward. Shane tried to contort herself to block, but pain erupted up her left arm as the knife sliced all the way down her arm.

"I was hoping this was going to be a better fight," Fritz said as Shane stumbled backward. Terror returned. "After all, you're so hellbent on destroying me."

"You have no idea." Shane spat at his feet; her free hand was cradling her wounded arm. "I hate you. I hate everything you stand for. Everything you've accomplished."

"That's too bad because I don't know you."

Shane's right foot caught on something that made her fall backward, her knife falling from her hand. She tried to get back up but couldn't. The room was spinning– she was losing too much blood.

"You are nothing more than an ignorant little girl who wants revenge for something I don't even remember."

Shane forced a smile to her face. "Are you sure about that?" She tore at her neckline, revealing the ugly brand marks that had haunted her day and night. Fritz took in a sharp intake of breath.

"You." He pointed his knife at Shane. "You were supposed to be dead."

"Well, I'm not." She grimaced as blood continued to leak from her arm. She reached for a knife strapped to her leg, but as soon as it was in her hand, Fritz kicked it away. She was out of weapons.

"I should've killed you when I had the chance." Fritz took a step forward, and Shane had nowhere else to go. She was pressed tightly to the wall. "Do you know how many people you and your assassin friend killed?"

"Quite a few?"

"You ruined my reputation!" Spit flew from his mouth and landed on Shane's forehead. "You should've died that day."

"I'm still breathing, aren't I?"

"Not for long." He stepped on Shane's outstretched leg, putting his full weight on her shin. She heard a crack before she felt any pain, but when she did it was blinding, and she screamed in agony.

She didn't feel the knife grazing her stomach. The pain in her leg was too tremendous to even be aware of whatever else hurt on her body. But she couldn't stop fighting. Couldn't stop until Fritz was dead in front of her.

As Fritz brought the knife down again to finish her through the heart, she caught his hand stopping it from finishing its deadly blow. Suddenly, all the months of training with Eli made sense. He was building her up for this exact moment. Her face contorted with determination as she used every single muscle she had spent months building up to force his hand backward.

"I'm not afraid of you anymore," she panted as she tore the knife away from his hands. She plunged the dagger straight into Fritz's beating heart.

CHAPTER 27

S hane felt his heart stop beating through the knife in her hand. She felt the life leave his body as his dark red blood soaked her hands. His body landed on top of her, a strangled scream escaping her when he hit her leg. She pushed him off with all her might. His eyes remained staring up at the ceiling as she grabbed the ring from his finger.

Shane yanked the knife from his chest. Her breaths came heavily, laboriously. She had already lost so much blood that pain was the only thing she knew. The world spun around her as she leaned against the wall, feeling at peace for the first time in over a year.

Shane should've felt something like guilt or anger, but instead all she felt was pure joy thrumming from her heart. The man who had tortured her, had beaten her nearly to death, was finally dead, by her hand. If there was one thing she felt badly about it was that he didn't suffer nearly enough for what he did to not only her but all the other prisoners who had suffered and died in Verscar.

A small part of her scolded herself for feeling the way she did. Her hands shook as she looked down at the monster that she had become. The monster that Reece had died to save.

"Shane." Eli's voice came as nothing but a whisper, but she whipped her head around forgetting nearly everything that went through her mind only moments before.

"Elias." Shane tried to stand, but the pain in her leg wouldn't allow it. She let out a cry and fell to the floor. "I'm here Eli," she sobbed.

"I couldn't see anything besides darkness, and when you stopped talking..." Eli took a shaky breath. "I thought you died, Shane."

"I'm alive." *But maybe not for long.* Already the edges of her vision were growing dim.

"Is it done?" The pain in his voice made Shane want to cry even harder, but that would do nothing to help either of them.

"Yes." Shane nodded. "I did it."

Shane tried crawling over to him. Though pain flared in her broken leg, she managed to push herself until she could feel his cold hand with her palm. Wet mixed with dry blood soaked his hand.

"Are you okay?" she managed to ask through her shock.

"Does it look like I'm okay?" Eli forced a laugh as he propped himself against the nearest wall. "I'm going to live if that's what you mean. He just hit my shoulder, and I've already dealt with that."

A sob of joy escaped Shane's mouth.

Blood dripped from her injured arm and landed on Eli's hand.

"Shane, you're bleeding."

"So are you." Shane moved her leg and let out a cry.

"Oh, gods." Shane could see Eli's face whiten. "Is your leg broken?"

"I think so."

Eli used the wall to help him up, placing his bloody hand on the dresser. He searched the room for a lantern and lit it. He gazed down upon Shane's shattered limb; eyebrows creased in worry.

"How bad is it?" she asked.

"You don't want to know." Eli set the lantern down on the dresser and took off his cloak. Using the knives strapped to both his arms and legs, he tore it into small cloth pieces and tossed a larger piece to Shane. "Put pressure on your arm and try to clean it as much as possible."

"I know how to treat wounds," Shane said, but she grabbed the cloth anyway. Drawing a deep breath, she brought it down on her arm. Pain raced down the entire length.

Eli told her to stop applying pressure and looked into the wound.

"It's not as bad as it looks." He dropped her arm and allowed her to reapply pressure.

"How about my leg?"

"Let's not talk about it," Eli quickly said.

She couldn't help but look down and gasp. Her leg was bent at an odd angle. Seeing it caused the pain to intensify.

"Don't look at it," Eli scolded. "It will only make it worse."

"Why didn't you tell me that sooner?" Shane's teeth clenched, looking up to the ceiling, tears running down her face. "Why does it hurt so damn much?"

"That's what broken legs do."

"Well, it sucks."

"Well, you've got to deal with it."

Eli grabbed her hurt arm lightly and tied a cloth around it tightly. Shane winced but didn't cry out. She was afraid that if she did, she would alert someone of their presence.

"If only we had some water," Shane mumbled under her breath. Eli heard her and slung his water flask from across her shoulder.

"Why didn't you remind me of it earlier?" he asked, tossing it over to Shane.

"Because I forgot." She unscrewed the top and poured some of it on her arm and the remainder over her leg. Immediate relief washed over her, but not nearly enough. It would take a whole lot more to heal it completely. "I've only been Mindalin's Chosen Hero for about a year."

"Most people remember stuff like that."

"I'm sorry, but with the whole fighting for my life, and being in more pain than I have ever been in before, it slipped my mind." Shane tossed the empty flask back to Eli and tried to stand on her leg. Pain instantly laced its way up her leg.

"Are you gonna make a splint?" Shane asked wearily.

"I can try. But it will hurt a lot."

"I don't care." Shane grimaced as she accidentally moved her leg across the floor.

"This is going to hurt. Like a lot. I'm gonna have to set your bones first."

"You said that already," Shane said through gritted teeth. "Just do it."

Eli was about to start, but hesitated. He tore a strip from his already ruined cloak, wadded it up, and stuffed it in Shane's mouth. "Just in case." His eyes darted to the door.

Shane didn't argue. She knew better.

Eli went to work. Without warning, he grabbed her leg gently, but that didn't stop her from screeching through the cloth in her mouth. He didn't give Shane a warning before pulling and straightening out the unnatural bend in her leg. When she regained consciousness, Eli was tying the two pieces of wood from the broken chair alongside her knee, immobilizing her leg.

"Better?" Eli asked as he stood up.

"You're funny," she said, upon pulling the rag out of her mouth.

"At least you still have a sense of humor."

Shane rolled her eyes and used the wall to help her off the ground. She winced but didn't cry out. She still couldn't put much weight on her leg.

It was then that a noise came from the hallway.

"Why isn't Fritz out here helping? Has anyone notified him of the escapes?" a woman's voice said, just outside the door.

"Hide." With Eli's help, they made their way quickly to the closet near the bed. Eli held her tightly, bringing her closer into his chest than ever before. Shane could hear his heart racing in his chest. She was grateful to have someone to hold onto when all hell was breaking loose.

The door creaked open, and Shane held her breath.

"Fritz, the prisoners are—" and before she could finish her sentence, she screamed. Shane could hear her footsteps leaving the room in a hurry. "Fritz is dead! Fritz is dead!"

Eli waited a few seconds before loosening his tight grip around Shane's shoulders. They both let out a collective breath. Shane met Eli's eyes and they said all she needed to know. They needed to leave, now.

Shane pushed open the closet door and stumbled out. She started limping quickly for the door before Eli got his shoulder under her own so she could use him as a crutch. His warm body shifted beneath her, getting into a more comfortable position before they started down the deserted hallway at twice the speed that Shane could've done on her own. They both knew the hallway wouldn't be deserted long. All of Haytorrow's Fallen Realm was about to break loose.

"What about your shoulder?" Shane asked.

"I'll manage."

Already she could hear footsteps making their way toward them from every direction.

Upon finding their exit, Shane quickly, but painfully, lowered herself out of the window. She used the ledge to support herself before sliding over and supporting herself with only her arms. Quickly, Eli quickly joined her as noises came from above and shadows rushed by. The sound of armor on running soldiers suggested more and more were sprinting down the hallway.

Shane found a sill to allow her uninjured leg to help support her weight. She started making her way down using the same rain gutter that had helped her up. The guards were too preoccupied with the prisoners to notice Shane and Eli descending from the building.

Shane fell to the ground as the bells stopped ringing, replaced by gunfire. There was a fire ablaze somewhere to the west. Everywhere she looked she saw dead bodies littering the ground.

Eli landed next to her and gave a nod before they started for the wall to the east. Hopefully, no one would notice two people when there was a crowd of prisoners mobbing together to escape.

They made it to the corner of the building, and they no longer had shadows to rely on. There were no guards to be seen at that moment, but she knew that wouldn't last.

The wall loomed over them ahead. Shane tried to pick up her limping pace, but she was already going as fast as her leg would allow. Halfway there, footsteps could be heard coming toward them. Shane froze in place, pulling out her knives as shadows came into view, and grew closer. Eli met her eyes. She held his gaze for as long as she could. She wasn't going to run and hide from fear anymore.

Two guards appeared ahead of them out of the darkness and skidded to a stop at the sight of Shane and Eli. Without hesitation, they pulled their swords from their sheaths and started toward them. Shane stood steady where she was. She wasn't going to run from this fight. She had done enough running, and she was tired of it.

She started forward, favoring her broken leg, meeting the guards halfway. With a clash of metal against metal, their blades met, and the fight began. Shane's injured leg prevented her from advancing. The guard backed her up against a small pile of dirt, her injured leg preventing her from pushing back.

He took one swipe up toward her stomach, and she easily blocked it. She brought one blade up while keeping the other pressed down on the guard's sword and stabbed the man through his thin armor. He tried to bring his sword up to defend himself, but it was too late. He let out a gasp as he fell forward, lifeless.

As Eli removed his own blade from the abdomen of the man he was fighting, they could hear even more footsteps coming their way. Shane didn't know how much longer she could keep fighting like this.

Eli grabbed her by the arm and dragged her toward the wall. He found a small nook and pulled Shane in with him without a moment to spare as more guards came rushing past.

"I don't think I can do this," Shane whispered to Eli as she looked up on the wall. "With my leg…"

"You either do this, or you die here." Eli looked behind her to make sure no one else was coming. "I would prefer it if you didn't choose the second option. I don't feel like training another partner."

Shane looked up at the wall and tried to muster the strength she so badly needed. "I'll try, but I probably won't make it."

"Then we'd better hurry." It was obvious to both that it wouldn't be long before more guards arrived, and Shane would prefer to be at least somewhat up in the air by the time they did. Taking a deep breath, she stepped up to the wall and began her climb.

Each step Shane took was agony. But she was determined to make it up no matter how much it took out of her.

Guards ran by underneath, not noticing her tiny body against the huge blackness of the wall. Screams could be heard throughout the fortress, but Shane couldn't tell if they were from the escaped prisoners or the guards. She wished she could do more to help the slaves, but she needed to get as far away from Verscar as she could, as fast as she could.

Eli climbed right behind her, making sure she didn't fall. Her bad foot slipped a few times, hitting him square in the face, but he kept climbing while cussing at her the tiniest bit.

After what seemed like forever, Shane miraculously grabbed the ledge at the top. She peered over the top to make sure that nobody was coming from either direction. One man stood there at the ready several feet away, his hands gripped tightly to a rifle. His eyes scanned the battlefield down below, his finger on the trigger.

Shane pulled her bloodied hood over her torn face before hauling herself silently over the wall. She was barely out of the man's peripheral vision. Carefully, she unsheathed one of her knives and circled around behind him before grabbing him by the hair and slitting his throat. He fell to the ground without making a sound.

"That was a little violent," Eli said as he brought himself over the wall.

Shane used her cloak cloth to wipe off the excess blood from her knife. "You would've done the same thing."

"Not after my first kill."

Eli looked like he was about to continue but just then someone came sprinting out of the shadows toward them. He saw them and stopped and aimed his rifle.

"Run?" Shane asked.

"Definitely!"

They both dashed away from the man with the rifle, Shane skipping along as fast as her broken leg would allow. A gunshot rang out, and Shane could hear the bullet whiz past her ear. The guard quickly reloaded.

"The lake." Shane pointed toward the large body of water ahead of them. If they could just get down there, then everything would be fine. The only problem was the guards standing between them and their goal.

"I hope you have a plan."

Shane did too.

Another gunshot and a small piece of the wall next to Shane blew apart. Fragments of the wall embedded themselves into her skin. With only a hint of a scream, she kept going.

A pair of guards were ready for them, guns at the ready. Shane and Eli skidded to a stop, glancing behind them to see the other guard rushing to catch up.

"If we die here," Eli whispered to Shane, "I want you to know I want my room back."

"Seriously?" Shane scolded him.

The guards aimed their guns at their hearts, but it appeared that there was no hurry in killing them now that they were surrounded.

"Who are you?" one of the guards yelled out.

Shane let out a fake laugh. "No way in Haytorrow's Realm I'm telling you that."

"Are you the ones who killed Fritz?"

"So, what if we are?" Shane allowed her bloodied hands to appear in the bright torch light.

"Shoot them," one of them barked.

Shane's heart accelerated. She looked over the side of the wall only to see the lake right below them. So close, yet so far away. Unless…

"Do you trust me?" she whispered into Eli's ear.

"What?"

She said a quick prayer to Mindalin, then before Eli could say anything else she used all of her weight to thrust herself over the edge of the wall, dragging Eli with her.

CHAPTER 28

Before Shane could even think about screaming, they slammed into the icy cold water. She somehow lost hold of Eli as she sunk to the bottom, leaving nothing but a thin trail of bubbles behind.

She wasn't dead, and she sent a silent thanks to Mindalin for that.

Eli!

Shane pushed up from the bottom, cold water cutting into her like a knife. "Elias!" She screamed, but it sounded more like a garbled cry, the words barely understandable through the water.

As Shane swam toward the surface, she saw something move out of the corner of her eye. She let out a cry of relief at seeing Eli swimming toward her. She kicked his way, grabbing his arms and pulling him in for a hug.

"I thought I lost you," she told him through the water, tears coming from her eyes mixing instantly with the water of the lake. "I was afraid you'd died."

Elis started to squirm uncomfortably in her arms, and she released him. How long had they been under water? A minute? Maybe two? In the cold water, it was almost impossible for a normal human to hold their breath for longer than that.

"Go." Shane pointed toward the surface. "I'll meet you there." She intended to wait for the water to stitch her arm and heal her leg completely. She needed a moment of peace before returning to the world above.

Eli wanted to protest, but he couldn't hold his breath any longer. Shane was sure that his lungs had to be screaming for air as he headed begrudgingly toward the surface. Finally, his head broke the surface, and with a gasp for air, he swam toward the shore.

Shane, meanwhile, sat at the bottom as the water reconfigured her leg to where it was no longer broken. The bones ground together and pushed at her skin, but she didn't cry out. She had learned that pain is only temporary.

She watched as the blood drifted away from her lacerated arm, replaced by a fresh new scar. It wasn't thick, but it was noticeable, disfiguring most of her arm.

Shane felt relief as the movement of the bones in her legs stopped and the pain that had been there before disappeared. Pushing herself off the sandy bottom, she kicked her way toward the surface. When her head finally broke the surface, she was almost to shore.

"Way to nearly kill us, Shay." Eli's voice came from across the lake. His dark silhouette slowly made his way around the lake, being lit by the chaos and the fires that had spread through the camp. Shane didn't hear any close gunfire.

"It was either that or die from being shot." Shane made her way out of the water and met Eli on the shore. "I would take a long fall any day over that."

"Where was that same energy when I first took you to the rooftops?"

Shane shrugged. "There was hard ground beneath me there," she said, trying to wring out her clothes without taking them off. She led the way to the forest not looking back at Verscar. "At least I knew there was a chance of me surviving the water."

"And you just brought me along to see if your water invincibility worked on me?"

A smile made it to Shane's face. "Basically, yeah."

"Great to know I'm expendable."

"Hey, I prayed to Mindalin to save you too."

Eli raised both eyebrows. "Glad she listened to you."

"You should be. You would've been dead otherwise."

They made their way to the tree line. Shane stopped and looked back through the trees at the smoke rising from Verscar.

"So, I'm a killer now..." Shane said, a trace of guilt on her face.

"You had to do it," Eli said after taking one look at Shane's guilt-ridden face. "If you hadn't, they would've done the exact same thing to you."

"I keep telling myself that."

"It's normal, especially with your first kill."

Shane allowed tears to swell up in her eyes. "Except I was relieved when Fritz's blood soaked my hands." She looked over at Eli with terror filling her face. "What if I'm becoming what he was."

Eli's face went blank. "Shane, look at me." She obliged, looking him in the eye. "You are nothing like him."

"I wanted to make him suffer." She didn't try to stop her voice from shaking. "I wanted to make sure he died the most awful way a human could, yet you say I'm nothing like him?"

"I know you're not." Eli grabbed Shane's shoulders, making sure she couldn't walk away. "He doesn't care about people's lives, but you do. All he saw were price tags over people's heads. If you're worse than him, then you wouldn't feel guilty about killing any of them."

Shane let tears flow down the sides of her already wet face. "Are you sure about that?"

"Yes. I've never been more sure about anything in my life."

Shane sniffled. "I'm not."

"Fritz was a monster, you are not."

"Except maybe I am." Shane shrugged Eli's hands off her shoulders and continued to walk toward their camp. She was too ashamed to meet Eli's eyes any longer. "When we were in there, a small part of me wanted everyone who wasn't a prisoner to suffer the way I thought they deserved."

"Do you think I expected you not to?" Eli ran a hand down his face. "Shane, you were tortured there. You have every right to want the people who did that to you to die a painful death. I would've done it myself if you asked me to."

The camp appeared through the trees. The sun had started to rise over the horizon, and a new tiredness had taken over Shane, but she wasn't sure she had the strength to sleep after all that had happened.

"If my family were here, they'd disagree with you too."

"But they're not here," Eli said. "Shane, you did what you had to do to survive. If you hadn't decided to come with Kyaina, you would've been discovered by Fritz and you would've died right then and there."

"That should've happened." Shane wiped the tears away from her eyes, but they kept coming. "Then I wouldn't hate myself as much as I do right now, and I would be able to see Reece." Her voice caught.

Reece.

"She would hate me if she could see me now," Shane said. "Knowing what I did after her death, I wouldn't be surprised if she wanted to get as far away from me as possible. I wouldn't blame her."

"She wouldn't be ashamed of you."

"How do you know? You didn't know her."

"But I know you." Eli let out a sigh. "I know what type of people you call friends, and I'm sure that Reece wouldn't hate you if she knew what you're doing."

"I— Thank you." She ran up to Eli and grabbed him for a hug. As usual, he tensed up at first, but relaxed and put his arms around Shane to return the hug. "I needed that."

"You keep thanking me, and I don't know why," Eli said, retreating from the hug. "It's not like I'm any good at this advice thing."

"No, you aren't," Shane agreed. "But somehow your pathetic attempts have managed to remind me that I'm not the only one with a messed-up past." Shane let out a yawn.

"You should go to bed." Eli looked behind Shane's shoulder to the rising sun.

Before Shane could argue, a wave of tiredness crashed over her. She hadn't realized how exhausting the journey had been until that exact moment. Now that Fritz was dead, she should have an easier time getting to sleep and staying asleep, but she didn't trust herself enough for that yet.

"We should move a little way away from the camp, and then I'll think about it," Shane said, thinking of an excuse not to fall asleep.

Eli opened his mouth, then closed it once again when he realized there was no way of winning the argument. "All right, but as soon as we're far enough away, you are going to sleep. No 'I'm taking first watch' bullshit."

A smile cracked on Shane's face. "Whatever."

***

Verscar was only a small plume of smoke on the horizon when they stopped to set up camp. The sun was high in the sky, cresting above the tall pine trees. Shane no more than laid down on her bedroll when she was asleep.

At first, her sleep was peaceful, but eventually dreams returned. She was back in the castle's dungeons, except the doors were unlocked. Hesitantly, she pushed them forward and was greeted by the squeak of the door as it opened wide. Shane took a step out and started up the staircase, unsure of where exactly she was going. She found her way into the empty throne room.

"I hate this place," a familiar voice startled Shane. She searched frantically for any weapons but somehow knew this was only a dream.

"Who are you!" Shane took a couple steps forward but didn't see anything besides pillars. "Show yourself!"

"I'm hurt, Shane, that you don't recognize my voice," the voice said. A blinding light appeared ahead of her and through it stepped a young girl. Shane scrunched her eyes to see who it was.

"Reece!" Shane ran forward over the murky floor. She wasn't sure it was real, but seeing her friend still brought tears of happiness streaming from her eyes as she embraced her friend fiercely in a hug. She shook as she felt the solidity of Reece's body under her fingers. She was real. She was here, at least in this dream. "I thought I'd never see you again."

Shane let go of the hug and let out an even bigger sob when she saw Reece's face clearly. "Are you real? Or is this just part of my dream?"

"Last time I checked I was real."

"But you died," Shane whispered, her eyes running up and down Reece.

Reece winced. "I did."

"Then how are you here?"

"Haytorrow is allowing me to visit you for a couple minutes."

"But how?"

"Death and dreams aren't so different." A huge smile cracked over Reece's face. "You've changed so much from the last time I saw you."

"And you haven't changed one bit." Even the clothes Reece was wearing were the same as before they left their world, not the nasty, washed out beige colored clothes she had died in.

"I can't tell you how much I wished that the roles would've been reversed." The smile on Shane's face faded. "I... I should've died instead of you."

"Are you hearing yourself correctly, Shane?" Reece asked.

Shane nodded. "It should've been me." She took a deep breath. "After everything I've done since your death... it just should've been me, or I should've at least been fast enough to save you." Shane touched the scar that divided her face. An ugly reminder that she wasn't good enough to help her friend.

"You aren't thinking straight."

"Yes, I am," Shane said, failing to hold back her tears. "If I had died, then maybe I wouldn't hate myself as much as I do now."

Reece's smile wavered. "You shouldn't hate yourself for doing what you had to do to survive."

"If you knew what I've had to do, you would hate me too."

"You mean becoming an assassin and killing the man who tortured you for six months of your life?"

Shane stared at Reece, her mouth agape. "How did you know...?"

Reece winced. "I've been... checking in on you periodically."

"Then you must know how much I've wasted my life, wasted your sacrifice." Tears clouded Shane's vision. "Your death was wasted on a useless, low life street rat like me."

"You aren't that." Reece pursed her lips and looked behind her warily. "You weren't chosen to be Mindalin's Chosen Hero for nothing, all right."

"Well, she made a mistake, choosing a mess up like me."

"No, she didn't."

Shane looked up at Reece, a questioning look in her eyes. "Do you know something I don't?"

"Let's just say that being dead has its perks."

"What is it?" Shane asked. "What do you know?"

Reece opened her mouth, then closed it almost instantaneously. "I can't tell you, unless I want Haytorrow to banish me to his Fallen Realm."

"What do you know?" Shane asked again, this time more insistent.

"I want to tell you. I truly do, but I can't."

"Can you tell me anything?"

Reece thought for a moment before saying, "You have a greater destiny than I ever did."

"What? What do you mean?" Shane asked, trying to pry the answers from her friend.

"I can't tell you much, but I can tell you this. The people of this world will know your name."

Shane couldn't breathe. She stumbled and she caught her hand on a pillar to support herself. "But I'm just an assassin."

"You're so much more than that." Reece grimaced and doubled over in pain. When Shane went to go help her, she waved her away. "I didn't tell her, Haytorrow," she yelled. Silence was all that answered her. "He can be such an ass sometimes."

Shane forced a smile. "Did you just call the god of death an ass?"

"Yes, I did." Reece gave out a small laugh. "At least I'm not one of his living servants like you are." She motioned to Shane's tattoo.

"I didn't want to be," Shane said looking down at her arm with the tattoo. It looked even blacker than it had when she had first seen it. "I still can't believe that this is real. This is my new reality, killing people for blood money." Shane felt her emotions build. "It's hard to believe that last year we were all too worried about who was going to win the football game." She brought her bloodshot eyes up to Reece.

"*You* were worried about who would win the football game," Reece said. "I was perfectly happy sitting at home, alone, but you forced me to come along with you."

"Do you blame me?" Shane swallowed down the thickness. "For ending up here? For dying?"

Reece shook her head. "Never." She smiled. "If I hadn't gone to that game, I never would've had something to die for."

"What do you mean?"

Reece's smile saddened. "Just wait and you'll see." She grimaced once again and took a forced step backward, almost like she was being pulled. "Haytorrow wants me to return to his realm," she explained, seeing the confusion on Shane's face.

A new panic took hold of Shane.

"If you make it back home, tell my dad and siblings I love them." Reece fought against whatever was pulling her back but was losing ground. "Promise me you'll do that, Shane." The words came out with her voice cracking.

So many thoughts were racing through Shane's mind. There were still so many things that she wanted to talk about, but not enough time. "I… I promise," she whispered over the wind that had picked up, whisking Reece away. There was a giant flash of light, and Reece was gone, leaving Shane lying down on her pad in broad daylight, breathing heavily with Eli sleeping right beside her.

CHAPTER 29

S hane was wide awake and sitting against a dead, rotting tree when Eli finally woke up. By that time, the sun was setting behind the mountain ranges, casting the world into a pinkish, orangish glow. It would've been beautiful and awe inspiring if Shane hadn't been preoccupied with the dream. She wasn't sure if what she saw was real, or just a figment of her imagination.

"Why do you look like you're thinking of different ways to kill me?" Eli asked as he stretched his arms out wide.

"If you weren't going to get up soon, I very well might have."

"Why are you up before me?" He got up and started packing his stuff. "You were the one near death from exhaustion when we finally stopped."

Shane shrugged. "I had a dream."

"Of the camp?"

She shook her head. "No. I'm not sure what it all meant."

She explained everything that happened in her dream. As she talked, the more she was convinced that it wasn't just a dream. Her dreams were always all over the place, never stopping long enough for her to figure out what was happening. Last night, everything seemed to slow down to a normal pace, and all the details were on point.

When she finished, her mouth was dry. The sun had finally set, leaving the world dark once again.

"You saw her?" Eli asked after a few seconds had passed. "Like you actually saw your friend?"

"Yes." Shane nodded. "And I don't think that it was just a regular dream. I know it's hard to believe—"

"I believe you."

Shane stared at him. "You do?"

"Yeah." Eli shrugged his shoulders. "I mean for all we know it could just be a hallucination because of your exhaustion, but I believe that you saw her."

Shane rolled her eyes. "You're insufferable."

Eli only smiled.

There was still something nagging at the back of Shane's mind, and that was whatever secrets Reece was keeping from her. Did she really know something about Shane's future? As far as she was concerned, her future held nothing more than killing random people and getting money for it. Not any of that nonsense about her having a destiny. Mindalin had chosen the wrong person to be her Hero, and that was that.

Shane didn't want to worry Eli with her thoughts, so she kept silent as they packed their stuff and got on their horses for the long trek home.

They traveled by night and slept during the day. It took them nearly a week to get back to the familiar mountains. By the time they entered Conlar everything on Shane's body was sore, and all her muscles screamed in protest when she dismounted her horse. Relief flooded her body as she moved her legs around to walk. She wasn't meant to sit on a horse for twelve hours of the day, only getting off to fall asleep.

Shane secured her horse in the stables near the Underground and waited for Eli before heading to the alleyway.

"What are you in a hurry for?" Eli asked as Shane itched to get a move on.

"I just want to get back to my room and sleep in a real bed."

"Your sleep schedule is messed up if you want to go to bed at midday."

Shane snorted. "So is yours."

"I never said that mine wasn't, but at least it isn't as bad as yours."

"At least I acknowledge it," Shane said as she opened the door and allowed Eli to go in ahead of her.

Eli pulled the lever to reveal the ramp, and they both headed down together.

"Before you get too settled in," Eli said when they made it to their doors, "we need to see Wikter."

"Why?"

"Because he'll want to know how it went, and if you succeeded in the assassination." Eli opened his door and was about to go in when he saw Shane's worried face. "Relax, all right. You did it, didn't you?"

"Yeah, but what would happen if I hadn't."

"You would be stripped of any weapon and put in an arena where Wikter would end your life."

Shane gulped. "Sounds fun," she said, her face lacking color.

"Very. Meet me in my room in ten minutes and then we'll get going."

With that, he shut his door behind him. Shane hesitated before going in.

With wet hair and clean clothes, she stood in Eli's room waiting for him to throw his shoes on.

"Why must you insist on putting those on so slowly?"

"I can't go any faster." Eli cracked a smile. "With my hurt shoulder, this is all I got."

"Stop using that as an excuse."

"It's not an excuse if it's true."

"Please, just hurry up. We're going to be late if you keep goofing off."

"Wikter isn't expecting us."

"Yeah, but I'm sure he would frown at people coming to his room at midnight." Shane raised her eyebrows. "Pretty sure that you wouldn't walk out of that room alive."

"Haha. You're so funny."

Shane only smiled.

They started out the door and down the passageway to the common area where they saw several assassins here and there, all talking in quiet voices, afraid that someone might overhear them. It was almost exactly as it was when Shane first arrived there six months before, but now she no longer felt like she didn't belong.

Shane's hands became unexpectedly sweaty as they walked toward Wikter's door. She knew that she was being stupid for being afraid, yet she couldn't help herself. She had completed the assignment, but nothing in the instructions said anything about freeing the prisoners. Was she going to be punished for starting a riot? Was she going to be stripped of the title of assassin, sent away for good and have to restart her life once again? Was it going to end the way Eli said it would when she first shared her idea?

It was too late to back down now.

Eli knocked on the door and a muffled reply came back. "Come in."

Shane was the first into his room. It had been nearly six months since the last time she had been there, yet nothing had changed. His desk still sat at the end of the room with almost the same amount of papers cluttering it, and the lantern still flickered on the wall. It was eerie.

"Shane." Wikter nodded in her direction as a greeting. "Elias. I was wondering when you were going to get back."

"It took a little longer than expected." Elias took a seat and Shane was quick to follow.

"Does that have anything to do with the prisoners that escaped, or the fires that burnt the place to the ground?"

Shane lost all the color in her face. "That was my doing," she explained before Eli could open his mouth to speak. "I thought it would be a good distraction to escape."

Right then she prayed to every god and goddess she knew that Wikter wouldn't kill her right then and there. By the look on his face, he was still debating.

"And it had nothing to do with the fact that you were once a slave there?"

Shane shrugged, trying to keep her emotions masked. Wikter couldn't know how truly anxious and afraid she was. "That also might have contributed to my decision."

There was a long silence as neither of them broke eye contact with each other before Wikter at last looked away back toward his desk. "My niece, Airel, always hated that camp."

"So, I'm not in trouble?"

"That depends." Fear struck in Shane's heart before he continued. "On whether or not you completed the assassination."

Shane let out an audible sigh of relief. "Yes. I did." She searched in her pockets and pulled out one of the rings Fritz always wore. "Exactly as you asked for."

Wikter grabbed the ring from the table and examined it in the flickering lantern light. "Are you sure this is his?"

"Yes," Shane replied. "I took it from his cold, dead fingers."

He turned to Eli. "Can you verify this?"

Eli nodded. "Yes. I was too busy bleeding out to help."

Wikter raised an eyebrow, so Shane told him the story, leaving out the part about Fritz breaking her leg and gashing her arm. He would ask too many questions about how she healed so quickly if she did.

When Shane finished, Wikter gave out a mighty laugh. "I must say that I'm impressed. I didn't think you had it in you." A smile was plastered on his face that made Shane feel uneasy.

"Neither did I," she said wearily.

"I honestly thought she would freeze up when she had the chance," Elias said. "I wouldn't put it past her."

Shane elbowed him and returned her attention to Wikter.

"I guess I should say congratulations," Wikter said. "For completing all the tasks you had." The smile remained on his face. "I can now officially call you an assassin."

"Wasn't I one before?"

"Technically, yes. But it takes the first kill to make it official."

And I killed three, Shane thought with a guilty smile.

"Now you're one of us." Wikter stuck out his hand and Shane shook it gratefully. After so long, she had finally done it. All the months that had passed, every painful day and training session felt so worth it now, just to be shaking Wikter's hand. "You'll receive your payment within a week."

"Thank you," she said through her smile, finally breaking away from his firm grip.

Wikter waved his hand for them to leave. "I'm sure that my daughter will be dying to know everything."

Shane got up to leave, feeling Wikter's eyes on her back. It wasn't until she closed the door behind her and Eli that she let out a sigh of relief.

"You see," Elias said. "Nothing to worry about."

"Despite the fact that Wikter scares the hell out of me," Shane said as they started down the hall to their rooms.

"Everybody here feels that way."

"It's like he knows something that I don't, and I don't like it. It makes me feel uneasy."

"Careful." Elias laughed. "He might be able to hear you."

Shane took one look over her shoulder as the main area disappeared behind a wall of the passage, shuddering.

When Shane got up the next morning, she was surprised to find a bag of Schulhers inside the door. She picked it up, the weight of it coming as a pleasant surprise. It was her first official payment, and she was going to put it to good use.

Her mind was set. She got dressed quickly and headed for the door. It was time for an overdue funeral. Time to finally let Reece go.

As she made her way up toward the surface, she went over a checklist in her head. Flowers, a boat, and flint and steel for a funeral without a body. Only the gods knew that Reece wasn't going to actually be physically part of it, but that didn't matter. The sentiment was the same either way.

She weaved her way in and out of the many people on the streets, her money bag jangled by her side, considerably heavier than before the assassination.

The sun was shining high in the sky, and not a cloud in sight. It was one of the few remaining nice days before winter, and people were going to try and make the most of what they could do before the first snowfall.

Shane stopped by a storefront on the main street that most people walked past without a second look. Not that Shane could blame them. Every time she looked at the sign, she was only reminded of her own mortality.

The inside of the shop was empty, save for the cashier behind the desk. Boats of all sizes were stacked on each side of the store, some shabbily made while others looked like they had taken weeks, maybe even months to meticulously craft to such perfection. Some were the length of a small child, and others were the length of a fully grown man. It was a shame, really, to know that someday they would be either at the bottom of a lake or sea or burned on the water.

"Can I help you with anything?" a balding, gray-haired old man behind the counter asked morbidly.

"Unfortunately." Shane didn't try to hide the distraught look on her face. Being so close to those boats reminded her of the day Reece died. She wasn't prepared for this. "My close friend died," she explained.

"You have my condolences." He said the words like he had spoken them countless times before, dull of any emotion.

"I need one of your best boats." Shane held back the sorrow that threatened to bring tears to her eyes.

"Do you know her measurements?"

"That won't be necessary." She averted her gaze from the man and wiped at her face.

"I see."

The words hung heavily in the air.

Shane wanted to hurry out of the shop, but the man behind the counter took his leisurely time showing her all the boats they had on display. It made her want to puke, but she maintained control all the while until she left the shop with her money bag considerably lighter, and a boat waiting for her at the back of the shop. When she needed it, she would send it down a small stream to a lake a little outside of Conlar.

But first she needed flowers.

She bought them at a small vendor, paying a heavy price for the best they had. But she didn't care. Reece deserved the best.

Shane didn't want to go back to the boat shop, but the sun was already rising steadily in the sky, and she knew that she needed to have at least some daylight to perform the funeral. With flowers in one hand and a heavy heart, she set off toward the back of the funeral boat shop. The boat was bobbing in a man-made stream, straw coating the bottom. The murky water glistened as she placed the flowers in the boat and untied it from the shore.

Shane took the light ropes and guided it to the lake, where at last the city was behind her and trees were tall around her.

Lake Burthalm. It was a huge mountain lake, and Shane wondered just how many bodies were under the water?

She secured the boat to the shore to a stump and took some time to rearrange the flowers in the boat. Shane felt she needed to place them in the exact right place. Thinking she was done, she would gaze at it until she decided that she had messed up and then would meticulously start all over again. Everything had to be perfect. Shane had waited a whole year to do this, and she wasn't about to settle for anything less than perfect.

When she finally stepped back once again, the sun was low on the horizon. What she had done had to be good enough because light was quickly being whisked away.

She pulled out a box of matches from her pocket and lit the boat on fire. With one spark, the straw of the boat caught fire. Shane pushed it out into the lake, tears stinging her eyes.

"May Haytorrow find you a place in his Realm," she recited, voice hoarse. "May he be kind to your soul and let you live the rest of eternity in the higher kingdom." Shane let the tears fall freely from her eyes as she continued reciting lines that she had memorized. "Let the fire be your light in the darkness and pave the way toward a brighter future."

Shane continued to cry as the rest of the lines fell freely from her mouth. When she finished, the boat was a quarter of the way across the lake burning brightly.

"This seems like a very sad funeral." Eli's voice came from above the rocky downslide. "What, with only one person here to attend it."

He slid down and joined Shane. She sat on the shore, hugging her knees close to her chest.

"I'm not sure that Reece would've invited you." Shane didn't even bother to look back. Her eyes remained fixed on the burning boat. "What with you being the reason we got arrested in the first place."

"Since she's not here, who's gonna stop me."

"I could stop you."

"But you won't."

He slid his way closer to Shane.

"My life has changed so much this past year that I'm no longer the girl I once was." Shane said as a giant flame rose into the sky.

"And who was that?"

"A naive girl from Idaho who thought the world was split in two and bad people got what they deserved." Shane placed her head on her arms and wiped away the stray tears that managed to escape her eyes. "But if that were true, I would've been dead a long time ago. Both of us would be."

"Are you calling me a bad person?" Elias laughed.

"Isn't that what I implied?" She looked over at Elias. His face was being lit by the orange glow of Reece's fire. "If it makes you feel any better, I put myself in that category too."

"Strangely it does." Shane returned her gaze to the burning boat, a single tear rolling down her cheek. The fire began to disappear as the boat began to sink beneath the surface, leaving them both in darkness, except for the stars shining brightly above.

"What do you do now?" Elias asked.

Shane looked over at Elias and smiled, the thoughts of Reece and of her old home fading from her mind and being replaced by what lay ahead of her in the future. "What you said I should do months ago. Move forward with my life."

CHAPTER 30

W ikter always hated Rotshall, yet here he was back in the place where he was born, gazing up at the castle ahead of him. Just being there made something crawl under his flesh.

But he had to be there.

He had to see his brother.

The brother that he hated since birth. Wikter had been pushed aside for the newborn Crown Prince even though he was born only minutes after him. The servants would pamper that spoiled brat, leaving Wikter to be a lonely child in a massive castle that he had called home for so long.

Until his parents died and Aarion became king.

That was when Wikter snapped. An immature man child as king was too much for him. He left the night of the coronation and headed north where he stumbled upon Conlar and the assassins, which he gladly joined. Why bother being royalty when he could kill those aristocratic brats for good money?

Wikter gathered his cloak as he sprinted for the castle. He knew exactly where the guards stood post, and he knew how to avoid them. He made his way toward a small cliff face below that almost everyone forgot existed, besides Wikter. When you're a lonely, unsupervised child let loose in a castle, you would explore every nook and cranny in the place.

His gloved hands gripped tightly to the stone as he started his way up the mountain leading to the base of the castle, fighting against the wind, until he made it to the plateau where he could finally stand. The castle was only a couple paces away, and a small, rusted, metal door stood against its walls, long forgotten by most.

Wikter pulled off his gloves with his teeth and started for the door. It looked like it hadn't been open in years. Wikter wouldn't be surprised if it no longer functioned but was surprised when it flung off its hinges on his second kick to the lock, rust dust flying everywhere. He managed to catch it before it hit the ground.

Taking a deep breath, he started down the long, dirt and stone tunnel that he knew led halfway through the castle to a hidden staircase that led to exactly where he wanted to be: a secret entrance to Aarion's room on the top story of the castle.

He followed the twisting set of spiral staircases until at last he made it to the small door that, last he knew, was hidden behind a tapestry in the king's quarters. He opened it slowly to not make any sound.

Gods, he hated the room. Suddenly he was a kid once again, running through the halls with servants chasing after him, finally ending up here, in his parents' room where he would hide in the passageway. He wanted to forget those memories all together.

Wikter walked over to the bed in which Aarion lay sleeping soundly. He would've been so easy to kill. Just a quick slit to the throat, and all Wikter's worries would be gone, but that would leave the kingdom to his heir, Vito Bourne, who wasn't even part of the family. He was just as cruel as Aarion, probably why he chose him.

But he came here on a mission that didn't require the spilling of blood.

"I'm surprised that you aren't dead already," Wikter said loudly as he sat down on one of the king's chairs. "I'm surprised that an assassin, like myself, hasn't already slit your throat."

Aarion's bright blue eyes, the exact same as Wikter's, flung open and he reached for a knife on his bedside table.

"Who are you?" he demanded. When he saw that it was his brother, his grip on the knife only tightened. "What are you doing here, Wikter?" He said his brother's name like venom.

Wikter only laughed. "Do I need a reason to see my dear brother?"

"Last time you came to 'see me' you nearly killed me."

"It was only an accident. You just so happened to be in the way of my knife."

Aarion let out a cruel, heartless laugh. "And I suppose you have a good reason for having a throwing knife, ready for use, at the dining table?"

"You got me there." Wikter smirked. He got up from the chair and started to walk around the room. "I see you haven't changed much around here since Mother and Father died."

"Why would I?"

"Oh, I don't know. Maybe to snazz it up a bit." Wikter grabbed the tapestry. "The place does appear rather dull."

"Cut the bullshit. What do you want?"

Wikter let out an exasperated sigh. "Do I really need to want something to see you?"

Aarion stared questioningly up at him.

"Fine," Wikter surrendered. "You got me." He allowed a small smile to tug at the edges of his lips. "I just wanted to ask you a question."

"And that is?"

"How many years has it been since Airel died?"

Aarion's face flashed with anger. "Did you come all the way from Conlar just to taunt me with that?"

"No, actually. I just wanted to know."

"You know damn well that she died fifteen years ago."

The smile on Wikter's face only widened. "Just needed the confirmation."

"Why?" Aarion spat.

"Because I know where she is."

A heavy silence filled the room before Aarion scoffed. "That's impossible. Her body's at the bottom of the ocean, it has been for years."

"Are you sure about that?"

"Yes, I am." He made a motion with his knife. "Now if you would be so kind as to leave—"

"I'm surprised that you didn't realize that Airel was alive," Wikter continued, cutting Aarion off. "After all, she was in this very castle about a year ago."

"Are you delusional?"

"No, I'm not." The smile on his face only widened. "In fact, I'm pretty sure that you sold her to Verscar of all places, you know, the place she hated and wanted wiped off the map?"

"I sell a lot of people to that place."

"You sold," Wikter corrected. "It was actually Airel who killed Fritz."

"What are you talking about." Aarion's face kept getting paler and paler.

"Your daughter is one of my many assassins." Wikter couldn't hide his joy from seeing the terror on Aarion's face.

"That's impossible. She would never—"

"She doesn't know who she is yet." Wikter continued. "She's trapped in the body of her fifteen-year-old self, but the similarities are uncanny. It's probably Mindalin's doing I suppose."

"You really are delusional."

"The only difference is an ugly scar running down her face. If I'm not mistaken, that was your doing."

"I don't know what you're talking about. I wouldn't have done that to Airel."

"Except she doesn't go by Airel anymore." Wikter couldn't stop the excitement from showing in his eyes. "She thinks her name is Shane Richards."

The End of *Mark of the Assassins*

SHANE WILL RETURN!

In *Legacy of the Assassins*

If you liked this story, please leave a review. This is the first book in a new series and reviews mean everything to us.

Keep reading as there is more…

I t wasn't a deadly poison, the one Shane carried in her pocket. Once ingested, it would hurt like hell and make the target's insides claw themselves nearly to death, but it wouldn't kill him. That job was left for the knife strapped to Eli's arm.

The client had been clear on when and where he wanted the victim to die, and since they were paying a huge sum of money, Shane wasn't going to argue with them. If there was one thing she'd learned over the last year spent as an assassin it was this: if you question your employer, you get paid less. And in the world she was now living in, money was one of the most important things for survival.

A cold ocean breeze swept up her black cloak as she made her way through the streets of Tagholden. Nearly every road in the city was empty. The only thing that greeted Shane was the salty taste of the ocean nearby. Not that Shane could blame anyone for remaining inside. If she didn't have an assassination to complete, she would be snuggled in bed in the inn she and Eli were staying at. Dark storm clouds had moved in with the breeze, and with it came the chance of a torrential downpour. Weather like that wasn't uncommon in that part of Lyconnexal, especially in the fall.

Shane looked over her shoulder before veering off to her left down an alleyway Eli had marked for her when they were planning the assassination. It was near the docks and perfect for what she planned to do. There were no windows for people to spy on her, and it was a dead end. One way in, one way out.

She made her way to the end of the alleyway before glancing over her shoulder once again to make sure no one was following her. Once she was sure the coast was clear, she began her climb, grabbing nearly every hand hold she could find. It wasn't until she made it to the top that the crook of her left elbow began to tingle.

"One second, Eli," she mumbled under her breath, rubbing the spot on her arm with the tattoo. The tattoo was nothing intricate, just a circle with mountains in the background and a bloody knife in the center. The assassin's mark.

She searched the roof of the building surrounding her, looking for Eli's silhouette. When Shane and Eli had left the inn, they went separate directions, agreeing to meet on the rooftop near the target's home. Two people wearing all black, making their way down the street looked suspicious, but people wouldn't look twice at only one.

Shane's eyes narrowed as she saw someone moving in the distance, and she assumed it to be Eli. She started toward him, leaping across chasms. When she finally got to him, she found him lounging against a tall chimney with his arms crossed and a blank expression on his face.

"Took you long enough to get here," he said, pushing himself away from the chimney.

Shane rolled her eyes. "I was making sure no one was following me."

"And were they?" Eli asked.

"No, but that's not the point." Shane gazed over toward the ocean's lapping waves. "I just didn't want to get seen."

"Sounds like you're a bit paranoid."

Shane laughed. "After what happened last time, I have every right to be."

"It wasn't that bad." A small smile crept its way to Eli's face. "It wasn't like I died or anything.

"But you did get shot multiple times."

Eli shrugged. "Mere grazes. Besides, if I had a Schuller for every time I'd been shot at or almost died, I would be rich." Shane raised an eyebrow. "Fine. Richer than I already am." Eli started to the edge, walking backward. "The point is you have to relax a bit and have some fun."

"Oh, yes. Because my definition of fun is definitely killing people in cold blood just to get some money." A few raindrops hit the ground, and a few seconds later, the skies opened. "Great," she said. "Now it's raining."

"I thought you said you liked the rain." Eli stopped at the very edge.

"Yes, but not when I have an assassination to finish." Rain made it more difficult to complete an assassination. It made everything slippery, and not to mention harder trying to hide their footsteps in a warm, dry room.

Also, Shane didn't enjoy the rain as much in Tagholden. It brought back too many memories of a couple years ago when she'd been forced to march to Rotshall before eventually being sold to Verscar, one of the worst labor camps in all Lyconnexal, by King Aarion.

Lightning cracked in the distance, followed seconds later by thunder that shook Shane to the bones.

"Do you remember the plan?" Shane asked.

"Yes," Eli said as he was about to drop. "Get to the target's house while he's away from his office, place the poison in his water, and wait for the target to drink if before I jump out and slit his throat. Simple."

"Simple on paper," Shane corrected him. "Not in practice."

Eli shrugged. "Same difference."

"And what do we do if that plan doesn't work?"

"Improvise."

"Exactly."

Nearly all the plans they made ended up going off the rails. Shane didn't see why they made them anymore, but where was the fun in life without a little excitement of the never-ending threat of death?

"Do you have the poison?" Eli asked.

Shane nodded and tapped the hidden pocket in her cloak. "Have it right here." Shane pulled out a tiny vial with a cloudy, translucent liquid in it.

"Make sure you don't ingest it," Eli joked.

"I'm not even stupid enough to do that."

"I mean…." Eli smirked. Shane gasped and slapped him playfully across the chest. "Hey!" He whispered fiercely. "That hurt."

"But you deserved it."

"Doesn't mean it was nice."

"Well, I'm not a nice person."

"You can say that again."

Shane ignored him and put on the hood and the mask. She was glad that the outfit was waterproof. Eli put on his mask as well before leaping off the building and rolling onto the roof. It didn't take long before they were in position crouching on a rooftop across the street from the target's house in a wealthy neighborhood

They'd spent most their evenings spying on the target from that location. Every day, an hour after the sun disappeared over the horizon, he always left for at least half an hour before coming back to his office and continuing his work as a successful merchant. It was no surprise when they didn't see him in there.

Shane took the lead as they dropped to the ground and ran through the shadows before climbing to the targets roof. They slid down to a small, covered balcony, just outside the target's office, hiding away from the glass door. Shane made an effort to ring out her cloak before opening the door and sneaking in, but water still dripped onto the carpet. All she could do was hope the target wouldn't be paying too much attention to the floor.

The room was small. A crackling fireplace sat in on the wall to Shane's right, and his desk sat opposite it. The desk was full of neatly stacked papers and quills, along with a glass of water. Perfect.

"You want to do it?" Eli asked as Shane took the poison out of her pocket.

"I thought we agreed that I would poison him, and you would slit his throat."

"I thought you'd like to switch it up a little bit."

Shane unscrewed the top of the bottle. It was odorless, making it perfect for assassins as it didn't waft toward the target's nose. She poured it into the water, stirring it gently with her finger. When she was done, the water looked no different than it had before, but Shane knew better than to drink it.

"Now we wait," Shane said as she wiped her finger on her cloak.

With no place to hide inside the room, they went out on the balcony and sat in silence as the rain hit the roof in a rhythmic way.

"I hate doing this," Shane said as she glanced into the room.

"Doing what?"

"Making them suffer before we deliver our killing blow." There was something inhumane about it.

Eli sighed. "So do I, but we have to." It sounded like he was trying to convince himself of that more than Shane.

"Have you ever wanted to be anything other than an assassin?" Shane asked him quietly.

Eli nodded. "I used to."

He didn't elaborate, and Shane was fine with that.

"How about you?" he asked. "I mean, I know you did, but what did you want to be?"

Shane laughed as she took off her hood and mask. Thinking about it now, given what she'd become, it was ridiculous. "I wanted to be a police officer, like my dad."

Eli stared at her, then started laughing. "Yeah, good luck with that. I'm pretty sure they frown on people with a criminal background."

She smiled over at Eli, and he reciprocated it.

Just then, there came the sound of the door opening and footsteps making their way toward the desk. Shane put her mask back on and glanced over to Eli as the sounds of the footsteps stopped and the sound of a sliding chair hinted that he was sitting at his desk. She peered through the window just as he took a sip of water. Seconds later, the cup shattered against the floor, and he slumped forward in his chair.

Now, Eli nodded. He went first through the doors, and Shane followed.

The target's eyes widened when he saw them. "Who are you?" he managed to croak out through the pain.

"Haytorrow's servants," Shane said as she circled around his desk. She felt for the knives against her side, calming her. She knew Eli had the right to kill him, but that didn't mean she didn't have to be prepared if things went awry.

The man thrashed in his chair, choking on his own spit. Shane knew the poison wouldn't kill him, but the victim didn't know that.

"Why are you here?" He sporadically twitched, knocking everything from his desk.

"I thought the answer to that question was simple." Eli brought his knives out of their sheaths and twirled them in his hand. "To kill you."

"Why?" He managed to gasp out.

Eli looked to Shane, and she shrugged. "Money, I guess," she said, taking a step closer to him. She recoiled as the man lashed out at her. You should ask our employer why they want you dead." She gave a nod to Eli, and he brought the knife closer to the target's neck.

"Wait!" He yelled, lunging forward to Shane. She tried to jump backward, but he hit her mask wildly with his hand, and fell from her face to the floor.

"Now you've done it," she seethed, fire burning in her eyes. Her fingers tightened menacingly around her blades, but the target gasped.

"Airel?"

"What?" Shane said, taken aback. She took an unsteady step backward. Eli brought the knife down on his neck, slitting his throat before he could say another word.

Shane had been called many things before, but that was the first time she'd been called the name of the long dead princess.

"Well, that went well," Eli said sarcastically as he wiped the blade on his cloak. He grabbed Shane's mask and tossed it over to her. "And not much went wrong with the plan."

"What?" Shane asked, her mind being torn away from what the target had said. "Oh, yeah. It did." She forced a smile as she put the mask back on.

But as soon as the words escaped her mouth, the doorknob started to rattle. Before either of them could even think about escaping, the door opened and a servant walked in, in his hands a tray of food. She closed the door and looked up, her eyes widening, dropping the tray as she found both Shane and Eli standing over her boss's dead body. A scream left her mouth, and she opened the door and sprinted out of the room.

"You seriously had to say it, didn't you?" Shane asked as the servant ran through the hallways, alerting everyone in the home that the man was dead. "You just jinxed us."

"Looking back, it wasn't the best thing to say, given the time and place."

"You think?"

They started for the balcony, but a young man sprinted into the room with a gun in his hand. "Don't move," he said shakily. Shane turned around.

"I wouldn't do that if I were you," Shane said. The young man's hands were shaking so much that she was surprised he hadn't accidentally pulled the trigger.

Eli was the first one to act, grabbing his throwing knives and sending them at the man. The first one collided with his chest. The next bounced painfully off his head, and the third stuck straight into leg. The man dropped the gun and took a step back before keeling over onto the floor.

"Really?" Shane asked. "Three knives? Was all that necessary?"

"No, but I wanted to make sure he didn't follow us."

More footsteps could be heard sprinting toward them through the hallways, and they were about to leave before Eli scrambled for the gun the boy had been holding. He tossed it over to Shane as the first person stepped into the room.

"Shoot for the kill!" Eli ordered.

"What am I supposed to say to that? Live for the thrill?" Shane asked as she fired, hitting the man in the chest, before turning and sprinting out the glass doors behind Eli. She stuffed the gun into one of her many pockets.

"Or you could just not respond at all." Eli scrambled up to the roof and then turned to assist Shane. People rushed to the street pointing at the rooftop. Gunfire erupted and Shane flinched. The only way to run was toward the ocean.

"So much for not wanting to attract attention," Shane scolded as they slid down an angled roof. Gunfire came from below them, and a chunk of the roof flew off. "And now they're firing at us."

"You're acting like this is your first time."

"And it's sad that it isn't!" A bullet *whizzed* over Shane's head as they ran. They jumped a gap. "We have to keep moving!"

"Really? I didn't know." They leaped over obstacles, but they couldn't leave their pursuers behind. "Where exactly do you plan on going? Because the ocean is right ahead of us." Eli skidded to a stop as realization hit him. "Oh, no."

"Yes," Shane said, yanking Eli along by the hand. A bullet hit where he'd been standing moments before."

"Don't tell me you're doing your Mindalin's Chosen Hero thing again?"

"So what if I am?"

"I hate when you do this."

"You're just jealous of my powers." Shane smiled over at Eli.

"Yeah, right." Eli said as they both ducked behind a small stone abutment. "That's one way to put it.

"Look," Shane said, letting go of Eli's hand. "It's easier to lose people when you're traveling alone." Shane heard people making their way around the house they were on and swore, looking out across the ocean. "Just meet me at the docks, alright?"

"Shay—" he tried to say, but it was too late. She'd already gotten up and sprinted toward the edge. She flung herself off the building, arms flailing wildly as she fell for the unforgiving, rough water below. She plunged into the water and sank toward the bottom.

It should've killed her, and it would have if she hadn't been blessed by Mindalin, but as it was, she had plunged into the water unscathed. Her only worry was being tossed by the rough waves that tried to bring her back to shore, but a couple kicks brought her out into the ocean.

The water seemed to revitalize all her senses. Everything was sharper than they'd been moments before. She could see for what seemed to be miles, and her hearing was impeccable. She could stay there all day if she hadn't promised Eli to meet him at the docks. Shane hoped he had escaped their pursuers. She knew if she'd stayed there with him, he would've had a more difficult time trying to escape, but that didn't mean she didn't carry a small feeling of guilt. He didn't have the easy option of diving into the water when things got too difficult on the surface.

Shane kicked away from the sandy bottom and started southward. Wooden pillars emerged from the darkness, rising from the floor of the bay. Large sailing vessels, most likely filled with goods to be transported to the colonies or elsewhere in the world, blocking out the light above her.

Shane carefully peeked above the surface. She heard people yelling from the shore, but they were heading away from the ocean. She climbed onto the docks and sat on the edge while she waited for Eli to show. She swore at herself as she gazed across the vastness of the docks. From far away, they looked relatively small, but now that Shane was there, they seemed endless.

She should've been more specific before she dove into the ocean.

Then a shadow caught her eyes. She spun around, her hands instinctively finding the hilts of her knives but relaxed when she saw it was only Eli. She stood and ran toward him.

"Thank the gods," she said, giving him a hug. "You're alive."

"Were you worried for me?" A smile formed on Eli's face.

"So, what if I was?" Shane said, her face burning. "You're my partner after all."

She broke apart the hug, and her hands met his warm arm. "Bloody knives, Shay. You're freezing."

"Outstanding observation skills. Was it my blue lips that gave it away?" Shane asked, pointing to her shivering lips.

Eli rolled his eyes and took off his cloak. He handed it to Shane. "Wear this. It'll warm you up."

"It's just as soaked as mine."

"Not on the inside." Shane took it and replaced it with her own. Her underlayers were still soaking wet but having a dry cloak did help warm her up the tiniest bit. "Unlike you, I don't have a habit of throwing myself in waters."

"Neither do I," Shane said as she started toward the shore. "It just so happened to be the easiest way out."

Eli scoffed. "Maybe for you, but poor, ordinary people like me don't have that luxury."

"You're the descendant of Fuerbrand's Chosen Hero. You're anything but ordinary."

"Ooh," Eli said sarcastically. "I can warm up my hands at will. So exciting."

Shane pushed him playfully. "Some people would kill to have those abilities."

"And more people would kill to have *your* abilities," Eli said. "The last person to have them was the princess of Lyconnexal."

That brought back what the target had said and the smile on Shane's face faded. "According to the target, I am her."

Eli looked at her skeptically. "What?"

"You didn't hear him?" Shane asked. "When he swiped off my mask, he asked if I was Airel."

"That's the most ridiculous thing I've ever heard," Eli laughed. "You? Airel?"

"That's what I thought."

But she still couldn't shake his words from her mind.

"Let me assure you, Shay, you are nothing like her. A cousin of hers? Sure. But not her."

"If I were her cousin, that would make Kyaina my sister and Wikter my father."

"I can see it. Both you and Kyaina share the same thirst for blood."

Shane rolled her eyes. "Sure, I do. And you'd better watch your back or you'll be the next person I go after to appease my 'thirst for blood.'"

"I'm just shaking in my boots."

... and there you have it, the first chapter in the next book, Legacy of the Assassins. Coming soon.

I f you liked *Mark of the Assassins,* we're positive you'll like the Not Enough series.

A series by Eden Wolfe and Craig Martelle

https://geni.us/NotEnough

What if our desires create fantastic worlds?

Fantastically flawed, as if every day were Christmas…

There are those born to it, and they're the ones who can break it, end the echoes and save those within, even if they don't want to be saved.

The weight of a false world falls on the shoulders of the young to fix.

For those who will follow and remain in the real world.

Who will persevere in this fantastic new coming of age trilogy?

Book #1 Echo Breaker

Book #2 Echo Chaser

Book #3 Echo Ender

Read them today.

Written November 2021

I worked with Landri's dad on the North Slope of Alaska, the oilfields inside the Arctic Circle. I retired from that gig because the weather was too harsh and I was away from home for too long. But Scott kept working while his daughter created a wondrous world in which to spend her time. When Scott first approached me about Landri's story, I was skeptical because many people want to write books and parents are always proud of their children.

But Landri's story wasn't a pipe dream. It was real with gripping dialogue. It was a story that the world needed to see. We hooked Landri up with an editor four time zones away and through the power of the internet, they collaborated on the final product you just read. It was a magnificent effort between Kristy and Landri. Two full rounds of edits, all the while Landri finished book two in this series. Keep in mind, Landri is also a junior in high school.

I've been writing and publishing full time for more than six years. I've learned a great deal, but also, since I run the 20Booksto50k® self-publishing group, I get access to great opportunities, like bringing Landri's book to market. This was my pleasure, especially since you will see her name again. You will know who she is as she continues her author journey.

Keep reading and keep dreaming. Both can be great places to spend time.

Peace, fellow humans.

Craig

* * *

If you liked this story, you might like some of my other books. You can join my mailing list by dropping by my website craigmartelle.com or if you have any comments, shoot me a note at craig@craigmartelle.com. I am always happy to hear from people who've read any title in my stable. I try to answer every email I receive.

If you liked the story, please write a short review. I greatly appreciate any kind words; even one or two sentences go a long way. The number of reviews an ebook receives greatly improves how well it does on Amazon.

Craig Martelle on Amazon—http://author.to/CraigMartelle

Facebook—www.facebook.com/authorcraigmartelle

BookBub—https://www.bookbub.com/authors/craig-martelle

Craig's web page—https://craigmartelle.com

Thank you for joining us on this incredible journey.

* * *

– <u>available in audio, too</u>

Terry Henry Walton Chronicles (#) (co-written with Michael Anderle)—a post-apocalyptic paranormal adventure

Gateway to the Universe (#) (co-written with Justin Sloan & Michael Anderle)—this book transitions the characters from the Terry Henry Walton Chronicles to The Bad Company

The Bad Company (#) (co-written with Michael Anderle)—a military science fiction space opera

Judge, Jury, & Executioner (#)—a space opera adventure legal thriller

Shadow Vanguard—a Tom Dublin space adventure series

Superdreadnought (#)—an AI military space opera

Metal Legion (#)—a military space opera

Battleship: Leviathan—military science fiction

The Free Trader (#)—a young adult science fiction action-adventure

Cygnus Space Opera (#)—a young adult space opera (set in the Free Trader universe)

Darklanding (#) (co-written with Scott Moon)—a space western

Mystically Engineered (co-written with Valerie Emerson)—mystics, dragons, & spaceships

Metamorphosis Alpha—stories from the world's first science fiction RPG

The Expanding Universe—science fiction anthologies

Krimson Empire (co-written with Julia Huni)—a galactic race for justice

Zenophobia (#)—a space archaeological adventure

End Times Alaska (#)—a Permuted Press publication—a post-apocalyptic survivalist adventure

Nightwalker (a Frank Roderus series)—A post-apocalyptic western adventure

End Days (#) (co-written with E.E. Isherwood)—a post-apocalyptic adventure

Successful Indie Author (#)—a non-fiction series to help self-published authors

Monster Case Files (co-written with Kathryn Hearst)—a Warner twins mystery adventure

Rick Banik (#)—spy & terrorism action adventure

Ian Bragg Thrillers (#)—a hitman with a conscience

Not Enough (co-written with Eden Wolfe)—a coming of age contemporary fantasy

Published exclusively by Craig Martelle, Inc

The Dragon's Call by Angelique Anderson & Craig A. Price, Jr.—an epic fantasy quest

A Couples Travels—a non-fiction travel series

Mischief Maker by Bruce Nesmith—A Norse Mythology Contemporary Fantasy (not superhero)

Love & Haight by Jean Rabe and Donald R. Bingle—a courtroom drama with the undead, humor, horror, and the law.

9 781953 062291